CLOCKWORK PHOENIX

Selected for the 2008 Locus Recommended Reading List

A neatly packaged set of short stories that flow cleverly and seamlessly from one inspiration to another . . . Lush descriptions and exotic imagery startle, engross, chill and electrify the reader, and all 19 stories have a strong and delicious taste of weird.

— *Publishers Weekly*

A very strong first volume . . . Established writers and new names all are in good form here.

— Nick Gevers, *Locus*

A lot of good stuff here, and the cover, an effective use of an old painting, is lovely.

— Gardner Dozois, *Locus*

Even if you're not into the genre, this is a welcome read that'll hopefully strike an emotional chord in you.

— *Bibliophile Stalker*

I would have bought this book for its mysteriously gorgeous cover art alone, but the stellar lineup of contributing writers sold me completely.

— *PhillyBurbs.com*

Clockwork Phoenix is by no means your average, everyday anthology . . . this is a collection of rare treasures and intriguing stories, pushing boundaries and making the reader think . . . it stretches out of the usual comfort zone, offering up entire new worlds and concepts to play with.

— *SF Site*

I highly recommend the book to anyone looking for top-notch fiction irrespective of genre labels.

— *The Harrow*

CLOCKWORK PHOENIX 2
More Tales of Beauty and Strangeness

Edited by Mike Allen

Copyright © 2009 by Mike Allen.
All Rights Reserved.

Cover Painting:
"Medicine (Hygieia)" by Gustav Klimt, c. 1901

Cover Design Copyright © 2009 by Vera Nazarian and Mike Allen

ISBN-13: 978-1-60762-027-3
ISBN-10: 1-60762-027-8

FIRST EDITION
Trade Paperback Edition

July 1, 2009

A Publication of
Norilana Books
P. O. Box 2188
Winnetka, CA 91396
www.norilana.com

Printed in the United States of America

CREDITS

Also by Mike Allen

Poetry
DEFACING THE MOON
PETTING THE TIME SHARK
DISTURBING MUSES
STRANGE WISDOMS OF THE DEAD
THE JOURNEY TO KAILASH

Fiction
FOLLOW THE WOUNDED ONE

As editor:
NEW DOMINIONS:
Fantasy Stories by Virginia Writers
THE ALCHEMY OF STARS:
Rhysling Award Winners Showcase
(with Roger Dutcher)
MYTHIC
MYTHIC 2
CLOCKWORK PHOENIX

Clockwork Phoenix 2
more tales of beauty and strangeness

Norilana Books

Fantasy

www.norilana.com

CLOCKWORK PHOENIX 2

more tales of beauty and strangeness

Edited by
Mike Allen

ACKNOWLEDGMENTS

This has been a tough year for me, for a number of my loved ones and for many of my friends in personal and professional spheres. But we all persevere; it's our duty. In terms of this book—well, Reader, the volume in your hand could not exist without Vera Nazarian, who insisted this book would go forward even when her own house briefly appeared to be in jeopardy of foreclosure. I don't see how I could ever ask for a more dedicated publisher.

Other thanks have to go to Michael M. Jones, who served as my assistant editor (translation: *slush slave*) while we fielded submissions for this volume. Also to Kathy Sedia, who gave invaluable advice for promoting the first volume far and wide; Amal El-Mohtar, for her enthusiasm and encouragement; Sonya Taaffe, for her insight; and to my wife Anita, who, aside from having to endure marriage to me for almost two decades, suggested the order in which these stories best flow (as she did for the first book). Trust me, neither of those things constitutes an easy task.

To Dad

CONTENTS

INTRODUCTION

Mike Allen

Below us the world burns, though the fires are not visible to the naked eye.

Yet when you look down through the remarkable prisms that form the razor-keen feathers of our steed and host, you cannot deny the oilslick rainbow of infernos that rages underneath those deceptively orderly urban rows. The city floats atop them just as the shell of this planet floats atop layers upon layers of molten hells.

The gears of the raptor that carries us spin and shift; great coiled springs compress and unwind; chains rattle through sprockets; wings contract; and we drop lower. Light bends through the body of our phoenix, bends so far in its dimensions that we can see under the rooftops and between the floors of these teeming towers, tall boxes now open to us like tesseracts, granting us shockingly intimate views of those who live inside these structures and what lies inside their lives.

See the ghosts of the slaughtered and the suicides as they rise past us or scream inside prisons of cathode and glass.

See the deformed lovers, their eyes too damaged to perceive—much less grasp—the desperate hands that grope beside them. See the perfect lovers, painful in their glory, steady their spears against the slavering hate lurching toward them from all sides, determined to smash them into easily consumed pieces. See the loves' children: boys buried deep, waiting for the dark robed ones to dig them up again; girls forced too soon into the harshest sunfire glare.

And watch out, my friend—for now they begin to see us. Look how they sing their screams at us, their combined voices like all the animals sealed together in the hold of the Ark.

These denizens: their eyes, like their throats, are not like ours. They spy us through crevices and spaces our own eyesight focuses too clearly to detect.

See that pair of egg-round men in striped sweaters who share one mouth at the corner of their massive dual skull—can you hear what that mouth yells at us? That we have no right to impose our visions over theirs, that we command this height simply to distract the gaze of the One On High from all the rest of them?

And what is this woman rushing out onto the next roof, scrambling to climb its steeple, her vestigial wings flapping behind her as her long reptilian neck snaps our way? She roars that we've nothing to tell, that we're made of pretty surfaces and all mirage beneath.

And they scream louder, exuberant, thrilled at the damage they're doing as feathers start to fall away.

No need, my friend, to clutch so tight. We won't fall. Not yet.

See how the sharp feathers spin faster and faster as they drop, how the rabble below so vigorously hurls their ragged voices that they don't notice how the feathers follow the sound, track the shouts to their sources. By the time each feather reaches its mark, it is spinning so fast the poor morsels can't possibly see what hits them.

Have you ever seen so many beautiful hues of blood? And more beautiful yet, when the fluids ignite and the iridescent fires bloom.

And so the hidden infernos beneath become vivid blazes above, an incandescent splendor at our backs as we abandon these erupting towers for the buttoned-down brick safety of the suburbs. These square domiciles beneath, loyal regiments of secretive red soldiers that fight with shale and mortar to keep us from knowing what's inside—I assure you, the things that combust within their furnaces burn even hotter than the conflagration we just left behind.

Why do you keep looking back?

You still smell the burning city, you say? No. Look closer. Look down.

Look how the gears shimmer under our feet. Look at the sparks that fly between them, thickening rapidly from trickle to multitude to flood. Look at how the edges of the pinions snake with orange glows, fireplace embers blown hotter, kindling to life.

A phoenix can only endure its own friction for so long.

I never promised you a safe ride, friend, and surely you never expected one. Surely you desire this end as much as I do. Surely, you do.

The pain is exquisite and all too short, and you and I are now ash scattered out through the sky, our last thoughts raining down upon this single lonely house, itself as burnt to gray as we are.

THREE FRIENDS

Claude Lalumière

Part 1
Out of the Summer and into the Grey

That morning, so very near the end of summer, the Boy Who Speaks with Walls emerged from his parents' house with his tote bag full of lollipops, just like he had every day since school had let out in June. As he walked down the three wooden steps of his front porch, he glanced back affectionately at the red brick wall of his house. He liked how, in summer, the corners were softened by the leaves and branches of oak trees. He wore a baseball cap to protect his bald head from the summer sun, faded beige corduroy pants (he never wore shorts because he disliked exposing his bare legs), and a T-shirt with an iron-on picture of Timothy Draxton, the star of his favourite television show, *The Adventures of Shade Savage*.

He crossed the street, to the house where the Girl Who Eats Fire lived with her parents. Actually, the Boy assumed that the Girl lived with her parents in that old broken-down house. He had never seen them, and the Girl never spoke about them. He knew better than to ask the Girl questions she didn't want to answer. The house stood in the middle of a large lot, far from the sidewalk and from the houses on either side of it. The chipped, dirty bricks, the rotten wood, the rusted metal, the broken windows all fused into one stern grey mass that forbade colour. There was one old, dead, grey tree near the porch. The ground around it—and on the whole lot—was paved in concrete. People said the house looked like something from Greytown, and they avoided the Girl Who Eats Fire because of it. But the Boy didn't care. The Girl was his friend, and that's all that mattered.

He knocked on the door (the doorbell had been broken for as long as he could remember). Sometimes, it took several minutes for the Girl to answer his knock, so he was prepared to wait. In the meantime, he sucked on a lemon-cherry lollipop and lost himself in that bittersweet pleasure. After he chewed off the last pieces of candy from the white stick, he tossed it in the paper sack he carried in his tote bag for just that purpose. He thought, *The Girl never takes this long. Maybe she didn't hear me knock?* He looked at the house; he noticed—not for the first time—that a few of the windows were boarded up and that old paint was flaking off the crooked brick wall. Out of respect for his friend, he resisted the temptation to reach out and touch that old wall and ask it to share its secrets. He knocked again, putting all of his strength into it. This time the door gave and opened slightly. He heard a loud crash coming from inside the house.

There was a second, louder crash. And muted laughter. The Boy pushed the door open a bit wider and shouted: "Girl! Are you in there?"

There was no answer, and that frightened the Boy. He was worried about his friend. He had never been inside her house, and the thought of crossing the threshold filled him with a dread he couldn't explain.

He forced himself to gather his courage. Sometimes, his friends teased him because of his cowardice, but he knew he was brave. It's just that there was so much that scared him. Every day there were new fears to confront. Yes, he cried and sometimes froze with fear. But he didn't run away, and he didn't pretend not to be scared. Every morning, after his mom had filled up his tote bag with lollipops and kissed him goodbye, she smiled at him and said: "My brave little man!" His mother would never lie to him.

Suddenly, just as he was about to push the door wide open and run into the house in search of the Girl (or at least when he thought he was just about to), the door flung open and the Kid Whose Laughter Makes Adults Run Away stepped outside the Girl's house. The Girl followed, holding hands with the Kid. Today her hair was white with jet-black streaks. She wore a torn button-up shirt. Black, of course. She always dressed in black. The shirt was so long that it covered up the usual black denim shorts that she was in all likelihood also wearing.

The Girl, her face impassive (as it so often was), closed the door behind her while the Kid, grinning wide, said: "Good morning, Boy!" The Kid chuckled. "Good morning! Ha! Did these walls tell you anything?" The Kid punched the wall of the house.

The Boy blushed. The Kid had been in the Girl's house! No one ever went inside the Girl's house. And why were they holding hands? Something new and different was happening, but he didn't know what. He felt left out. No—more: he felt betrayed by his two friends, but he couldn't articulate or even guess at the nature of this betrayal.

The Boy tried to speak, not really knowing what he was going to say, but the words were trapped by a stutter, and he repeated the same indeterminate sound several times until the Kid tickled him and then bolted from the porch, daring both the Boy and the Girl to catch up.

Without meeting his eyes the Girl squeezed the Boy's shoulder, and they ran off together after the Kid. The long-legged Kid ran much faster than either the Girl, who tended to be easily short of breath, or the plump, short-legged Boy, who never cared much for physical exertion. After a block and a half of heavy breathing, they completely lost sight of the Kid.

The Boy, drenched in sweat, and the Girl, so pale now that she almost looked like a skeleton, plopped themselves against the wall of Venus & Milo's High-Class Discount Beauty Salon, Coffee Shop & No-Nonsense Aquarian Therapy Clinic. The Boy, hunched over with his eyes half-closed, trying to catch his breath, heard the Girl giggle wheezily. He looked up at her, and she pointed at the large window of Venus & Milo's. Inside, the Boy saw Milo parading around like a runway model, in what looked like a fancy, expensive dress. He walked in those spike heels like he was born to it. Venus lounged back in one the swivelling chairs that customers sat in to get their hair cut or styled, smoking a long cigarette and clapping his hands in delight. Milo's legs were thick and hairy, and, to the Boy, the dress had a comical effect, but from the loving expression on Venus's face the Boy Who Speaks with Walls knew that Milo was showing off for someone who thought he looked radiant.

The Boy laughed along with the Girl. It was such a rare treat to hear her laugh. He caught her eye and was rewarded with a conspiratorial wink that soothed away the betrayal he had felt earlier.

Suddenly the door to Venus & Milo's pushed open, and out poured Milo, in his low-cut blue velvet dress that showed off a thick patch of chest hair. "Boy! Girl! What a pleasure! Come on in!"

The Boy and the Girl sat down on the swivelling chairs, and, as they often did, spun them around, enjoying the dizzy feeling. Milo lit a cigar and then snapped open a Tupperware container, offering the children some doughnuts. "I made these last night. Go on."

The two children each grabbed a sugar-sprinkled doughnut. "Thank you," the Boy said for the both of them. "Where's Venus? We thought we saw him through the window."

Blowing out thick rings of smoke, Milo said, "He'll be right out. He just went to—" Just then, Venus walked through the bead curtain that separated the front from the back of the shop, holding a tray, saying, "Herbal tea, darlings?"

Venus was slim and elegant. He wore black wool pants, a pocketless and collarless white shirt with the top button open, a trim black vest, and shiny black shoes. Black eyeliner highlighted his dark blue eyes. A red scarf, tied around his neck, added a flash of dazzle that was echoed by the red belt across his waist. His jet-black hair was gelled tightly on his head, and a pencil-thin mustache decorated his upper lip. He moved with the grace of a cat.

Venus winked at the children. "The usual?" The Girl nodded her assent, while the Boy grunted his: lemon-ginger zinger for the Girl, three-berry blend for the Boy, both heavily laced with honey. The adults drank mint.

"Isn't the Kid with you today?" asked Venus. "That one dresses so well." His eyes lost focus, as if he were staring into a dream.

The Boy, interrupting his attempt to cool down the tea by gently blowing on it, answered, "We were all together this morning, and then the Kid ran off, daring us to catch up." The Boy took a sip of tea. "That Kid sure runs faster than we do. A lot faster. But we'll find the Kid. We'll get the Kid."

For the next minute or so, everyone sipped their tea in silence. All around the shop, there were plastic plants ("So much cleaner!" Venus always said) in hand-painted pots ("It's the inner me," Milo often repeated about the loud colours and abstract designs). A long and narrow counter showcased a spectacular variety of coffee pots, coffee grinders, coffee makers, and all kinds of coffee paraphernalia that looked very strange to the Boy. Most of it was for sale, but some of it was to prepare coffee for customers. One wall featured a rotating gallery of Milo's paintings ("The outside world's not ready yet," he would sometimes remark sadly). The wall facing it displayed Venus's most recent photographs. The current series were all self-portraits in extreme closeup. Next to the door, hung a giant sign advertising the different products and services offered at Venus & Milo's High-Class Discount Beauty Salon, Coffee Shop & No-Nonsense Aquarian Therapy Clinic.

The Girl Who Eats Fire slipped out of her chair and went to take a closer look at Venus's photographs.

It occurred to the Boy that he had never been inside Venus & Milo's without the Kid. "C-C-Can I ask you guys a question?" The Boy Who Speaks with Walls stuttered only when he was scared. (He scared easily.) It was much easier to speak with walls. He wasn't confronted with all kinds of imagined expectations and judgments by gazing into the pool of their eyes, because they didn't have any (at least not the way people understood such things). There was something about the question he wanted to ask that made him feel as if his feet were dangling off a precipice.

He didn't usually stutter much with Venus and Milo. They were different from other adults. Most adults forgot they had ever been children, but the Boy felt that Venus and Milo, even all grown up, had never completely stopped being children.

"Of course, Boy, anything!" Venus laughed reassuringly, lighting a long thin white cigarette.

"Ask away," chimed in Milo, waving the butt of his cigar and brushing ashes off his dress with his free hand.

"Well . . . How- How c-come you guys aren't afraid of- of the K-Kid? Most grownups always wanna run away from our friend. Especially when the Kid laughs, which is almost always, and then you should see the look in their eyes! B-but, you guys, you . . . you like the Kid! Why?"

"Well . . . " said Venus. Milo noisily coughed up some cigar smoke.

"That Kid is pretty special, you know," continued Venus. "Milo and I, well, we . . . We like to be friends with people who need good friends. We're your friends, too, Boy, and you, too, G—"

Milo nudged Venus and pointed toward the door with his cigar butt. There was the Kid, inside the shop, leaning on the doorframe and smiling an especially scary smile. The sunlight glowed like a crown around the Kid's thick auburn curls.

The Boy exclaimed, "Kid! How did you—When did you —I m-mean, no one heard—"

Across the room, the Girl grinned.

"So, I'm special, am I?" That smile was really scary, thought the Boy. *If I were a grownup, I'd be running away so fast!*

"Special!" That smile was getting scarier and scarier.

The Kid moved slowly toward Venus and Milo, smiling.

Both Venus and Milo trembled a little bit. That smile sure was getting to them. Milo said, "Kid, we—we're—we're happy to see you." Venus's eyes looked like they were trying to retreat into his head.

"Special! I'll show you special!" And then the Kid Whose Laughter Makes Adults Run Away laughed—a soft, menacing laugh. No one laughed quite like the Kid.

The laughter seemed to grow and take up physical space in the shop, although no one could actually see it. Venus and Milo squirmed, as if the laughter were crawling all over them. They both opened their mouths as if to speak, but then suddenly fled from the front of the shop, to hide behind the bead curtain.

The Girl now stood next to the Kid, her face back to its neutral expression. "Let's get out of here," said the Kid to the other two children and winking at the Girl.

The Boy was angry with the Kid. What was the matter with his friend today? Why was the Kid acting so mean and tough? The Kid always had an edge, but not like this, not like this at all.

Outside, the Kid said, "Why'd you guys go in there! Why didn't you try to find me? Some friends you are."

Did the Boy imagine the quickly suppressed sadness on the Girl's face? Unusually, his anger was stronger than his fear. He confronted the Kid. "What's wrong you today, Kid? Why are you trying to make everyone so miserable? We were gonna leave there soon to find you, you know. Why d'you do that to Venus and Milo? They're our friends! They like you!"

"Ha! Venus and Milo! They think I'm a boy." The Kid sneered, then grabbed the Girl's hand. She let the Kid hold it, but she looked uncomfortable.

"What are you talking about? They never said anything like that! Besides, they like the Girl, too." The Boy's earlier feelings of betrayal had resurfaced, and they further fueled his anger toward the Kid.

"Boy!" The Kid grinned at the Boy. "What are you so mad about? You're so sensitive. I was just fooling."

It was true that the Kid always enjoyed giving adults a good scare. The Kid liked seeing how uncomfortable they could become, liked being responsible for it. The Boy was mollified, at least for now, and he mumbled, "Okay, sorry."

The Kid let go of the Girl's hand and started gesticulating nervously. "We have to do something fun today. Something really exciting! Dangerous!"

"Like what?" The Boy was not quite successful in hiding that he was once more suspicious of the Kid.

The Kid glared at him, but then the Kid's smile unexpectedly turned from menacing to friendly. "Like . . . like . . . Come on, help me out. I want this to be fun for all three of us."

"I want to eat."

The Boy reflexively picked a lollipop out of his bag and gave it, unwrapped, to the Girl. The Girl never spoke unless circumstances prevented her from staying silent. Her friends knew it, and because they were her friends they rarely required her to speak. Whenever circumstances forced her to talk, the Boy Who Speaks with Walls offered her a lollipop.

The Boy and the Kid watched the Girl suck on the banana-orange lollipop, both of them stunned into silence by the Girl's unexpected utterance. She was very thin, so thin her bones looked like they were about to puncture her flesh.

When she finished the lollipop, she dropped the chewed-up sticky white stick on the ground. The Boy had to stop himself from reprimanding her. Littering was bad, but he felt it was the wrong time to point it out to his friend for the zillionth time.

"That was good. Now I want to eat something hot. Really hot." There was cruelty in her eyes when she spoke.

The Kid quickly took charge again. "Okay, Boy, do your stuff. Find us an abandoned building. One with lots of wood!" The Kid took out a lighter and flicked it on and off three times.

It was a little-known fact that buildings spoke to each other. Not that every building got along; not every building was community-minded, but that's true of people, too. The Boy pressed his hands against the wall of the nearest building, Tim Tom's Fast Food, Fast Photo & Fast Surgery Service Centre, and asked it if it knew of any building suitable for their needs. It did, and it gave the Boy directions. The Boy thanked it, then turned to his friends.

The Girl Who Eats Fire brought a new lollipop to her mouth—she must have grabbed one from the Boy's bag while he was distracted—and as the grin spread to her eyes, she rubbed herself against the Kid, like a kitten. The Boy was shocked at the grin that spread across the Girl's face and at her uncharacteristically coquettish behaviour.

The Boy said, "There's a place, but it's next to Greytown."

The Girl's face betrayed a flash of fear, but the Kid didn't see it. "Let's go! I love watching the Girl eat." The Kid walked off excitedly without a backward glance. The Boy and the Girl hesitated, but then followed their friend.

Everyone knew about Greytown, but nobody ever went there. Ever. When adults wanted to scare children into submission, they'd threaten to send them to Greytown. They'd point to old homeless men and women—with their crooked spines, broken teeth, and torn, drab clothes, coughing so hard it was easy to imagine pieces of blackened lung flying out of their mouths. They'd say, "That's what happens to you when you go to Greytown!"

The children took a detour to avoid running into Cop Carla; that decision was taken wordlessly. When they saw her help old Ms. Blossomglow cross the street to get to Sir Harold's Personalized Skin-Pigment Treatment Spa & Imported Rug Warehouse, they all knew they had to take a less direct route so the police officer wouldn't spot them. Cop Carla was always trying to meddle into their affairs. When Cop Carla wore her uniform, the Kid just couldn't seem to scare her. But a few times, in the evenings, when she wore civilian clothes, the Kid had run into her, and those times she'd run away screaming from the Kid. At least, that's what the Kid had said to the Boy and Girl. The Boy had never seen Cop Carla out of uniform; all he'd witnessed was the Kid's humiliatingly unsuccessful attempts at making her run away.

As they neared the edge of Greytown, the Boy looked at the smog that spewed skyward out of the grimy suburb like lava from a volcano.

The Boy told his friends, "We n-n-need to t-t-tu-t-turn left here."

The Kid was jubilant when they reached their destination. "Good work, Boy! This is perfect!" The faded sign above the front door of the abandoned building was still legible: Captain Willy's Printing Press, Lumberyard & Comprehensive High School. "A school! We're gonna burn down a school!"

"What do you kids think you're doing?" It was Cop Carla, of course. She always seemed to find them, like the time they'd broken into the lollipop factory, or the time they'd started digging a tunnel in the mayor's backyard, or the time they'd cut out nude photos from a picture magazine and taped them inside the pages of the giveaway prayer books at the Holy Evangelical Steak House, Flagellation Hut & Gas Station. The Boy never did find out how or where the Kid got that magazine.

The children ran. Cop Carla ran after them. Ahead of the children was a thick wall of smog, the border of Greytown.

Cop Carla was catching up to them. It was her or Greytown.

As the Boy hit the smog—it was so thick it almost felt like swimming in mud—Cop Carla shouted something at the children, but he didn't make out her words. For a second it felt as if the smog held him aloft, but then he almost twisted his ankle with his next step. Suddenly, the ground was rough and uneven, like a bad paving job after an earthquake.

At first, the Boy couldn't see anything. He'd stopped running and was now walking deeper into Greytown. After a few minutes, he could see small spheres of light cutting through the grey haze. "Hey guys, lights!" He shouted at his friends, hoping for some response, because he was afraid they'd all become separated in the darkness. From close by, he heard the Girl hiss a sharp "Shh!" Then, he felt her hand on his arm and they walked together, in silence, toward the nearest globe of light.

The pair stood under the source of light. The flame flickered in the old-fashioned street lamp. Forgetting the Girl's warning, the Boy shouted, "Kid! Where are—"

The Girl Who Eats Fire slapped her hand against his mouth to shut him up. She whispered, "Don't talk. Don't bring attention to us. And don't let go of me. This is important: Do. Not. Let. Go. I don't want to lose you, too." Shocked at hearing her speak so confidently and spooked by his surroundings, the

Boy forgot to offer her a lollipop. After a few seconds the Girl reached into his tote bag and drew out a kiwi-flavoured one. She let the wrapper fall to the ground. The Boy watched the wrapper fall, following its descent with the help of the flickering reflection of light on the transparent plastic, but the feeble illumination was insufficient to penetrate the thick haze as far as the ground. He couldn't even see his own feet.

He opened his mouth, almost speaking to the Girl, but an impending stutter gave him pause, and he closed it again. He wanted to ask her questions, but he realized he didn't know which questions, exactly, to ask.

The Girl's gaze panned from the Boy's face to the wall behind the lamppost. He nodded at her, and they walked together to the wall. The Boy firmly pressed one palm against it. "It says the Kid hasn't been by here," he told the Girl in a soft whisper as he removed his hand from the wall.

Was the Kid continuing the hide-and-seek game that had been interrupted earlier? Or were all three of them lost in this unfamiliar place? The Boy asked himself these questions while he waited for the Girl to indicate what they would do next. She seemed more focused than usual and wasn't behaving as lost as he felt. He had no idea what to do next.

Suddenly, he heard the trot of hooves against the pavement. The sound was coming toward them. The Girl pulled at his arm, and together they ran away, to hide from the sound and the light.

When they stopped, the Boy panted heavily from the exertion and the thick smog invading his lungs. The Girl had no trouble breathing.

The Boy looked around him, but he couldn't see anything. The smog was too thick, the atmosphere too dark. He felt completely lost. He couldn't imagine ever being able to find his way out of this thick mist that made everything invisible. He missed the blue sky; he missed his parents; he missed his house; he missed his mom's meals; he missed Venus and Milo;

he missed *The Adventures of Shade Savage*; he missed his
comic books; he missed the smell of the old paperbacks on the
shelf next to his bed; he missed the weekly Sunday phone calls
from his old grandmother who always seemed so interested in
everything about him; he missed going to the movies on the
weekends with his father and Jules (his dad's best friend); he
missed the stray cats he fed in his backyard; he missed the
Kid, who had been his friend longer than anyone; he even
missed Cop Carla's constant vigilance. It felt as if all of these
things had been forever swallowed up by Greytown, even
though the Boy had only been here for a short while, no longer
than half an hour. His eyes watered up, stung by the smog, and
in no time he was crying.

The Girl squeezed his hand, allowing him to come
through his fit. After a few minutes, he murmured, "What are
we going to do, Girl? Where will we go?"

Again, the Girl spoke: "Close your eyes, Boy. Keep them
shut and count to two hundred. And then open them slowly.
And you'll see. You'll see."

The Boy opened his mouth . . . to complain? . . . to ask
questions? . . . to disagree? He never found out. There was an
urgency to the way that the Girl's hand tightly held on to his,
an urgency that refused to be questioned. He shut his mouth
and closed his eyes. And he counted, abandoning himself
entirely to the string of numbers. One. Two. Three . . .

. . . Two hundred! Slowly, like the Girl had instructed
him to, he opened his eyes—and found that he could see; not
clearly, but he could make out the shape of some nearby
buildings and details of their close surroundings, even though
there were no lampposts in sight or any other visible light
source to pierce the dense smog. His eyes had adjusted to the
slight amount of sunlight that diffused through the grey
atmosphere.

They were in a dead-end alley, some three buildings
deep and one wide. Across from the wall on which the Boy and

the Girl were leaning, cylinders pumped out grey smog: some in quick currents, others in slow streams, others still in irregular explosions like old diesel engines struggling to get started, and still others in steady bursts, as if they were obeying the beat of a military march. The cylinders were of all sizes, some as small as household plumbing, others as big as a patio door. The Boy couldn't see as far as the roof of the middle building. It was so high it seemed to meld with the smog. The surface of its wall was spotted with all sizes of cylinders, sometimes in thick clumps, sometimes spread out haphazardly. The building to the left, the one closest to the dead end, was only two storeys high, and a huge cylinder, spewing a thick slow stream of smog, sprouted out from the centre of its wall. The building to the right, where the alley opened out, was three or four times as high as the short one and only had one small cylinder out of which smoke leaked out slowly. The Boy could just barely make out the jutting stone that bordered its roof.

The Girl pulled him up, and they left the alley.

Again, the Boy was struck by the definite purpose in the Girl's steps. She seemed to know where she was going. But how could she? And where did she think she was leading them? Back where they'd come from? To the Kid? How could she know where the Kid was in this place? Was all of this a plan the Girl and the Kid had concocted earlier, before the Boy had met them at the Girl's house? Was this a prank to scare him, to make fun of him? He wished he could voice these questions, but both his potential stutter and the Girl's stern command of silence stayed his voice.

They hadn't walked far when a loud, familiar voice boomed from behind them, "There you are!" And there was Cop Carla, as always, right on their heels. The Boy had never been so grateful for her unshakeable presence. Cop Carla would get them all out of this horrible place that smelled like an old, unventilated garage.

The Girl screamed, "No!" Her grip on the Boy's hand was so tight that he thought his bones would break. She started to run away from the police officer. The Boy was taken by surprise by the Girl's abrupt movements, and they both stumbled to the ground, scraping their hands on the asphalt.

Again, the Girl screamed, "No!" She reached for the Boy. "Don't ever let go of me, or they'll see you!"

The Boy had no idea what the Girl was talking about.

Cop Carla knelt down. "Are you kids alright?" She furrowed her brow. "What were you thinking? Coming in here! This is the most dangerous stunt you've pulled all summer!" She squinted quizzically at the children and asked, looking the Boy right in the eye, "Isn't the Kid with you? I saw all three of you brats run in here."

"I-I-I ha-he d-d-did we—" The Boy erupted in tears, overwhelmed by the shame of his impediment, the intimidating presence of the adult, and the fear his surroundings inspired.

In a menacing tone, the Girl answered, "We got separated. Okay? We don't know where the Kid is. Leave us alone. This is none of your business." Her voice betrayed absolute hatred for the intruding adult.

"Well, we'll see what your parents think about that! Come on! Get up! I'm taking you back home!" Cop Carla stood up, towering over the fallen children.

The Girl shouted, "Like you know my parents! How could you?"

Cop Carla's mouth hung open in silence for a moment. The children never knew what she would have said next because, right then, her head burst into flame. The Boy had never heard such a terrible shriek in all his life. But even more frightening was the deep, guffawing laughter that was just as loud as Cop Carla's screams. Who or what was laughing like that? It was a laugh, the Boy was sure, that would scare even the Kid, were his friend to hear it.

"D-do something!" He shouted at the Girl, "Eat the fire! You c-c-can s-save her!"

"It's too late," the Girl answered. "Like I would anyway. I hate her."

A voice erupted from the darkness: "Are you here, wayward daughter? We have your friend. That confused child who doesn't know whether to be a boy or a girl. Would you like to see what we've done to your friend?"

The Girl dug her fingers into the Boy's arm, hurting him. She ran, dragging the stammering Boy behind her, leading them both deeper and deeper into the dark greyness of Greytown.

The Girl spoke again. "I'm getting you out of here. It's too dangerous for you. Too dangerous for me, too, to have you with me. The only way I'll be able to save the Kid is alone."

"The Kid is my friend, too. I'm n-n-n-ot going to ab-aba-abandon you. Either of you. I'm not a c-coward."

The Girl leaned forward and pressed her lips against the Boy's.

"I never said you were. But . . . this is where I come from. I escaped when I was five years old. I'm invisible to them. But you, you're a stranger. They can sense you, find you. I can hide you a little when we're touching, but that won't save you forever. I can find the Kid—or at least I can try—but if you stay I might lose both of you."

"What about m-m-me? What if I l-lose the two of you? We're all three of us friends together."

"I'm sorry, Boy." She kissed him again, and he shivered when her tongue touched his. Then he felt smoke pour out of her mouth and into his throat. He tried to break free, but her grip was much stronger than he expected. He lost consciousness.

Part 2
Home Is Where the Friends Are

The Boy woke up coughing. Milo held his hand and said, "Welcome back, Boy." Milo wore red overalls and a pink shirt. Then Venus, dressed as elegantly as ever, walked into the room, holding a tray with a tea set and a glass of water. "Three-berry blend?"

The Boy's throat was too raw, and he almost choked when he tried to speak, so he nodded instead.

Venus poured the tea for all three of them. He said, "The Girl brought you here, carrying you in her scrawny arms. Who would have thought that little thing could be so strong?"

Milo added, "She said to tell you that she was going back, and that you shouldn't follow. But she didn't say where. And then she ran off."

The Boy drank some water and found his voice again. "We have to go to Greytown. To save the Kid. Please." The Boy jumped out of bed.

Venus and Milo exchanged a glance. Venus said, "Greytown?" The two men clasped hands. Milo asked, "Is that where your friends are, Boy?"

The Boy nodded.

"Are they in danger?"

"Yes."

"Then let's go."

En route, the Boy filled them in on what had happened. Venus and Milo listened solemnly to the Boy's story. But when the trio reached the edge of Greytown . . . the suburb was nowhere in sight. Where Greytown used to be, they found a big empty parking lot—the size of several city blocks—with sickly weeds growing out of the cracked asphalt.

None of the nearby walls could tell the Boy what had happened or how to find his friends again.

* * *

The next morning, the Boy Who Speaks with Walls left his parents' house at dawn, before his mom woke up, before she could fill up his tote bag with lollipops, give him a kiss, and tell him that he was her brave little man. Stepping outside without the comforting weight of his tote bag was an unusual experience, but he found that he liked the sensation. He felt both lighter and taller . . . and perhaps a little naked.

The previous evening he had fallen asleep overwhelmed by despair, but the night had given him an idea.

He crossed the street and stepped onto the porch of the Girl's house, that house that looked so much like something out of Greytown. He stood there for a few seconds and breathed in the cool morning air. Summer was almost over. His eyes were moist with memories of his friends, the Girl Who Eats Fire and the Kid Whose Laughter Makes Adults Run Away.

He didn't knock. He turned the doorknob and pushed open the unlocked door.

He stepped inside and touched the walls. The Girl's house spoke to him and revealed its secrets.

Years ago, when she first emerged from Greytown, the Girl Who Eats Fire barricaded one door of the house across the street from the Boy's. The door was in the basement, under the staircase. The slanted wall there remembered the hammering and the nails.

She had emerged from that door, five years old, and dirty with blood and soot.

The Boy tried to pull off the planks with his bare hands, but he wasn't strong enough. He looked around and found a hammer. It wasn't much of a tool, but it was probably the same hammer the Girl had used. If it had been good enough to put up these planks, it would have to be enough to take them down.

* * *

Crossing the threshold of the long-condemned door, the Boy
felt suspended in nothingness, a sensation not unlike what
he'd experienced when he first penetrated the smog of
Greytown, but then he emerged into a narrow passageway.
Nails stuck out from the walls. They kept ripping his clothes
and scratching his skin. The passageway smelled like a
laundry hamper stuffed with old socks drenched in sour milk
and rotten eggs.

To his right, there was a thumb-sized hole in the wall.
When he looked through it, he saw an old man and an old
woman sitting at a kitchen table. They looked almost the same,
except the man was bearded and their clothes were different.
They were very thin, much like the Girl, but their backs were
crooked, their chins hanging halfway down their chests; their
long grey hair was thin and wispy. Their clothes, also, were
grey: the man wore a rumpled suit and tie badly in need of
mending; the woman, a shapeless dress riddled with holes.
Their skin was sickly grey.

The woman stood up and opened a cupboard door. She
took a small box from the shelf, closed the door, and sat next to
the man.

Together, they opened the box and took out its contents,
one object at a time. The Boy thought it looked like a ceremony
of some sort.

The first thing they took out was a candle, and then a
candleholder, and then a matchbox. The woman placed the
candle in the candleholder, and the man struck a match and
lighted the candle.

Next, the woman took out baby pyjamas. The man
reached in the box and brought out a pacifier. And then the
Boy noticed that the old couple was crying quietly, tears slowly
travelling down their grey cheeks. They continued to pull
objects from the box: a rattle, baby shoes, a small frayed

blanket. They laid these objects in a tidy arc around the candleholder's base. Suddenly, the woman let out a deep sob. The man reached over, put an arm across her back, and tenderly kissed her cheek. His hand stroked her neck and his fingers rubbed her scalp. He held their heads against each other's, and they cried together.

A lump formed in the Boy's throat. He wanted to cry along with them. It felt wrong and dirty to be spying on these people, but he couldn't bring himself to stop watching.

And then they took out a photograph of a little girl. The Boy gasped when he recognized the younger face of his lost friend.

The old man said, "Who's there?"

The Boy answered, "I'm a friend of the Girl. I've come to rescue her." The wall told him how to get out of the secret passageway. He stepped down nine steps in the darkness, ripping his clothes and flesh on yet more nails. Then he crouched down and found the hidden panel. He slid it open and, being so plump, was barely able to squeeze through it.

He emerged in the pantry, with the old couple staring at him.

The woman said, "Where did you come from?"

The old couple served the Boy tea while they listened to his story. He sipped at the tea as politely as he could, but it smelled—and tasted—like garbage sprayed with cat urine.

There was a lot of commotion outside. Hoofbeats. Banging doors. Crashes. Shouts. Screams.

The old couple shushed away all the Boy's questions. They wanted to know everything about the Girl, who was their granddaughter. But the Boy grew impatient with them and their curiosity. His friends' lives might be in danger, and he needed this old couple to answer his questions, to give him a clue as to how to go about finding the Girl and the Kid in this forbidding place.

"What's going on out there? Answer me! Is it always like this?"

"No . . . they must know the Girl is back. They don't like it when people leave. They're going to punish her, make an example of her." The old woman cried as she said this, and the old man, pacing around the room, balled up his fists so tightly that his long, cracked nails drew blood from his palms.

"Who's they?"

"The mayor and her husband, the prime alderman," said the woman, hiding her eyes. "Our daughter and her husband. The Girl's parents."

The Boy gathered his courage and wandered deeper and deeper into the darkness of Greytown, doing his best to steer clear of the mayoral forces roaming the streets. He kept his hands firmly on the walls of the closely packed houses, so he could remember his way back to the house of the Girl's grandparents. He could always tell one wall from another, even when he couldn't see anything.

But the walls of Greytown were only too eager to share with the Boy all they'd witnessed: the years of brutality; of houses being broken into by semi-ethereal smog creatures in black uniforms; of broken, gnarled old people dragged away by smoke-spewing, coal-powered mechanical soldiers; of a laughing man with a mouth of fire riding on horseback, cracking his whip, and running down burning, screaming children. Occasionally, the walls gave him brief, shadowy glimpses of the Girl's face, but he couldn't tell if they were of her younger self or more recent memories. Also he was shown a grown woman, riding in a chauffeur-driven red convertible, whose face strongly resembled the Girl's. With a handgun, she aimed at the heads of fleeing passersby. Too often, her aim was true.

And then, within this barrage of unwelcome images and sounds, the Kid appeared, tied up and bloodied, being dragged on the cobblestoned street at the end of a rope. The image flashed by so quickly that he couldn't figure out in which direction his friend was being dragged, or any other detail that might, however improbably, help him accomplish his mission. The Boy sharpened his focus, asking the wall of this abandoned printing press to tell him more.

But then . . . "Boy! How did you get back here?"

The Girl!

The Boy couldn't see a thing, but the wall shared what it perceived: in her arms, the Girl held the wounded Kid, naked and covered with bloody gashes.

The Boy led the Girl to the house of her grandparents.

When the three children burst into their house, the old couple yelled out in alarm, but then they gasped when, as one, their gaze fell on the Girl. Before anyone had time to say anything, the Girl spoke: "No time to lose. They're on my trail, and they're bound to figure out where I went. They closed the city off from the outside world. This is our only way out, and we all have to leave right now!"

The Girl's grandparents crowded around her, but the Girl shooed them away. "There's no time for that. Granma, Granpa, I missed you so much. I thought you were dead after what happened, but—"

The old man said, "Your parents tortured us, but they finally let us go."

The Girl was speechless for a second, and her face scrunched up like she was about to cry, but then she turned to the Boy. "Get into the pantry and make the hole larger, or we'll never get the Kid through there."

The Boy ran to the pantry, bent down, slid open the secret panel, and gripped the wall. He quickly apologized to the wall, then set about his task. The wall was old and thin, and it came apart as he tore at it barehanded with all his strength.

The noise outside was growing louder.

"That'll have to be enough. Let's go."

The old couple sat down at the table.

"Granma! Granpa! You too!"

The old woman said, "No, Girl. Our old lungs are used to Greytown. We wouldn't survive in the outside world. Besides, this way, we can stall them, steer them in the wrong direction. We're proud of you. That you're so brave. That you have such good friends."

The Girl looked like she wanted to protest; instead, a tear slid down her cheek. She gently laid the Kid on the floor and rushed to hug her grandparents. But she quickly disentangled herself.

Without another word, the Girl and the Boy carried the Kid up the nine steps hidden behind the kitchen wall, wincing every time they noticed a nail tearing into the Kid's already lacerated flesh.

Venus and Milo, both of whom were licensed Aquarian therapists, nursed the Kid back to health. It turned out that the Kid's father had thrown his child out of the house the day before the three friends' adventure in Greytown, so the Kid moved in with Venus and Milo. They had plenty of space for one more.

After the Kid recovered, Venus, Milo, and the Kid invited the Boy and the Girl to dinner every Thursday night. The Girl didn't show up every week, but the Boy was there every time. The Boy had never seen the Kid so relaxed, as if all that rage had finally stopped piling up.

Greytown never did reappear. So the city started construction on a shopping mall to go next to that huge, empty parking lot. The Girl and the Boy tried to use the doorway to visit the Girl's grandparents again, to make sure the old couple was safe, but the door under the steps now opened onto a concrete wall. The Boy tried talking to it. The wall stayed resolutely mute.

For months, the Girl cried herself to sleep. Often, the Boy would be there to hold her. Once her breathing had calmed and she was finally asleep, his shirt wet with her tears, he'd cross the street and go back to his house. When spring came along, her mood finally lightened.

The next summer, the afternoon school let out, while the Boy, the Girl, and the Kid were hanging out and sipping smoothies at Max the Guru's Hip-Hop Diner & Secondhand Nautical Gear Emporium, the Boy asked, "Do you miss making adults afraid?" The Kid—who still bore, and would always bear, scars that would forever remind the three friends of Greytown—hadn't laughed that way since the previous summer. Whether the laugh was gone or whether the Kid had chosen not to use it anymore, the Kid wouldn't say.

"No. Not really. I think I was making myself afraid, too. Afraid of adults, I mean." The Kid paused, scrutinizing the Boy. "Hey! I just realized something! You don't stutter anymore!"

"No, not since I had to go and rescue you guys."

The Girl let out a big whoop. "Rescue us? I did all the rescuing, buster!"

Staring at the clock behind the cash counter, the Kid shushed the other two and whispered. "Wait for it."

The Boy said, "It . . . ? What's going to happen? What did you—?"

The Kid's smile grew just a tad menacing, and the Girl's eyes widened in anticipation.

SIX

Leah Bobet

Six and Joe bunk together nights in the smallest north-side billet on the twentieth floor. "Take care of your brother," Mama said when she gave them the key to the rooms. They shut the door behind them on their brand new domain: polished parquet floors and a fresh-netted balcony, a mattress in the corner and walls white as white, ready to be decorated with scribbles or artwork or sun, moon, and stars. And Joe pulled a face.

"She meant it to me," he said, with a flip of his curly girl's hair, and strutted into the tiled bathroom to wash.

That's not when Six started hating him, but it's when he knew it to the bone.

Six's name is really Charlie, but he's the devil's boy right through, and they've been calling him by the devil's number since he was old enough to walk. Sixth son of a seventh son; "You're bad news," the brothers' wives tell him afternoons between rows of peas trained up to the ceiling on the seventeenth floor. A couple of them ruffle his hair after they say it, fix him with a crooked, between-you-and-me smile. A couple of 'em don't.

Nobody ever tells Joe he's bad news.

Six locked him out twice when he pulled faces behind Six's back, and he wailed in the halls 'til Mama gave him his own key at seven, and *no* Higgins ever got their own key at seven. Six hid Joe's stuffy toy next and Mama strapped him for the first time ever over that, and now Six is Bad News. Six won't punch Joe in the nose for that insult 'cause Joe's still the baby, and it's his job to take care of the baby no matter what Joe thinks Mama said to who.

But Joe gets away with murder, gets the steals of pastry and half-days off that Six never got even before he was Bad News. Joe's seventh, Sunday-born seventh, and he's had a destiny since he was yea high.

It drives Six clean nuts.

"I'll die," Six whispers, late at night, curled up in his bedroll on the edge of the fat mattress that the littlest Higgins boys share. "I'll throw myself off the tall pasture and then you won't be seventh no more."

This used to freeze Joe mid-breath. He's nine years old now and got himself wise to it. "You're fulla shit," he says proudly—nobody ever boxed his ears none for saying *shit* like a street-picker's boy—and puts a pillow over his ear.

"I will," Six breathes. Imagines leaping, the tug of wind, falling, falling. "I will and you'll go to the devil."

Of course, Joe squeals in the morning.

Six gets hauled into Father's office after breakfast with last year's blackberry jam still on his mouth. "What're you telling your brother?" Father says, back to his desk and leaning heavy in his big black leather-backed chair. There are papers scattered on his desk, Market language that Six can't yet read. Interrupting Father's work used to be worth a spanking too, when more of the brothers and sisters were young. Father is a busy man. Except when it comes to Joe.

"Nothin'," Six mutters, knowing there's no good answer to give.

Father clucks his tongue, and Six bounces back and forth from foot to foot, rearing, raring to go. The air in Father's office smells dry and sweet like paper. All the other air in the clan building smells like dirt and green.

"Saturday's child has far to go," Six's father sighs under his fat moustache, and Six hates him. Father is the agribaron of the whole central district. Everyone in central knows him; he has three whole cars on the Moving Market staffed by Six and Joe's big sisters, and on Sunday market the papermen and water-sellers and the three rich owners of Hydro tip their hats at his clan through the windows.

Six isn't allowed to work the Market cars. Six makes trouble. The last time, he threw fresh tomatoes at the tailor's little boy, and Mama went white with rage and sentenced him to garden work until he knew the value of good food.

So now Six works in the gardens, underfoot between his big sister Lucinda and stupid little Joe, who's small enough and spoiled to only do half-chores in the kitchen and be a pain in the ass the rest of the day. All the Higgins children know their sums and their letters, but Joe's gonna go to the alchemists when he's ten. Seventh son of a seventh son's strong magic by them, so he doesn't do full-chores and hasn't learned the garden. There's no use in it if you're going away.

Six weeds tomato beds all afternoon in whispery silent disgrace, stared at crinkle-eyed by sisters and brothers and their wives, but he doesn't throw them at no one. He goes up to the tall pasture, spread over the soaring rooftop, and feeds the ducks that lay in the pond that used to be a tiled swimming pool. And Joe follows him everywhere, kicking and pinching and chattering so loud the mama ducks flutter their wings and stick their necks out in case Joe's starting something with their brats.

Sunshine comes through the windows around the pond, through the thick glass door that goes out to the pasture and the wall that keeps the goats and sheep from the thirty-floor drop below. Six goes to the rail and looks down, way down: the cracked pavement streets and rubbled-out buildings stretch all the way to the lakeshore, empty of people, of ships. He turns around, fingers tight on the rail, tries to glance casual over the backs of the Uncles' prize flock of sheep.

Joe watches him. He don't even flinch.

It's halfway down to dinnertime before Six finally loses Joe, trailing him into the kitchens Mama keeps on floor twenty-six and making a run for it when Joe's eyes stray to the fat raisin cake for dessert time. He runs pounding down the stairs down to floor number six, still uncleared, full of pigeon shit where the screen doors came open once upon a time.

When Father and his brothers claimed the clan building for their own they started cleaning from the top: the work hasn't gone down past nine these days, not with all hands busy with the milking and shearing and growing and weeding and tending to the biggest clan farm in all of central district—and with the cousins clearing their own buildings, taking up their trades and moving out. The twenty-second floor was once Uncle Elmer's yarnshop. The twenty-first, Uncle Ignatz's dairy. The nineteenth was Uncle Eddie's garden, but Uncle Eddie grew devil's weed and the rest of them kicked him out.

Uncle Eddie was a sixth son. He smoked little brown cigarettes that smelled like cinnamon toast and talked with his hands open like he was bringing fire into the universe. Six was too young to remember much more when they threw out Uncle Eddie and burned his crop on the wasteheap, but Mama called Uncle Eddie a bad seed. Bad seeds don't grow when you put them in the dirt, but Six doesn't know why that meant burning. Bad seeds don't hurt anyone else.

They cleaned out Uncle Eddie's garden when they booted him out, but Six snagged a lamp and hid it real good from Father. Over the years he's got himself a bunch of Uncle Elmer's spare string, old herb stakes, cracked pots, odds and ends and unwanted things too busted to recycle. It all gets smuggled down to the sixth floor, through the peeling walls and dust-stink carpets, where Six has set up his workshop.

The workshop's behind a broken-locked door, or never locked by whoever lived there once when the world fell one night between evening and dawn. Six cleared it all by himself, broken machines and moldering paper snuck out to the waste on odd, switched-up days. The water's dirty here, but the water runs. It keeps Six's little garden.

Six plants the flawed seeds. He plants the bad seeds, the ones that don't grow when you lay 'em down, or grow crooked, or bear limp and yearning fruit. He sneaks down and waters them every other day, shoos flies away from the opening leaves and nibbles the produce at night when the whole clan's down asleep.

"I'll take care of you," he tells the bum seeds. They make spindly, delicate, blight-prone plants. Half of them die before they can strengthen out. Six has to tie them to popsicle sticks with Uncle Elmer's old grey string, and they lean like addled sheep against the snap-end, dirty wood.

Six don't think they're beautiful. He knows the difference between strong and busted, good and no-good.

He and his plants, they stick together. They're bad news.

The alchemists run their long black train only at full midnight. Market girls tell stories about it, rushing through the platforms like a ghost of what the city used to be, rustling the flyers and wrappers and dust into a hiss against black book-magic.

People talk 'bout the alchemists only in whispers. They bring the good weather. They bring the out-of-district news and keep books, mounds of books written in faded-out scripts that no one can read since the world fell two generations past. Nobody ever sees their faces, knows their names.

They give out magic, and they take sons.

They take sons to their Destinies.

Father throws a feast for Joe's tenth birthday. He gets paper from the papermen and the sisters take a whole day off to pen the invitations, and come the afternoon of Joe's nativity the whole clan gathers in, cousins and uncles and aunts and brothers, and holds a festival day in the downstairs meeting-hall.

Six helps set the buffet table. The sisters and brothers'-wives boss him around, dump basket or plate in his arms to ferry one to the other, every single one of them sharp-voiced and mad. None of the brothers'-wives ruffle his hair today. Everyone's edgy. Everyone's bad.

The clan puts on its best Sunday clothes and Father holds up his glass, handed down from before the world fell and full of out-district oaked white wine.

"To our son," Father says, and the whole clan roars.

To our son!

Six slides out of his chair between the stamping and cheering and weeping. He boots it around the cousins and the table with the soup tureen down the rattletrap metal-gray stairs to the sixth floor.

His workshop's quiet. Six floors above, he can't hear the cheering and congratulations and condolences, the aunts touching shoulders and saying how brave one is to give up a loved little brother for the good of the district, the world. "They didn't have a party for you," Six tells the empty air, the bent-stemmed plants and his green and growing bastard-born potatoes.

The absence of Uncle Eddie says no, they did not.

The air ducts whisper and clank, and go silent.

Someone's watching.

Six feels the gaze like spider legs on his neck, somewhere behind him where he can't see, in the dark. But there's no one on the balcony, no one in the closets, no one in the bedroom of the billet he's made his own. He peeks careful careful out the never-locked broken-locked door, but nobody's picking their way through the sixth floor, through the piles of debris that only little kids can get around.

"Uncle Eddie?" Six whispers, skin prickling, belly aching, but there ain't nobody there but the ghosts.

He hides from the dead men. From the dead Uncles haunting through the uncleared halls and the live ones drinking up Father's wine and laughing up their sleeves at his first, his one misfortune, this demand of a seventh son by the alchemists in their black train. He hides upstairs in the clan quarters, in the billet he'll share for one more night with goddamn Joe the special kid, Joe who'll be gone from the sheep-fold and the dirt.

When the party breaks up goddamn special blond-curls smartmouth Joe comes up full of sweet cream and holiday raisin cake. Six stares up at him with his empty mad eyes.

"I'll jump," Six whispers, holding his pillow against the length of his body. His tummy feels hot and terrible, like the fall of the whole big world. "I'll die, and they won't want you anymore, and they'll send you back tomorrow night and that'll show you."

"*So do it,*" Joe screams clean as torchlight, and leaps.

Joe punches like a girl. Six's never been punched by a girl, but Joe sure's hell don't punch like a boy, and half the hits don't even hurt. Six just holds him off, catching his fists with his own hands or the soft bits along his belly, until Joe lands him one right in the nose and the night goes bright with sparkles.

"God*damn!*" Six roars and throws Joe off him, throws him clear across the mattress and into the wad of baby blanket that he sleeps with every night. He rears back to go after him, to beat the sense right good into his special stupid skull, and his breath comes hot and bitter, liquidy. Wrong.

Six wipes his nose. There's blood stinking up his mouth and something else: hot and wet and bitter.

It's crying. Not his. The baby's crying.

Six feels the red from his face to his elbows, hot right down to his toes. "Hey," he says, then softer: "Hey. Cut it out."

But Joe doesn't cut it out, he just hugs himself down in his padded corner and cries without making one sound, cries like the sisters getting ready to throw another nephew, in the worst part where Six gets sent out for water so he can't hear them stop pushing and make a sound that's all the lost hope in the world.

Six scrubs at the blood on his right hand with the sheet and it don't come off.

He goes running down the hall for Mama.

There's fighting behind the door where Mama and Father make their billet. They always fight in low polite voices, more polite than anyone ever speaks in the clan farm where usually it's yelling across whole rooms and floors. Six presses his ear to the old brass mailslot in the brown wood door, heart running up against the inside of his chest like it might run right out. *Please be done with it,* he thinks, the first time he's thought please to his parents since Joe got himself a key at seven years old. Maybe when they're done with it he can knock, pretend he don't know nothing about it. Get one of them to make that soundless crying stop.

But "They never come back," Mama's saying, far and near and far and near. Six pushes up the mailslot, slow and careful hands, and she's rocking on the long black couch that Father bought her for a bearing-gift after she had Marabel. Her Sunday dress is all wrinkled. Her face is puffed-up crying.

"They'll raise him up right," Father rumbles. He's standing behind her, both hands on her shoulders, resting heavier than they should to hold her back straight. "There's good education there. Book-smarts. He'll learn things to help us all build back up."

"How d'you know that's what they do?" Mama asks, her voice going high and thin as the fingers she's got clenched in her lap. "Maybe they kill them. Maybe they use them. *Nobody comes back.*"

The blood smears down Six's lip and drips onto his chin. He has never heard his Mama scared, not in his life.

"Talk sense," says Father, the agribaron of the central district. The most respected man from the north stations to the lakeside where the sugar factory churns. "They're learned. And they're the only men in this district or the next who seem to care about—about *why*, about more than eating and shitting and dying."

"Nobody comes back," Mama repeats, and shakes off Father's hands, paces back and forth across their soft-carpeted floor. "I've tried to let the boy have fun. I've tried to make his life here good—"

"It's done."

"He's only a baby—"

"Martha—"

"I wish you'd never let them in," Mama says, and slaps Father's face so hard the silence echoes for a three-count after. And soft, polite and very very soft: "I wish I'd not given you enough children that you can spend them so very cheap."

Father doesn't move. He stands still as a pigeon scarecrow, hands straight at his sides and not one single feeling on his face.

Six backs up. He shuffles back on the carpet, eyes big as the bright blue sky.

The mailslot clangs, and the silence spreads out like a strapping.

Six runs.

He scrambles up and runs hard down the hallway, back to the billet and inside and locks the door fast behind him. "Pretend you're sleeping," he pants to Joe, and Joe, red-faced and still dripping baby snot, doesn't say one word against him.

They lie together silent, eyes pressed shut and gulping down their breathing for five minutes, ten, until there's no steps down the hallway and there isn't gonna be. Six sits up, lets himself cough. He's tacky with sweat.

"Is it safe?" Joe asks, curled up in the blankets, one eye open as if the other can keep the nightmares out.

"Yeah," Six whispers, pats his little fist. Taking care of the baby. "C'mon. I'll show you a special thing."

The sixth floor is scary at night. Lucinda's new beau hasn't drawn down the power to the uncleared floors, and the emergency lights are long burned out, dead as dead for twenty-five years.

Six's workshop runs on filched batteries, a beat-up old charger he hides under the laundry pile in their billet on the twentieth floor. He hits one of the old slap-lights and it clicks into glowing, casts shadows across the dusty floor. There's no feeling like ghosts. Joe holds his hand tight, and it keeps the ghosts away.

"You got a garden," he says, just as breathless in wonder as he was in fear, and Six feels something he hasn't in a long time, not since Father let them all know about Joe and his destiny. He feels things going right.

"Yeah. It's a secret," he says, and brushes a curled-up leaf with his free right hand.

"What'd you make?" Joe whispers, hugging himself in outlines, in the dark.

"Mint plant," Six says, and his head comes up a little, his eyes go bright with pride. "Strawberries. The little potatoes Mama didn't want last year. Spinach."

"The old seeds."

"I saved them."

Six and Joe sit on Six's old emergency blanket and share out the crop on a beat-up kitchen plate. Their fingers poke each other on the way to strawberries and light-washed spinach. It washes the taste of blood away.

"Thanks," Joe says sleepy when the harvest's all done. "S'good."

Joe's not a little kid anymore. He's not half as light as a chicken or a goat. But Six carries him up fourteen floors of stairway to their billet, mouth smeared with strawberries, fast asleep.

The alchemists' train is the black train that comes down the tracks come midnight. Six has never seen it up close: by midnight every good kid and even the bad ones have locked the doors of their billets and are fast asleep, full knowing they've got a six a.m. wakeup.

The turnstile men don't guard the station gates when the alchemists' train comes in. They unlatch the metal bars that're for strollers and wheelchairs and market-buggies, and everyone walks free to the platform, free out again until the sunlight spills sickly down the stairs and announces it Market time.

The boy who comes through the gate, hooded, face covered 'gainst public eyes is too big for a ten-year-old if you look hard, or look twice. His arms are too thick, his legs too thin and gangling.

He doesn't say goodbye to his father, who stands at the stairway under his best Sunday hat, mouth a tight line under his bushy moustache.

But midnight's so that nobody notices: the too-long cloak, the shaky step. The blond-haired brother smuggled down early evening to a broken-backed sixth floor garden, holding himself in outlines, in the dark, with the taste of secret strawberries on his tongue. Midnight's the alchemists' hour, and in their hands things go strange.

The wind rises from the tunnel, from the dark. The train comes in.

The midnight train is dark as stars. The midnight train's painted up with planets, each car banded with the swoop of a heavenly body ringed or striped or pitted. It moves like a snake along the tracks every child in central's seen so many times on Market days, cheering as the rumble gets loud and the Moving Market comes in.

The doors all open. Nobody cheers the midnight train.

At the staircase, somebody sobs.

The boy in the black rough cloak looks into the dark of the lead car. There's no lights at midnight on the platform, in the train. He steps from dark to darker; he steps inside.

"Greetings," say the alchemists, and their voices are sharp like devil weed, bad seed, breaking the rules. The alchemists in their black train, learned men, terror-men, are hard to see for a boy who grew up billeting in a place where it's never full dark. They're flashes of patched knees and sunless skin. They're eyes that reflect metal and never close.

The train doors shut behind him with a hiss of dead men watching. The sobbing's sliced clean from his ears with metal and rubber seal, and then the only sound's one he hasn't heard since he was littler: the train, whish-whisper, the moving of wheels on track.

It's too much to close his eyes, hands up and ready to fight. But he counts three, counts the deepening of the shadow that's tunnel-not-station before the boy lets down his cloak.

"I'm not the seventh son," Six says, and his voice is all squeaky like a kid's. "I'm bad news. Bad seed. You won't have him," he says, and waits to be struck down.

It won't keep secret more than a day. They'll open the billet door for breakfast and it'll be the wrong baby boy lying curled up in the blankets, arm around his stuffy, ruined from Great Destiny by complicity with his bad boy, bad seed big brother. They'll be so mad. They'll be furious.

They'll hug little Joe to their chests and cry happy for his keeping and teach him the garden and the chicken-feed times.

"You must love your brother very much," the alchemists say, circled, leaning close and closer. Their train smells like paper and dry sweet. No, their breaths. Their breaths are hot and paper. They eat tales. They eat children.

"No," Six chokes out, and lifts his chin up high even though deep inside he's crying, crying right to his belly now that there's no chance of scaring the baby. Pictures himself falling, falling. The tug of the wind. "I hate him."

There's a silence.

Then: "Good," one of the alchemists laughs, crackling, crumple-paged. "I like bad sixth sons."

His eyes are working again, in the dark; his eyes work enough to see the turn of a chin, the half-light of eyelids drooped low. "We didn't agree—"

"I *like* bad sixth sons," the alchemist repeats sharp as a papercut to the tongue, and breaks the hovering circle, steps in close.

His robes rustle like pigeon wings, like the wind going through the tall pasture, and his hands are clean-nailed but rough as any farmsman's. The walls are covered, lined, padded with books and books and books. His eyes are dark. His eyes are dark as stars, and the smell of his hands and books and eyes is burnt cinnamon toast and the devil.

I'm a brave boy, Six tells himself, breathing shallow so's to not get the smoke and devil in. *I grew right. I saved things. I didn't hurt no one else.*

He takes him by the hands. He leads him into the black, black car as the train pulls free through the tunnels to travel the nighttime tracks.

"Come along, bad seed," he says, in a voice that echoes like a child's tunnel scream, a voice that might be kind or hard or mocking. "There's much to do before morning."

ONCE A GODDESS

Marie Brennan

For eleven years Hathirekhmet was a goddess, and then they sent her home.

She didn't understand. They explained it to her, in patient tones just bordering on the patronizing, and she didn't understand. They told her, again and again, right up until the moment it ended, because they had done this before and they knew the goddess never understood.

She didn't believe them until the ceremony, when a little girl with wide, dark eyes came into the sanctum and touched her on the brow. That little girl, blessed with the seventeen signs of perfection, was Hathirekhmet now.

After eleven years, she who had been Hathirekhmet was Nefret again—and then they sent her home.

They said the woman in the wattle-and-daub house was her mother. And Nefret accepted it, numbly, as she had accepted everything since that little girl took her place.

No—not her place. Hathirekhmet's place, and she was Hathirekhmet no more; that honor passed now to another, as it always did. They told her to be proud; eleven years was a long time. Few girls retained their perfection for so long. Most ceased to be the goddess much younger.

The woman in the house no more knew what to do with Nefret than Nefret knew what to do with herself. She introduced herself as Merentari, and the two of them embraced while the priests looked on with benevolent smiles, but it was brief and unbearably awkward. They parted, and did not touch again.

Slaves carried the priests' litters away, and the plainer one Nefret had occupied. And that simply, the last vestige of her temple life was gone.

But casting off that life was not so easily done. "You are dusty from the road; no doubt you wish to bathe," Merentari said, and Nefret stood dumbly, waiting for slaves to come and wash her. "I have prepared food; please, eat," Merentari said, and Nefret stared at the spiced paste and flatcakes laid before her, the small bowl of dried figs. "You will sleep here, with me," Merentari said, and Nefret turned her face from the straw mattress, willing herself not to cry.

Hathirekhmet did not choose her vessels according to caste. The seventeen signs of perfection could appear in the meanest hovel as easily as the imperial palace. As indeed they had, eleven years before.

Awkwardness gave way to rage quickly enough. Nefret was accustomed to luxury, servitude, and instant obedience. She did not know how to do the simplest of chores, and became furious when Merentari tried to teach her. "Wash these dishes," Merentari said, and Nefret slapped them from her hands. "Sweep the floor," Merentari said, and Nefret hurled the broom out the door. "Bring in more dung for the fire," Merentari said, and Nefret fled the house.

Had her father been alive, she would have been curbed quickly enough. No woman so useless would ever be bought as a wife; she had to learn a wife's place and a wife's skills, soon, before age rendered her a spinster. Nefret's father would have beaten the willfulness out of her, rather than abandon her to that fate. But he died two years after she became the goddess' avatar. She had no memory of him, no more than she did of Merentari.

Huddled in the lee of the riverbank, out of the punishing sun and free, however briefly, of the life that now trapped her, Nefret entertained a vision of something different. The priests said this woman was her mother, but what if they lied? Surely Hathirekhmet would not have abandoned her to this, to flies and dust and fires built of dung. For eleven years Nefret had been her vessel; did that mean nothing to the goddess now?

Tears leaked from beneath Nefret's tightly closed lids, tracking through the grime on her cheeks and falling to the thirsty earth, where they vanished without a trace.

Merentari's younger brother found her there a short while later, and dragged her back to the house. He was not cruel, but he tolerated no resistance, and there were marks on her arm when he finally released her inside the hut. Merentari scowled, her patience worn thin by Nefret's intransigence. "There you are. Get washed up, and quickly; we don't want to miss this chance."

A tub of water waited out back, and a hard-bristled brush that Merentari used to scrub Nefret clean. Her brisk ministrations were as unlike the gentle service of the slaves as the dull, repetitive food was to the feasts of the temple, but it did the work; Nefret was as clean as she'd been since coming to this place she refused to call home. Her mahogany skin glowed, and Merentari scraped her thick hair back into two braids so tight they made Nefret's head ache. Instead of Merentari's cast-off clothing, she wore a thin robe she had never seen before, plain, but neatly pleated, and of good linen.

When Nefret was clean and dressed, Merentari took her roughly by the chin and forced the girl to look at her. Taller than this woman they said was her mother, Nefret felt calm superiority envelop her. She might be in exile, but she still had her pride.

"You keep your mouth shut, except when he asks you a question," Merentari said. "You be polite and meek. This might be your one chance at any kind of future, girl. If you spit on this, you'll end your days as a beggar in the streets. Understand?"

Nefret did not, but she learned quickly enough. A man came to inspect her—Nefret's mind would not let go of that word. *Inspect*, as a temple servant might inspect a cow offered for sacrifice. There were men, it seemed, who would pay a good bride-price for a woman who was once a goddess, men interested enough in prestige that they did not care how bad a wife they bought.

Nefret kept her mouth shut, but not for the reasons her mother might have wished. She thought she might be sick. Reduced to this, after the life she had lived: bought and sold, like livestock.

The man did not speak to her at all, questions or otherwise. When his inspection was done, he turned to Merentari. "Can she cook? Weave? Sew?"

Lying was not among Merentari's talents. Her hesitation was answer enough.

"I didn't expect it," the man said. His own robe was finely woven, with azure embroidery along the edge. Such as he would have some servants, possibly even slaves. Wealth, by the standards of this hovel. "Teach her basic domestic duties. If she passes muster by flood-time, I'll buy her."

Merentari's weathered face showed gratitude that bordered on fawning. She was not old, but hard work had aged her young. Beauty was a luxury few peasants could afford. "Yes, noble one. Thank you. I will make sure she learns."

When the wealthy man was gone, Merentari turned to her daughter. "You *will* learn. Or you will starve."

* * *

In the dark hours before dawn, when Nefret so frequently lay awake, she knew that Merentari did not mean to make her suffer. The woman was harsh because there was no other choice; she did not want her daughter to end like this, scraping the barest existence out of the hard-packed dirt. Pity would not buy her a better future.

In the bright hours of day, Nefret hated her mother with a passion she fancied rivaled the rages of Hathirekhmet herself.

Merentari bent grimly to the task of making her daughter into a suitable wife. A thick reed from the riverbank became an all-too-familiar fixture in Merentari's hand, laying burning lines across Nefret's back when she rebelled. Never before had she been beaten; rarely had she even suffered pain, and then slaves had raced to bring soothing ointment, tea to numb her senses. Pride kept Nefret's jaw clenched; she cried out the first few times, but soon forbade herself such weakness.

She tried—if only because it was a path for her to follow, and promised a life more like the one she knew. But the shuttle and thread were alien in her hands, the cook-fire smoky and foul. Other girls learned these skills from childhood, practicing them for years under their mothers' eyes. The priests had taught Nefret all the wrong things, and then dropped her into a life for which she was wholly unprepared.

She tried, and she failed, until one day she could endure no more and ran away again, her feet this time taking her in a new direction.

Nefret smelled the market before she saw it, a confusing welter of dust and sweat, food and animal dung. She crested a rise and saw the clustered buildings, mud-brick structures huddled up against each other, with sun-bleached awnings branching out from their walls. A market was a recognizable thing to her, though this one was shabby and small. She had gone through markets before, during festival processions.

Her bare feet led her down the slope and toward the market as if of their own accord.

At first no one took notice of her. Nefret felt like a ghost, drifting down the strip of sunlight between the awnings on either side. Silent amidst the market's clamor, she could almost believe she didn't exist. But this was a small market; strangers were rare, and even moreso strangers like her, beautiful and unweathered by a peasant's hard life. A middle-aged woman bent to whisper to another, and then someone else pointed, and little by little, the market fell into stillness.

The stillness was broken by a young woman who hesitated at the edge of the crowd, then darted forward and flung herself facedown onto the hard-packed soil at Nefret's feet. "Mistress of the desert winds," she said, her voice ragged and unclear, "bless me, I beg you."

The words struck Nefret like the chilled water the slaves had poured over her for the Ceremony of the River's Coming. Her fingers twitched, reflexively: in learning to weave, they had not forgotten how to form the sign of blessing.

But she was not the goddess.

She ached to reach out, to make the sign above the young woman's head, perhaps even to move her foot forward so the supplicant could kiss it. To these people, she was not Nefret, daughter of nobody; she was Hathirekhmet, the Divine Face, the Sand-Mother. Relentless and harsh as the desert and sun, but not without mercy.

But she was not Hathirekhmet. Not anymore. To bless this young woman would be blasphemy.

The magnitude of her loss gaped before her, stretching into the endless distance like the desert itself, even more barren of life.

Nefret stared down at the young woman, stricken and shaking, while the silence stretched tighter and tighter. Then she spun without a word and fled, back to the house, to weep for her loss where no one could see.

* * *

But Merentari was waiting for her there, reed switch in hand and fury on her face.

Nefret stopped dead, facing the woman in the doorway. Her mother, they said, and to deny it was childish. A peasant, whose daughter was born with the seventeen signs the priests looked for. An ordinary woman, whose ambition could rise no higher than to sell that same daughter to a man that wanted for his wife a woman who was once a goddess.

That man—she did not even know his name—wanted her for who she had been. No: for who she was now, the loss she had suffered. Hathirekhmet he feared, but Nefret he could own.

To go into his house would mean accepting that her loss was her only value now.

"I am not Hathirekhmet," Nefret said to her mother. The words came out steady, with a deadness that could pass for calm. "But I will not sell myself as her leavings."

Merentari's face twisted, as she saw Nefret's one chance —*her* one chance—withering into death. "No one else will take you!"

Nefret nodded, slowly. The logic was inescapable.

"Then no one else will have me," she said. "I would rather be nothing than be his."

Merentari's expression showed that she did not understand. Nefret did not know when her mother realized the truth; by the time it happened, she had turned her back, and walked away from the hut, into the desert.

The sand burned against Nefret's forehead and arms, scorching her body even through the cotton of her robe, cooking the flesh beneath, but she remained motionless, accepting the pain.

In the temple, there were slaves whose sole duty was to stoke the fires beneath raised platforms of sand, so the penitents above continually felt the sun's heat against their bodies. Here, without slaves, the sand grew cool. Nefret rose and crawled sideways, then stretched out again, burning herself anew.

She did not pray. No words could express the screaming need in her heart. She did not know whether she wanted to be purified, made perfect again so she could once more be Hathirekhmet's vessel; to deny and disfigure the flesh that had known divinity and lost it; to die, and feel this pain no more.

All of them. None of them. She did not know.

I would rather be nothing than be his.

She would rather be nothing than what she was now.

When sunset came, the sand chilled quickly. At first it was a pleasant change from the heat of the day; then it became unpleasant, and the desire for self-punishment withered. She rose and walked unsteadily to a rocky upthrust nearby, and there she found a tiny spring; she drained it in moments, then had to wait for the pool to refill. But it was enough to keep her alive.

She did not want to die.

It was more than she had known that morning.

"Very well," Nefret said to the night sky, to the pale and envious crescent of Hathirekhmet's younger brother. "I will live. And I will stay alive, until—"

She paused, thinking. Looking at the tiny, glittering pinpricks of the stars, cast off when the moon's folly caused his power to explode outward and be lost.

"Until I am the goddess once more."

They came to her refuge, there among the rocks.

She had not fled so far as to vanish. Men went out into the desert's edge, to hunt lions, to trade with distant oases. They saw her silhouette atop a ridge, or glimpsed her hiding when they came to her tiny spring. A ragged figure, her robe sand-brown with dust, her fine black hair tangled into whips. She was far from perfect now. But Nefret could not regain the qualities she had lost—not now, when blood ran from between her legs, answering the moon's call. If she was to be Hathirekhmet again, she would have to find another way.

So she remembered what the scriptures said about Khapep, how the holy man had survived upon the flesh of lizards and the venom of scorpions, and she learned to do the same. It was bitter fare, even as the desert was bitter, and she welcomed it.

Hathirekhmet was the sun and the sand. Nefret would be the same.

They came to her among the rocks and brought gifts of food, the finest they had to give: dried figs and dates, fish from the river's bounty. But Amuthamse was, the priests said, why Hathirekhmet always withdrew; the goddess departed when the blood came, for it was the sign of the river-god's touch. His fertility was alien to Hathirekhmet. Nefret ate scorpions, and left the fish to rot in the sun.

They came for her blessing, and she turned them away. Holy woman? She was no such thing. She would be, someday, and when that dawn came she would extend her hand once more. But until then, she was only Nefret, who let her skin dry out and her hair turn brittle, and tried to remember what she had once known by instinct, by divine grace.

She barely spoke a word until Sekhaf came.

Nefret woke before dawn and went to the spring; she would drink no more until the sun left the sky. She scooped water into her mouth with dirty hands, wishing she could do without, wondering if that was what Hathirekhmet wanted. Wondering if the goddess would touch her in the instant before death. She was not ready to try, and perhaps that was why she failed.

When she lifted her head, a man sat on a boulder across from her. Nefret had heard him approach, but hoped if she ignored him he would go away. He was not a villager, as she had assumed; he wore a traveler's robe and bore a staff, but he did not have the look of a pilgrim. His weathered face was seamed with patient lines.

"Dawn is near," he said—a fact she knew as well or better than he, but he did not have the tone of one lecturing. Rather he seemed to acknowledge the intrusion of his presence. "When it has passed, I hope you will spare me your time."

Nefret's voice came out smoothly from her newly-wetted throat, not its usual dry rasp. "I have no blessing to give."

"I do not seek your blessing."

She scowled. "I will not marry you, either."

"I do not seek your hand."

"What, then?"

The lines of his face settled in the pre-dawn light. "Your knowledge."

She stared for a moment, curious against her will. But the sun drew near; she had no time to spare for him. Nefret turned away and climbed the rocks, greeting Hathirekhmet from the pinnacle, basking in this, the goddess' gentlest touch. Soon enough heat would scorch the water from her, as she hunted lizards to eat.

When she descended, the man was still there, patient as stone. "I know nothing," Nefret said, and picked up several likely rocks.

"You know something shared only by a four-year-old girl in a temple," the man said. "You know Hathirekhmet."

Nefret's fingers curled around a sharp-edged fragment of flint. "I *knew* her," she answered, voice roughening to harshness. "She is gone from me now."

The man nodded. "And that makes you unique. Nineteen years ago, I tried to find her who had been Hathirekhmet, only to discover she had been sold into marriage, to a husband who let her speak to no other. She is dead now, in childbirth. Eleven years ago, I tried again, only to discover she who had been Hathirekhmet hanged herself from her father's great loom. She, too, is dead. There is only you, who understands the goddess better than any man or woman living—who *understands*, but is herself. I cannot ask these questions of Hathirekhmet. I ask them of you." He paused, still seated on his rock. "If you will let me."

The stone hung heavy in her hand. The man's eyes rested unwavering on her—on *her*, Nefret. Who was once a goddess, and for that he valued her. But not like the man Merentari would have sold her to. Her worth lay in what she kept, not what she had lost.

"Ask," she said.

The man stood and bowed his gratitude. "Then I will begin. Of temple life, I have heard; I know the ceremonies and indulgences, the luxury in which the goddess' avatar lives. But only you can tell me: what is the divine presence like?"

The stone fell from Nefret's limp fingers, thudding into the dust. Staring unseen into the brightening sky, she whispered, "I cannot remember."

It was the truth no one spoke, and Sekhaf believed her. In the early years, Hathirekhmet dwelt often in the body of her avatar, but as the child grew the goddess came less and less. She still performed the ceremonies, for they had merit even if the divine presence was not in her; the avatar was the conduit from earth to heaven.

But as Hathirekhmet retreated, the priests began their search for the new vessel. Nefret had not felt the goddess' touch for a year before she left.

Sekhaf sat by as Nefret sliced open the belly of a lizard and said, "Why? Why does she leave?"

He was a philosopher, and did not ask out of cruelty. He had been with her among the rocks for several days now, carefully probing, shifting between topics arcane and obvious, questioning everything. Nefret licked the blood from her fingers and answered him. "Amuthamse. A woman is of the river's world, not the desert, and Amuthamse is friend to

Hathirekhmet's brother the moon. Once we begin to bleed, we are no longer fit for her presence."

"But you said she leaves earlier, sometimes."

Six months after the last visitation, Nefret had bled for the first time. She had no such name to give herself on that day; the avatar thought of herself as Hathirekhmet, even when the divine presence was not in her. She knew no other identity. But Hathirekhmet did not bleed; Nefret did. She had stayed longer than most, the priests said, her voice remaining high and clear, her skin unblemished, her limbs slender—a far cry from her appearance now. Most girls lost Hathirekhmet sooner, before they ever bled.

"She can sense Amuthamse's approach," Nefret said; it was the answer the priests gave. She could feel Sekhaf's dissatisfaction with it. He loved the purity of thought, the clean lines of truth. Anything blurry or untidy displeased him.

No one at the temple thought as he did. They had their scriptures and their answers; they had rituals to carry out, ceremonies to conduct, comforting patterns to shape their lives. None of them had Sekhaf's restless, questioning mind. Nefret did not blame them; she had not questioned, either. Not until the philosopher came.

And his presence, which she had feared would distract her, honed the blade of her own thoughts. If Nefret tested her body less often against the sun, she tested her mind more, contemplating the nature of Hathirekhmet. When Sekhaf went to the village for food, she meditated in silence; when he returned, she had new answers for him, new fragments of memory dredged up from the forgotten corners of the past.

In the desert, there was no time. The rains fell in the mountains and brought the river's flood, Amuthamse's bounty for mankind; Nefret knew nothing of it. The villagers left their offerings and she ignored them, fish bones drying to glass in the sun.

Other men came.

One by one, following word of Sekhaf. Philosophers, men of the mind instead of the temple, their fingers stained from scribing. Some, meaning well, tried to hunt lizards for Nefret, so she might spend more time in thought. Sekhaf taught them better. They waited with patience as she dug out scorpions; they trailed after her in silence as she walked the rounds of her rocks, bare feet hard and cracked as horn against the stone. They did not lust after her, as that man had in Merentari's house; one might as soon lust after the desert. But they asked her questions, and listened when she answered.

"They say it is because we cannot draw near Hathirekhmet ourselves," Nefret said, breaking a new flint to use for butchering lizards. Her hands had turned into bony, calloused things, strong as old leather. The sun warmed her filthy hair. "The ancient priests built a pyramid that reached up to the very sky, seeking the goddess, and were burnt when they climbed to the top. Ordinary people cannot bear her presence and live."

Men both older and younger deferred to Sekhaf here; they spoke among themselves, but only he spoke to Nefret. He said, "But the perfection of her avatars protects them?"

"Imperfections are flaws that can break the vessel," Nefret said, cracking a clean face off the flint. Pottery would be more appropriate, but she had no pots out here. "I do not think that is why she takes avatars, though."

The philosopher thought about it. One of the younger men murmured to him, and Sekhaf nodded. "They allow us to experience the divine presence safely. Yet why should that matter to Hathirekhmet? She is the sun's hammer, the desert wind; humans are not *meant* to be close to such."

Nefret tested the edge of her flint with her thumb, feeling it press against her calloused skin. "It is not for us. It is for her, for the goddess—so she may experience the world without destroying it. That is what I think."

Why else should the avatar live so lavishly?

She ate foods sweet and spicy, had garments of smooth linen and supple leather and delicate fur. It was a feast of the senses, for one who otherwise could never know such. If the sun descended to earth, she would burn it to a cinder. Hathirekhmet chose avatars because she was curious about the world she saw so far beneath.

Nefret sometimes wondered if the goddess did not envy Amuthamse, who enjoyed all the earth's bounty without fear.

The men whispered to each other, voices rising in excitement. Sekhaf clapped his hands, sharply, and they ceased. "We distract her with our chatter," he said. "Nefret, our thanks. You have given us much to think about. We will return tomorrow."

She rose from her crouch, feeling the flex and contraction of her wiry muscles. A body, imperfect as avatars never were. Yet if the goddess sought sensation, why choose only the slender, the unblemished, the young? There was a whole world of experience, and Hathirekhmet felt only the merest sliver of it. "No," Nefret said. "I will spend tomorrow in contemplation. When I am ready, I will leave a sign for you."

A lizard skull, placed at the foot of the path leading up to her shelter. Nefret had demanded solitude before. Sekhaf bowed. "As you wish."

The others began climbing down the rocks, talking more loudly as they went. Sekhaf stayed, hesitating, until they were well away, and he and Nefret stood alone atop the flint-littered plateau. "You have my thanks as well," he said. Startled, she found herself wondering how long ago the others had come— how long it had been since they were just two, the philosopher and the young woman who was once a goddess. "I came to you hoping to understand something I could never experience for myself. I know now the impossibility of that—but you have given me something far greater. You may not be holy, as Khapep was. But you, Nefret, have wisdom no priest or scripture could ever grant. The world beyond this place will benefit from that wisdom for ages to come."

She blinked eyes dried by sun and wind. That men had come to debate these questions, she knew; she had never thought beyond that. What did the priests think of this woman in the desert, who spoke so familiarly of Hathirekhmet? Did they revere her, as the villagers did? Fear her? Dismiss her as a simple madwoman?

Nefret might have thought herself mad, were it not for Sekhaf. He saw wisdom in her words. But if it was there, they had created it together, questions and answers dancing around and ever nearer to the truth.

He bowed and left her, climbing down the rocks after his companions, and not until he was gone did she whisper "thank you" in reply.

She greeted the dawn from the pinnacle of her rocks, as she had for countless days.

The soft breeze of morning blew over her skin, bringing warmth to banish the night's bitter chill. Soon it would be heat, punishing and fierce, growing through the day, until at last the sun retreated, and night claimed the desert once more.

Nefret understood that cycle as well as she did her own body. She knew Hathirekhmet's shifting arc through the sky, and the way the wind answered it; she knew the textures of limestone and flint and the restless dance of the sand.

She knew the seventeen perfections had nothing to do with any of it.

Oh, the priests did not deceive. Those were the sign of Hathirekmet's choice—but the priests mistook the sign for the cause. That certainty had grown in Nefret's heart through all the long debates with the philosophers. The goddess did not occupy a body because it had skin of a particular shade, or a voice of a particular timbre.

If that was not what drew her to a body, then it followed that the loss of those perfections was not why she left.

Something else drove the goddess from her avatars.

This was the question upon which Nefret fixed her mind. She put aside all other thoughts—lizards and scorpions, Sekhaf and the philosophers, Merentari and the man who would have bought her. Nothing but Hathirekhmet. She sat under the eye of the sun, not moving, letting the wind scour her dry. She had drunk no water since the previous dawn, and would drink none until the sun set tonight. She did not seek death—not as she once thought she did—but she seared all the river's gift from herself, the better to know Hathirekhmet. To know the answer to this one question: why the goddess had left.

The sun beat more strongly upon her with every passing moment. She felt the sweat dry upon her skin, until no more came; she heard the pounding of her own heart, marking the incremental movement of the sun.

And she remembered.

The presence she had gradually lost. The blazing glory of Hathirekhmet, pitiless as stone, but not cruel; cruelty implied a desire for suffering in others. Hathirekhmet did not desire. She simply *was*. And to pour a fragment of herself into an avatar was to be as she otherwise could not be, to feel and see a world otherwise distant to her.

The luxury was the doing of the priests, because they thought the goddess wished it. They honored the one they believed Hathirekhmet's gift to them, thinking it the respectful thing to do.

They did not understand. And Nefret had not, either.

She remembered that blazing presence, annihilating all other thought. As a child it had been easy: she lived in the moment, thinking neither of past nor future. She *was* Hathirekhmet. But as she grew, she changed; thoughts entered her head and did not leave. Dislike of one temple maiden, amusement at an elderly priest. Curiosity about a story from the scriptures. Ideas and feelings, which had to be pushed aside to make room for Hathirekhmet. It grew harder and harder, and the goddess came more rarely.

Because she could not be both Hathirekhmet and herself.

Understanding swirled through the reeling dizziness of her head. The goddess chose children because they were unformed, empty—vessels she could fill. Life was the imperfection, the cracks through which the world entered, changing little girls into young women. And day by day, year by year, the avatars pushed the goddess out to make room for themselves.

Which meant she could reverse it. The sun's hammer beat upon her, seeking entrance. All she had to do was step aside, and let the goddess in.

Let go of Nefret, and become Hathirekhmet again.

Then the goddess could experience something new: a grown body, twisted hard by the desert; a life austere instead of luxurious. Her skin pulsed, a fragile barrier between humanity and divinity. It was easy. Simple. The kind of pure answer Sekhaf sought.

Sekhaf.

She held in the palm of her hand all the things that barred Hathirekhmet from her. All the other thoughts, all the desires and annoyances and knowledge, all the things he called her wisdom. All the things that brought the philosophers to her desert refuge, that fueled their debates in the long heat of day.

Everything that made her who she was.

She could regain what she had lost—by losing what she had gained.

Once, she would have found it no choice at all. Nefret had nothing; Hathirekhmet, everything. But in her seeking, she had found another life. One of lizards and scorpions, a muddy spring and a hard bed, and questions always to be answered. It was not the life she had known in the temple, but it was hers.

Hers. Not Hathirekhmet's.

I was once a goddess. Now I am myself. And myself I shall remain.

Nefret curled her hands around herself, filled her mind with thoughts of life—and bid Hathirekhmet farewell.

She awoke to stone, rough under her cheek and hand. Nefret opened eyes that felt dry as dust. She knew without thinking that it was sunset, heat slipping quickly from the air, familiar shadows consuming the world around her.

One shadow was out of place.

She spoke, and the word went little further than her lips. "Sekhaf."

He heard her anyway, or perhaps just saw her move. The philosopher rose from hiding and came to her side, shamefaced. "I should not have disturbed you," he said. "But I watched from below, and saw you collapse. And I thought—"

For once he did not share his thought. He did not have to. Nefret reached out, and he gave her the skin bag at his side. She drank greedily, tasting the leather, letting water spill over her cheeks and chin.

When at last she stopped, he asked quietly, "Did you find your answer?"

The one she had sought, and more besides. Hathirekhmet bore her no grudge for her choice; a grudge implied desire, and Hathirekhmet desired nothing. Not as a human might.

Not as Nefret desired the life she had chosen to keep.

"I found myself," she said. "That is answer enough."

She could feel Sekhaf's dissatisfaction with it. But that was all right. It was one of Sekhaf's favorite sayings, that questions bred answers, and answers, more questions; he would ask her more before long.

Together they would create wisdom, a new understanding of the goddess. And the time had come, Nefret thought, for that wisdom to go beyond this desert refuge, into the world without. To the priests, and the temple, and the little girl who was Hathirekhmet, who someday would become someone else.

When she did, Nefret would be there to greet her.

ANGEL DUST

Ian McHugh

It was a day when autumn's bitter rain swept in off the strait. It rinsed the filth from the streets and beat against the black tower that rose from the heart of the city's sprawl.

In the plaza before the tower's gate, a pair of statues stood on man-high plinths, rendered from the same black stone as the tower and overgrown with climbing briars. A female figure and a male, they wore the long-bodied forms of the race of Avalae, the city's first masters, and had the high-domed skulls and small round ears, set low behind the jaw, distinctive of that vanquished folk. The statues reached, left-handed, towards each other, as though they longed to cross the space between, their unseeing gazes locked together. The woman's outstretched arm ended in a stump above the wrist.

Being statues, they were inert and unknowing, but had they ears to hear, they would have known the cry of dismay that arose from the ghettos below.

The angel was returned.

Always in the past, the angel's homecoming had been greeted with joy, and the ears of the city dwellers had pricked up to listen for the strident chorus of the returning songships. But on this day, as copper sunshine found the gap between horizon and clouds, there arose no triumphant song from the harbour. Had the statues eyes that saw and legs of muscle and sinew to walk among the people, they would have seen the faces that turned up and watched the angel's passage, tight with worry, and they would have marked his course, erratic as a butterfly's, the beat of his grey swan wings laboured and inconstant.

"Where is the fleet?" the people whispered. Their whispers turned to wails when they saw the scant dozen ships that limped into port, and heard the mournful dirge they sang.

The rest would not return, the statues might have heard the sailors say. They were burned or sunk, along with the armadas of Melkurr and the Gil-Gadin. Melkurr was defeated, its capital sacked, and the sheikdoms were falling one by one.

From their plinths before the gate, the statues could have watched the angel battle to reach his tower roost. Were their eyes acute, they might have seen the trail of blood that mingled with the rain, and seen that, as it fell, it turned to glimmering dust.

Had the statues walked the city streets, they might have witnessed the wonders where the dust alighted. Cobblestones turned to clumps of poppies. Some grew legs and scuttled away. Downpipes turned to twisting vines, or pythons that insinuated themselves through the windows of the houses. A colony of pigeons grew arms, and minds that thought, and plotted war against the rats and starlings who raided their nests. People who were touched by the dust burst apart into clouds of copper bees, or turned inside out, for golden-boughed trees to spring from their quivering guts.

The angel slumped gratefully over the high balustrade of his refuge. Had the statues chanced to look up, they would have seen a last drop of blood turn to dust as it fell.

* * *

Her eyelids fluttered. She heaved a raw breath, then another. For a long time, that was all she did, her new mind aflood with the sensations of her body, and all the memories of things she would've seen and known, had she always had eyes that saw, ears that heard. Centuries of days and nights overlaid the deserted plaza. Harvest dances and winter stillness, the red crackle of solstice bonfires and the smoke and clamour of war. Changeless through it all was the petrified stare locked on hers, stone fingers always reaching, never touching.

She swayed, wincing as the briars that wreathed her hooked their barbs into newly soft skin. She shifted her arms, to extricate herself, and cried aloud when she saw the flat stump that ended her left arm above the wrist.

A memory swam to the surface, of Yng'finail Reavers fighting the beast-headed slave warriors of Avalae, a massacre dance of iron blades on bronze, swirling about the plinths. A wild-swung halberd struck her wrist, splinters showering the wielder. She remembered the fractures spreading through her arm as the temperature fell and rose in the nights and days and weeks that followed until, with a crack one frosted morning, the hand tumbled from her wrist.

Her breaths became sobs. The briars stabbed her anew. Moving slowly, whimpering at every tear of her skin, she freed herself from their embrace and shoved the mess of vines from her plinth. She sank down into a crouch, and shivered in the cold rain. The sounds of the restless city assailed her, disorienting. She crept her toes forward until they found the edge of the plinth, and clung there, vertiginous and confused.

A flicker of lightning caught a glint of wet stone in the edge of the briar patch. With a yell, she leapt from the plinth, powered by muscles that did not know, yet, how to properly obey command. Hip, hand and stump met the cobbles. She lay, winded and gasping, staring up through the rain at the black silhouette of the tower that filled half the sky.

When the breath had found its way back into her lungs, she rolled over and crawled to the spot where she'd seen her severed hand. She cradled it, cold and unfeeling against her breast.

Her gaze strayed up again, to the statue of her mate, like her hand still etched in stone. He was all but featureless in the gloom. Higher still, to the balcony that marked the angel's roost, where the mages of Avalae had summoned their fabulous winged beasts to take them hunting, once upon a time. She saw in her mind the angel's latest, agonized return. The tower gate was closed, and there were no windows in its face to show if light and life existed within, except the balcony, and it was dark.

A hand gripped her arm, hard fingers bruising new skin. A rough voice said, "'Allo, lovely." Sniggered.

She twisted, lashing out blindly with her stone hand. Her ears rang with memories of screams cut short, terrible sounds of fright and injury in the shadows at the plaza's edge.

The man retreated, cursing loudly, cradling a forearm bruised, at least, or fractured.

She registered an answering shout from across the plaza. Another man, or several, she didn't wait to see. Clutching her stone hand to her chest, she fled.

She ran down well-lit streets, where the private guards of the well-to-do eyed the first nervous citizens ascending from the city below to come demand the angel's counsel. All stopped to stare, amazed, at the naked woman who sprinted past.

At the foot of the hill, the streets grew darker. She heard the grumble of larger crowds ahead. She slowed, clutching at the stitch in her side, and turned from the main avenue. The cold air burned her lungs, her legs shook and her uncallused heels ached from pounding on the cobbles.

The doorways along this street were alcoved, the frontages colonnaded with the long bones of giants, the doors themselves shrouded in shadow. Blankets spilled into the rain from one, nearby. Shivering violently now, she crept over and reached with tentative fingers. She began to tug at the wet hem of the topmost blanket, then abruptly withdrew her hand. There was a body underneath the covers. She waited, but there came no cry of protest.

She tugged on the blanket again, gathering it into her lap, ready to flee at the first sign of movement. Her hand touched an outflung limb. The flesh was cold.

She drew the first blanket around her shoulders and dragged the remaining covers from the corpse. Bundling them to her chest, she crept to the next alcove along the street. She wrapped herself as tightly as she could, tucking her legs against her chest and pulling the blankets over her head, holding them closed with her single hand. After a time, her shivering stilled and she felt something approaching warmth.

She slept, and her dreams were filled with the black stone features of her mate.

Consciousness returned slowly. The clatter of hooves punctured her dreams, then the creak and crack of a cart following, the drum of passing feet, random snatches of conversation. With a start, she came fully awake.

She raised her head to peer beneath the blanket's fringe, blinking against the morning light. The rain had ceased, but the clouds remained heavy. The street was filled with people.

Most were Yng'finail, the city's current masters, red of skin and silver-pale of eye and hair. Slight figures wove among them, coal black skins stark against white robes and shining gold-in-gold eyes—Gil-Gadin, she had seen their like beneath the angel's tower. A trio of brown-skinned warrior women stalked past, their spiny manes held erect, open vests displaying the scars left by severed breasts.

Others in the crowd were stranger and less human. She remembered them, the cruelly fashioned playthings of the Avalae. Folk with the furred heads and naked tails of rats, scuttling on four limbs or two as the need took them, their eyes the glowing gold of Gil-Gadin. A hairless Yng'finail, pushing himself awkwardly along on a serpent's coils. A gargoyle leaning on a cane, too old to fly anymore, her once powerful wings twisted with arthritis, copper feathers tarnished green.

All of them, human and less so, had an agitation about them. They moved with a step more hurried and a nervous indecision, both, that on a different day might have been absent. Tempers were quick as people got in each other's way. But only threats and curses were exchanged. It seemed no one had the stomach for trading blows.

A rumbling beat penetrated the hubbub. It resolved into the sound of dozens of feet—booted, hoofed or clawed—treading in not-quite-unison. A company of soldiers marched by, their armour an irregular assortment of lamellae and baked leather, only a handful with helms of any kind, the rest in felt caps or bareheaded. The weapons on their shoulders made an ugly forest of mismatched steel.

"And what's this, cluttering my step?" said a deep voice, startlingly close.

The door had opened behind her. A cassocked figure filled the frame. Blue human eyes glared down at her from a horned bovine face. Sparse hair covered a hide as thick and dimpled as citrus peel. She had seen his kind stand like colossi on the last day of Avalae while Yng'finail Reavers slaughtered their lesser brethren around them, until weight of numbers and iron blades brought them down, too.

"Be gone," the minotaur said, lifting an arm to strike backhanded.

She scrambled back, shaking her good arm free of her blankets. She raised the stone hand in warning while she got her feet under her. The minotaur's eyes widened as she retreated into the sunlight.

He followed, raising his hand again, but palm outward this time. "Wait."

But she was already running. A carthorse flapped its neck frills in warning as she skipped in front of it. She ducked the half-hearted swipe of the carter's crop and pushed on through the crowds.

The cobbles were cold and slippery wet, her feet bruised and aching from her running the night before. She soon slowed to a hobbling walk. She had no direction in mind, no knowledge of the city beyond the plaza where she had stood. She passed terraces of shops and houses walled with brick and stone and black iron plate, others roofed in bright canvas to resemble the sails of ships. Others still were grown of living trees woven tight together.

Lost, she let the pedestrian tides carry her where they would, until her attention was arrested by the aromas of a pie seller's stall. His wares were heated over a bed of coals in the iron belly of his spider-legged cart. Her stomach knotted painfully as she watched a man walk away with a steaming pastry. She sidled closer, wondering if she might snatch a pie and run.

She noticed a boy staring at her, narrow-eyed and blunt nosed, a younger, leaner version of the pie seller. He tapped a leather cosh meaningfully against his thigh.

Downcast, she retreated, and walked on.

She passed a golden tree, growing in the centre of the thoroughfare. Beneath it, a trio of hook-beaked gargoyle men confronted a party of soldiers with axes. A gargoyle woman knelt between them, wailing and tearing at copper breastfeathers.

The black tower loomed above the rooftops. She turned towards it. Her pulse quickened as she ascended the hill, a twinge of fear as she remembered the man she had injured the night before.

Reaching the plaza, she saw that her anxiety was needless. A mob had gathered before the angel's keep, demanding entry. Soldiers watched them, but made no move to intervene. No one had any attention to spare for her.

She stopped beneath the petrified figure of her mate. His features were opaque with the sun behind him. She stretched up, but his outstretched hand was too high for her to reach. She pulled aside the briars that covered his foot and ran her fingertips over the shape of his toes. The stone was as ungiving as the severed hand she clutched against her belly.

A loaded cart arrived, and people started piling wood for a bonfire. She cleared a nest among the briars, on the side of her mate's plinth that faced the tower, then sank down and curled her limbs around the hollow misery of her belly.

She started from a torpid daydream, of her mate smiling, his stone visage turned to flesh, his fingers grasping hers.

The minotaur looked down at her.

She levered herself up, fumbling for her stone hand. Panic made her clumsy, and she dropped it in the briars at her feet. With a yelp, she bent to grab it.

"Be still," the minotaur said. "I'll not hurt you."

She paused, warily, the stone hand half raised. He gazed at her in silence for a time, then his blue eyes shifted to look at the male statue.

"How did this come to be?" he asked.

She opened her mouth, struggling to shape a response. Although she understood him, like a small child, she lacked the skill to form words of her own. She pointed to the grand balcony.

The minotaur gave a bovine snort and took her by the wrist. Dragging her along in his wake, he marched towards the tower.

A few, braver or more angry than their fellows, still beat at the gate with mallets and staves. The blackened iron seemed to drink the sounds of their blows into itself. The hammerers fell back at the minotaur's arrival. He raised his fist, muttering beneath his breath, then struck the door, three times. With each blow a boom like the striking of a gong echoed inside the tower.

For a time, there was stillness. Then a postern cracked ajar within the surface of the gate and an Yng'finail head peered out. The man's hair was yellowed with age and his skin a jaundiced orange. His pale eyes blinked and watered in the daylight.

"We seek audience," said the minotaur.

The old man licked his lips. His eyes flickered to the minotaur's companion, still caught by the wrist, and back again.

"Forgive me, m'lord," he said. "There'll be no audience today."

He began to withdraw, but the minotaur raised a hand to stay him. "When?" he asked.

The man started an answer, thought the better of it and stuttered to a halt. "I cannot say."

He shrank back as the minotaur leaned towards him. "If he is hurt, I might aid him."

The old man's eyes went wide. He stepped back abruptly through the door and shut it behind him.

An angry mutter passed through the crowd. The minotaur snorted. A human might have sighed.

"Go to your homes," he said, and turned on his heel. He let go his captive's wrist. "Go."

She stared at his broad back as he strode from the tower. The hammerers closed again around the gate. She struggled free, buffeted and bumped, and hurried after the minotaur. She tugged at his sleeve to stop him, and pointed to the male statue.

The slump of his shoulders was answer enough. He said, "Only he who gave life to you can give it to your mate. I cannot help."

She fought with her tongue. "When?"

The minotaur glanced back at the tower. He shook his head. "Come back tomorrow, and see." The pocked skin around his eyes was tight, as though something pained him. "Come. I will see you fed. You can bed in front of my hearth. Cassiann, is my name."

She looked back over her shoulder, at her mate in his cloak of briars. Her gaze travelled up the black face of the tower, to the balcony, silent to the entreaties raised below.

They returned to Cassiann's house. He had to duck his head to fit through the door, and remain stooped, inside, so as not to scrape his horns on the ribs of the ceiling. Inside, a wooden bench stood along one side of the hall. The door of the front room was open, the room lined with shelves of jars and vials and tins, every one labelled in meticulous script. A high table with an ornate set of scales stood in the centre and, to the rear, a padded couch and scale curtain to pull around it.

He was an apothecary, Cassiann said, and when it was plain she did not know the word, explained that he healed people with magic and medicine. He led her down the hall to the kitchen and parlour in back. He pointed to the stairs, leading up to rooms where he slept and studied, and showed her the larder, the lavatory chute and the water pump. He tossed a fresh log onto the hearth, set out fruit and cheese, and a bowl, and cloths, for her to wash herself, should she wish. Then he said he had customers to prepare for, had missed appointments already. He closed the hallway door, and she was alone.

She stuffed the food into her mouth, hardly chewing before she swallowed. Finished, she wriggled back in the seat of his solitary chair, so that her feet dangled clear of the ground. Her stone hand was cold beneath her living palm. She stared into the flames that licked inside the hearth. Her stomach still grumbled, but her hunger lacked the urgency it had before.

Presently, she heard voices, the minotaur's and another, higher in pitch. She listened for a while, idly trying to discern their words. Her gaze wandered around the room, settled on the staircase, then up the curve of the wall to the joists of timber and giant ivory that crossed the ceiling.

She slipped down from the chair.

The lowest stair creaked beneath her foot. She crept quietly up, across the small landing at the top and into the bedroom. She padded past the long bed, to the window that opened over the street. The panes of polished leviathan scales let in light, but revealed only the murkiest outlines of the world beyond. She examined the latch, gave it an experimental tug. The window swung outward. She pushed it open.

Cool air brushed over her face and arms. She leaned her elbows on the damp sill and gazed up at the dark tower, high on its hill. She saw a black stone face, and fingers reaching for her own.

She awoke early the next day, in the dull red light of the coals in the hearth. Her mate's face faded slowly from her mind's eye.

Cassiann was already in his surgery, mixing powders. He paused when she appeared in the doorway. "I hope I didn't disturb you."

She shook her head.

The minotaur returned to his work, tipping a measure of pale green powder into a jar already half filled with white. He stoppered the jar and shook it vigorously to mix the powders together, then placed the jar on a shelf. His hand lingered. He seemed to be gazing at something other than the shelves in front of him.

"It is a lonely thing, to be unique," he said, suddenly. "My people's shaping occurred elsewhere in the realms of Avalae. Our nation holds the islands to the west of here. It has been a long time, since I was forced to leave them."

He fell silent again, ordering the ranks of jars. He stopped, faced her. With an abrupt stride, he closed the gap between them. He reached out, jerkily, to touch her cheek. "My people were made to adore those whose shape you wear," he said.

His fingertips were dry and smooth. He traced the shape of her ear, the rapid pulse that arose in the side of her neck. His hand paused at her collarbone, then slowly eased the blanket from her shoulder.

Carefully, she stepped backwards through the doorway. The minotaur hung his head. His outstretched fingers curled back into his palm.

"Forgive me. I did not think I would be so overcome."

She fled, out into the morning fog.

The greyness was disorienting, and she stayed close to the buildings as she hurried along. Her heart thumped against her ribs—terror at what he might've done during the night, had his compulsion overcome him sooner.

The top of the hill was clear of the mist. The black tower stood stark against the chill blue sky, unrelieved by the bright sunshine. The buildings at the plaza's edge stuck up like jagged teeth, the city beyond them lost beneath a white blanket of cloud.

Yesterday's near-riot had become an encampment. Handcarts and wagons did service as sleeping shelters. Would-be supplicants hunched around cookfires. There were soldiers among them, now. A delegation of Reaver captains camped closest to the gate.

She rubbed her mate's frigid toes.

The Reaver captains thumped on the gate and hollered up to the angel's balcony. The tower remained silent. The captains argued briefly among themselves, and several left with their men.

A cloud of copper-coloured bees buzzed around her head. She watched them dance patterns in the air. A starling swooped, scattering the cloud. The bird alighted on her mate's outstretched arm. One beady eye met hers. A bee struggled vainly in its beak. The rest buzzed about erratically.

The starling flapped its wings and was gone.

"Bet you're hungry, eh?"

She jumped. An Yng'finail soldier in mismatched conscript armour held up a torn loaf of bread, just out of her reach. Her stomach complained loudly.

"Need to agree on a price first, love," he said. "It's not coin I have in mind, you understand."

She backed away, only to bump into a second man.

He sneered. "Too good for the likes of us, eh?"

She cried out and swatted at him with her stone hand. He caught the blow on the shoulder of his cuirass, cursing. His companion grabbed her arms from behind. The man she'd struck pulled back his fist and punched her in the mouth.

She tasted hot metal and salt. Pain radiated from her crushed lips. They took her by an arm each and began to drag her away. She struggled feebly, dazed from the blow.

The man to her left punched her again, under the ribs, driving the air from her lungs. She sagged, gasping.

She heard a sharp enquiry. A Reaver captain had risen, over by the tower gate, and stood watching them with hands on hips. His scrutiny was enough to make the two men falter. Their grip on her arms slackened.

She wrenched free. They shouted after her as she tottered into a run. One of them started to pursue, but a bark from the Reaver captain stopped him. Only their curses chased her from the plaza.

She didn't run far. The press of traffic soon forced her to slow. She found refuge in a doorway alcove. Gradually, her pulse slowed, her panic settled.

A memory floated to the surface of her thoughts, of festival dances beneath the tower: Avalae twirling in silk and gauze, each the focus of a ring of ecstatic slaves, competing for their masters' attention with the energy of their dancing. Every so often a slave would be chosen, and their masters would lead them by the hand through the black tower's gate.

She paused, thinking of cold and hunger, curled in her nest of briars and not knowing when the angel might open his gate. She thought of the men who'd seized her today, of the one who'd first found her, and thought of what might have happened had the first man been more wary, or had the Reaver captain not taken an interest.

She weighed the price of Cassiann's roof and hearth. *Made to adore those whose shape you wear*, he'd said.

She found his door unlocked, the apothecary speaking to a patient in his surgery room. He faltered, as she went past down the hall.

She perched on his tall chair, until she heard the front door shut, and Cassiann came into the kitchen.

"Our angel keeps his tower closed, then," he said.

She nodded.

Heart hammering, she placed her hand on his belly. She slid her fingers downward, felt him quicken. He grunted and caught her wrist. He touched a finger to her battered lips, questioning. She held his gaze, resolute, for the long moment that he stared.

He swept her up and carried her up the stairs.

He was gentle, but hurried. She cried out in pain when he entered her, wound her one fist in his cassock and buried her face against his chest as he thrust between her thighs.

Afterwards, she felt between her legs, found the blood there. She wiped her fingers on the bedsheet, and for a long time couldn't sleep.

When at last she did, she dreamed of her mate. He stood with his back to her, and no matter how fast she ran around his plinth, his face remained stubbornly turned away.

She awoke to find Cassiann kneeling beside the bed. His mouth was agape, his eyes squinting half shut. She realised he was smiling.

He held up a plain-spun dress. "I got these for you." He showed her a felted cloak and sheepskin boots.

"And this." He held out his palm. Across it was draped a simple wire necklace. Twined in its grasp was a small black orb.

Hesitantly, she reached out and touched it with her forefinger.

"It's a pearl," he said, then shyly: "I thought it a good name for you, since you lack one."

Her eyes felt suddenly hot. She tried the word out, under her breath, "Purr."

"Here."

He held the wire loop to her throat and clasped it behind her neck. She held the pearl between her fingertips and let him nuzzle at her neck, as his arms came around her.

Snowflakes greeted her when she pushed the window open. The street was clogged with wagons and handcarts and families afoot. A flock of gargoyles flew low over the rooftops, bearing infants and bundles of trinkets. Soldiers passed along the traffic jam, dragging men and boys from the line.

She felt the boards beneath her feet shift with the weight of Cassiann's tread. His hand clasped her shoulder. He peered down into the chaos below.

"Come," he said.

He tarried only long enough for them both to dress. She had to run to keep up with him as the minotaur ploughed through the press. She tucked her stone hand into the crook of her stump and hooked her fingers through his.

She felt a guilty relief when he turned downhill instead of up. She'd lost count of the days since she'd last gone back to the tower. The guilt she felt, standing beside her mate's plinth, touching him, had been too much to bear. She'd taken to lingering at the edge of the plaza, just long enough to see that the gate remained closed, and to drink in the sight of her mate. Then she'd stopped doing even that.

Cassiann's hurried pace brought them quickly to the harbour, emerging onto the waterfront near the city's arsenal.

The songships, few that survived, slept in a row, hulls bumping gently together as they rocked on the tide, their figureheads with faces bowed, arms folded across their wooden chests. They awoke a bitter longing in her, who would awake from their stillness, where her mate would not. But the songships were guarded by soldiers in armour and helms of good steel. She averted her eyes from their unfriendly regard, and hurried after Cassiann.

Further on, the docks became crowded. Gil-Gadin dhows lined the piers. Quar-Akech was fallen, were the words on many lips—the last of the sheikdoms, these ships escaped from the jaws of the invading fleet. Cassiann stopped to question some sailors. "Grahodden," she heard, in regard to the conquerors, and "Uiggrahodd," from whence they came, terms she did not know but she heard the fear and hate they owned when spoken.

These dhows were not staying, save a handful of battered warships. People on the docks shouted their bids for passage to the crews. A few were allowed to board. Other merchantmen were readying to flee as well, offering refuge on their decks for a price. A pair of Melkurran triremes remained aloof, their crews of flat-chested warrior women treating the goings-on about them with stoic indifference.

All along the harbourfront, soldiers were fortifying buildings and barricading streets. Cassiann led her past one such barrier, through a gap left just wide enough to allow foot traffic, past an angry carriage driver and his passengers, arguing with soldiers who wanted to divert them two streets over.

The minotaur did not speak until they were back inside his house. He went straight into his surgery and started filling a long wooden case with jars. She put her stone hand on the bench beside the scales and watched.

"The city will fall," he said. "If the angel will not come from his tower, the city's mages will not suffice to turn the invaders back. I must flee while I can. The Grahodden slaughter magic users in all the realms they conquer. And those who rule in Uiggrahodd have styled themselves as gods, and tolerate no other shapings of men, so I am doubly damned."

He stopped his packing and took her flesh hand in both of his. "Come with me. We'll take the East Road, through the mountains. Winter will not have closed the passes, yet."

She looked into his human eyes, sincere in his inhuman face. She thought of her mate, still stone, and the angel in his tower—and her hope, the same—alive or dead, she did not know. And though she could form its sound upon her tongue, she could not bring herself to say the word, "Yes."

Cassiann withdrew his hands, and smiled, sadly, insomuch as his face allowed. He rummaged in the pockets of his cassock, and placed on the table beside her stone hand the key for his house, and a drawstring purse that clinked, full of coin. She knew, then, that he had expected no different answer.

She followed him about the house as he gathered food and a few small, precious things. He tied them in a bundle and slung it from his shoulder, then stood, his head bowed beneath the ceiling, and looked down at her once more.

He brushed his fingers on her cheek. "Live, Pearl," he said.

He turned away abruptly, and strode down the hall. He scooped up his case of medicines as he ducked to get through the front door, and was gone.

She sat alone for a while, touching the key, and the purse, and her stone hand. Then she too, went to the larder, and made a bundle of food. Upstairs, to find a blanket to supplement her cloak. Then she picked up the key and the hand from the table and went out, locking the door behind her, and up the hill, to wait for one last time.

Most of the crowds had fled. The tower gate stood unscarred by their efforts. She stroked her mate's petrified ankle, gazed up at cold stone features, male mirror of her own. She cringed from the disdain she saw there.

Her fingers strayed to the black pearl at her throat as she lowered herself into her briar nest.

After a time, the wind brought the brave chorus of the songships, leading the war fleet out to meet the enemy. She heard the song disintegrate, before it faded, into the bitter laments of the dying. She twisted to peer around the plinth's edge. In the spaces the streets made between the buildings, she saw galleys beaching outside the city walls.

Too soon, the sounds of battle reached her ears: the clatter of steel and the hoarse shouts of officers rallying their men, the whine of killing spells and the wails of the injured.

She remembered those sounds, covered her ears with hand and stump, unwilling, yet, to abandon her mate, as the last diehards fled the plaza. Defenders ran past, few of them armed. Arrows cut some down. A rat-headed soldier dodged around the plinth, barely an arm's length away, and sprawled, a white-feathered shaft between his shoulder blades. He reached out, to drag himself onward with his fingers. He spat blood and shuddered violently, his jaw smacking the cobbles, and was still.

A rock smashed into the tower's face. Another followed, then a barrage. She screamed in terror. Missiles lit with magic were tossed among the stones. They spattered on impact, their fires eating gouges in the tower's face. Some fell short. A rock hit the cobbles only yards away, showering her with splinters of stone.

It was too much. With a howl, she broke from the shelter of the plinth. A spinning rock bounced in front of her. She tripped and fell. Her stone hand slipped from her grasp. She watched helplessly as it arced to strike the cobbles, broken pieces skittering apart.

A fireball detonated near her mate's plinth. Its flaming offspring rained around her. She thrashed and rolled as the magic flame ate through her cloak and into tender flesh beneath. Sobbing and wailing, trailing embers from her hair, she fled.

She ran through streets already littered with corpses, houses already aflame. Hulking figures loomed out of the smoke. She reached Cassiann's house. Mad with fear and grief, she gave no thought to the key tucked into her waistband. She sat, moaning more than weeping, rocking herself back and forth, in the alcove before the door.

In time, she calmed, but remained where she was, shocked and numb, feeling keenly the absence of the cold weight from her lap.

Ash-blackened snow began to fall. People slunk past, hollow-faced and cowed, snowmelt leaving streaks of soot on their faces. Others emerged from the houses, to ask where they were going.

"They've brought our angel from his tower," was the reply.

Her heart thudded. She joined the flow. The snow settled as slush, soaking through her boots and freezing her toes. Only those of fully human shape were abroad. Whatever others had survived had gone to ground.

She got her first clear sight of the city's conquerors, squads of Grahodden soldiers guarding the intersections of major streets. They were huge men, Cassian's size, and as burly, with skins like brown citrus peel. Their bulk was made greater by the cloaks of mottled feathers and fur caps they wore against the cold. In their fists they gripped halberds and glaives with cruel curved blades.

She stumbled past the ruined barricades that had walled the harbour. A great throng was gathered on the waterfront, its focus a gigantic quinquereme, pulled tight against the wharf. The bare masts of other war galleys filled the harbour, a skeleton forest through swirling snow.

The crowd was packed tight, but she threaded through, crawling in the slush when she could find no other way, desperate to see the angel. A voice rang out, unnaturally amplified, but she did not know its language. She wriggled between the last few rows of legs, heedless of the curses and kicks she earned. She tucked her burning cold fingers beneath her cloak and peered past the kilted thighs of a Grahodden soldier.

The angel knelt in the centre of a wide semi-circle of clear ground, the crowd held back by a ring of halberd blades. A wooden block was set before him, and a basket. A giant Grahodden stood over him, stripped to the waist to reveal the slabbed muscle beneath his pocked hide, a headsman's axe in his hands.

The angel's back was bowed, his complexion drained from Yng'finail red to leprous yellow. Shudders wracked his limbs. His grey swan wings drooped behind him, broken and roughly plucked.

Gazing down at him from the rail of the ship sat three lords of Uiggrahodd. They wore the heads of Grahodden folk, but outsized. Their bodies were those of lions. One raised a prehensile paw, a black talon springing from the thumbtip.

The headsman pushed down the angel's unresisting neck, then stepped back and took a grip on his axe.

The moment dilated. The thumb turned down.

The crowd groaned and surged at the soldiers' line. The Grahodden kept their discipline, laying about the rioters with the butts of their weapons as they closed ranks.

Like a rabbit breaking from cover, she sprang past the soldiers' legs and dashed across the space. Deep voices bellowed behind her.

She skidded to her knees in front of the angel. Holding hand and stump before his face, she shaped a word: "Please."

The angel raised his head, looked at her through a veil of filthy feather-hair. Grey eyes, half-mad with pain, stared into hers. The brows above them creased, as he recognized the shape of those his Reavers had vanquished, generations before. The frown cleared, eyes widened, as he perceived the stuff of his own self that animated her.

"Please," she said again.

His cracked lips worked. An incantation. A string of blood-flecked drool fell. She caught the precious spittle in her palm, closed her fingers around it as the headsman's boot came up under her ribs.

She balled around her hurt, rolling away through the slush. Rough fingers caught her hair and dragged her by it. She gritted her teeth against the pain, clutching her hand against her chest as she felt the phlegm become dust. She saw a halberd silhouetted against the sky.

A voice rose above the melee, a roar of command. It came from the ship. The command repeated. The soldier who held her lowered his weapon. Again, the sphinx spoke, and the noise of the crowd stilled.

The soldier jerked into motion, towing her backwards across the cobbles. The angel was forced down again. The axe rose, fell. The basket rocked. The broken body flexed, a pump of blood from the severed neck. A gasp and a sigh from the crowd. The tattered wings folded limply around the corpse.

The soldier deposited her at the feet of the mob, delivered a casual thump from the butt of his halberd as she found her feet. She averted her face from wondering eyes, pushed past the front rows, moving then in the roil of the crowd, toward and away, the collective beast suddenly lacking its head. She kept her fist pressed tight against her.

She trekked alone up the hill to the tower, past Grahodden soldiers, splintered doors and smouldering frames, and defenders' corpses already vanishing under drifts of snow. The black tower's gate hung twisted on its hinges, rent aside by magic, the stone face a mess of scars. Soldiers leaning in the shelter of the arch glanced at her, and away, dismissive.

Her mate was gone from his plinth. Only the stumps of his legs remained. Her stomach convulsed, she dry-retched. The dust in her palm felt like ash.

She crossed the space to the plinth at a faltering run, tripping once but catching herself, the ground turned unsteady beneath her. She slowed, had to force her feet to take her around the plinth, visions of her hand shattering on the cobbles replaying before her eyes.

She heaved again, this time with a sob of bittersweet relief. Her mate lay on a bed of briars, broken off whole above the knees, his left arm raised plaintive to the sky. Scars from magic fire pocked the length of his right side, a finger gone from the hand and his ear ruined in the mess along his neck and jaw. She sank to her knees beside him.

She caressed his undamaged cheek with her stump. Her fist ached, closed tight around the angel's dust.

Her hand shook as she held it over his chest.

She lowered her arm.

Unbidden, her stump brushed the necklace at her throat.

"Pearl," she whispered.

She wondered where Cassiann was, if he was safe.

Her clenched fingers began to cramp in the cold. Snowflakes drifted down. Her gaze fell on black stone shards, still lying where her stone hand had slipped her grasp. She looked at the broken stumps of her mate's legs. Could she do it to him? Bring him into this world, a cripple?

Could she not?

Made to adore him.

But did that mean she had no choice? She thought of Cassiann's gentleness, his kindness. Cassiann had made a choice: to leave, and live, when his compulsion would have bid him stay with her and die. His choice must have hurt him, but he had made it even so, and he was better for it.

The East Road, he'd said. *To the mountains.*

But did she want to follow? Did she need to? Her gaze fell on the soldiers, over by the tower gate. What better did Cassiann offer but a measure of gentleness?

Live, he had bid her. She touched the roll of her waistband, felt the key still there.

Pearl bent and touched her lips to cold stone. She tasted the salt warmth of her own tears. Gritting her teeth against a cry, she pushed herself away, and up.

She touched the roll of her waistband, felt the key still there. With unsteady steps, she walked from the plaza.

Glittering dust trailed from her fingers. Poppies sprang from the cobbles in her wake.

THE ENDANGERED CAMP

Ann Leckie

After the terrible push to be free of the Earth was past, we could stand again. In a while, the engineers had said, everything would float, but for now we were still accelerating. We were eight in the small, round room, though there were others on the sky-boat—engineers, and nest-guardians examining the eggs we had brought to see how many had been lost in the crushing, upward flight. But we eight stood watching the world recede.

The floor and walls of the room were of smooth, gold metal. Around the low ceiling was a pattern of cycad fronds and under this scenes from the histories. There was the first mother, ancestor of us all, who broke the shell of the original egg. The picture showed the egg, a single claw of the mother piercing that boundary between Inside and Outside. With her was the tiny figure of her mate. If you are from the mountains, you know that he ventured forth and fed on the carcass of the world-beast, slain by the mother, and in due time found the mother and mated with her. If you are a lowlander, he waited in the shell until she brought the liver to him, giving him the strength to come out into the open. Neither was pictured—the building of the sky-boat had taken the resources of both mountains and lowlands.

On another panel was Strong Claw, her sharp-toothed snout open in a triumphant call. She stood tall on powerful legs, each foot with its arced killing claw, sharp and deadly. Her arms stretched out before her, claws spread, and her long, stiff tail stretched behind. The artists had worked with such skill that every feather could be distinguished. Behind her was the great tree that had carried her across the sea, and in the water were pictured its inhabitants: coiled ammonites, hungry sharks, and a giant mososaur, huge-mouthed enough to swallow a person down at a gulp. Before Strong Claw was forested land, full of food for the hunting, new territory for her and her daughters yet unhatched.

A third panel showed the first sky-boat departing for the moon that had turned out to be farther away than our ancestors ever imagined. That voyage had been a triumph—the sky-boat (designed, all were ceaselessly told, by lowlander engineers) had achieved a seemingly impossible goal. But it had also been a disaster—as the mountain engineers had predicted, and the lowlanders refused to believe until the last, irrefutable moment, there had been no air on the moon. But as we had now set our sights on Mars, the artist had left off the end of the tale, to avoid ill-omen.

The engineers had used mirrors to cast an image of the Earth on the last, blank panel of the curved wall. It was this that held our attention.

As we watched, disaster struck. A sudden, brilliant flash whited out the image for an instant, and after that an expanding ring began to spread across the face of the world, as though a pebble had been dropped into a pond. Almost instantly a ball of fire rose up from the center of the ripple and expanded outward, obscuring it. I blinked, slowly, deliberately, sure that my vision was at fault. Still the fire grew until finally it dissipated, leaving a slowly-expanding veil of smoke.

There was silence in the sky-boat for some time.

Out of the speaking tube came the quiet voice of an engineer in the chamber below us. "A great stone from the void." There are many such, it seems, but no song speaks of them, no history tells us what happens when one strikes the Earth. This would not hinder the engineers, who are full of predictions and calculations.

"I was not informed," said White Ring into the tube. She was facing the image, her back to us. "Why?"

"We did not know," came the faint voice of the engineer.

"Do we not watch the skies?"

"The skies are vast. The stones are dark. We might have seen it if we looked in precisely the right place, at the right time. Or perhaps not."

"And now?"

Around me, not a feather stirred. "The cloud will continue to expand. The impact will leave a crater." Here the voice hesitated. "My colleague thinks perhaps twenty-five to thirty-five leagues wide, though I believe she has miscalculated the object's size. Perhaps forty-five to sixty leagues." White Ring's killing claw clicked on the floor. "I have not calculated how long it will take the cloud to disperse," the engineer continued. "I fear it will grow to cover the whole world. There may be fires as rocks fall back down to the ground. It hit water, so—"

"Silence!" ordered White Ring. "How far will the damage reach?"

A moment of silence from the tube. "It depends," came the voice, slowly, carefully. "On how thick the cloud is, and how long it stands between the Earth and the Sun. And if there are fires. And other things we haven't calculated yet."

For just a moment White Ring's feathers ruffled as though a breeze had stirred them. Nearly every other face was turned towards the view of Earth, but I looked at her, sidelong, without moving my snout. I felt the muscles in my back and my legs tense, and I forced them to relax lest the click of my largest claw on the deck betray my thoughts.

"We must go back," White Ring said. Snouts turned towards her in surprise. She turned her head to look behind her, and then turned fully, her daughter ducking low to avoid her tail. Others in the ring ducked and turned so that all who had faced forward could face the center of the circle. "We can stay above until the cloud disperses, and then land."

"*Can* we go back?" One of the younger females.

"We must," said White Ring, her tone admitting no dispute. "This venture was risk enough with the world safe behind us. If we are the only ones left alive . . . "

White Ring's daughter called through the speaking tube, and an answer came back. "We might be able to, if we act soon enough. We will have to make some calculations. But..."

"Make them," said White Ring. Her daughter eyed the rest of us, watching.

They had told us that leaving the Earth would be difficult. Three of our number had died in the punishing climb. But all of us standing here had survived it. Could those so silent and still around me be willing to throw that away, to throw away everything we had worked for? It seemed so.

The engineer had said *If we act soon enough*. A question of fuel, no doubt. If I did not speak up now, the time would be gone.

But here was my difficulty: every other person in the room was a lowlander. The superiority of mountain optics had ensured that some of the engineers aboard were highlanders, but I was one of only two surviving who was not either an engineer or an egg tender. If I spoke now, no one else would speak in support of me, unless they were completely convinced of my argument. Or unless I killed White Ring, in which case they would likely follow me out of fear if nothing else. But as things stood, I would not be allowed even to strike.

But I am no coward. "We must *not* go back," I said.

My neighbors sidled away, as far as they could in the cramped space, claws clicking on the metal floor. I stood face to face with White Ring.

"I hear nothing," said White Ring. Her killing claw tapped once, twice.

"This ship won't be built again," I said, "not in our lifetimes. Look!" I gestured at the picture with one clawed finger, at the still-spreading smoke. "Will we reach Mars, or will we die having made all this effort and accomplished nothing?"

White Ring looked around the circle, watching the faces and the demeanor of the others. I did not dare take my eyes off her to make the same survey. "I hear nothing," she said again.

"Coward! You disgrace our ancestors!"

Instantly White Ring's neck snaked forward and she snapped her teeth together a breath from my neck. I stood still as stone.

"Will you challenge me?" White Ring hissed. "At this time? Is your ambition so great?"

I would not allow my feathers to lift, or flutter. I would not allow a single twitch that I did not intend. "Did Strong Claw turn back?" I asked. I would have pointed to the picture, but I did not wish to move.

"She knew all was well behind her," said White Ring. "If none survive on Earth, and we die attempting Mars, what then?"

"We don't know there's air to breathe where we're going," said the daughter beside White Ring, when I didn't answer. "There was none on the moon."

"What a wonder this is! You lowlanders disbelieved when the engineers from the mountains said there was no air on the moon. Now you disbelieve when you are told that Mars certainly has an atmosphere."

"Bent light," White Ring began, her voice scornful.

"There is more than just the bending of light to prove it. There are plants, the astronomers have said so. We see them wax and wane with the seasons. There is no reason to think that Mars will not be much like Earth."

"The astronomers are not all agreed. Not even those from the mountains."

"But you have staked your life on it," I pointed out.

"While other lives were sure to continue," said White Ring. "What if everyone else is dead?"

"Then they are dead because Earth is now unlivable," I said. "And in that case, why turn back?"

"I know your ambition of old," said White Ring. "I had not thought you would exercise it at a time like this."

My feathers twitched then, I couldn't avoid it. I allowed them to tremble and rise. White Ring and her daughter watched me with malice, the other five with fear, or perhaps something else.

The moment stretched out. Time—time might be an enemy or an ally. Prolong the contention, and the moment to turn back would have passed. Allow the return to begin, and there would be only a short space, if any at all, in which it would be possible to correct our course.

"You call me ambitious," I said, "and I am. I would reach Mars! Did any of us embark without a similar ambition? But now you abandon what we have all worked so hard to attain! And when I point this out, I am threatened. Why is this? If one of you," and here I pointed around the circle, "had spoken, would this have been the response?" Had I seen movement among the others? Someone about to speak, some thoughtful twitch of feathers? "You may kill me if you like, as I am clearly outnumbered. But it will not change the truth."

One of those who had been silent spoke. "There is something in what she says."

White Ring was silent a moment. "It would be best not to fight," she said. "I would not lose more of us. Bring out the histories."

"Bring out the histories," I agreed.

She scratched at the unyielding metal ground with her foot, never taking her eyes off me. Then she barked a short order to her daughter, who repeated White Ring's word into the speaking tube.

The ladder well was behind me. I did not look as I heard the singer climbing into the room, or move as he squeezed past into the center of the circle in front of White Ring. I never moved my eyes from her, and let the others shift to let him by.

He was shorter even than most males, and his feathers were a dull brown, specked with black. He was an unprepossessing thing until he opened his mouth, as I well knew. He was my son.

He lowered his head in front of White Ring. "You choose first," she said to me. I should have been daunted—if I chose first, hers would be the last word. But I was not.

"I choose *Strong Claw's Voyage*," I said.

We are all susceptible to the power of song. The songs you've known since hatching, in the mouth of a great singer, will quicken your pulse and stop your breath. As my son called out the opening lines to the history I had chosen, all in the room were compelled by his voice to listen. Feathers ruffled and then settled, and all were still and there was no sound but his song.

There is no need to give the details here. The story is told, in its essentials, in the picture on the wall of the sky-boat, and in any event I might have chosen anything from the histories I wished, so long as White Ring would feel safe making the obvious choice when her turn came.

No, the song, and its argument, is already clear to you. Instead, I will tell you about my son.

When I was younger, and looking for a mate, I had resolved to have only the strongest, wiliest male I could find. I wanted large, strong daughters. I wanted children who would distinguish themselves on a hunt. I turned down suitors who were stupid, or weak, or too short. Some I killed. I would have killed the little brown-feathered thing that approached me last, but he opened his mouth and sang.

His voice! I lost all reason.

When the first clutch of eggs hatched, I had five daughters and six sons. Three of the daughters seemed strong enough. Three of the males were small and weak, and I thought they might die. But one of those, as I bent near to it, tiny, naked-looking thing, let out one barely audible peep.

I ate the four weaklings and fed them to him. His health was all my care in the coming months, and he grew strong.

He was undersized, but he was clever. I taught him what I could, and when the day came, that comes for all male children, the day to leave his mother and sisters behind forever, I instructed him to seek out the singers guild.

For most mothers, when that day comes it is as though they never had male children. The boys go off to other territories, and if they're seen again the sight raises no sentiment in the breast of the formerly doting mother. Your daughters are yours for life; your sons cease to exist when they leave the nest. But I took what steps I could to ensure that my son would be mine, no less than my daughters, even after he had gone to the singers guild.

I didn't know then that I would be on the sky-boat, or that a giant rock would hurtle out of the heavens and destroy the Earth. And even had I known, I could not have predicted that the lowlander singer would die during the launch, leaving my boy the only historian on the ship. But I knew that a singer's voice has a power entirely different from claws and teeth. White Ring had said she knew my ambition of old, but she did not realize its true extent.

The song ended. Strong Claw, victorious through all dangers, never turning back though she knew not what the end of her voyage would be, stood at last on the shore of the land she had discovered. Every listener sighed to hear it. It is an old song, and a pleasing one, with a clear lesson—the strong and resolute prevail.

It was no more than I had already said. And as I had hoped—expected!—White Ring answered with *The Endangered Camp*.

It is a story older even than Strong Claw's. It begins when a party of hunters goes out looking for iguanadon. (I myself have never seen an iguanadon, but they thunder through the oldest stories in vast herds.) They leave behind them in the woods their camp, a nursery. "Mounds of earth and leaves," the singer sang, "the infants waiting their time to come forth, and the guardians of the nests watchful."

An idyllic scene! But while the hunters are gone, the camp is attacked. The beast's tearing claws and rending teeth kill one guardian, and the others circle the nests as well as they can, and cry out together, *Let the hunting party return!*

Close around me, the listeners were rapt and their eyes wide, and they barely breathed, such was the power of the singer's voice.

The hunting party did return, of course. They heard the cries of the guardians, and ran with desperate speed back to the camp. Three guardians were killed, and four hunters, but they drove off the beast, saved the eggs, saved the pack. So the history tells us.

Now, this is the strange thing about history. When we are in doubt as to what course to take, or there is some debate, we examine the histories, we say, "So our ancestors did then, and so we should do now." And we think of the past as a solid, unbreakable rock that will always have the same form. But by accident or design, the rock is shaped. A singer drops a line here, a verse there, knowing or unknowing. And if you change the past, you change the future.

Stop with the beast defeated, and the eggs safe, and the salutary moral is clear. The lowlander singers I had heard had always stopped there. But it's not the end of the story. The four dead hunters had been among the most experienced, many of the others were injured, and food was scarce that year anyway. The seven dead from the attack fed the pack for a while, but after that they plundered the nests to survive, and no children were born that year.

I did not think White Ring would expect the singer to continue, even if she knew of the ending. The ill-omen of it would be too strong. Any singer would know what she meant by requesting it, and know, if he knew the end, to leave it off. But oh, my clever boy! He sang the rest of the song.

For a moment, as he continued where she had expected him to stop, she stood paralyzed. The others blinked in surprise, but his voice transfixed them and they were silent. White Ring drew her head back, and I saw her killing claws twitch. Even so she waited until he had finished.

"You made that up," accused White Ring's daughter when he fell silent. White Ring still held her threatening pose, ready to strike. But she dared not touch the singer; there was no other on board.

"You're very young," I said, my leg muscles tense with the desire to jump. "It's fashionable these days to leave that verse off, but anyone of any experience and education knows that's how the story ends." I swiveled my snout towards White Ring, and bared my teeth. "Isn't that so?"

"I have never heard it," said White Ring, still poised to strike. Her gaze was fixed on the boy, a small, brown-specked shape in the middle of the circle. "You have violated your obligation as a singer. Why? There can have been no collusion. Can you have done such a terrible thing merely from a hatred of lowlanders?"

Even if I had told her he was mine she would not have been able to imagine why such a thing would matter. And besides, he had sung truly. I might have laughed, but I did not; this was a dangerous moment.

"I have heard it," said a quiet voice. The others turned their heads but I never took my eyes off White Ring. She never took her eyes off my son.

"My great-aunt's mate was a singer," the voice continued. I placed it—a sturdy, handsome male, gray and black feathered, still young. He had kept quiet before now, as was proper. "He died when I was still a chick, but I remember he sang it in just that way." Silence. And then, even more timidly than before, "I was surprised to hear it requested. I wondered if you would signal the singer to leave the ending off. But then I thought, *he won't sing the ending, no one ever has except my uncle.*"

White Ring and her daughter would have no qualms about killing the black and gray male. They drew their heads back, hissing.

In that instant, a voice came from the speaking tube. "We have completed our calculations."

The low ceiling made it impossible to jump. Instead I drew my head back and then struck forward with all the force I could muster, hoping the boy would be quick enough to move out of the way.

The room erupted in screams and shouts. My teeth snapped together where White Ring's neck had been an instant before. I grabbed her shoulder and as she raked me with her claws I brought my foot up with its deadly killing claw. White Ring grabbed me and sank her teeth into my shoulder, but she was too late. My foot came up, and I drove my claw into her belly, and pulled my leg convulsively back.

Her jaws opened in a scream, and I let go of her and stepped back. The black and gray male was locked with the daughter. No one else was in the room—they must have fled down the ladder well.

"You are dead, White Ring," I said. Pink entrails sagged out of the bleeding slash in her belly. "I need only keep out of reach for a while."

"Return to Earth," she said. "What if we're all that's left?"

I wanted to take a step back and lean against the wall, but I wasn't sure if she still had strength for a last charge, and I didn't want to show any weakness.

"You have doomed us," she said, and fell to her knees, and then onto her side, guts squirting out with the force of her fall. Still I did not approach. Until she was reliably dead she was a danger.

Instead I looked over at the black and gray male, who stood now over the daughter's corpse. His feathers drooped, and he was covered in blood, whose it was impossible to tell. "Are you hurt?" I asked. I hoped he wasn't. He was handsome, and obviously strong.

"Yes," he said.

"Go down to the doctor. On your way, inform the engineers of the change in command." He bowed his head low and limped to the ladder well. My son had climbed up, and made way for him.

I stepped over to the daughter and pushed her with my foot. She was dead. Carefully, tentatively, I did the same for her mother.

Dead.

"Well, my chick," I said. "There will be new songs, and they will be yours." I turned to see him standing at the well. He bobbed his head. We had always understood each other.

My shoulder hurt, and my neck, where I had been clawed. I would have to see the doctor soon enough myself, but not this very moment. I turned around to see the image of the smoking, burning Earth. "Earth is dead, or if not it may as well be. Mars will be ours." If anyone still lived on the Earth, perhaps one day they would venture away from the world and find, on Mars, the evidence of our triumph.

Let cowards retreat. We go forward. We live!

AT THE EDGE OF DYING

Mary Robinette Kowal

Kahe peeked over the edge of the earthen trench as his tribe's retreating warriors broke from the bamboo grove onto the lava field. The tribesmen showed every sign of panicked flight in front of the advancing Ouvallese. Spears and shields dropped to the ground as they tucked in their arms and ran.

And the Ouvallese, arrogant with their exotic horses and metal armor, believed what they saw and chased the warriors toward him. The timing on this would be close. Kahe gathered the spell in his mind and double-checked the garrote around his neck. His wife stood behind him, the ends resting lightly in her hands. "Do it."

Bless her, Mehahui did not hesitate. She hauled back, cutting into his throat with the knotted cord. Kahe tried not to struggle as his breath was cut off. Black dots swirled in his vision, but he could not afford to faint yet.

With each breath he could not take, with each step closer to death, Kahe's power grew. As the tribe's warriors reached the trench and leaped down, he scanned the lava field to make certain none were left behind. Vision fading, he unleashed the spell coiled inside him.

The heat from the firestorm singed the air as it swept out from his trench. Even through his graying sight, the blue flame burned like the sun as it raced toward the Ouvallese battalion. Screams rose like prayer as his spell crisped the men in their armor.

As soon as the spell rolled out, Mehahui released her hold and Kahe fell against the damp red soil. The grains of dirt blended with the dots dancing in front of his eyes, so the very earth seemed to move. Air scraped across his tortured throat as life flooded into him. He gasped as the goddess's gift of power faded.

Beyond his own wrenching sobs, Kahe heard the agonized screams of those Ouvallese too distant to be instantly immolated. He prayed to Hia that his spell had gotten most of them; the goddess of death and magic had rarely failed him. Still, the kings of the tribes would have to send runners out to deal with the burned soldiers; a dying enemy was too dangerous to allow to linger.

Mehahui patted him, soft as a duckling, on the back. Her round face hovered in the edge of his vision. "Stay with me."

Kahe coughed when he tried to speak. "I am." His throat scraped as if it were filled with thorns. He knew she hated seeing him downed by a spell, but flirting with Hia was the only way to get the power he needed for a spell this big. Pushing against the earth wall, Kahe sat up.

His head swam. The dirt thrummed under his hands.

The vibration grew to a roar and the earth bucked. A wall collapsed. Dirt spilled into the trench, as the earth quaked.

No. A sorcerer must have been at the edge of his firestorm and by almost killing him, Kahe had given him access to Hia's power—only a dying man would have enough power to work magic on the earth itself. As the trench shifted and filled with falling rocks, the spell he needed to counter it sprang to his mind but without power. He turned to Mehahui even while knowing there wasn't enough time for the garrote to work. He fumbled for the knife at his side.

The tremors stopped.

Dust settled in the suddenly still air but he had not cast the counter-spell. Even if he had, it would have been as a rush lamp beside a bonfire.

Around them, men in the earthworks called to each other for aid or reassurance. Trickles of new dirt slid down the wall in miniature red avalanches. King Enahu scrambled over a mound, using his long spear as a walking staff.

"Hia's left tit! You're still alive." He slid down the side of the trench, red dirt smearing his legs with an illusion of blood. "When you stopped the earthquake, I didn't think you could have survived the spell. Not so soon after working the other."

"I didn't stop it." Kahe watched Mehahui instead of the king. Her skin had bleached like driftwood and she would not meet his eyes.

Beside him, King Enahu inhaled sharply, understanding what Kahe meant. "There's another sorcerer in the ranks? Hia, Pikeo, and the Mother! This could be the saving of us. Who?"

Mehahui hung her head, her hair falling around her face like rain at night. "It's me."

Kahe's heart stuttered, as if he had taken makiroot poison for a spell. Hia only gave her power to those on the road to death. "That's not possible."

"I'm dying, Kahe." His beautiful wife lifted her head and Kahe could not understand how he had missed the dark circles under her eyes.

With only a thin blanket covering her, every breeze in the hut chilled Mehahui. She shivered and kept her attention focused on the thatched pili-leaf ceiling while the surgeon poked at her.

Iokua stepped back from the table. "Why didn't you come to me sooner?" he asked.

Clinging to the blanket, Mehahui sat up. "Could you have done anything?"

"I could have tried."

They had studied under the same masters at the Paheni Academy of Medicinal Arts; she didn't need Iokua to tell her that only palliative care was possible. "Are you finished?"

He nodded and Mehahui wrapped her felted skirt back around her waist. Her hands shook when she tucked in the ends of the fabric. "Will you tell Kahe? I can't." She pulled her hair away from her face, securing it with the tortoiseshell pins Kahe had given her for their fifteenth anniversary. She tucked a red suhibis flower behind her left ear so her married status was clear—not that she needed it. Everyone in the united tribes knew Kahe.

Iokua tugged at his graying doctor's braid. "As you wish." He paused to pick up the sandalwood surgeon's mask and settled it on his face. The image of the goddess hid his worry behind her fragrant, smooth cheeks. Carved filigree of whale bone formed the mask's eyes, giving no hint of the man beneath.

He pushed aside the hanging in the door of the hut. Outside, Kahe was pacing on the lanai. He stopped, face tightening like leather as he saw the surgeon's mask, but he came when Iokua beckoned him.

Mehahui could not say anything as she took her husband's hand. The scars on the inside of his wrists stood out in angry relief.

Iokua bowed formally. "Your wife has a tumor in her abdomen." The mask flattened his voice.

"Can you cut it out of her?" Kahe sounded like she was still strangling him.

"No." The surgeon's mask was impassive. "I'm sorry."

Despite her husband's touch, Mehahui felt herself shrink into the far distance.

"How long does she have?"

The mask turned to her, cold and neutral though the voice underneath was not. "I suspect Mehahui will know better than I."

And she did know. Underneath the constant ache in her belly, the mass hummed with the goddess's power. She had known she was dying, but until today she had been afraid to prove it.

Kahe grasped her hand tighter. "Mehahui?"

Blindly, she turned toward him. "Weeks. Maybe."

As soon as they were alone, Kahe said, "Why didn't you tell me?" When had the soft curves of her face turned to planes?

"You would have tried to heal me."

Hia dealt out the power to kill but was more sparing with her willingness to heal. She would grant a life only in exchange for another. Kahe could have healed Mehahui, could still heal her, but only if he were willing to be taken to Hia's breast himself. And to do that would leave the king without a sorcerer.

He stood and paced the three strides that their tiny house allowed. The pili-leaf walls pressed in on him and his throat still felt tight. After all the times Mehahui had nearly killed him, only now did he feel the impact of death. He went over the list of poisons in his kit. "Makiroot acts slowly enough that I could work spells for the king until it was time to heal you. I'd be stronger than I am from strangling, so—"

"Stop. Kahe, stop." Mehahui clutched the sides of her head. "Do you think I could live with the guilt if you wasted your death on me?"

"It wouldn't be a waste!"

"Will you look beyond me? Paheni is being invaded. The South Shore Tribe have allied with the Ouvallese and we are overwhelmed. Hia has given us this gift and—"

"A gift!" If the goddess presented herself right then, he would have spit in her face.

"Yes, a gift! It's like Hia and Pikeo's Crossroads all over again. Can you imagine a better meeting of death and luck? It's not as if I am a common housewife—I've worked at your side; I know all the spells but I've never had the power to cast them. Hia gave me this so we can win the war." Mehahui held out her hands to him. "Please. Please don't take this from me."

Kahe could not go to her, though he knew she was right. Her power would only grow, as his mentor's had at the end of his life. In short order, she would surpass what he could do, and the tribes needed that to turn the tide in their favor.

But he needed her more. "How long do you have? Think deeply about it, and Hia will tell you the time remaining."

Mehahui's gaze turned inward. He watched her, sending a prayer to Pikeo for a little bit of luck. Hia's brother could be fickle, but Kahe no longer trusted his patron goddess.

"Eighteen days." Those two words shook Mehahui's voice.

But a tiny seed of hope sprouted in Kahe. "That might be enough."

"What? Enough for what?"

"To get you to Hia'au." Pilgrims from every tribe went to the goddess's city to die and sometimes—sometimes Hia would grant them the power to heal with their dying breath.

Mehahui looked at him like he had lost his senses. "But we lost Hia'au to Ouvalle."

Kahe nodded. "That's why we have to win this war quickly."

King Enahu's great house, despite the broad windows opening onto a terraced lanai, felt close and stifling with the narrow thoughts of the other kings who had gathered to meet with him. Kahe's knees ached from kneeling on the floor behind Enahu.

King Waitipi played with the lei of ti leaves around his neck, pulling the leaves through his fat hands in a fragrant rattle. "We are sorry to hear of your wife's illness, but I fail to see how this changes any of our strategies."

Kahe bent his head before answering. "With respect, your majesty, it changes everything. Mehahui will be stronger than me in a matter of days. What's more, she can cast spells at a moment's notice. We can take the battle right to the Ouvallese ships and handle anything that they cast at us."

"I'll admit it's tempting to retake Hia'au." The bright yellow feathers of King Enahu's cloak fluttered in the breeze. Across his knees lay the long spear he used in battle as a reminder of his strength.

King Haleko said, "I, for one, do not want to subject our troops to another massacre like Keonika Valley."

"I understand your concern, your majesty. But the Ouvallese only have one full sorcerer from their alliance with the South Shore tribe. With Mehahui's power added to mine, we can best them."

"Of course I do not doubt your assessment of your wife's power"—King Waitipi plucked at a ti leaf, shredding it—"but it seems to me that the South Shore tribe is making out much the best in this. Should we not reconsider our position?"

So many kings, so few rulers.

King Ehanu scowled. "Reconsider? The Ouvallese offered to let us rule over a portion of *our* land. A portion. As if they have the right to take whatever they wish. I will *not* subject my people to rule by outlanders."

"Nor I." King Haleko nodded, gray hair swaying around his head. "But this does raise some interesting possibilities." King Haleko's words raised hope for a moment. "Would the infirm in our hospices offer more sorcerers?"

"You would find power without knowledge. Hia's gift only comes to those who study and are willing to make the sacrifice of themselves."

"But your wife—"

"My wife . . . " Kahe had to stop to keep from drowning in his longing for her.

In the void, King Enahu spoke, "The lady Mehahui has studied at Kahe's side all the years they have been in our service."

Kahe begged his king, "This war could be over in two weeks, if you let us go to the South harbor. It would not divert troops; only a small band need come with us. No more than ten to protect us until we reach the South Harbor where the Ouvallese are moored. We could wipe them out in a matter of minutes." And then, though he would not say it out loud, he could take Mehahui to the Hia'ua and pray that one of the dying in the goddess's city would heal her.

King Enahu scowled. "Pikeo's Hawk! You're asking me to bet my kingdom that your wife is right about how long she has to live. What happens if we extend ourselves to attack and are cut off because she dies early? Everything is already in place to stop Ouvalle's incursions into King Waitipi's land. I need you there, not at the South Shore."

"Well." King Waitipi let the lei fall from his hand. "You've convinced me this merits more discussion and thought. Let us consider it more at the next meeting."

Kahe slammed his fists on the floor in front of him, sending a puff of dust into the air. "Eighteen days. She has eighteen days. We don't have time to wait."

The men in the great hall tensed. Kings, all of them, and disrespect could mean a death sentence.

Half-turning, Enahu let his hands rest on the spear across his knees. "Kahe. You are here on my sufferance. Do not forget yourself."

Trembling, Kahe bit his tongue and took a shallow breath. He bowed his head low until it rested on the floor. "Forgive me, your highness."

King Waitipi giggled like a girl. "You are no doubt distraught because of your wife's condition. I remind you that she will find grace with Hia no matter the outcome of our meetings."

Kahe knew that better than any king could.

But to wait until they made up their mind was worse than trusting Mehahui's life to the hands of Hia's brother god, Pikeo—luck had never been his friend.

If they did not decide fast enough, he would take Mehahui and go to the goddess's city without waiting for leave. He tasted the chalky dust as he knelt with his forehead pressed against from the floor. Leaving his king would mean abandoning his tribe in the war.

Surely Hia could not ask for a higher sacrifice. Surely she would spare Mehahui for that.

Mehahui could not remember the last time she had seen a crossroad instead of the usual roundabout. Most people went out of their way to avoid invoking the gods with crossed paths, connecting even forest tracks like this with diagonals and circles.

She half expected Hia and Pikeo to materialize and relive their famous bet.

A cramp twisted in her belly. Mehahui pressed her fist hard into her middle, trying to push the pain away. It was clear which god would use her as a game piece if they appeared. Doubling over, a moan escaped her.

She tried to straighten but Kahe had already returned to her. "Are you all right?"

Mehahui forced a laugh. "Oh. Fine. Hia's gift is being a talkative one this morning." She unclenched her fist and patted him on the arm. "It will pass."

"Can I do anything?" He caught her hand and squeezed it. Every angle of his body spoke of worry.

"Just keep going." Mehahui wiped her face. Her hand came away slick with sweat, but she smiled at her husband. "See. It has already passed."

She pushed past him onto the main road to Hia'ua.

As if she had said nothing, Kahe took her hand and pulled her to a stop in the middle of the crossroad. "You should take something for the pain." He knelt and fished his sorcery kit out of his pack.

Amid the ways of dying lay the remedies. Some spells needed a long slow death and he had poisons for that. Others needed the bright flash of blood flooding from the body, and he had obsidian knives, bone needles and sinew for those. But all of the deaths brought pain. Mehahui had nursed him back from all of them. The painkiller had been one of the most faithful tools in her arsenal.

She held out her hand to accept one of the dark pills from him. "Thank you."

A drumming sounded on the main road, heading toward the harbor.

She dropped the pill. A queasy tension in her belly held Mehahui rigid. Three creatures came into view—men whose bodies were twisted into something like massive storks with four legs. Her fear raced ahead of her mind and she had already begun to back away from the road before she recognized them as men riding horses, the exotic animals the Ouvallese had brought with them from overseas.

Warriors, clearly, and wearing the green and black Ouvallese colors—outriders, returning to the main band. If the gods were replaying their age-old game, then this unlucky chance was clearly Pikeo's move.

Which had more influence on mortal lives: Death or Luck? Would Hia win again in her battle against her brother?

The man in front saw them and shouted. She could not understand his words, but his intent was clear. Halt. Kahe placed his hand on his knife.

In moments, the three riders had cut them off, pinning them in the middle of the crossroad. The one who had shouted, a small effete man with blond curls showing under the bottom of his black helm, pushed his horse in closer. He pointed at Kahe's knife.

"Not to have!" His Pahenian was slow as if he spoke around a mouth of nettles.

Kahe glanced at the other riders. "I don't understand."

The blond pointed to the ground. "There. Put!"

Kahe nodded and reached slowly for the tie of his knife belt.

Despite the shade of the trees, heat coursed through Mehahui. The knot in her stomach throbbed with her pulse. Hia could not have brought them to this crossroad only to abandon them.

She looked around for an answer. The soldier closest to her lifted a bow from his saddle. Without giving Kahe time to disarm, he pulled an arrow from his quiver. Aimed it at her husband. Drew.

"Kahe!"

Her husband flinched and turned at her cry. Before he finished moving, the arrow sprouted from his cheek.

Mehahui shrieked. The soldier turned to her, bow raised.

Kahe flung out his hand and a palpable shadow flew through the air to engulf the soldier. His face was visible for a moment as fog in the night, then he vanished.

Blood cascaded from Kahe's mouth down his chest. He staggered but raised his arms again.

Spooked by its rider's disappearance, the soldier's horse reared and came down, nearly atop Mehahui. She danced back and grabbed at the dangling reins, trying to stop the bucking animal.

Ignoring her, the other two soldiers closed on Kahe. She flung the same spell she had seen him use, sucking a living night into being.

In that moment of inattention, the horse crashed into her, knocking her down. A hard hoof slammed against her belly.

Mehahui rolled, frantic to get away from the horse's plunging feet. Fetching up against a trunk at the side of the road, she struggled to get air into her lungs. Dear goddess, was this what Kahe felt when she strangled him?

The hard crack of metal on obsidian resounded through the forest. Kahe somehow had drawn his knife and met the remaining soldier's blow, but the glass shattered on the steel.

Mehahui pushed at the ground, but her arms only twitched. The bright pain of Hia's gift flared in her belly, almost blinding her. Her thighs were damp and sticky.

The soldier raised his sword again to bring it down on Kahe's unguarded neck.

Mehahui cried out, "Stop!"

It was not a true spell, but the soldier stopped. His arm, his horse, everything froze in mid-motion.

Kahe shuddered. Then, he slipped sideways and fell heavily to the ground.

The soldier, a statue in the forest, did not move.

Mehahui crawled across the dirt road to her husband. The pain in her stomach kept her bent nearly double. Her skirts were bright with blood.

Something had broken inside when the horse had knocked her down.

No matter now, Kahe needed her. During the years of aiding him, she had seen almost every form of near-death and learned to bring him back. She grabbed the smooth leather sorcerer's kit. With it in her grasp, Mehahui set to work to save him.

The arrow had entered his cheek under his right eye, passing through his mouth and lodging in his jaw opposite. Kahe was bleeding heavily from the channel it had cut through the roof of his mouth, but she knew how to deal with that.

Shaking, Mehahui turned him on his side, so he would not drown in his own blood. She broke the arrow and pulled the shaft free. Then with a pair of forceps, she tried to pry the arrowhead out of his jawbone. The forceps slipped off it. She gripped it again, but her hands shook too much to hold it steady and his mouth open. If she could not get it out, the wound would suppurate and Kahe would die despite all her efforts. Again, she tried and gouged his cheek when the forceps slipped.

Mehahui looked at the sky, tears of frustration pooling in her eyes.

The frozen soldier still stood in arrested motion. His cape stood away from his body showing the bright gold seal of the Ouvallese king on the field of dark green. A bead of sweat clung to the edge of his jaw in unmoving testament to her power.

She did not need the forceps. She had Hia. Praise the goddess for giving Mehahui power when she needed it most.

Mehahui focused on the arrowhead and sent a prayer to Hia. Channeling the smallest vanishing spell possible, she begged the arrowhead to go. For an instant, a new shadow appeared in Kahe's mouth and then blood rushed from the hole where the arrowhead had been.

"Praise Hia!"

The other wounds would answer to pressure. From the kit she took pads of clean cloth, soaked them in suhibis flower honey and packed them into the wounds. When all was tied and tight, Mehahui looked again at the soldier. There was no time to let Kahe rest.

She held smelling salts under his nose and braced herself for the next task.

K ahe retched and his world exploded with pain. Every part of his head, his being, seemed to exist for no reason but to hurt.

He tried to probe the pain with his tongue and gagged again. Cloth almost filled his mouth.

"Hush, hush . . . " Mehahui's gentle hand stroked his forehead.

Kahe cracked his eyes and tried to speak, but only a grunt came out. Bandages swaddled his head and held his mouth closed.

"You have to get up, Kahe. The rest of the warriors will be coming."

Battalion. He had to get up. Kahe could barely lift his head and somehow he had to stand. With Mehahui's help, he rolled into a sitting position.

A soldier stood over them. His sword was raised to strike.

Kahe tried to push Mehahui away from the man and fell face forward in the road. All the pain returned and threatened to pull him back into Hia's blessed darkness.

"It's all right! He's—he's frozen." Mehahui helped him sit again.

He looked more carefully at the soldier. The man's cloak had swung out from his body, but gravity did nothing to pull it down. Kahe did not know of a spell that could do such a thing.

He looked at Mehahui. The shadows under her eyes were deeper. In the hollows of her cheeks, the bone lay close beneath her skin. Blood coated her skirts and showed in red blotches at her ankles.

He tried to ask, but his words came out more garbled than a foreigner's.

Still, Mehahui understood enough. "Hia granted my prayer." She stood, the effort clear in her every movement.

Kahe grabbed her skirt and gestured to the blood. What price had Hia demanded for this power?

She pushed his hands away. "You have to hurry. I think the main road is the fastest way back, yes?"

Kahe forced a word past the cloth in his mouth. "Back?" They could go around the battalion in the forest.

"Yes. Back." Mehahui stood with her hands braced on her knees, swaying. "You have to go to King Enahu."

He shook his head. "Hia'au."

"I am not going to Hia'au. The goddess gave me the power to save Paheni, not myself. I am staying here."

She could not mean that. Kahe clambered to his feet. The forest tipped and swayed around him, but long practice at being bled kept him standing. He had to make her understand that going to Hia'au would save both her and Paheni. No possible good could come from her staying here.

As if in answer to his thoughts, Mehahui said, "Look at the soldier, Kahe. Do you see the badge on his shoulder?"

Kahe dragged his eyes away from her. The coiled hydra of Ouvalle shone against a field of green. Where the necks sprouted from the body, a crown circled like a collar.

"That's their king's symbol, isn't it? He's landed. It's not a single battalion, but his army." Mehahui beckoned him. "Please, Kahe."

He would not leave her here. Kahe clawed at the bandages surrounding his head. If he could only talk to her, she would understand.

"Please, please go. Hia—" her voice broke. Tears wiped her cheeks clean of dirt. "Hia has given me more power, but I only have until this evening before she takes me home. I want to know you are safe while I meet the King of Ouvalle."

Thunder rumbled in the distance.

Kahe had freely dedicated himself to the goddess but she had no right to demand this of his wife. Mehahui was his wife. His. Hia had no right to take her from him. Not now. Not like this.

Death combined with Luck showed the hands of Hia and Pikeo and they stood square in the middle of a crossroads. The Mother only knew what else the gods had planned.

"Hate her."

"No. No! Do you think this is easy for me? The only comfort I have is that I am serving a greater good. That this is the will of Hia and Pikeo and the Mother. You will *not* take my faith from me."

How could he live without her? The thunder grew louder, discernible now as the sound of a great mass of men marching closer.

Mehahui limped to his side and took his hand. She raised it to her lips and kissed his knuckles tenderly. "Please go."

Belling through the trees, a horn sounded.

Kahe cursed the goddess for cutting their time so short and leaned in to kiss his wife. The pain in his jaw meant nothing in this moment.

The sound of approaching horses broke their embrace. Kahe bent to retrieve his sorcery kit; if he took one of the faster poisons, then he could match Mehahui's power and meet Hia with his wife.

Mehahui put her hand on his shoulder. "No. I don't want you to go to the goddess. Someone must bear witness to our king."

He shook his head and pulled out the tincture of shadoweve blossoms.

"I have spent our entire marriage helping you die and knowing I would outlive you. Have you heard me complain?" She spoke very fast, as the army approached.

Kahe glanced down the road. The first of the men came into view. It seemed such a simple thing to want to die with her.

A mounted soldier separated from the company and advanced, shouting at them until he saw his immobile comrade. Moments later, a bugled command halted the force a bowshot away.

Men crowded the road in the green and black of Ouvalle. Scores of hydras fluttered on pennants, writhing in the breeze. Rising above the helmets of the warriors were ranks of bows and pikes. In the midst of them were towering gray animals, like horses swollen to the size of whales, with elongated, snaking noses that reached almost to the ground and wicked tusks jutting from their mouths. Each whale-horse glimmered with armor in scales of green lacquered steel. The black huts on their backs brushed the overarching trees. What spell had they used to bring these monsters across the ocean?

Mehahui squeezed Kahe's shoulder. When she stepped away from him, the absence of her hand left his shoulder cold and light.

She spoke; a spell amplified her voice so the very trees seemed to carry her words. "Lay down your arms and return to your homes."

Involuntarily, the closest warriors began to unbuckle their sword belts. Their sergeant shouted at them and looks of startled confusion or bewildered anger crossed their faces.

Then, at a command, the front rank of archers raised their bows.

Kahe reached for what little power was available to him. A rain of arrows darkened the air between them and the army. Kahe hurled a spell praying that Hia would allow him to create a small shield. As the spell left him, the air over them thickened, diverting the leading arrows but not enough.

Mehahui wiped the air with her hand; arrows fell to the ground. Their heavy blunt tips struck the road creating a perimeter around them. Designed to bludgeon a sorcerer to unconsciousness, without risking a wound that would bring more power, these arrows meant the Ouvallese army had recognized what the two of them were.

How long would it take them to realize that *he* was without power? Kahe turned to his kit when the air shuddered. A spell left Mehahui and the trees closest to the road swayed with a breeze. A groan rose from their bases. The trees toppled, falling like children's playthings toward the road.

Horses and men screamed in terror. Trumpeting, the tall whale-horses were the first to feel the weight of the trees.

On the lead whale-horse, the cloth curtains of the black hut blew straight out as a great wind pushed the trees upright.

The curtains remained open. An ancient, frail man stood at the opening, supported by two attendants—Oahi, the

South Shore king's sorcerer. Another spell left the traitor king's sorcerer, forming into a bird of fire as it passed over the warriors' heads.

Screaming its wrath, the phoenix plummeted toward them. The counter-spell formed in Kahe's mind and he hurled it, creating a fledgling waterbird. The phoenix clawed the tiny creature with a flaming talon and the waterbird steamed out of existence.

Moments later, Mehahui hurled the same spell. Her waterbird formed with a crack of thunder. The roar of a thousand waterfalls deafened Kahe with each stroke of the mighty bird's wings.

As it grappled with the phoenix, dousing the bird's fire in a steaming conflagration, Kahe saw the power of the goddess. *This* was why Hia wanted them both there; Mehahui had the power and the knowledge, but not the instincts of a sorcerer.

Without waiting for her waterbird to finish the phoenix, Kahe attacked the Ouvallese. The pathetic spell barely warmed the metal of the whale-horse's scales. But when Mehahui copied him, the animal screamed under the red hot metal, plunging forward in terror. Its iron shod feet trampled the warriors closest to it.

On its back, the attendants clutched Oahi, struggling to keep him upright as he worked the counter-spell. Even though he cooled the scales, the panicked creature did not stop its rampage. A blond, bearded man, with a gold circlet on his helm staggered forward in the hut to stand next to the old man. What would the King of Ouvalle do when all his animals panicked?

Kahe croaked, "Others."

Mehahui nodded, and heated the scaled armor of the whale-horse next to the first.

As quickly as she heated it, the Ouvallese sorcerer cooled it, but the frightened animal turned the disciplined

In Kahe's arms, Mehahui stirred and opened her eyes. She gulped in air. "Oh, Hia. No!"

Her skin was clear and flushed with life. Kahe took her face in his hands, feeling the warm vitality of her flesh. "How?"

"They healed me," she groaned. "The goddess has left." She looked past him at the archers. Her eyes widened.

They had no more blunt arrows. A field of sharp points sprang toward them.

"Pikeo save us!" Kahe threw himself across her, turning to cast a shield at the deadly arrows. It stopped most of them.

A familiar pain tore open his cheek. Another arrow plunged into his left shoulder and the third went through his right arm and pinned it to his thigh.

But none of them hit Mehahui.

Kahe waited for Hia's power to come to him, but the wounds were too slight. So he sent a prayer to Pikeo begging for good luck. They were in a crossroads, if ever Luck were going to play fair with him, it would be here and now.

And this would be the moment to strike. Oahi sagged in the arms of his escort, already gone home to Hia, but Kahe lacked the power for any large spells. He tried to reach for his dagger but by unlucky chance, the arrow bound his right arm to his leg.

His left arm hung limp. This was how Pikeo answered his prayer?

Mehahui pushed him off of her and got to her knees. He saw her prep for a spell with a sense of despair. Flush with life, she had even less power than he.

The spell fluttered from her, almost dissipating by the time it reached the army. She had thrown an unbinding spell. It was a simple childish spell, good only for causing a rival's skirt to drop.

One tie on the king's hut came undone.

Kahe held his breath, praying that Pikeo would notice that chance and play with it.

As the animal lurched onto the road, the king's hut slid off and toppled among the remnant of the Ouvallese army. The hut splintered as it crushed the men unlucky enough to be caught underneath it. As the debris settled, Kahe gasped at what the hand of Pikeo had wrought: the pike of one of the Ouvallese had impaled the king like a trophy of war.

He convulsed once and hung limp.

At the sight of their dead monarch, a rising wail swept through the remaining warriors. Those closest to Mehahui and Kahe backed away. Others, seeing their decimated ranks, threw down their arms and ran.

Mehahui leaned her head against Kahe's back. Then she patted him, soft as a hatchling. "Stay with me."

Kahe coughed as he tried to speak, gagging on the mass in his mouth. She knelt in front of him.

Looking at his wife's fair and healthy face, Kahe sent a prayer of thanks to both gods.

"The arrow in your cheek appears to have followed the same path as the other did; it is lodged in your bandages. I'd say we have Luck to thank for our survival today." Mehahui picked up the sorcery kit. "And now, my love, I intend to keep you out of Hia's hands."

She placed a hand against his cheek and Kahe had never felt anything so sweet as his wife's touch, proving they were both alive.

HOOVES AND THE HOVEL
OF ABDEL JAMEELA

Saladin Ahmed

As soon as I arrive in the village of Beit Zujaaj I begin to hear the mutters about Abdel Jameela, a strange old man supposedly unconnected to any of the local families. Two days into my stay the villagers fall over one another to share with me the rumors that Abdel Jameela is in fact distantly related to the esteemed Assad clan. By my third day in Beit Zujaaj, several of the Assads, omniscient as "important" families always are in these piles of cottages, have accosted me to deny the malicious whispers. No doubt they are worried about the bad impression such an association might make on me, favorite physicker of the Caliph's own son.

The latest denial comes from Hajjar al-Assad himself, the middle-aged head of the clan and the sort of half-literate lout that passes for a Shaykh in these parts. Desperate for the approval of the young courtier whom he no doubt privately condemns as an overschooled sodomite, bristle-bearded Shaykh Hajjar has cornered me in the village's only café—if the sitting room of a qat-chewing old woman can be called a café by anyone other than bumpkins.

I should not be so hard on Beit Zujaaj and its bumpkins. But when I look at the gray rock-heap houses, the withered gray vegetable-yards, and the stuporous gray lives that fill this village, I want to weep for the lost color of Baghdad.

Instead I sit and listen to the Shaykh.

"Abdel Jameela is not of Assad blood, O learned Professor. My grandfather took mercy, as God tells us we must, on the old man's mother. Seventy-and-some years ago she showed up in Beit Zujaaj, half-dead from traveling and big with child, telling tales—God alone knows if they were true—of her Assad-clan husband, supposedly slain by highwaymen. Abdel Jameela was birthed and raised here, but he has never been of this village." Shaykh Hajjar scowls. "For decades now—since I was a boy—he has lived up on the hilltop rather than among us. More of a hermit than a villager. And not of Assad blood," he says again.

I stand up. I can take no more of the man's unctuous voice and, praise God, I don't have to.

"Of course, O Shaykh, of course. I understand. Now, if you will excuse me?"

Shaykh Hajjar blinks. He wishes to say more but doesn't dare. For I have come from the Caliph's court.

"Yes, Professor. Peace be upon you." His voice is like a snuffed candle.

"And upon you, peace." I head for the door as I speak.

The villagers would be less deferential if they knew of my current position at court—or rather, lack of one. The Caliph has sent me to Beit Zujaaj as an insult. I am here as a reminder that the well-read young physicker with the clever wit and impressive skill, whose company the Commander of the Faithful's own bookish son enjoys, is worth less than the droppings of the Caliph's favorite falcon. At least when gold and a Persian noble's beautiful daughter are involved.

For God's viceroy the Caliph has seen fit to promise my Shireen to another, despite her love for me. Her husband-to-be is older than her father—too ill, the last I heard, to even sign the marriage contract. But as soon as his palsied, liver-spotted hand is hale enough to raise a pen . . . Things would have gone differently were I a wealthy man. Shireen's father would have heard my proposal happily enough if I'd been able to provide the grand dowry he sought. The Caliph's son, fond of his brilliant physicker, even asked that Shireen be wedded to me. But the boy's fondness could only get me so far. The Commander of the Faithful saw no reason to impose a raggedy scholar of a son-in-law on the Persian when a rich old vulture would please the man more. I am, in the Caliph's eyes, an amusing companion to his son, but one whom the boy will lose like a doll once he grows to love killing and gold-getting more than learning. Certainly I am nothing worth upsetting Shireen's coin-crazed courtier father over.

For a man is not merely who he is, but what he has. Had I land or caravans I would be a different man—the sort who could compete for Shireen's hand. But I have only books and instruments and a tiny inheritance, and thus that is all that I am. A man made of books and pittances would be a fool to protest when the Commander of the Faithful told him that his love would soon wed another.

I am a fool.

My outburst in court did not quite cost me my head, but I was sent to Beit Zujaaj "for a time, only, to minister to the villagers as a representative of Our beneficent concern for Our subjects." And my fiery, tree-climbing Shireen was locked away to await her half-dead suitor's recovery.

"O Professor! Looks like you might get a chance to see Abdel Jameela for yourself!" Just outside the café, the gravelly voice of Umm Hikma the café-keeper pierces the cool morning air and pulls me out of my reverie. I like old Umm Hikma, with her qat-chewer's irascibility and her blacksmithish arms.

Beside her is a broad-shouldered man I don't know. He scuffs the dusty ground with his sandal and speaks to me in a worried stutter.

"P-peace be upon you, O learned Professor. We haven't yet met. I'm Yousef, the porter."

"And upon you, peace, O Yousef. A pleasure to meet you."

"The pleasure's mine, O Professor. But I am here on behalf of another. To bring you a message. From Abdel Jameela."

For the first time since arriving in Beit Zujaaj, I am surprised. "A message? For me?"

"Yes, Professor. I am just returned from the old hermit's hovel, a half-day's walk from here, on the hilltop. Five, six times a year I bring things to Abdel Jameela, you see. In exchange he gives a few coins, praise God."

"And where does he get these coins, up there on the hill?" Shaykh Hajjar's voice spits out the words from the café doorway behind me. I glare and he falls silent.

I turn back to the porter. "What message do you bear, O Yousef? And how does this graybeard know of me?"

Broad-shouldered Yousef looks terrified. The power of the court. "Forgive me, O learned Professor! Abdel Jameela asked what news from the village and I . . . I told him that a court physicker was in Beit Zujaaj. He grew excited and told me to beg upon his behalf for your aid. He said his wife was horribly ill. He fears she will lose her legs, and perhaps her life."

"His wife?" I've never heard of a married hermit.

Umm Hikma raises her charcoaled eyebrows, chews her qat, and says nothing.

Shaykh Hajjar is more vocal. "No one save God knows where she came from, or how many years she's been up there. The people have had glimpses only. She doesn't wear the head scarf that our women wear. She is wrapped all in black cloth from head to toe and mesh-masked like a foreigner. She has spoken to no one. Do you know, O Professor, what the old rascal said to me years ago when I asked why his wife never comes down to the village? He said, 'She is very religious'! The old dog! Where is it written that a woman can't speak to other women? Other women who are good Muslims? The old son of a whore! What should his wife fear here? The truth of the matter is—"

"The truth, O Shaykh, is that in this village only *your* poor wife need live in fear!" Umm Hikma lets out a rockslide chuckle and gives me a conspiratorial wink. Before the Shaykh can sputter out his offended reply, I turn to Yousef again.

"On this visit, did you see Abdel Jameela's wife?" If he can describe the sick woman, I may be able to make some guesses about her condition. But the porter frowns.

"He does not ask me into his home, O Professor. No one has been asked into his home for thirty years."

Except for the gifted young physicker from the Caliph's court. Well, it may prove more interesting than what I've seen of Beit Zujaaj thus far. I do have a fondness for hermits. Or, rather, for the *idea* of hermits. I can't say that I have ever met one. But as a student I always fantasized that I would one day *be* a hermit, alone with God and my many books in the barren hills.

That was before I met Shireen.

"There is one thing more," Yousef says, his broad face looking even more nervous. "He asked that you come alone."

My heartbeat quickens, though there is no good reason for fear. Surely this is just an old hater-of-men's surly whim. A physicker deals with such temperamental oddities as often as maladies of the liver or lungs. Still . . . "Why does he ask this?"

"He says that his wife is very modest and that in her state the frightening presence of men might worsen her illness."

Shaykh Hajjar erupts at this. "Bah! Illness! More likely they've done something shameful they don't want the village to know of. Almighty God forbid, maybe they—"

Whatever malicious thing the Shaykh is going to say, I silence it with another glare borrowed from the Commander of the Faithful. "If the woman is ill, it is my duty as a Muslim and a physicker to help her, whatever her husband's oddities."

Shaykh Hajjar's scowl is soul-deep. "Forgive me, O Professor, but this is not a matter of oddities. You could be in danger. We know why Abdel Jameela's wife hides away, though some here fear to speak of such things."

Umm Hikma spits her qat into the road, folds her powerful arms and frowns. "In the name of God! Don't you believe, Professor, that Abdel Jameela, who couldn't kill an ant, means you any harm." She jerks her chin at Shaykh Hajjar. "And you, O Shaykh, by God, please don't start telling your old lady stories again!"

The Shaykh wags a finger at her. "Yes, I *will* tell him, woman! And may Almighty God forgive you for mocking your Shaykh!" Shaykh Hajjar turns to me with a grim look. "O learned Professor, I will say it plainly: Abdel Jameela's wife is a witch."

"A witch?" The last drops of my patience with Beit Zujaaj have dripped through the water clock. It is time to be away from these people. "Why would you say such a thing, O Shaykh?"

The Shaykh shrugs. "Only God knows for certain," he says. His tone belies his words.

"May God protect us all from slanderous ill-wishers," I say.

He scowls. But I have come from the Caliph's court, so his tone is venomously polite. "It is no slander, O Professor. Abdel Jameela's wife consorts with ghouls. Travelers have heard strange noises coming from the hilltop. And hoofprints have been seen on the hill-path. Cloven hoofprints, O Professor, where there are neither sheep nor goats."

"No! Not cloven hoofprints!" I say.

But the Shaykh pretends not to notice my sarcasm. He just nods. "There is no strength and no safety but with God."

"God is great," I say in vague, obligatory acknowledgment. I have heard enough rumor and nonsense. And a sick woman needs my help. "I will leave as soon as I gather my things. This Abdel Jameela lives up the road, yes? On a hill? If I walk, how long will it take me?"

"If you do not stop to rest, you will see the hill in the distance by noontime prayer," says Umm Hikma, who has a new bit of qat going in her cheek.

"I will bring you some food for your trip, Professor, and the stream runs alongside the road much of the way, so you'll have no need of water." Yousef seems relieved that I'm not angry with him, though I don't quite know why I would be. I thank him then speak to the group.

"Peace be upon you all."

"And upon you, peace," they say in near-unison.

In my room, I gather scalpel, saw, and drugs into my pack—the kid-leather pack that my beloved gifted to me. I say more farewells to the villagers, firmly discourage their company, and set off alone on the road. As I walk rumors of witches and wife-beaters are crowded out of my thoughts by the sweet remembered sweat-and-ambergris scent of my Shireen.

After an hour on the rock-strewn road, the late-morning air warms. The sound of the stream beside the road almost calms me.

Time passes and the sun climbs high in the sky. I take off my turban and caftan, make ablution by the stream and say my noon prayers. Not long after I begin walking again, I can make out what must be Beit Zujaaj hill off in the distance. In another hour or so I am at its foot.

It is not much of a hill, actually. There are buildings in Baghdad that are taller. A relief, as I am not much of a hill-climber. The rocky path is not too steep, and green sprays of grass and thyme dot it—a pleasant enough walk, really. The sun sinks a bit in the sky and I break halfway up the hill for afternoon prayers and a bit of bread and green apple. I try to keep my soul from sinking as I recall Shireen, her skirts tied up scandalously, knocking apples down to me from the high branches of the Caliph's orchard-trees.

The rest of the path proves steeper and I am sweating through my galabeya when I finally reach the hilltop. As I stand there huffing and puffing my eyes land on a small structure thirty yards away.

If Beit Zujaaj hill is not much of a hill, at least the hermit's hovel can be called nothing but a hovel. Stones piled on stones until they have taken the vague shape of a dwelling. Two sickly chickens scratching in the dirt. As soon as I have caught my breath a man comes walking out to meet me. Abdel Jameela.

He is shriveled with a long gray beard and a ragged kaffiyeh, and I can tell he will smell unpleasant even before he reaches me. How does he already know I'm here? I don't have much time to wonder, as the old man moves quickly despite clearly gouty legs.

"You are the physicker, yes? From the Caliph's court?"

No 'peace be upon you,' no 'how is your health,' no 'pleased to meet you.' Life on a hilltop apparently wears away one's manners. As if reading my thoughts, the old man bows his head in supplication.

"Ah. Forgive my abruptness, O learned Professor. I am Abdel Jameela. Thank you. Thank you a thousand times for coming." I am right about his stink, and I thank God he does not try to embrace me. With no further ceremony I am led into the hovel.

There are a few stained and tattered carpets layered on the packed-dirt floor. A straw mat, an old cushion and a battered tea tray are the only furnishings. Except for the screen. Directly opposite the door is a tall, incongruously fine cedar-and-pearl latticed folding screen, behind which I can make out only a vague shape. It is a more expensive piece of furniture than any of the villagers could afford, I'm sure. And behind it, no doubt, sits Abdel Jameela's wife.

The old man makes tea hurriedly, clattering the cups but saying nothing the whole while. The scent of the seeping mint leaves drifts up, covering his sour smell. Abdel Jameela sets my tea before me, places a cup beside the screen, and sits down. A hand reaches out from behind the screen to take the tea. It is brown and graceful. *Beautiful*, if I am to speak truly. I realize I am staring and tear my gaze away.

The old man doesn't seem to notice. "I don't spend my time among men, Professor. I can't talk like a courtier. All I can say is that we need your help."

"Yousef the porter has told me that your wife is ill, O Uncle. Something to do with her legs, yes? I will do whatever I can to cure her, Almighty God willing."

For some reason, Abdel Jameela grimaces at this. Then he rubs his hands together and gives me an even more pained expression. "O Professor, I must show you a sight that will shock you. My wife . . . Well, words are not the way."

With a grunt the old man stands and walks halfway behind the screen. He gestures for me to follow then bids me stop a few feet away. I hear rustling behind the screen, and I can see a woman's form moving, but still Abdel Jameela's wife is silent.

"Prepare yourself, Professor. Please show him, O beautiful wife of mine." The shape behind the screen shifts. There is a scraping noise. And a woman's leg ending in a cloven hoof stretches out from behind the screen.

I take a deep breath. "God is Great," I say aloud. This, then, is the source of Shaykh Hajjar's fanciful grumbling. But such grotesqueries are not unheard of to an educated man. Only last year another physicker at court showed me a child—born to a healthy, pious man and his modest wife—all covered in fur. This same physicker told me of another child he'd seen born with scaly skin. I take another deep breath. If a hoofed woman can be born and live, is it so strange that she might find a mad old man to care for her?

"O my sweetheart!" Abdel Jameela's whisper is indecent as he holds his wife's hoof.

And for a moment I see what mad Abdel Jameela sees. The hoof's glossy black beauty, as smoldering as a woman's eye. It is entrancing . . .

"O, my wife," the old man goes on, and runs his crooked old finger over the hoof-cleft slowly and lovingly. "O, my beautiful wife . . . " The leg flexes, but still no sound comes from behind the screen.

This is wrong. I take a step back from the screen without meaning to. "In the name of God! Have you no shame, old man?"

Abdel Jameela turns from the screen and faces me with an apologetic smile. "I am sorry to say that I have little shame left," he says.

I've never heard words spoken with such weariness. I remind myself that charity and mercy are our duty to God, and I soften my tone. "Is this why you sent for me, Uncle? What would you have me do? Give her feet she was not born with? My heart bleeds for you, truly. But such a thing only God can do."

Another wrinkled grimace. "O Professor, I am afraid that I must beg your forgiveness. For I have lied to you. And for that I am sorry. For it is not my wife that needs your help, but I."

"But her—pardon me, uncle—her hoof."

"Yes! Its curve! Like a jet-black half-moon!" The old hermit's voice quivers and he struggles to keep his gaze on me. Away from his wife's hoof. "Her hoof is breathtaking, Professor. No, it is *I* that need your help, for I am not the creature I need to be."

"I don't understand, Uncle." Exasperation burns away my sympathy. I've walked for hours and climbed a hill, small though it was. I am in no mood for a hermit's games. Abdel Jameela winces at the anger in my eyes and says, "My . . . my wife will explain."

I will try, my husband.

The voice is like song and there is the strong scent of sweet flowers. Then she steps from behind the screen and I lose all my words. I scream. I call on God, and I scream.

Abdel Jameela's wife is no creature of God. Her head is a goat's and her mouth a wolf's muzzle. Fish-scales and jackal-hair cover her. A scorpion's tail curls behind her. I look into a woman's eyes set in a demon's face and I stagger backward, calling on God and my dead mother.

Please, learned one, be calm.

"What . . . what . . . " I can't form the words. I look to the floor. I try to bury my sight in the dirty carpets and hard-packed earth. Her voice is more beautiful than any woman's. And there is the powerful smell of jasmine and clove. A nightingale sings perfumed words at me while my mind's eye burns with horrors that would make the Almighty turn away.

If fear did not hold your tongue, you would ask what I am. Men have called my people by many names—ghoul, demon. Does a word matter so very much? What I am, learned one, is Abdel Jameela's wife.

For long moments I don't speak. If I don't speak this nightmare will end. I will wake in Baghdad, or Beit Zujaaj. But I don't wake.

She speaks again, and I cover my ears, though the sound is beauty itself.

The words you hear come not from my mouth, and you do not hear them with your ears. I ask you to listen with your mind and your heart. We will die, my husband and I, if you will not lend us your skill. Have you, learned one, never needed to be something other that what you are?

Cinnamon scent and the sound of an oasis wind come to me. I cannot speak to this demon. My heart will stop if I do, I am certain. I want to run, but fear has fixed my feet. I turn to Abdel Jameela, who stands there wringing his hands.

"Why am I here, Uncle? God damn you, why did you call me here? There is no sick woman here! God protect me, I know nothing of . . . of ghouls, or—" A horrible thought comes to me. "You . . . you are not hoping to make her into a woman? Only God can . . . "

The old hermit casts his eyes downward. "Please . . . you must listen to my wife. I beg you." He falls silent and his wife, behind the screen again, goes on.

My husband and I have been on this hilltop too long, learned one. My body cannot stand so much time away from my people. I smell yellow roses and hear bumblebees droning beneath her voice. *If we stay in this place one more season, I will die. And without me to care for him and keep age's scourge from him, my sweet Abdel Jameela will die too. But across the desert there is a life for us. My father was a prince among our people. Long ago I left. For many reasons. But I never forsook my birthright. My father is dying now, I have word. He has left no sons and so his lands are mine. Mine, and my handsome husband's.*

In her voice is a chorus of wind-chimes. Despite myself, I lift my eyes. She steps from behind the screen, clad now in a black abaya and a mask. Behind the mask's mesh is the glint of wolf-teeth. I look again to the floor, focusing on a faded blue spiral in the carpet and the kindness in that voice.

But my people do not love men. I cannot claim my lands unless things change. Unless my husband shows my people that he can change.

Somehow I force myself to speak. "What . . . what do you mean, change?"

There is a cymbal-shimmer in her voice and sandalwood incense fills my nostrils. *O learned one, you will help me to make these my Abdel Jameela's.*

She extends her slender brown hands, ablaze with henna. In each she holds a length of golden sculpture—goat-like legs ending in shining, cloven hooves. A thick braid of gold thread dances at the end of each statue-leg, alive.

Madness, and I must say so though this creature may kill me for it. "I have not the skill to do this! No man alive does!"

You will not do this through your skill alone. Just as I cannot do it through my sorcery alone. My art will guide yours as your hands work. She takes a step toward me and my shoulders clench at the sound of her hooves hitting the earth.

"No! No . . . I cannot do this thing."

"Please!" I jump at Abdel Jameela's voice, nearly having forgotten him. There are tears in the old man's eyes as he pulls at my galabeya, and his stink gets in my nostrils. "Please listen! We need your help. And we know what has brought you to Beit Zujaaj." The old man falls to his knees before me. "Please! Would not your Shireen aid us?"

With those words he knocks the wind from my lungs. How can he know that name? The Shaykh hadn't lied—there *is* witchcraft at work here, and I should run from it.

But, Almighty God help me, Abdel Jameela is right. Fierce as she is, Shireen still has her dreamy Persian notions —that love is more important than money or duty or religion. If I turn this old man away . . .

My throat is dry and cracked. "How do you know of Shireen?" Each word burns.

His eyes dart away. "She has . . . ways, my wife."

"All protection comes from God." I feel foul even as I steel myself with the old words. Is this forbidden? Am I walking the path of those who displease the Almighty? God forgive me, it is hard to know or to care when my beloved is gone. "If I were a good Muslim I would run down to the village now and . . . and . . . "

And what, learned one? Spread word of what you have seen? Bring men with spears and arrows? Why would you do this? Vanilla beans and the sound of rain give way to something else. Clanging steel and clean-burning fire. *I will not let you harm my husband. What we ask is not disallowed to you. Can you tell me, learned one, that it is in your book of what is blessed and what is forbidden not to give a man golden legs?*

It is not. Not in so many words. But this thing can't be acceptable in God's eyes. Can it? "Has this ever been done before?"

There are old stories. But it has been centuries. Each of her words spreads perfume and music and she asks *Please, learned one, will you help us?* And then one scent rises above the others.

Almighty God protect me, it is the sweat-and-ambergris smell of my beloved. Shireen of the ribbing remark, who in quiet moments confessed her love of my learning. She *would* help them.

Have I any choice after that? This, then, the fruit of my study. And this my reward for wishing to be more than what I am. A twisted, unnatural path.

"Very well." I reach for my small saw and try not to hear Abdel Jameela's weird whimpers as I sharpen it.

I give him poppy and hemlock, but as I work Abdel Jameela still screams, nearly loud enough to make my heart cease beating. His old body is going through things it should not be surviving. And I am the one putting him through these things, with knives and fire and bone-breaking clamps. I wad cotton and stuff it in my ears to block out the hermit's screams.

But I feel half-asleep as I do so, hardly aware of my own hands. Somehow the demon's magic is keeping Abdel Jameela alive and guiding me through this grisly task. It is painful, like having two minds crammed inside my skull and shadow-puppet poles lashed to my arms. I am burning up, and I can barely trace my thoughts. Slowly I become aware of the she-ghoul's voice in my head and the scent of apricots.

Cut there. Now the mercury powder. The cautering iron is hot. Put a rag in his mouth so he does not bite his tongue. I flay and cauterize and lose track of time. A fever cooks my mind away. I work through the evening prayer, then the night prayer. I feel withered inside.

In each step Abdel Jameela's wife guides me. With her magic she rifles my mind for the knowledge she needs and steers my skilled fingers. For a long while there is only her voice in my head and the feeling of bloody instruments in my hands, which move with a life of their own.

Then I am holding a man's loose tendons in my right hand and thick golden threads in my left. There are shameful smells in the air and Abdel Jameela shouts and begs me to stop even though he is half-asleep with the great pot of drugs I have forced down his throat.

Something is wrong! The she-ghoul screams in my skull and Abdel Jameela passes out. My hands no longer dance magically. The shining threads shrivel in my fist. We have failed, though I know not exactly how.

No! No! Our skill! Our sorcery! But his body refuses! There are funeral wails in the air and the smell of houses burning. *My husband! Do something, physicker!*

The golden legs turn to dust in my hands. With my ears I hear Abdel Jameela's wife growl a wordless death-threat.

I deserve death! Almighty God, what have I done? An old man lies dying on my blanket. I have sawed off his legs at a she-ghoul's bidding. There is no strength save in God! I bow my head.

Then I see them. Just above where I've amputated Abdel Jameela's legs are the swollen bulges that I'd thought came from gout. But it is not gout that has made these. There is something buried beneath the skin of each leg. I take hold of my scalpel and flay each thin thigh. The old man moans with what little life he has left.

What are you doing? Abdel Jameela's wife asks the walls of my skull. I ignore her, pulling at a flap of the old man's thigh-flesh, revealing a corrupted sort of miracle.

Beneath Abdel Jameela's skin, tucked between muscles, are tiny legs. Thin as spindles and hairless. Each folded little leg ends in a minuscule hoof.

Unbidden, a memory comes to me—Shireen and I in the Caliph's orchards. A baby bird had fallen from its nest. I'd sighed and bit my lip and my Shireen—a dreamer, but not a soft one—had laughed and clapped at my tender-heartedness.

I slide each wet gray leg out from under the flayed skin and gently unbend them. As I flex the little joints, the she-ghoul's voice returns.

What . . . what is this, learned one? Tell me!

For a long moment I am mute. Then I force words out, my throat still cracked. "I . . . I do not know. They are—they look like—the legs of a kid or a ewe still in the womb."

It is as if she nods inside my mind. *Or the legs of one of my people. I have long wondered how a mere man could captivate me so.*

"All knowledge and understanding lies with God," I say. "Perhaps your husband always had these within him. The villagers say he is of uncertain parentage. Or perhaps . . . Perhaps his love for you . . . The crippled beggars of Cairo are the most grotesque—and the best—in the world. It is said that they wish so fiercely to make money begging that their souls reshape their bodies from the inside out. Yesterday I saw such stories as nonsense. But yesterday I'd have named *you* a villager's fantasy, too." As I speak I continue to work the little legs carefully, to help their circulation. The she-ghoul's sorcery no longer guides my hands, but a physicker's nurturing routines are nearly as compelling. There is weakness here and I do what I can to help it find strength.

The tiny legs twitch and kick in my hands.

Abdel Jameela's wife howls in my head. *They are drawing on my magic. Something pulls at*—The voice falls silent.

I let go of the legs and, before my eyes, they begin to grow. As they grow, they fill with color, as if blood flowed into them. Then fur starts to sprout upon them.

"There is no strength or safety but in God!" I try to close my eyes and focus on the words I speak but I can't. My head swims and my body swoons.

The spell that I cast on my poor husband to preserve him —these hidden hooves of his nurse on it! O, my surprising, wonderful husband! I hear loud lute music and smell lemongrass and then everything around me goes black.

When I wake I am on my back, looking up at a purple sky. An early morning sky. I am lying on a blanket outside the hovel. I sit up and Abdel Jameela hunches over me with his sour smell. Further away, near the hill-path, I see the black shape of his wife.

"Professor, you are awake! Good!" the hermit says. "We were about to leave."

But we are glad to have the chance to thank you.

My heart skips and my stomach clenches as I hear that voice in my head again. Kitten purrs and a crushed cardamom scent linger beneath the demon's words. I look at Abdel Jameela's legs.

They are sleek and covered in fur the color of almonds. And each leg ends in a perfect cloven hoof. He walks on them with a surprising grace.

Yes, learned one, my beloved husband lives and stands on two hooves. It would not be so if we hadn't had your help. You have our gratitude.

Dazedly clambering to my feet, I nod in the she-ghoul's direction. Abdel Jameela claps me on the back wordlessly and takes a few goat-strides toward the hill-path. His wife makes a slight bow to me. *With my people, learned one, gratitude is more than a word. Look toward the hovel.*

I turn and look. And my breath catches.

A hoard right out of the stories. Gold and spices. Jewels and musks. Silver and silks. Porcelain and punks of aloe.

It is probably ten times the dowry Shireen's father seeks.

We leave you this and wish you well. I have purged the signs of our work in the hovel. And in the language of the donkeys, I have called two wild asses to carry your goods. No troubles left to bother our brave friend!

I manage to smile gratefully with my head high for one long moment. Blood and bits of the old man's bone still stain my hands. But as I look on Abdel Jameela and his wife in the light of the sunrise, all my thoughts are not grim or grisly.

As they set off on the hill-path the she-ghoul takes Abdel Jameela's arm, and the hooves of husband and wife scrabble against the pebbles of Beit Zujaaj hill. I stand stock-still, watching them walk toward the land of the ghouls.

They cross a bend in the path and disappear behind the hill. And a faint voice, full of mischievous laughter and smelling of early morning love in perfumed sheets, whispers in my head. *No troubles at all, learned one. For last night your Shireen's husband-to-be lost his battle with the destroyer of delights.*

Can it really be so? The old vulture dead? And me a rich man? I should laugh and dance. Instead I am brought to my knees by the heavy memory of blood-spattered golden hooves. I wonder whether Shireen's suitor died from his illness, or from malicious magic meant to reward me. I fear for my soul. For a long while I kneel there and cry.

But after a while I can cry no longer. Tears give way to hopes I'd thought dead. I stand and thank Beneficent God, hoping it is not wrong to do so. Then I begin to put together an acceptable story about a secretly-wealthy hermit who has rewarded me for saving his wife's life. And I wonder what Shireen and her father will think of the man I have become.

THE PAIN OF GLASS
A STORY OF THE FLAT EARTH

Tanith Lee

1. The Third Fragment

That very afternoon a caravan had entered the city. It had journeyed from the Great Purple Sea, which lay far to the west and was so named for the preponderance of purplish weed that massed its waters, and at certain seasons dyed them. After the coast, the caravan negotiated many lands. It had crossed serpentine rivers, dagger-like mountains, and finally the Vast Harsh Desert, renowned for waterless and unobliging terrain. Small wonder then that the caravan might be supposed to bring with it much valuable stuff, not to mention travellers' tales, whose vividity was matched only by their tallness.

Prince Razved stood on a balcony of his palace, staring out over high walls and lengthening shadows, to the marketplace.

"Oh, to be merely a merchant," sighed the Prince. "Oh, to have no destiny but the discovery of new things, adventure and commerce."

He did not mean this. What he actually meant, and partly he knew it, was that he yearned to be freed from the direly irksome situation into which Lord Fate had thrust him. For though he ruled the city, he might enjoy neither it nor his full power in it. A single awful obstacle kept him always from his rights.

Just then a voice arose at his back. It was wild, quavering, and disrespectful.

"Are they *here*? Are they *near*?"

The Prince clenched his jaw and his fists. He paled white as fresh ivory. Young though he was, the weight of extra decades slumped upon his shoulders.

There in the chamber behind the balcony stood a filthy and dishevelled old man. Two hundred years of age he looked, and the colourless thin wires of his hair rained round his face, which was like that of a demented hawk. He was mad as the word, and none could help him. Now too he began to weep and scream. Razved locked his fists together behind his back, and bellowed for assistance.

It came instantly in the person of three men, frenzied with dismay, who rushed into the room, where they flung themselves on their faces before the Prince.

But Razved only said to them, in tones of steel, "He has got out again. How has he done this? Are you not meant to care for and contain him?"

"Mighty Master—only a moment was the door undone—"

"Only ever is it undone for a moment," replied Razved, his tone now composed of stifled rage and black despair. "Or it is the window-lattice. Or some other pretext. Take him away. *Hide* him from me. If you transgress again, you will meet the doom those of his last retinue suffered."

Whispering shrieks of terror, the jailor-retinue leapt to their feet and gathered in the mad old man, bearing him instantly off, crying and calling, along the corridor to renewed detention.

But Razved could not rid himself of the memory of the encounter, which had been so often repeated through countless years. He strode to another chamber. There he donned a disguise he sometimes employed when wandering about the city. Razved believed none of the citizens had ever penetrated this. And although, of course, many of them had, and did, none were recently foolish enough to confess to him.

As the sun burned down behind the palace, the Prince also descended. Before the first star blinked, he was in the marketplace.

Soon the whole market, infused by the caravan and lighted with torches, was like a lamp against the blue night.

Razved strolled from place to place, forgetting for a while his plight. He beheld an indigo snake of extreme size and patterned with gold, that danced to the intricate beat of drums. It twisted itself into hoops and spirals, coils and knots, that each time seemed impossible for it ever to unravel—yet always it did so, rising and bowing to the crowd. They threw coins which the snake caught in its mouth. And there was a silk from the edge of the Purple Sea, coloured with the purple weed-dye, and this material seemed to burn with sapphires in the shadows and rubies in the torchlight. Also Razved tasted bizarre fruits with thick cream skins, that had no juice but gave up the flavour of honey. Elsewhere stood books the height of a man and twice his width, with covers of hammered bronze, and pages of blond wood incised with silver—but often what they said was nonsense. Or there were birds which could recite poetry in the voices of beautiful boys or women, tiny exquisite models of temples and shrines cut from green pearls, wines which were black and scented with roses, swords both straight and curved, in the blades of which were supernaturally written spells of invincible power . . .

After a while Razved grew weary. He sat down by the booth of a seller of glass, and drank some black wine.

Behind him the Prince could hear how the glass-seller was complaining, some tale of half his wares, including the most expensive mirrors, being broken, the fault apparently of a vulture-like desert witch. Razved paid little heed, only thinking, *The man does not know his luck. He has only loss of trade, and poverty to fear. While I—*And once more he clenched his fists, pondering how the full rule of the city might never come to him, nor the title of King. Dwelling too upon the awful haunt of the insane old man in the palace. *I shall never get what I am owed. I shall never be free of* him. *Would not death be preferable?*

But despite his bitter thoughts, Razved was not yet ready to make the close acquaintance of Lord Death. And presently he turned his head to glare at the complaining glass-seller.

At once the man broke into smiles. "Best sir, what might I show you that may tempt? It is true, many of my finest articles were destroyed as I travelled here, but even so certain elegancies remain which, though quite unworthy of your discerning gaze, may yet briefly amuse you."

Razved yawned. He passed a jaundiced look over a surviving mirror so liquid it suggested a tear from the full moon, and a curious magnifying glass that stared back at him like an elemental eye.

"Well," said Razved, with unencouragement, "what is your finest *remaining* piece?"

The glass-seller, whose name was Jandur, bowed his head as if in thought. He had heard rumours concerning the city, and of a strange delaying fate which hung over its King-in-waiting. Jandur had also been told that sometimes this Prince went about the streets in disguise, but was easily recognizable, the disguise being a sloppy one and the Prince himself equally brooding, ill-tempered, and unmissably regal in his manner. Yet those who gave away their recognition, the rumour added, were normally found deceased not long after. Jandur now guessed that here sat the very man. To be cautious was therefore prudent. To make a *sale*, however, must be a prize. Besides, there was too another matter.

"Wise sir," said Jandur, after a moment, "one item there is that I feel inclined to show you—though I am uneasy at doing so."

"Come," snapped Razved, "your task is to sell, is it not?"

"Quite so, intelligent sir. My unease rests on two counts. Firstly, I hope you will pardon me—but I perceive from your garb you are neither rich nor high-born—"

Razved seemed coqettishly pleased. "You speak honestly."

"—yet," continued cunning Jandur, "what strikes me forcefully is a great refinement of spirit and judgement immediately apparent about your person. Because of these qualities I would wish to reveal a treasure. Yet again—"

"Yet again!" Razved had now risen and was impatient to be shown.

"—I am loathe to part with the thing. It is charming, and unusual beyond all my other wares, yes, even those exquisites smashed to bits amid the desert sands of the Vast Harsh."

"Come," said Razved, with a dangerous glint in his eye. Life had baulked his wishes, this pedlar should not.

Jandur gauged all perfectly and now exclaimed, "You shall see the wonder! Pray follow me, illumined sir, into the back premises of the booth."

In the dark beyond the light beyond the dark, then—that was, the shadowed space inside the lighted market and city, which themselves rested in the dish of night—the ultimate inner brilliance shone. It was very small.

As Jandur lit the candle to display it, Razved peered. What did he see?

"Only that?" he said, in ominous disappointment.

The object was a little drinking vessel, about as tall as the length of a woman's hand. The stem was slender, and the cup wide, like the bowl of an open flower, but it would hold, Razved believed, less than three gulps of wine. "And this is your most astonishing vendible, is it? Your brain must be as cracked as your broken mirrors."

"Pray examine the item."

Razved sullenly reached out, and wondered somewhat why he bothered to do so. But then his fingers met the texture of the glass. As they did this, the candlelight caught all the vessel's surfaces, and for a second it seemed to the Prince he held in his hand a mote of softest living flame—it was like phosphorescence on water, or like fireflies glimmering on a marble trellis. The colours of the goblet woke, shifted and merged, now dawn-pink, now flamingo-red, next a limpid golden green. Not meaning to, not knowing quite what he did, Razved touched his other fingers to the lip of the cup. Instantly there came the sweetest and most poignant note of music, slender as sheer silk passed through a silver ring. And in that moment, standing in the cramped booth, Razved felt within his hands not the glass of a vessel—but two perfect breasts—crystalline, silken—that sang back against his palms, while on his lips he tasted the glass-girt wine of a longed-for lover's kiss.

Jandur, who had predicted with some cause an intriguing result at contact, stepped swiftly forward, and steadied both Razved and the precious goblet, though Jandur wrapped the latter in his sleeve.

Razved seemed nearly in a swoon. Jandur sat him on a bench, and replaced the foremost treasure of his stock safely out of reach.

"What occurred?" eventually Razved asked. He no longer had the voice of a Prince, he sounded like a child. "Is the cup ensorcelled?"

"I cannot definitely tell you," Jandur answered. It was a fact, he could not.

"It is—*what* is it?"

"Alas. I cannot say. Mystical and magical certainly."

"Does it affect all—who—touch it?"

"In various ways, it does. Some weep. Some blush. Some begin to sing."

"And *you*," said Razved, with another warning note suddenly entering his voice: that of jealousy, "what do *you* feel when you take hold of it?"

"Fear," Jandur replied simply.

"Ah," said Razved. "It is not meant for *you*, then."

For a while after this exchange, neither man spoke or moved. Jandur stood in the dark beyond the candle, thinking his own thoughts. The Prince, still physically overwhelmed, his manhood urgently upright and his blood tingling and thundering, slumped on the bench. At length however, he bethought himself of his status, and drew himself together.

"Well, an astonishing trifle," said he, with the most ludicrous dismissal. "But what price do you set on it?"

Jandur now realized his peak of cunning bravado.

"I will confess, sir, I am so taken with admiration for your natural gifts that, while acknowledging your obvious penury, I believe you may after all be able to summon the amount. For surely such a man as yourself will have *another* admirer from whom you will command the present of the vessel —an admirer even more smitten than I. The value I require is seventy sevens of white gold."

Razved snorted piggishly. He now cared, it seemed, less for his deception. "You are astute, glass-vendor. Just such a sum was handed me by a lover, in order I might buy myself a trinket." And reaching into his poor man's apparel. he drew forth a bag and spilled the contents at Jandur's feet. "Wrap the thing in a cloth," he commanded in a feverish undertone.

Jandur, ostensibly ignoring, even stepping on the spilled money, did as he was bid, he himself taking great care not to touch the goblet once. In a few more minutes the King-in-waiting had hurried from the booth, and any who noted his rushing figure, saw it fly off around the high outer wall of the palace.

But Jandur sat down on the bench and murmured a prayer of thanks to a god of his own country—both for the riches Razved had given him, and for his release from proximity to the glass goblet.

Deep in the dark thereafter, Prince Razved repaired alone to his most isolate chamber. Not even the moon might look in, save through the sombre vitreus of thick windows clad in gauze.

Dark was in the flagon, too, the black wine aromatic of roses, which he had had his servants bring him.

The haunting madman had been locked away, shackled tonight for good measure. Not only were merchants prudent, after all.

Razved, bathed in hot water and spices, clad in loose and sensuous garments, unwrapped at last the goblet. Holding it only through a piece of fine embroidered cloth, he set it on the table by his couch.

Despite the lack of light, even so the faintest and most mellifluous tinctures of colour began at once to flutter to and fro in the glass. They were like birds in a cloud, or fish in a ghostly pool. Dilute crimson melded to opalescent rose—to amber—to emerald. All this—just from his touch through cloth, his hungry gaze upon it.

In a while he leant forward and filled the vessel full of inky wine. Rather than dim the spectrum in the glass, the blackness seemed to bring it out. Gold shot through the other tints like benign lightning.

Razved sighed. He had put away his woes.

He placed his fingers upon the rim of the goblet. At once, it sang for him. He could hear again a woman's voice in the notes, clear as a silver bell, and as he kept just one finger on the vessel, the melody—and melody it was—went on and on. Razved was not afraid. Unlike the shoddy glass-seller, he was royal, a warrior of a warlike and powerful line—although he had never ridden to battle, nor seen what battle may produce aside from valour. The glass was neither evil nor any threat. It was enchanted, and enchanting. It was a delicious toy the gods had sent him, in recompense for all the other frustrations of his days.

Unable any longer to detain himself, the Prince now put both his hands on the goblet. Intoxicating heat raced through his arms and filled his body, as he drew the brim towards his lips. He drained the wine, and the act of drinking became instead the act of kissing, while the singing notes entered his brain, and floated there like iridium feathers.

He found he had lain back, the cup held firm against his heart. And then it seemed the cup too had taken hold of *him*. Female arms, slender and strong, encircled his body. For an instant he glimpsed, lifted above him, a maiden made of flames and waters, flowing down on him in waves and foam and sparks, more sinuous than any serpent. Then a mouth famished as his own fastened on his lips, a tongue like smoothest myrrh and ice-hot quicksilver, drank deeply. Against him in his delirium he felt the movement of a frame that was softness and succulence, pliable and limber as a young cat's—but all this, the plains of skin, the pressure of slim muscle, the downfall of shining hair—even the narrow hands whose tips were like bees, the flawless breasts whose tips were like buds—all this was cool and composite, and made all, *all* of it, of *glass*.

Yet still Razved feared nothing. As his hands swept over the crystal curves of a phantasmal yet actual shape, as he drowned in the silver notes of a song that had, as yet, no words, as he began to ride in the primal race of desire, not one qualm interrupted Razved's intense and scalding pleasure. For it did not trouble him *she* was all of glass, and that *she* flamed with shades of flowers and gems, and her tongue was of glass, her lips and hair, her little feet that gripped him, glass that kissed, caressed, and sang in ecstasy. Even her centre, the core of her glory, that too, where now he lay, fixed and explosive as a sun, *that* was formed of glass. And it rippled and embraced and grew molten, better than any human vessel; wine and darkness; jasper, asphodel: fire, ash, sand.

2. *The Second Fragment*

That very morning they had entered the expanse of the terrible desert known as the Vast Harsh, Jandur the glass-seller received an omen. He did not, at the hour, much consider it, but later it came to him he had been awarded one of those useless portents the gods tended to throw before mankind. What the omen presumably was, had been a solitary black vulture crouched on a sycamore, which weirdly held upright in its beak a shard of glass. This caught the light and flashed, amusing many who saw it. But they, and Jandur, soon forgot, since a mile or so later the desert began.

There lay before the caravan now countless miles of that inimical landscape, which separated the more abundant lands from the towns and cities of the north and east. And though provided with all necessities, none of the travellers viewed the desert prospect with much joy. The Harsh was famed not only for its personal cruelties, but for those of various men driven out there, and making their desperate livelihoods by the robbery and murder of passing human traffic. Well-armed guards had joined the caravan at Marah, the last town on the desert's edge.

The Harsh opened to receive them, grinning.

Jandur journeyed glumly among the rest.

By day the caravan wended, though sheltering some-times at noon, when the predatory eye of the sun centred the sky. Once there it turned both heaven and earth into a furnace any glass-maker might have valued. *Perhaps*, thought Jandur then, *the gods also are glass-makers. The earth is their kiln and we, mortals of silicious sand, suffer, turn and burn in this sunfire, and likewise the flames of pain and sorrow, in order to become creatures as pure and beautiful as glass.*

But really he was well aware that people rarely grew beautiful or pure through suffering and burning. Normally ill-treatment made them worse, and wicked. Those that did achieve virtue no doubt might have become just as wonderful, even if they had *not* had to suffer, or to burn.

At night the caravan spread itself out like an exhausted yet demanding beast. It lit torches and fires, cooked its meals, sometimes told stories or danced, frequently bickered, argued, or even came to blows. Above, the myriad stars blazed bright. *If each were a glass,* thought Jandur, *what a fortune they would make for those that formed them. But alas, when they fall,* he added to himself, seeing one which did, *they shatter.*

Jandur had himself never made a single piece of glass. He only *sold* glass, but that in quantities. In the very next town they would come to, which was called Burab, and which still lay ninety days and nights across the Harsh, Jandur's brother-in-law had charge of the family's second glass-makery. He was a quarrelsome brute, dark red from heat; and scarred all over with the white bites of burns. But Jandur had already enough stock, and thought he would not need to trouble his brother-in-law. Which thought cheered Jandur in the desert, even when jackals howled, or the dust-winds blew.

D espite the reputation of the Harsh, they met no robbers. Probably any robbers spied them first and found their numbers, and their armed escort, off-putting. Meanwhile, on a certain evening, they reached one of the few oases that served the waste.

This was a poor enough specimen. A handful of spindly trees led to a well no bigger than a washtub, the margin spiked with black rushes that discontentedly chittered.

Leaving his servant to go for fresh water, Jandur dismounted from his mule and took a walk among the stunted trees. The sun was already low and veiled in sandy gold, and a reluctant breeze smoked along the dunes. The impromptu caravanserai was being settled for the night, cookfires breaking into red blossom. Jandur went up to a little rise, idly following the prints of some now-absent, small desert animal. From here he looked about at the world, as mortals did and yet do, both pleased and displeased with it, suspended in the quiet melancholy of dusk.

"Where is the glass-maker?" shouted a baleful voice behind him.

"I do not know," muttered Jandur. But he turned nonetheless.

And there on the rise with him perched a most ungainly and uncouth female figure. She was clad in a mantle of vulture feathers. More, her long and ragged hair, lucklessly dark as was the hair, they said, of demons, was stuck with other such feathers. On her wrists and at her long, thin neck were ornaments of what Jandur, not illogically, concluded to be vulture bones. She smelled of vultures too, a smell that was of chickens, and of carrion.

If he had been going to admit to an acquaintance with glassware, perhaps now he thought better of it. But this was all in vain. For she announced immediately, "You are *he*. You are the one named Janpur or Jinkor, a glass-maker and vendor of such."

"What, assuming I am he, would you have with him?" inquired Jandur.

The female ruffled her feathers. It was difficult to be sure, when she did this, if rather than a mantle, they were not actually growing from her skin. "I am Morjhas. I perambulate the desert. I have no trepidation in the Harsh, for my powers bring me all I need."

She was a witch. Jandur nodded politely.

But she reached forward and thrust her skinny talon of a finger at his breast. "Come you with me. I will show you a strangeness. I am bound to do this, for my talent carries with it a certain onus. A strangeness, I say. And what you do thereupon I shall advise you."

"I may not leave the caravan," protested Jandur. "If you are often here, you will know the place abounds in villains."

"What care I for villains? They are all afraid of Morjhas —and rightly. Those who annoy me," she added, fixing Jandur with a tar-black eye, "regret it. If you behave, you will be safe enough in *my* company."

They flew.

He had not, and maybe he might have done, expected this. But the bird-hag lifted him straight off his feet and bore him away. He suspected he screamed, but none heard him over the din of the caravan; twilight doubtless screened the view. And she—she spread her wings and rushed both of them on.

However, they did not travel a very great way. The 'strangeness' Morjhas meant to reveal lay only some half mile from the camp.

At first, having been landed, Jandur gaped about him. No trace of sun remained, only the huge translucent violet dome of nightfall, where they were lighting the million cobalt, ferrous, and pewter cookfires and torches of the stars.

The vulture witch pointed with her eldritch claw.

"See there."

Some sixty or seventy paces off rose a mesa, scorched black by weather, and below, as elsewhere around, lay sand, slightly patched paler or darker, denoting seemingly depth, variance of consistency, or only shadows.

"At what do I look? That rock?"

"Hush, fool. Look and listen and learn."

So there they stood, and the night gathered all about, glowing as always in such open places, yet also black behind the stars. And coldness came too, for the desert, even the Vast Harsh, presented two faces, furnace by day and iceberg by night.

Jandur was frightened, but not out of his wits. He stared at the patch of sand below the mesa that his unwanted guide had indicated, and in a while he started to note a disturbance in it. A dust devil appeared to be at work there, but one which did not move from its origins. And after a time, the motes which circled upward and round and round commenced also to shine.

"Is it a ghost?" asked Jandur in a whisper.

"*Hush*," said the witch.

And exactly then the spinning busyness began to chime. An eerie carillon it was, bereft and lorn, like the cries of the wolves and jackals which prevailed in the desert. Yet too it had profound beauty, an insistent music. Like a song it seemed, lacking words, though once perhaps words had belonged to it, a song of longing and loss that only a poet might create, and a human throat emit.

This uncanny and emotive recital continued for several minutes. Then came the night wind, and breathed on the spot, as a mother might with a weeping child. And the song ended, and the dust of the sand drifted down. It slept, whatever it had been, whatever it was. And silence returned, composed of the shift of the dunes, the sigh of the flimsy wind.

Morjhas spoke. "There, then."

"But *what* then?" asked Jandur.

"I cannot tell you. I, even *I*, do not know. But it cries out, does it not? I cannot ignore that cry, nor shall you."

"But what am *I* to do with it?"

"*Fool* of a *fool*, *son* of fools to seventeen generations, *father* of fools and *grandsire* of *imbeciles!*" ranted the vulture-witch. "Are you a glass-maker? Gather up the sand there, take and make it into glass, for glass is made with sand and fire. Take it and shape it and see what *then* it does—for long enough it has lain and lamented here, unheard by any but myself and now you, O *fool.*"

"Take and make—" cried Jandur in horror, for he did not want any part of this scheme.

"Take and make. For my powers are generous and I must be kind in turn to the tragedies of the Harsh. But you I will punish if you fail in this. Heed me, Jumduk, if so you are named. Either scoop up the sand there and have it worked, or I will send my minions to smash every item of your saleable glass, even within the cosy caravan. I will begin, O *fool*, with a certain mirror—" here the vulture held up her wing and gave a screech, and from far away—about half a mile in fact—the appalled merchant seemed to detect a glacial splintering. "I will smash all and everything, until you have dug up that place of sand which sings and sobs. Go now. Hasten back to the camp and get your slaves and your spades, for with every second you delay, another delicacy *breaks*. Be assured also, that if the sand is not then rendered to glassware before three more months elapse, I will break anything you may have left, or thereafter acquire! You had best believe this."

Jandur was uncertain if he had only gone mad, but he credited every word. He bolted for the camp, and endlessly along the route as he ran, he heard the shattering of glass—the whole while becoming louder and louder.

Indeed, Jandur's bivouac lay in some confusion, when he reached it. People stood about amazed, and bits of glass lay around sparkling prettily in the firelight, but there was a deal of shrieking and praying too. "Vile winged shadows fell upon your wagon, Jandur!" some explained, hurrying gladly to convey bad news. "We heard the vandalism upon your wares but dare not enter! No other among us is attacked—only you, poor Jandur. Whatever can you have done to incur this supernatural wrath?" While as a background to their verbiage, yet other breakages sounded.

But Jandur paid no heed. Seizing his servant, two spades and some sacks, Jandur pelted back again, now on foot, across the desert. Regaining the spot where the dust had lifted and sung, the two men dug and transposed sand for all they were worth, until they had filled the sacks.

No sign of the vulture-witch remained, and truly the general site was so unremarkable that, saving the mesa, it was probable Jandur would not have found it again. A large dug hole now marked the dunes. Yet soon enough the sands would refill it.

"Hark," said Jandur. "Does it seem the wrecking has ceased?"

Presently he and the servant were agreed, any noises of destruction had stopped.

They trudged back to the caravan then and loaded the sacks into the wagon, where there was now some space for them, Jandur having lost a fair portion of his most valuable goods.

No other event of any moment befell the caravan, or Jandur, until they had entirely crossed the Harsh, and reached the town of Burab.

Jandur went, albeit with no delight, to the house of his brother-in-law Tesh, the glass-maker, which lay behind the smoking chimney of the makery. Here Jandur's sister, Tesh's wife, greeted Jandur with affection tempered only by her husband's censure. Tesh himself banged in and out of the place, upbraiding Jandur for the loss of his goods— "A witch broke them? Ha! A likely tale. Your donkey of a servant packed them improperly, either that or *you* lost them at gambling. What a simpleton you are, Jandur. Your father must whirl in his grave at your incompetence."

"Nevertheless," said Jandur, gravely, "I have collected in the desert a most fascinating sand, and this I would request you put to use instantly. Fashion some fresh articles that I may sell them in the great city markets."

Tesh was not the man to be given orders by such as Jandur. He made a colossal fuss, shouted at his wife, tried to kick the dog—which eluded him without effort, being well-practiced in the skill—and rained curses on the earth in general. However, since Tesh had had no items in the original wagon-load, and might now get profit from future sales, he eventually complied, making out that he did Jandur the sort of favour that was known, in those parts, as a 'Full day's holiday, with a feast at its end'.

Jandur then retired exhausted to his bed. The caravan would not quit Burab for some while, and there was time enough. The sand had filled three sacks to the top, and he expected several pieces to result. Unease he put from him. If the sand were possessed by some supramundane force, Jandur himself had had no choice but to take it on. What the resultant glass might be, or do or cause, Jandur did not permit himself to consider.

The next morning the chimney of the makery gouted, as always, thunders of smoke and sparkling cinders.

Jandur busied himself about the town, buying presents for his sister and the dog.

Evening fell and the smouldering chimney cooled. A little after the regular hour, in came Tesh—both Jandur and Tesh's wife jumped up in startlement.

The red-hot man was pale as one of his burn-scars, and glassy tears trembled from his eyes.

"My darling wife," said he, and she so addressed almost fainted with the shock, "can you forgive me for my temper and my foulness?"

"Are you ill?" she cried in panic. "What ails you?"

"Alas," wept Tesh, and gentle as a lamb he went and knelt before her, burying his face in her skirts. And when the dog came worriedly to sniff him, Tesh, without looking, stroked its head and murmured, "Poor boy, you shall have a bone, you shall have a dish of meat. I will buy you a collar that reads: *Faithful Under Duress*." After which his words were drowned in his tears.

As she embraced this strange, new-made husband, Jandur's sister said urgently to Jandur, "Go to the makery and see what has gone on!"

And Jandur did as she asked, his mind buzzing between curiosity, amusement, pity—and sheer fright.

The makery was a significant and hellish area. It rose up on many levels, that were dominated by the dark yet fiery hulks of kilns and braziers, and silvered stoops and founts of water, and all the while the crackle and bubble, the trickle and shiver, the rush and gush and whoosh and push—things altering, melting, expanding, blooming or dying. And always, even now, the ebb and flow of fire flickering on walls and roof, the glycerine rivering and drip of molten glass, the stench of hot metal and clay and combustion, and gaseousness, the nasal glitters and sumps of stone-dust, silica, calcium, and black natron.

Below on benches sat Tesh's work-gang. One was nursing a blowing pipe, three or four some smallish empty moulds. These fellows seemed bemused beyond speech. At a table sat one though, who was polishing little beakers with the rubbing stone. He glanced up and said to Jandur, "I will tell it. There has been a peculiarity here. Either you have brought us bad luck—or good luck. We are not sure as yet."

Jandur put a substantial coin before the man. "I hope you will all take some wine to comfort you. But for now, go on."

"The sand," said the stone-rubber, "when emptied, was only enough for a single slight item."

"But it had filled three sacks!"

"So we thought, too. But opening and emptying them, all that was there was this miniature amount. Be sure, Master Tesh ranted he would waste none of his *other* sand to pad it out, and next he made oaths worthy of the demonkind. But by then he must make something else of it than vulgar language, so we set to work. Then, when all goes in the crucible, a wild scent comes from the mix."

"A scent of what?"

"Of women's sweet skin and garments and young clean hair . . . so *then* we are all afeared, but Tesh rants on, so on we make. Then when he comes to blow the piece, soft light shines up above the brazier. Like green iron, or the rose-red that comes from glue-of-gold. But Tesh blows on, and then the vessel comes from the fire and is finished and firmed with a speed not very usual."

"What had been made?" demanded Jandur.

"One slender goblet with a flower-like drinking-bowl."

"And then?"

"Master touches it," put in one of the other men. "And his face goes rapt, as if he saw the gods. And then white. And then he staggers out to his house."

Jandur collected his wits. "Where is the goblet?"

"He took it with him."

When Jandur pelted back in at the house door, he halted as if he struck a buffer of some sort.

For there sat his sister, with Tesh adoringly leaning on her, and the dog with its head on Tesh's knee. And Jandur's sister sang in a light and lovely voice, an evening song. And in her hand Jandur beheld a glass drinking cup, no *longer* than a woman's hand, and full of mutable colours, as the stone-rubber had said. But just then the servant girl came in, and singing, Jandur's sister handed her the cup.

In consternation and excitement, Jandur watched the girl, to see what her reaction to the goblet might be.

For a moment she only stood quite still, and gazed at it. She was not more than thirteen years, and next she turned away, rather as a child would who has found out a secret. Jandur though saw she smiled, and her face blushed like one of the tints in the glass.

Jandur went to her and softly said, "What is it you feel?"

"Oh," said the girl, without either shyness or boldness, "only that one day I shall be in love."

"You must give me the cup," said Jandur. "It is mine."

Without any hesitation the girl did so, but the smile did not leave her, just as Tesh was yet affectionate, and his wife yet sang to him.

When Jandur took the cup he braced himself, thinking all manner of insanities or ecstasies might overwhelm him, and that despite them he must not let it fall and break. But all he felt was a speechless fear, the very same which had already visited him on the goblet's account.

He walked out into the little garden of the house. The moon was rising over the wall, where a mulberry tree grew, its leaves tarnished by exhalations of the makery. Jandur raised the glass, and the moon shone through it, grey and silent, telling nothing.

What shall I do with you? Jandur thought. *You may work miracles or do much harm. I will take you with me because it seems I must, and in the first city I will sell you, if such is possible. If I am wrong in that, forgive me, spirit of sand and glass. I have no other notion what is to be done.*

Then the wind blew through the mulberry leaves, and the wind said *Yes*, as sometimes, they reported, it did. *Yes*, said the wind among the leaves. So Jandur wrapped the goblet carefully and placed it in a box. A handful of time later he bore it to the city, where Prince Razved was King-in-waiting, and the Prince bought the goblet at the price of all the other broken glass. And after that Jandur took his own way through the world again, in prosperity or misfortune, as each man must.

3. The First Fragment

That very night, years before, the King of another country was to enter the town of Marah.

In the south, on the coast of the Great Purple Sea, there had been a war and much skirmishing, and this King, whose

own city lay north of the desert, had brought his troops to assist a southern ally. The battles done, and victory secured, now the young King was returning home. The bulk of his army had marched ahead of him, but he himself stopped here and there on his route. That he should honour Marah was a source to the town of pride and pandemonium. Most of the townspeople too were knife-keen to view the King. He was said to have that rare combination, pronounced beauty of person, intelligence of mind, and goodness of heart.

Marah however, was not then as it would come to be in the time of Jandur's maturity—which time was yet some two decades in its future. Preparations were frantic and extreme.

Came the night, the young northern King rode through the main avenue of the town. In the glare of many hundred torches, it was seen that while his black horse was caparisoned in silk from the Purple Coast, which burned sapphire in shade but like ruby in the light, the King was dressed well but plainly, and his only jewel was the ring that signified his kingship. In himself though, he was jewel enough. His hair was like darkly gilded bronze, his face and figure were so handsome he might have been some wonderful statue come to life.

All about exclamations rose, and sighs, and after these dumbness. How lucky was that northern city, to be ruled by such a paragon. How lucky his young wife, who had already borne him a son. How lucky his son, in such a father. How lucky the very sky there, and the air itself, to be seen by *him*, and breathed into *his* lungs.

Her name was Qirisn. She was by trade a musician, adopted and trained by an ancient school of the town, for her parents had died when she was only an infant. Marah, and the desert beyond, were all Qirisn knew, or supposedly. Since also she knew music, and knew it flawlessly, for she possessed great natural talent both as a player of stringed instruments, and as a singer. Music had, it seemed, taught her that

incredible elements lay beyond the mere facts of existence, and far outside the scope of human law and rational thought. A fine and feral inner landscape existed within the brain and spirit of Qirisn, and something of it showed in the night-blue of her eyes, though few noticed her until she sang. Her voice was of an almost supernal quality, very flexible and silken, and superlative from its lowest to its highest notes. "So stars must sing," her last tutor had remarked of her, although not in her hearing. But she did not need to be made either modest or vain. She knew her worth and where it lay; it made her happy, and others happy also: there are few greater gifts than such genius.

It had been arranged that the best musicians of Marah should entertain the northern King, but they would do so, as was the custom then in the town, behind a screen. That being so, they went out on a little terrace above the street to watch, with various others, the monarch's arrival at the hall of banqueting.

Among these witnesses there was no change of opinion from that of all the rest who had glimpsed him.

"How fair he is!" they said. "Better than sunrise."

Only Qirisn did not say a word.

She was not, certainly, the only one to look upon the King and love him instantly, but with her the blow sank much deeper. Not simply had she never experienced the lightning strike of physical love before, she had, conversely, when involved in making or listening to music, experienced the phenomenon over and over, never then having a point of reference. It had seemed to her always until this moment, that the passion of her inner sight was impossible to realize in the outer world. Now she found otherwise. Panes like ice shattered before her. Her heart itself seemed to break like a mirror. To her, love was the most familiar and least known of any emotion. She went in to play and sing, moving in a trance, aware solely that he would hear her music. As of course he

must, since now he would be the cause of it, and even in the past, before ever she looked at him, he had been so. It was plain to her, if in the most dreamlike way, she had known him elsewhere, in some other life perhaps, or on the outer fringes of this one. Or else, she had known him forever. And yet, in her current sphere, they would never meet.

The banquet began, the lamps burned bright, flowers and incenses released their perfumes. The diners were regaled by performances of magic and mystery. Doves burst from bottles and flew away, lions spoke riddles and could not be answered, diamond rain fell dry, and cool as the moon's kisses.

The musicians played and sang too. If they were noticed above the general hubbub, who could be sure. Yet, when Qirisn sang, and tonight it seemed she sang more exquisitely than ever before, some did fall quiet to listen. And the King? It was noted he turned his head a fraction, and for a second he frowned. But he was not unkind, not capricious, not heartless. Perhaps only he did not much care for music?

On the following day the King resumed his journey, which, having once left Marah, must take him out over the boiled shield of the Vast Harsh.

He had, naturally, no concern for robbers, his retinue of servants and soldiers were more than enough to make cautious the most vulpine robber band. Nevertheless, he himself led forays among those bandit strongholds which were sighted, wiping many felons from the desert's face with efficient economy.

Otherwise, the King seemed somewhat preoccupied. He had trouble sleeping, and restlessly walked about the nightly encampments, chatting with the guards. Or he might write a letter to his wife—a foolish exercise since he would see her in a pair more months.

A sunset happened which was the colour of a damson. The King stood watching it, and then he turned to one of his

officers, a man who had been close to him during the recent campaign.

"Did you hear ever, Nassib, was there much witchcraft in that last town?"

"In Marah, my lord? No, rather the opposite. Some of them talked of a witch who will shape-change to a vulture, but she is a desert hag and who knows, may only *be* a vulture and nothing more, save in a story."

"Quite so."

"Why do you ask, sir?"

"Oh, a little matter." The King watched the last of the sun's disc as it hid itself in some slot of the horizon. He added rather slowly, "I heard a girl sing at Marah, one of the musicians at the dinner. She had a lovely voice. But it is more than that."

"You fancied her, my lord? Surely you might have had her brought to you?"

"Well, but I never saw her even. And I do not wish to force any woman."

The officer laughed, between approval and envy, for very few women would not desire the King.

Returning to his tent, the King however wrote on the paper he had left ready for another letter, only these words: *In Marah, at the desert's brink, I heard a girl sweetly sing. And ever since that night, her voice has stayed with me, I do not know why. It seems I have been much disturbed by her song.*

The crossing of the desert, what with the forays upon bandits, and the King's mood, lasted longer than it might have otherwise.

But they lay over at a small oasis when the King called Nassib to him.

"Listen, my friend, I have a task for you if you will accept it." Nassib declared he would willingly do so. "Wait first to hear the commission. If you wish to refuse I will find another to undertake it. You know I have been wed these past three years, and my wife has given me a healthy son." Nassib agreed he did know this. "Custom allows me to take other women, and also to wed them, but I have never thought either act necessary since my marriage. Now I am in love. I am in love with a *voice* and— oh, Nassib, you will think me insane—with a vision I see of her in sleep, or awake, when sunlight fails a certain way, or a cloud scarfs the stars. Am I bewitched? I do not know, nor any longer care. Go back if you will to Marah, and seek out there the woman with the voice of silk and crystal. Though never having seen her, I can tell you how she is. Little and slender, with light hair, and eyes like blue midnight. If you doubt, ask her to sing a single note. Then you may be sure. Give her this ring with a crimson stone. Tell her, you will bring her to me, if she will go with you. I think she will. Her soul calls out to mine, Nassib, as mine to hers. Long ago, on some other earth, we have been lovers. More, we have been two halves of a solitary whole, and so remain. Tell her she shall be my second queen. Tell her," and here the King's face assumed such a look of bliss, his words rang strangely with it, "tell her I am dead without her, and wish to come alive." Nassib stood bereft of speech. He was shocked beyond calcula- tion at his own response. For it was as if all this while he had known the King uttered only the truth, and there could be no other choice. But "My regrets, Nassib," said the King, taking his hand. "No, I do not think I am mad. I am at the sanest moment of my life. If you will trust me, do what I ask. If not, remain my friend, and I will send another. For she must be brought with some subterfuge to the city. There will be many obstacles to overcome, both of courtesy and faction. There may be dangers."

"My lord," said Nassib humbly, "I believe the gods have taken you and she into their hand. I cannot gainsay the gods. I will do everything you ask as best I am able."

Before moonrise Nassib, accompanied by eight hand- picked men, was racing back across the Harsh to Marah.

* * *

She had dreamed of him every night, as he had of her. Awake, in changes of light she had seen him, in the faces of others or the faces of statues, or in the pouring of water, or the dazzle of sun on the strings of an instrument.

Qirisn grieved yet, seeing him so often, still she did not lose her quite unfounded hope. She could be nothing to him—yet surely she was. They could never meet—yet surely they would.

Some months after the night of the banquet, a young man, garbed like a desert wanderer, sought her in the court of the musicians' school.

He asked her if her name was Qirisn, and if she had sung in the hall when the King of the northern city dined there. He looked intently at her soft hair and small frame, and long into her eyes.

He asked she sing him one single note. She sang it. "I am Qirisn," she replied.

"Yes, so you are," said he. Then he gave a savage laugh. Then he begged her pardon for it. "When he was here in Marah, did you see the King?" Qirisn assented. She was very calm, long trained in means of control, as the musician must be, but pale, so her eyes seemed black rather than blue. Nassib took a breath, and asked her, "Would you see the King again?" To which Qirisn quietly answered, "I would give my life to do so."

Then the rest of the message was detailed, and the ring of rose-red topaz pressed into her hand. And she carried it to her lips and kissed it. Nassib next told her how they would leave the town before sunset, and start out over the desert, he and his eight men her escort. She nodded but asked nothing at all, only the colour of her eyes came back and filled Nassib's mind with a kind of blank serenity, and after this all was easy to do.

How easy indeed it was, as it had been easy to say to him, as she had, she would give her life to see the King once more.

And thus, while Qirisn and Nassib were crossing the waste, at long last the King reached his city.

Near to evening he entered the palace, and his wife the Queen came to meet him, her look radiant, her glorious hair twined with hyacinthine zircons. He greeted her publically with great affection, and then they went away into their private apartments, and here, after a slight interval, during which the radiance faded from her, the young King spoke of his love and respect for her, but then told his wife what had befallen him, and what presently must come to be.

She paid close attention. When he had finished, she raised her face, now like a paper never written on.

"What of your son, the Prince?"

"He shall continue as my heir. I will love him always— love does not cast out love, only increases it. He shall reign as King long after me."

"And I," she said.

"You will ever be my first wife, First Queen, and I will hold you dear. You need be afraid of nothing."

"Need I not," she said. And then, "Well, my lord. I wish you every felicity in your life with this second queen, who is your highest love, your spiritual mate through time. After the aeons you have waited to regain her, how marvellous will be your reunion." And rising she bowed to him and went away.

The Queen paced slowly to her own rooms, and there she drew off her body every rich thing which she had gained through her marriage. She called in the nurse, and gazed at her son, less than one year of age. "Be blessed, my darling," she said to her child, and gave the nurse seven zircons from her hair. Alone again, the Queen went into her compartment of bathing, and there she lay down on the marble floor and cut the vein of her left arm. Some while she watched the white stone alter to topaz red. She said to it, "He has not broken my heart, he has broken my soul." But then she fell asleep, and soon thereafter she died.

Such was the rejoicing at the King's return, no one discovered what had gone on until that night had passed. The

King himself did not receive the news until noon of the next day. When he did, he wept. It was proper that he should, and his court and subjects revered him for his tender sorrow. The Queen meanwhile they reviled for a madwoman. Even those who knew the truth avowed he had not meant to hurt her, she was unreasonable. And of course he had *not* meant to, for no man wants, unless an utter monster or fool, to saddle himself with such a dreadful scourge of guilt. Yet through the anguish of his tears and remorse, his love for Qirisn stayed like a pearl within contaminated water. The days of mourning would be long and scrupulously he would attend and mark each one. Beyond them, heaven-upon-earth awaited him. He could endure till then.

A storm was coming to the desert, it blew from the north. Lightning flared through the clouds, littering them with thin fissures of grey-gold. The thunder drummed on the sky's skin, as if to break through and plummet to the ground below in heavy chunks like granite, and each larger than a city. No rain fell. The dunes lit white, then brass, flickered to black, seemed to vanish underfoot.

To begin with they rode on, the escort of nine men on their horses, the girl in the little open carriage, she and its driver protected only by a canopy. But in another hour a strong wind gusted from the mouth of the storm, smelling of metal and salt. Soon enough it had the horses staggering, and snapped the posts so the canopy flew up to join the roiling cumulous above.

Nassib came to the carriage.

"There are tall rocks there. We must shelter, Qirisn-to-be-queen. No other way can we keep you safe."

They sought the rocks then, a narrow mesa like one segment of the backbone of a dead dragon.

Lightning carved about them still, and the thunder rolled. Men and animals waited, stark or trembling, and only

Qirisn was composed, afraid of nothing since her fate had found her, and she had trusted it.

Eventually another sound grew audible. It was that of men, unlike all others. Around the rocky hill came a cavalcade of sorts. They had lighted lamps too, and they were jolly, smiling and calling out invitingly to those who took shelter at the mesa's foot.

One of Nassib's men spoke in a voice of death.

"In number there are at least thirty of them. They are bandits. This is their stronghold. The gods have abandoned us."

Nassib drew his sword. It made a rasping, jeering noise, as if it mocked them. "While we may, we fight. Do not let them take you living." He had seemingly forgotten the girl. If he had remembered, he would have turned and offered to slay her at once. He could see his men had no chance, and nor would she have any, since these felons were everywhere noted for their profligate viciousness.

After this the bandits sprang from their donkeys, and rushing up they killed every other man that was there, Nassib too, the bandits grabbing and their leader beheading him at one blow. They recalled Nassib from the King's forays on their kind, but tonight they lost none of their own.

When even the carriage-driver had been slaughtered, they drew the valuable northern horses aside. That done, the leader went swaggering and laughing to Qirisn. "And what are you? Not much, for sure. Yet a woman, I will grant you that."

Perhaps she had gone mad in those minutes. Perhaps she had only been mad from the instant she fell in love.

She addressed the bandit reasonably, without fear or anger.

"You cannot touch me. I am meant for a king."

"Are you? His loss then. You shall have me and my lads instead."

The storm watched, missing no detail of what was next enacted at the foot of the dragon's backbone. In the lightning, flesh blazed white, or golden, or grew invisible; blood ran like blackest adders, or inks of scarlet or green. Cries became only another melodic cadence for the thunder and the gale. Storms frequently carried, and carry yet, such crying. Who can say if it is only imagined, or if it is the faithful report of the elements which, since time's start, have overheard such things.

At length, no one was there beneath the rock, but for the dead and Qirisn. In her, one ultimate wisp of life remained, although swiftly it was ebbing. *Come away*, life whispered to her urgently, *come away, for you and I are done with all this now.*

But Qirisn's eyes fixed on the sky of storm. The gods had forsaken her, love had, truth had. Worse than all these, *she* must now forsake *him*.

Something in her screamed in mute violence, a wordless, unthought prayer to the sky. Which, pausing, seemed to hear.

The cacophony of the cloud settled to a kind of stasis. The flutter of the lightning fashioned for itself another shape, that of an electrum knot. From this, long strands extended themselves, like searching arms. Long-fingered hands, resembling tentacles, reached as if most delicately to clasp the world. Then, from the core of heaven, a levinbolt shot downward. A flaming sword, the white of another spectrum, struck deep into the ground, at the spot where Qirisn lay dying. And after this it stood, the bolt, joining heaven to earth, pulsing with a regular muscular golden spasm. It fused all matter, sand and soil and dust, body and bone and blood, together in a disbanded union of change. Then the sword diluted and was gone. Everything was gone. And darkness sank into the space which was all the heaven-fire had left.

It is said, and possibly only Jandur, those twenty years later, propagated such a tale—for he was secretly a romantic —that hours on, when the storm had melted, demons came up on to the Harsh to enjoy its refreshment under a waning moon.

Passing the spot, those beautiful dreamers, the Eshva, paused only to sigh, before wandering away. If Vazdru princes passed, they paid no attention. But two Drin, the dwarvish, ugly and talented artisans of Underearth, did halt beside the silicate residues of Qirisn's death.

"Something is here worth looking at!"

But a desert hare, a female, gleaming platinum under the watery moon, and with ears like lilies, galloped over the dunes. And lust stirred up the Drin at such loveliness, and they vacated the area to pursue her. Such a master was love, then, for demons, and for men.

4. The Fourth Fragment

That very moment, as he entered the highest vortex of pleasure, Razved heard his phantasmal partner call out his name in her joy. It was not a moment otherwise for anything, let alone for thought. Nevertheless, it seemed not inappropriate she should know his name. Then the colossal wave bore him through the gate and dashed him among stars, and after that flat on his back again amid the pillows, with a maiden of glass gripped in his arms.

Only now did he unwillingly feel the chill and ungiving texture of her unflesh, and sense the folly, and maybe the *error* of what had just been done.

Only *now* also did he understand it was, after all, not exactly *his* name that she had called aloud in her voice of glass.

No, not *Razved*, that was not the name she had uttered. It had been Raz Vedey. *Raz Vedey, my beloved lord*.

Drained by ecstasy, stupified by confusion, Razved lay there. There rushed through his befuddled mind a memory of his mother, who had slain herself before ever he had known her, and of an old man locked up and enchained in a dirty room below. Down there, amid the irons and the skittering of rats, that was where *Raz Vedey* might be located.

In his mind, Razved asked of himself, *Whatever she is, what would she have with my father?*

Because, of course, the mad old man, who constantly escaped his imprisonment, but who haunted Razved even when safely stashed away, *was* that father, that very Raz Vedey.

Razved himself knew well that, along with a disgraced mother who had cut her wrist and died, he had a male parent who, while yet young and strong, the victor in a southern war, had one night, during a galvanic storm, started up shouting that his soul had perished in the Vast Harsh. And who, despite the subsequent care and attention of the best physicians and maguses, quickly became and stayed entirely lunatic. Razved, growing to maturity, was reared sternly by tutors, and when only thirteen made the regent of his father. Since then Razved had ruled the city, but without full authority and without the essential title of *King*. For did the King not still live? The city's moral code forbade his removal save through natural decease, and crazed though he was, the King ungraciously refused to die. Razved, to be sure, had engineered a clutch of clandestine attempts upon the wretch's life. All of these had failed. Yes, even the strong poison, or the block of stone cast from an upper roof. It was as if, Razved had long decided, his devilish sire awaited some news, or even arrival, and would not himself depart the world until assured of it. His constant wail: "Are they *here*? Are they *near*?" seemed infuriatingly—or piteably— to confirm this last suspicion.

The Prince's eyes now remained tightly closed. He was partly afraid to open them, for the fragile weight of *her* still lay over him. What would he see? What must he do?

"Remove yourself from me," he muttered, but there was no reaction.

Instead his brain brimmed suddenly with uncanny images—a glassy girl, shimmering green and rose, who drifted through the chamber on feet of glass, and her eyes, curiously, were dark, and gazed at him and did not see him. Perhaps they saw nothing, for they were made—not of eyes, nor of glass—but of *pain*, of *agony*, and of despair. A bride, brought forth from the carcass of Harsh Desert, the true meaning of whose title was *The Illegitimate Vessel*, a bride who had died in horror and waited in blind lament for two decades, next entering the city of her lover, her beloved, and mistaking for him one who *was* flesh of his flesh, if *never* spirit of his spirit. Where now then for her? Where else was there to seek or to fly?

On Razved's skin the glacial glass turned to ice, and with a howl he burst from his trance.

He bounded off the couch, slinging the succubus-creature from him, and opened wide his eyes. And in that instant he saw and heard a shattering of glass—as if a million crystal windows had blown in and whirled about him.

"Help me!" yowled Razved, King-in-waiting, descendant of warrior-lords, spraying his robe with the waters of his bladder. "Assassins! Demons!"

But when his terrified servants entered, they found him quite alone, not a mark upon him, and on the floor by his couch only one little plain drinking goblet, smashed into bits like sugar.

Qirisn was now finally and fully dead. Free therefore, she glided through the wall of the prison-chamber and stole quietly to King Raz Vedey. She touched his ravelled face, and looking up he saw her, her light hair and blue-midnight eyes; he saw her soul. And shedding his ruined mind and form, he came out to her, strong and young and beautiful as he had been in Marah, and kissed her hands and her lips. After which they went away together, wherever it was and is that lovers go, after physical death, when they are two halves of a faultless solitary whole.

But in the red dawn, when someone came to tell the Prince that his father had abruptly departed the world, Razved buried his head in the pillows and wept, over and over: "At last, at last, *I am the King.*"

THE FISH OF AL-KAWTHAR'S FOUNTAIN

Joanna Galbraith

In the fountain of Faris Al-Kawthar's courtyard swim eight orange goldfish who sing jubilant Os as they reel round and round. Weaving amongst water plants, reeds green as tree frogs, they seldom pause to breathe, just to reach a higher note. They never smile as they sing for what fish ever does? They just stare, eyes unblinking, though their gills burst with song.

The fountain in which they swim is as old as the earth. Made from three ribbons of rare, Parian marble, it is shaped like an olive, the curve of a woman's eye. At each end is a tap that has been fashioned from worn brass and in the middle is a stone spout wrought in the shape of *Anahita*. It is from here that fresh water springs eternally to the sky. High and then higher still, it is reaching for the stars.

The fountain is celebrated but not for its fish; though a fish warbling *Don Giovanni* would surely be celebration enough. No. Its fame is of a quiet sort; not of the kind to attract hoards and yet its reverence is well-known throughout the lands which surround it. From the glittering alleyways of

Souq-al-Hamidiyya to the cypress hills of *Qala'at Salah ad-Din*; from the riverbed of the Euphrates to the ramshackle port of Tartus, it is venerated; it is celebrated; for being the source of all life. Not directly, one understands, for it does not sow any seeds but rather it is the source of all rain, it is the source of all water. Every storm, every raindrop, has been conjured in its pool before being thrown into the sky by the mighty spring of this fountain. Propelled into the air where the clouds take their shape, its water is the sweetest thing that any child will ever taste. It brings life to arid soils; it brings life to withering crops. It is a life-giver to all people.

It can be a life-taker as well.

Visitors are frequent though they come on their own: a grateful farmer, a curious boy, an irrigation engineer. They never come in frenzied masses; they are calm, deliberate sorts.

Scientific in their thinking, methodical in their approach; they come because they must know; they seek to understand, how it is that a humble fountain can be a weather goddess as well.

Now Faris Al-Kawthar's courtyard is a kaleidoscopic whirl of mosaics, mother-of-pearl mirrors and painted pottery from *Tell Sabi Abyad*. Green vines dangle from internal windows and the circling balcony above; and latticed doors lead to small rooms with high ceilings and dawdling fans—some fans are so slow they are turning with the earth.

Elaborate tapestries hang from the courtyard walls, Islamic whisperings of Allah's peace; they are the first thing a visitor admires when they walk through the front door, followed by the immaculate floor, the green vines and the fountain of course.

It is Faris Al-Kawthar himself who tends to the fountain. He keeps the marble spotless. He knows that he must. Dirty water must not reach the skies or else it will fall dirty too.

He can only scrub it with his bare hands; he cannot use any other products. Once he used bleach and the sky rained acid for days after.

He is a young man, Faris, beautiful and lean.

His eyes are graphite-coloured; they burn like bright diamonds. No one can possibly believe that someone so beautiful might ever suffer from loneliness, even though he is without family, without a wife or his own child.

How could any man ever feel lonely when people are always coming?

Coming to Faris Al-Kawthar's courtyard to gaze upon his fountain; coming to thank him specially for tending the fountain the way he does.

But Faris *is* lonely; he is lonelier than forgotten bones.

A baker from Hama once offered him a bride but Faris declined politely, saying he was waiting for true love. It is difficult though, he admits, to believe that true love will ever find him when the only women who come visit him come to see the fountain first. Smart, educated sorts who are interested in gravity; Faris does not want a scientist; he wants a dreamer for his wife.

The eight fish in the fountain pool can sense their Master's great loneliness. They see it in his face as he quietly tends to their water garden. They feel it in his skin when he dips his hand in the water and they nibble at his fingertips with their open, songful mouths.

They know he cannot hear them but they hope all the same that somehow their jubilant songs will fuse into his bones. For even fish know that a good melody can get caught under a man's skin. Frank Sinatra's life-affirming *My Way* seems to do it every time.

* * *

It isn't just their Master's loneliness though that is disturbing to these fish.

Of late they have heard rumblings in the thunder overhead that all is not well across the lands which surround them. They have heard complaints that the rain is far more bitter than it is sweet and that its drops are so heavy that they are bruising all the harvests.

The fish can see it for themselves too as they reel round and round. Their water has become murky, the reeds are slowly dying. Their Master has stopped caring in the way that he should. He no longer scrubs the fountain in exact, watchful detail; his attempts are half-hearted. It seems that his loneliness has repercussions far beyond himself. The fountain is suffering, so too is the world.

"We must save the fountain," the fish cry. "Before it is too late."

But if the fish are to save the fountain then they must save Faris Al-Kawthar first.

"Let's stage an intervention," says the biggest of the fish.

"Yes, an intervention," trills another in a perfectly pitched high C.

The other fish nod their heads in approval—at the idea and the splendid C.

"Come," says the biggest fish. "We must all think as one. Perhaps if we all think together we can come up with a plan."

It is difficult though for the fish to come up with a plan because they are not known for their acumen and their brains are very small. They huddle closely together so their heads are almost touching and as they think they sing Puccini's *Humming Chorus* because they find it helps them to stay focused.

"Well," sighs the biggest fish eventually when no plan is forthcoming. "Let's break this down a bit. Perhaps that will help. Let's start with what it is that *we think* needs an intervention."

"Faris Al-Kawthar's loneliness," the smallest fish volunteers.

The other fish murmur in quick agreement; the smallest fish is right.

"And how do we solve that?"

The fish huddle closer, they hum a little more fervently as well.

"We must find Master Faris a wife," croons one of the fish suddenly.

All the fish nod together and blow delicate bubbles in unison.

"But how," they all ponder as they huddle closer still. Eyeball to eyeball, they are willing on a plan.

"We must think outside the fountain," the biggest fish finally suggests. "We're not going to find his wife in here. Our world is far too small."

The other fish shake their heads. The biggest fish is right. How are they ever going to find the right woman if they are stuck inside a marble bowl?

"I know," says one of the smaller fish thrashing his tail about with glee. "I shall swim right into the fountain spring so it flings me high into the air. Then I can take a look all around me to see what I can find. Perhaps if we can see outside the fountain we will think outside it too."

The bigger fish think it is too risky but the smaller fish is adamant. His life may be at stake but so too will many others if they don't cure Faris Al-Kawthar of loneliness before it is too late.

The smaller fish wastes no time, he is an impetuous sort of fellow, and with one enthusiastic flick of his golden tail he flings himself into the fountain's path. The other fish gape below as he spins away from their world. They try to muster up a buoyant song to send him on his way but only silence follows; they are too nervous for a song.

Meanwhile the smaller fish is being thrown high and higher into the air. He is somersaulting and twirling, flipping head over flapping tail. He is terrified and exhilarated; he has never seen so much colour. He can't believe anything has ever existed beyond sky blue and reed green.

Very soon though he is descending towards the fountain pool, finally slipping back underneath its watery surface with barely a splash from his spun tail.

"Are you alright?" the fish ask anxiously, crowding all around him.

The smaller fish nods his head; he is too winded yet to speak.

"What is the world like? Did it give you new ideas?"

"No," the fish confesses finally catching his breath. "It was all a bit of a blur but I did see a little boy standing by the front door. He was talking with Master Faris while they shared a piece of bread. You should have seen how the boy smiled when he saw me flipping through the air. I think Master Faris saw me as well because he started smiling too."

"Master Faris was smiling?"

"Yes, though it was only very slight."

"Well, then you must do it again if it makes Master Faris smile."

"No," replies the biggest fish. "This time I shall go. I have bigger eyes than our smaller friend here. I shall be able to look around a little more. Making Master Faris smile is important but curing his loneliness even more so."

The other fish nod their heads; they can see wisdom in his thoughts and without another word the biggest fish has disappeared—an orange rocket to the sky.

A few seconds later though, he returns with a choppy, violent splash; it seems he lacks the flying finesse of the smaller one in the air.

"Quickly," he pants. "Start swimming in circles. Master Faris and the boy are coming. They want to see what we're up to."

The fish begin to swim, trying their very best not to look conspicuous; as if they are going about their normal day the way normal fish are supposed to do. They understand how important it is that they look like normal fish; wide, vacant eyes, mouths open and shut, for they know there is nothing more suspicious than a fish that has been caught in the act of vigorous thought. It unnerves human beings when they see fish this way; makes it harder for them to reconcile the use of barbed hooks and spear guns. Normally the fish would not care, they would quite like to unnerve, but the last thing they want to do is upset their Master now.

"That was amazing," says the little boy leaning over the fountain edge. "I've never seen a fish dance before. Did you see the way the first one twirled? So many somersaults and pirouettes, he was beautiful don't you think?"

"Yes," Faris agrees. "Very beautiful indeed."

"Can I bring my older sister back another day? She is in Aleppo with my Uncle now but soon she will return. I am sure she would love to see your fish dance. She loves everything that dances."

"Of course," says Faris, patting the boy gently on his shoulder. "Though I cannot promise you the fish will dance again. I've never seen it before myself."

Later when the boy has gone, and Faris has retreated to his room, the fish congregate amongst the reeds and mouth the word "dance" in joyous unison. Of course, they should dance; it will bring all the women to Master Faris's door.

Don't women love their dancing as much as they love their glittering heels?

Such a gloriously simple idea, they wonder how they hadn't thought of it any earlier until one of the fish rather wisely says: "Yes, well though I am very familiar with the song; I am not so certain of the dance."

"We can learn it," says the biggest fish instantly, for he is not one to be deterred. "Tell us smaller fish, what exactly it was you did."

The smaller fish drops his head; his wee mind has drawn a blank. He remembers being high up and seeing gold letters in woven tapestry. He remembers the boy's face smiling and thinking he might die.

"Never mind," says the biggest fish. "We shall ask the universe for help. Someone out there will be able to teach us how to dance!"

The fish ask the universe in the very next storm; threading their message through the water before it is conjured to the sky.

> We are the fountain fish of Faris Al-Kawthar.
>
> We must learn to dance.
>
> It is a matter of great consequence for the fountain and the land.

They listen as the storm carries their words across the sky; they listen and they hope that their answer will soon arrive.

Unhappily for the fish though, the universe is not forthcoming and most of the creatures who hear their message choose to ignore their plea instead.

Why do fish want to dance anyway?

It sounds preposterous and frivolous; a little high-faluting as well.

In the end it is a Desert Lark who takes pity on the fish. She has looked down on the land from the blue sky above; she has seen how it is dying a little more with each passing day. She may not understand why the fish want to dance but she understands that it is something that they feel they must do.

She comes late one evening after the dusk light has faded and sings to the fish of all the dances that she has seen. Of dolphins she has seen skipping between the white tips of the sea. How they twirl high into the air, both backwards and then forwards. How they vault, leap and cartwheel across the surface of the water and wave with their fine flippers to each other in joyful harmony. She tells them of other dolphins, and of whales and seals too, whom she has seen performing in grand theatres to wild, rapturous applause.

The fish feel heartened as they listen to her accounts: if their fellow fish can dance then surely so too can they?

Soon they begin to secretly practice every night as Faris sleeps. The Lark tells them what she has seen; they listen and they learn. They find it much easier if there is a beat they can follow so the Lark invites a Syrian Woodpecker to come join her fountain side. He drums out a merry rhythm with his slim slate-black beak.

The fish are good studies and they work very hard. Sometimes they even slop water over the edge of the fountain. In the morning Master Faris mops the floor, shaking his head at the mess; he never questions why it has happened, he just cleans it half-heartedly and moves on with his chores.

Finally, after all the phases of the moon have made one journey across the sky, the fish decide that they are good enough; that they are ready to perform.

"We are ready," chorus the fish all together. "Now all we must do is wait for the boy."

Their waiting is soon rewarded. The boy returns two days later. He has brought his older sister with him too and she has brought her many friends. They crowd curiously around the fountain while Faris Al-Kawthar hovers in the periphery: he is preparing tea and *kanaf* should the fish fail to satisfy. But the fish will not fail; they are ready to perform and as the afternoon

Asr Prayer ends they begin their special dance. Shooting up with the fountain they spring out from each side like small exploding firecrackers; writhing orange flames. They spin, twirl and twist, while singing harmonic chords, before swooping back towards the water in synchronized dancing pairs. Then once under water they begin their formations: a flowering lotus, a revolving sun, a layered quilt of weaving fish.

Everyone is spellbound, even young Faris. Unable to speak, they simply watch on in wonder, mouths open and mouths shut and then mouths open once again. When the show finally ends with a triumphant fistful of springing fish the women cannot help but turn to each other and whisper how much more interesting Al-Kawthar's fountain is now it is the host of dancing fish.

"We shall come back with our sisters, our friends and our mothers. Every woman must come to Faris Al-Kawthar's fountain now to see its dancing fish."

The fish are delighted when they hear what the women say. Surely their young Master's loneliness will be cured before too long.

Soon the fish are dancing every day after the *As* Prayers. Tantalizing crowds of enthralled women as they dance, twirl and spin. Of course men come too, largely male relatives and showboat types. But it is the young women that the fish want to please; they want to charm them most of all.

Unfortunately, however, Faris does not see what they see. He is too busy being mesmerized by the tricks the fish perform to notice all the beautiful women who are now congregating in his home. He simply stands, widely gaping, watching his fish as they dance; clutching clenched fist to beating chest such is his pride in their fine work.

"He looks like a stunned mullet," the fish mutter in disgust. "Hell *never* find his true love if he simply stands there and stares."

"I shall try and draw his attention," says the biggest fish to the others. "Away from we fish and towards the young women."

"But how?" the fish chorus back in six chord harmony.

"I'm not sure but I shall try. It is imperative that I must."

The next day as the fish dance the biggest fish does his best; trying to catch his Master's eye as he somersaults through the air, while nodding his head vigorously towards the pretty young woman seated to Faris's right. It seems that after a few attempts Faris has begun to notice the biggest fish's efforts for he stops staring at the dancing fish and stares at the young woman instead.

But then something terrible happens!

The biggest fish is thrown out of orbit from all the vigorous nodding of his head. Confused and disoriented he misjudges his descent so he no longer falls back down towards the fountain but instead shoots across the room like a small orange dart. He lands on the lap of another watching woman but the landing is hard and causes him to bounce; twice on her covered knees and then once on her shoe, before hitting the marble floor very hard and with some clip. The whole crowd falls silent; many avert their eyes. No one wants to bear witness to this tragedy that is unfolding.

The young woman quickly kneels on the floor by the fish. She does not care that the cold marble will tear at her skin. She only cares about the fish lying so lifeless on the ground.

She cradles him in her hands, willing him to breathe. But the biggest fish does not stir. He is as still as Palmyra stone.

She carries him to the fountain, carefully cupping him in her hands, and then lowers him into the comforting embrace of the fountain spring. She prays the little fellow will feel his watery home once again. But the biggest fish feels nothing. He remains perfectly still; a limp, autumn leaf in the palm of her cupped hands.

Faris Al-Kawthar hurriedly joins her as she stands fountain side. His eyes are very bright. They shine like wet coals.

"I am sorry Brother Faris," she says gently, pouring the fish into his hands. "He was a beautiful fish. He lived a full life."

She then steps away from Faris and disappears with the crowds; leaving him alone by the fountain, his head bowed in sorrow.

The other fish congregate below the place where their Master now sadly stoops. Eyes wide, mouths stretched open; they are screaming silent Os. Faris leans over and lowers his cupped hands into the water. He knows the other fish will want to see their fallen friend one last time. They nudge at Faris's fingers and caress the biggest fish with their heads; all the time they are singing, though Faris cannot hear them. They are singing *In Parades;* they will never sing *Fauré* again.

That night Faris goes to bed without cleaning the fountain at all.

"Now the situation is worse," the fish weep. "Far worse than ever before."

The next day Faris Al-Kawthar's courtyard is inundated with visitors. They don't come because they expect to see the dancing fish again. They come because they want to express their sorrow for the biggest fish; because they want to embrace Faris Al-Kawthar and to bring him baked bread.

Yet as the *Asr* Prayers end there is a sudden surge in the fountain pool and the fish rise up once again; they rise up just the same. They don't feel much like dancing, their souls still freshly torn, but the fish know they must: that the biggest fish would have said so; that it is more crucial now than ever that their Master finds his true love.

It is difficult; however, for the fish to freely dance because they are nervous in the air and their hearts weigh them down. They can only hum intense melodies, most of which are by *Wagner*; melodies even the fish concede are not the most conducive to merry dance.

When the dancing finally ends and the applause has petered out, Faris clears his throat. He has an announcement to make.

"Thank you my good well-wishers for sharing your thoughts and your bread but I have decided that my fish shall no longer dance to great crowds."

He says this even though he knows he cannot stop the fish from dancing. Even though he knows he holds no power over what his fish choose to do. If the fish wish to dance, they will dance all alone; no crowds to distract them and divert their small minds. Perhaps without distraction no more fish will fall.

The fish are appalled when they hear their Master's words.

"How will he ever find his true love now," they sing in minor chords.

The following day there is a knock on Faris Al-Kawthar's door. Faris opens it expecting to find a small crowd of well-wishers begging him to rethink his ban on the dancing fish. Instead he finds a young woman standing alone on the doorstep. She is wearing a khimâr, all the colours of the rainbow; it is too cheerful for Faris, he wants to turn her away.

"The fish are not dancing," he says. "Now if you must excuse me I must go."

"I am Hayam," the woman answers, blocking the door with her foot. "Don't you remember me, Brother Faris?"

Faris looks closely at the woman. Now he remembers. Her ebony eyes, narrow and bright; and the knitted frown of her forehead. He remembers the way her hand had brushed his as she gave to him the biggest fish.

"I have made something for you," the woman continues. "May I come in and show you?" Faris nods at the woman and he ushers her quickly in. He is in no mood for visitors but he is curious just the same.

The woman removes a square package she has been hiding behind her back. It is wrapped in brown paper and then secured with jute twine. She hands it to Faris and then looks to the floor.

Inside is a painted canvas; even more colourful than her khimâr. It is of the biggest fish dancing. Dancing high above the fountain. She has caught him in full flight; he is living in the paint.

"It's just like him," says Faris, holding the painting out in front. "Thank you my Sister Hayam, I shall hang it in the courtyard."

The woman lifts her gaze; she is pleased Faris is happy.

"Won't you join me for some tea? A little thank you for your work."

"Sorry I cannot. I am already expected elsewhere today."

Faris is disappointed. "But I would so like to thank you for giving me this gift."

"Perhaps you can," Hayam says, nodding her head towards the fountain. "I should like, if I may, to return with my easel and paint all the other fish that live in your fountain. I am a painter as you can see and I delight in painting nature. But of late I have been sad and unable to paint for there has been nothing in nature I have felt inspired to draw. Everything is dying: trees, birds and flowers. These fish are the only things I have seen that have rekindled any sort of desire."

Faris pauses for a moment and then quietly nods his head. "It is true that I have said that my fish shall dance no more but if they are your one muse then I would be most honoured if you should come."

* * *

Hayam returns the next morning with her easel and paints. She looks into the fountain. It is sicker than ever. She can barely see the fish; they are slowly choking amongst the weeds.

"Brother Faris," she says, while rolling two rubber gloves over her jilbâb sleeves. "Would you mind very much if I cleaned your fountain first. I want to paint the dancing fish but I can barely see their golden scales."

Faris nods his head; feeling the smallest pinprick of reddening shame. "There is a special way to clean it. I will show you how it's done. As you have seen I have been neglectful. Please accept my apologies."

"It's not me you should be apologizing too," says Hayam, running her gloved finger across the water pool. "It's the poor fish I feel sorry for, fancy dancing in such squalor."

"Yes, fancy!" chorus the fish who are listening down below; before breaking out rather boisterously into *The Hallelujah Chorus* by Handel.

It takes Faris and Hayam most of the morning to clean the fountain properly. They trim away the strangling weeds and scrape dead algae from the marble walls. They cart away the stagnant water and polish the brass taps until they gleam. Their work is not easy. Their space is confined. Sometimes they brush limbs as they work side by side. Each time it happens and their limbs coincide, the fish feel a charge, a wild current through the water. It makes their tails spin and for a moment they feel giddy; unable to remember anything but the transient flutter of complete joy. This feeling swiftly passes and their grief soon returns but these currents are like nothing the fish have ever felt before.

At a little after one o'clock the fountain is declared clean and Hayam sets up her easel so she can begin painting once more. The dancing fish are coy at first and hide amongst the reeds. They have never been a painter's muse before and are not entirely sure what it is they should do. Fortunately Hayam knows exactly how to put the fish at ease and she begins by feeding them bread—not enough to leaden their stomachs but enough to make them surface. Soon the fish are nibbling and growing bolder with each breath; by afternoon they are dancing wildly, more wildly than ever before. They want to delight this painter woman; she makes them want to soar. There is something different about Hayam they have never sensed in a woman before.

By sundown Hayam has finished her first painting and she is ready to return home. Faris wants to admire her work but he is too nervous to be near her. He doesn't know why he is nervous he just feels it in his bones. Like if he stands too close he will forget how to speak, how to think, how to breathe.

"It's beautiful," he says, standing a few feet behind her.

Hayam jumps at his sudden words and drops the paintbrush from her hand. It falls into the fountain; its bristles thick with colour.

The fish watch entranced as the brush drifts to the fountain bottom; leaving a small contrail of vivid colours: orange and yellow; blue, red and green; traces of indigo and of sweet violet too.

It is Faris who retrieves the brush; soaking his tunic to the shoulder. Hayam must be nervous too; to have dropped her brush that way. He feels better for this somehow; knowing she is nervous too.

"Will you come back tomorrow?" he asks handing her the brush.

Hayam nods her head shyly.

They both lower their heads and smile.

That night as Faris sleeps, his fountain throws a grand storm. Flowers crawl from parched deathbeds to drink its nourishing rain and frogs find their voice again after having been silenced for so long. The rain water is pure again and even sweeter than before. Olive trees have stopped wilting. The rapeseed is turning yellow.

And in Faris Al-Kawthar's courtyard swim seven orange goldfish who sing jubilant Os as they reel round and round. This time though they are smiling; they are smiling as they sing. For they know when the dawn comes all they will see in the sky is a rainbow of orange and yellow; blue, red and green; traces of indigo and of sweet violet too.

THE SECRET HISTORY OF MIRRORS

Catherynne M. Valente

"*A mirror is an imp that eats light,*" the Queen said. "*An imp aligned with the moon, the dark, and women. It is the nature of silver, both quick and slow. The imp has blue, veiny wings, and its eyes flash like a cat's. Its heart has two parts: one of glass and one of mercury, which are the essential materials of a mirror. These parts war with one another; the glass is adamant and the mercury is soft, one cuts and one absorbs. You can see the results of their war in the mirror itself. The victory of the glass is in perfect reflection. The victory of the quicksilver is that the reflection is reversed.*"

The Queen closed her knurled, black-gloved hand around her daughter's little fingers. She guided the paintbrush in the child's grip, its bristles sodden with quicksilver like the long, braided hair of the moon. Together they made sweeping strokes over the surface of an oblong sheet of pristine glass.

* * *

I.

There is only one mirror. If we can all of us agree on one thing, it is most certainly that. However, from that perfect singularity, our society breaks down into a riot of squabbling angels inspecting the pinhead for minute differences in color, clarity, and metallurgic content. Definite statements of fact, phrased in declarative sentences, draw our wrath and contort it into impenetrable knots of red-faced, sweat-sprung fury. We are a tiresome band.

The essential material of a mirror is glass. *Say you not,* my brother will cry out! *It is silver! It is only that the world has so poisoned itself that the true substance of the primordial mirror tarnishes in our foul wind!* My sister will spit at my feet and demand if the first mirrors recorded in Anatolia were not obsidian. Yet another will scoff and extol the virtues of the bronze mirrors of Japan, and call bronze the prime element of the universe. But I am telling this story, and the honor of refracting the angle of the reader's vision is mine and mine alone. I shall hoard it, and pore over it in the dark.

The essential material of a mirror is glass. Sand, earth, fused self to self: all the world yearns to become a mirror in which the stars might stare. Obsidian, bronze, silver: these things are *reflective*, but they are not mirrors. The first mirror was a marriage of glass and mercury—and no differently from marriages of less pure materials, it shattered.

Ah, but they pound so upon the door of my cell, and demand their sides be told! Have you ever heard of such disagreeable folk? As if this was the first manuscript written from within our hexagonal chambers! As if vellum and gall were so rare as to be hunted across the fields like harts and hares. Leave me be, harridans, ruffians!

One of them enters without permission: Alba the Mercuress, her body wracked by quicksilver into a terrible, alien beauty, as a tree which once bloomed and bore scarlet fruit may, under the influence of winter, gnarl and bend, whiten and warp until it is a bald corkscrew, plashed with red and black where parts of it has died, or given life to some invasive species. So Alba seems to us, we who were spared in the lottery from service in the cinnabar cellars, squeezing the most beautiful of all poisons with a dropper onto perfect glass. She places her ruined, claw-curved hand over mine. Her mouth is so red, swollen and crimson with her peculiar suffering.

"Sister," she says, "you must tell all the truth, even the parts which are lies."

Because she is of my faction, and because she is hideous, I yield.

"It is my duty as a mother to introduce you to this imp," the Queen said. Her black collar shone in the candlelight, high and forbidding. The child looked up from the newborn mirror, her face wan and grey, pale as snow, her dark hair lank and limp.

"I'm hungry," the child whispered.

"Hunger is for beggars and gluttons," the Queen scoffed. She extended her ancient, broken hand to the surface of the mirror, and touched it gently. Out of the silvern surface, a tiny creature formed, no bigger than a thimble, with delicate, spiky wings and flashing eyes. It had breasts, furred with frost, dripping with quicksilver like mother's milk, and a tail, shivered already and covered with fractures like crushed ice. It grinned; its teeth were perfect and straight, mirror-sheened, reflecting the faces of the old woman and the young woman thirty-two times. The Queen pressed her finger to her daughter's and tilted it upward. The imp slowly, hesitantly slid from one hand to another like a ladybug passed between children.

II.

There are three schools of thought as to the nature and origin of the original mirror.

The first, and oldest, and therefore the most respectable and first to the dinner table, is that the earth was once a flat disc—there was a kind of truth in the poor, befuddled Church astronomers' assertions. When the dark was young, the earth was a flat disc. The sunward side was pure glass; the moonward side was mercury. Upon the glassy surface, folk lived in the fashion of Laplanders: they spun fur hoods from the fine glassy reeds that grew beside rivers of lugubrious molten crystal. They rode upon massive, shaggy tigers of quartz whose pale pelts drooped to the limpid steppe. They hunted the hyaline mammoth whose tusks were stained glass of a dozen colors, but the cobalt cows were most highly prized, shaking their prodigious heads at the silver sun. Those were days of innocence, of pellucid joy.

On the mercurial side of the world, another tribe dwelt on an endless sea of quicksilver. They lived in the manner of ancient Hawaiians, on ships of cinnabar, which stone floated still hither and yon upon the silver sea, remnants of some antediluvian birth—for cinnabar is the native rock that gives life to mercury like a scarlet womb, as all men worth their flesh know. With red oars and red hulls they moved through the black winds of the moonward side of the world, spearing the great vitreous whales what moved in silence and long thought within the mercurial tide. In those untroubled days, quicksilver had no poisonous quality, for it did not yet know how to harm.

Thus the great Edenic mirror was itself the world, and those who dwelt upon each side could not see one another. But the nature of paradises is to be lost, and it happened that a sunsider called Koh rode so far in his pursuit of a blue mammoth that he came to the edge of the mirror-world and looked over, into depthless space—and into the eyes of Tain, a moonsider who had pursued a glass-boned whale so far that she too reached the extremity of her universe. This would not be a very long story if they did not fall in love, and so they did their duty by narrative, coming together as it is the natural desire of glass and mercury to do, the one flowing over the other, until the end of time. But Tain could not bear the hard, bright land of the sunward side, where light reflected over and over in the great crystal mountains until she was blinded by it.

Koh for his part could not bear the liquid moonward side, where no firm land was to be had, save at the center, the pole, where the mercury froze into a jagged peak where only a few brave pioneers made their homesteads in towering whale-rib barracks.

Being young, they could not simply resolve to meet and mate but once a year in the manner of logical agrarian folklore. Instead, Koh, determined to make his home one in which Tain could smile, traveled to his favorite spot, a grove of glassapple trees in which loons keened, low and long. Tain, no less stubborn, sailed to her favorite shallows, determined to find a way to bring up sweet, clear land for her lover. Koh plunged his spear through the crystal earth, and Tain dove into the thick silver water, piercing the seabed with her own cinnabar harpoon at the same moment. They were true lovers: their timing was perfect, and the points of their weapons met precisely, the strength of their blows identical, the places they had chosen lying one on top of the other.

They broke the world between them.

Mercury erupted into glass and glass exploded into mercury. The stars cried out and the perfect disc warped, bending and breaking, shattering over and over, down to its most secret core. It collapsed into an orb, (the first school is somewhat non-specific as to the physics of this) and the glass shivered into a billion grains of sand, and the mercury hid itself away within the stone once more. Thus, all the mirrors of the world are smelted from sand which once belonged to the perfect, unified mirror of the ancestral world. More importantly, every mirror remembers having been a world, and longs to be one again.

In grudging acknowledgment of her contribution to such few pleasant things as this fallen world has to offer—wine, roasted pheasant, tobacco—the silvered side of a mirror is still called the Tain.

* * *

The child trembled.

"I have known this creature all my life, daughter," the Queen said. "It binds me to the mirror, but it also binds the mirror to me. Together, we have accomplished extraordinary things. Beauty, yes, but also power, for there is no power so great as the ability to reflect a thing—or a person—back to itself as it truly is, naked, unvarnished—and just slightly skewed. Women and mirrors made a bargain in the beginning of the world. The mirrors eat our light; we use theirs."

"I don't want to," whispered the child.

"You do not have a choice. You are my child. How many times did I ask the mirror when I would have a daughter, a girl like me, to love and to punish? The imp promised you to me, and I promised you to it. I have already told it that it can eat your heart, like a huntsman devours a deer's."

The child shuddered and began to weep. The imp stirred on her finger. Its voice was like glass grinding to dust.

"Don't cry," it said. "In a plane mirror, parallel beams of light change their direction as a whole, yet remain parallel."

III.

The second school, which is the second oldest, holds that a thing cannot exist without a maker. Now, you and I may know that that is silly, but very learned men have said it, and their beards are so long that we are required to listen politely while they blather on about clocks or else to cut their beards in their sleep, and they are very light and cunning sleepers.

Thus it is clear, according to their beards, that Abd-al-Qadir, an orphan child who lived deep in the catacombs of Edessa, feasting upon rats and hedgehogs, accomplished a great and monstrous thing in the autumn of ——. Like most orphans, the mind of Abd-al-Qadir was a magpie-mind. Edessa was at that time a vibrant outpost in the silver trade, the long and winding trail that led from the Caucasus to China and back again like a necklace-chain. My brothers are correct at least in that

silver was once an immutable metal, like gold. In the world
before factories vomited sulfur into the air, silver never did
tarnish, but glowed with an unearthly, moon-bright sheen
through years stacked end to end. Into the dark skirts of Edessa
many silver baubles dropped, and the quick hands of Abd-al-
Qadir snatched them all. Earrings and buttons, knives and egg-
cups, hair-combs and thimbles, spoons, signet rings, coins,
hatpins, brooches, shoes, bells, umbrella-handles, false eyes, false
teeth, false noses. Abd-al-Qadir lived in a perpetual rainfall.

In his hovel beneath the city, the child became obsessed
with his treasures. It is a sign of his peculiar genius that it
seems never to have occurred to the young master that he
could have bought himself a house on the highest hill with all
that silver. It was not a house he was after, so houses did not
exist for him. Instead all his soul bent towards the silver,
poring over it in the dark, pressing it to his cheeks, sleeping on
a bed of discarded wonders like an infant dragon.

My bearded brothers must, in their canonization of the
young Abd-al-Qadir, explain the fact that the archaeological
record clearly shows mirrors extant well before the incident in
Edessa. Some few of the objects the orphan-saint collected
must, in fact, have been hand-mirrors. *Think not on them*, they
snort. *They are mere pre-figurations of the great work to come.
A mirror is more than gross reflection.* And if that much is true,
it does not mean the rest of their argument must follow. But
you see how they argue, and how oppressed we all are by their
clumsy, toothsome hippopotamus-logic.

So it came to pass that Abd-al-Qadir grew dissatisfied
with his many treasures, and built a great fire in his sub-urban
cavern. Day and night he stoked it with rubbish and refuse,
and by and by it became hot enough to melt silver. Into a great
pot went earrings and buttons, knives and egg-cups, hair-
combs and thimbles, spoons, signet rings, coins, hatpins,
brooches, shoes, bells, umbrella-handles, false eyes, false teeth,
false noses. And not a few hand-mirrors. Abd-al-Qadir stirred
his witch's brew in silence, staring into the shimmering soup.
When he judged it complete by some unguessable internal

gauge, the child tilted the pot to his lips and drank it down, to the last drop, the silver scalding and burning him, an agony beyond my ability to imagine. My bearded brothers would say he wished to merge with the silver, to become more than flesh, to ascend, an apotheosis of metal and bone.

I think he was a lonely child, and could not bear to be parted from his toys.

It hardly matters, I suppose. From that moment Abd-al-Qadir ceased to be human in any reasonable way. His skin grew hard and sharp, his features smooth. When he finally ventured into the streets of Edessa, the market crowd drew back, and then drew in again to peer into his perfect body, to see themselves reflected in his skin, the boy who had become a mirror. He was feasted and feted at all the fashionable houses; women took him to bed, men took him to tutor, which is much the same thing. He remained placid through all these attentions. He did not eat, nor drink, nor ply his own kisses over attared flesh. He received only, and reflected his lovers back to themselves, as is the nature of a mirror. But with every dove killed for his sake, every grape crushed, every spasm of pleasure spent within him, he grew, and the expanse of his mirror-flesh widened.

When Edessa was besieged—not the famous siege, but one of the many others to which a city steeped in silver is prone—the gargantuan mirror that had once been a child named Abd-al-Qadir set the enemy ranks ablaze when he turned towards the sun. But soldiers are canny, and a mirror is only glass, after all. A shower of arrows shattered the surface of him, his breast and his knees and the smooth depressions that had once been his eyes. In the looting of Edessa, the shards were prized higher than diamonds, and the caravans carried them far across the world. In all the lust for enchanted glass, no one could be expected to notice a small silver skeleton, blackened as if burnt, huddled against the broken walls of the city.

The second school believes that all mirrors extant today are shards of the primordial mirror of Abd-al-Qadir, and must be guarded and protected as one would guard and protect a beloved child. The shards yearn to be brought together once more, to be kissed and feasted and feted, to receive the adoration and plenty of a nation of attentive lovers. Through their beards, they pant with anticipation.

"I feel sick," said the child. Her dark hair hung around her sallow face.

The Queen nodded. "You are becoming a woman."

The imp danced a little on the child's finger. "No one can devise tortures like a mother," it said. "It will only get worse."

"I feel as though my ribs are being squeezed by corset stays drawn too tight," the little girl whispered.

IV.

The third school, the newest and most avant-garde, holds that the mirror did not originate on this terrestrial sphere at all, but on a planet orbiting the star known as Shedir, in the constellation of Cassiopeia, bathed in the blue light of sixteen moons. These iconoclasts have no beards, and therefore no one listens to them, or sits with them at lunchtime. But we must be understanding of the ridiculous, or else how will they grow up to be the venerable?

It is said among these motley backbenchers that the society of Shedir's single habitable planet once utilized light as currency. Fishwives with cobalt skin and ice-clung loincloths harvested a certain substance from the bed of the great violet sea known as *aln*, which was much like our glass, yet pliable as a soap bubble. Within orbs of this substance the light of any of the moons could be trapped, or the cool white rays of Shedir, or even candlelight as soon as it left its tower of tallow. The rarer the light, the more valued the orb which contained it. The whole of this strange world was obsessed with light, its capture, its use, its philosophy. *Does light have a will?* asked the sophists of Shedir, passing among them an aln-goblet of what we might call walnut-wine. *Does it experience pain?*

Unlike the sophists of our own world, and I daresay unlike the sophists of the third school, the thinkers of Shedir were ambitious. They worked for years upon end to build a ship which could travel to the aln-beds, the source of that strange stuff in which light allowed itself to be caught, captured, loved. I suppose they might have asked the fish-wives, but if they had I should not have the opportunity to explicate absurd theories of dubious academic merit, so it is all for the best. Their ship was a wonder of trilobite shell, pressurized hydraulic mechanisms of pure gold, and the nacreous swim-bladders of a certain species of marine serpent that once flew the pale skies of Shedir before growing bored with aether and returning to the sea. Stunted, vestigial wings the color of new snow still adorn their black bodies, and the sophists fashioned those hoary, spined wings into passable rudders for their machine.

And so the ship of thinkers descended to the depths while the fishwives stood on the pier in their loincloths, smoking ruefully and taking bets on how many of them would drown. Into the black the ship sped, illuminating the darkness with lanterns in which the captured light of the seventh and greatest of the sixteen moons swam and gurgled. They passed over the oft-harvested and artificially seeded aln-beds, traveling faster and more urgently into the black and frigid sea until they came upon the deepest virgin an of the uttermost ocean floor. The bed was a vast mirror, the glassy stuff lying against the black rock, and showed the extraordinary ship gliding over its surface in a thousand faceted dimensions. Finally, the doctors of philosophy ventured outside in shimmering suits of oiled, no-longer-flying serpent skin, which kept their extremities warm and did not buckle under the pressure. Stretching out their arms, they touched their fingers to the most secret deposits of an.

Their hands, so sadhe the third school, passed through the aln-bed and into this world.

At this point in their lectures, most of us make our excuses. *I seem to be out of pickle-relish,* or, *can I freshen anyone's tea?*

But they are so very earnest, and that is why, despite all, we love the adherents of this school, who believe themselves to be descended from those selfsame philosophers of Shedir, who dragged behind them the whole of the virgin aln-bed, and thus brought mirrors with them into our world, and along with that great submarine mirror, some few fragments of light from a far-off star, seen through miles of violet sea. Thus, they say, every mirror that hangs on a wall or is closed up in a drawer, is descended from the gargantuan aln-mirror of old, just as they are descended from the exiled thinkers —does not their skin look a little blue, they ask, in this light? For as the tain of a mirror does not reflect, they could not pass through again and return home. But the third school retains hope—if but the right angle could be discovered, or the glass of a mirror removed while keeping the mirror itself intact (for in their scrambled cosmology the glass is really the tain and the tain the glass) then they might step through and find themselves in the ice-bamboo forests of Shedir once more, and hear the song of the equatorial winds through the stalks.

They say a little girl by the family name of Liddell managed it once, through a mirror on top of a mantle in her house outside London sometime in 1865. She brought her cat with her. This proof is usually met with thrown bread and protestations that popular fiction is not, in fact, the basis for sound science.

"Still, she loves you," hissed the quicksilver imp. "She has devised terrible fates for you, so that you will be like her, hook-handed and mad, with mercury dripping from every pore. That is what mothers do. They do not do it to be cruel, they do not sell their daughters' hearts to huntsmen and drive them alone and weeping into the black wood of the world because they are wicked, but only because these things are necessary to make a

woman in their own image, in order to make a lonely little girl into a Queen."

"I feel as though my scalp has been pierced by a poison comb," gasped the child.

The imp rubbed its silver stomach in satisfaction.

V.

The Mercuress places her other hand over mine. We are old, the two of us. We have grown old together. We hold the highest offices of our school. Alba the Mercuress and I, I, whose name does not matter. I am no more than a humble glass-blower, all my flesh scored with burns and scalds as Alba's is scored with the tracks of the quicksilver that moves still through her veins. My lips are a blister, while hers are bloody and violent red, the last stage of her slow poisoning. We have suffered so for our brief brushes with the truth of this world.

Once I lived in the desert, among all that sand yearning to become more, to reflect light, to capture it, to remember it, and I supposed I yearned for those things, too. Personal history is inferior to institutional history. But there was a day when I was not a nun in the service of light, there was a day when I looked into a mirror hanging in a university and believed it was holy. Believed that there was a reason that every tale of strange things contained somewhere in it glass and a mirror. Glass shoes, glass coffins, glass houses, mirrors that whisper: you are the fairest, the fairest of them all, mirrors that are really doors that are really mouths that are really endless seas whereon the throne of God floats like a golden buoy. I believed instinctively those solemn pronouncements that each school repeats in its most secret rituals: mirrors are memory, mirrors yearn to hold us within them, mirrors are the way home.

Light has a will. Light experiences pain.

And because I could smile and incline my head and know all those things, because I could laugh at all tales and believe them too, I have been allowed to stay within that

strange desert college, to boil the sacred glass and lay it flat
again, to smooth it for Alba's silver brush, to be the first face
reflected in any newborn plane. Alba and I converse with our
hands, our mouths, our glass, our mercury. We move in a rigid
line, pantomiming the origin story that pierces us like a shard
of mirror, showing our hearts on both sides. So it is that I, the
stewardess of glass, lay down upon the frail body of the
governess of mercury, as Koh lay over Tain, as the lovers of
Abd-al-Qadir lay over his glassy belly, as the philosophers of
Shedir lay over the an-bed, and between the two of us, we
make the world whole again, a perfect mirror.

*"I am sorry," the Queen said. "We dwell in a plague of mirrors.
It is best to give in, to understand that your youth is spent
staring into a glass, your middle-age is spent walking in glass
shoes, and upon your death you will be closed up in a coffin of
glass, in whose lid you may see yourself decay with perfect
clarity. This is the fate of a woman. Perhaps there are worlds
where it is otherwise. But here, the imp holds sway." The Queen
did indeed look pained, and thick, rheumy tears formed in the
corners of her eyes.*

    *"I feel as though a slice of apple has become lodged in my
throat," choked the child, clawing at her neck. She looked up,
pleading, into her mother's impassive face, her lips startlingly,
violently red, flush with poison, her face the tain of her mother's
mirror.*

    *The imp grinned for the third time, an expression
containing something of pity and something of triumph. "Did I
not promise just exactly this?" it cried. "A child with hair as
dark as ebony, with skin as white as snow, with lips as red as
blood?"*

    "You did promise."

    *Satisfied, the imp sighed passionately and melted into
the finger of the Queen's daughter. Slowly, the child collapsed
onto the worktable, and no breath fogged the mirror that bore
her up.*

VI.

The Mercuress my lover pulls my hand from the page. Her bluish skin is warm with the last light of the day, caught in the crystal lanterns of my cell, where it dances and flickers, caught, captured, loved. Her mouth is so beautiful, so red. In the hall we can hear the voices of our brothers and sisters, squabbling over the chemical content of an or what sign of the zodiac Abd-al-Qadir must have been. The novices, still flush with new knowledge, whisper and laugh, repeating to each other old tales of queens and imps and apples and snow in the corners of the refectory. How everything shines for them now, how every tale they have ever heard must be taken apart to find the secret story creeping there, just behind the glass. These are pleasant, comforting sounds, like those of children playing in the courtyard.

The bed in my cell is narrow. She will pull me onto her, and breast to breast we will sleep, whispering to each other of that perfect, lost world where we might have raced on glass tigers and swum in seas of silver too pure to ever harm us. The light will gutter and dim, spending its last crimson onto our joined skin, two old women watching each other in the mirrors of their eyes.

I will go to her. There is time enough for manuscripts tomorrow.

NEVER NOR EVER

Forrest Aguirre

I. The Twain

“It's coming.”

“THE CROW?!”

“Not the crow,” he shook his head, disappointed by the other's naiveté. They had not spoken of the crow since The Rattle Incident, fifty some years ago. “No, not the crow. Contrariwise, inevitability, death.”

“Oh, that.” And he knew it was true, that “that” was coming. That despite the unchanging DUM on his collar—his clothes had not aged a day—the grey hairs that nowadays shed from beneath his unchanging beanie would continue to fall like desiccated leaves on the autumn ground, and that the pace at which they fell would approach a lifetime's asymptote until time rearranged the equation completely, allowing infinity to shrink to naught.

“What now?” Dum asked.

Dee's face waxed dour. “Contrariwise. No now.”

"Know what?" Dum was perplexed, not knowing what information he lacked, of course.

"No now. There is only one way out, and that—or avoiding 'that'—is out of time."

Dum nodded, hand to chin, soaking in Dee's meaning. After a silence, the hand raised, finger pointed upward, his eyes widened.

"Perhaps we can slow time to a standstill!"

"It is not enough," Dee said gravely. "We must escape. Clearly we could slow our aging, every two-bit apothecary offers cures for the maladies of senescence. But inevitability will reign supreme, no matter what our age. We cannot ignore it. It will sneak up on us and . . . "

"The crow . . . " Dum said ominously.

"Yes, the crow," Dee agreed, non-contrariwise. "The crow, highwaymen, disease, the fickle nature of the queen."

They both involuntarily cringed, thinking of what had happened to Queen Alice since she had hit puberty, maturity, then menopause. It was not a pretty picture. The crow seemed inviting, by comparison.

"You are right," Dum conceded. "We need out. But how?"

"There are two of us," Dee observed. "Perhaps we should look in different directions and share what we find with one another."

"Agreed," said Dum.

"Agreed," said Dee.

"Agreed," said they, in unison. And they turned their backs on each other.

II. Dum

In the beginning was the word. And the word was God. Is God. Will be God. God is the beginning and the end, thus the word is the beginning and the end. The ends need unraveling, the word needs breaking. Broken words means no beginning and no end means no time, no how. Contrariwise, no words means no time at all. And no times means no decay, unless I says so. I will decay the word and become God. "Be" because I Am, "come" because I will be. Because. "Be" because I AM, "cause" because I will make it be. Because I says so. And no one won't stop me, no how!

III. Dee

Dum is becoming more and more unstable. I shan't tolerate his irregularities much longer, no how. I am so close to discovering the secret, and I try to impart my knowledge to him in discrete portions, but he deconstructs my words, even deconstructs his own words mid-sentence. He seems obsessed with pulling apart my very meanings. He makes no sense half the time. Contrariwise, he borders on insanity. I wonder if, perhaps, it is too late for him, if senility has already dug its talons into poor Tweedledum's skull. His brain seems scrambled.

Perhaps he misunderstood the concept of time and timelessness, blinded by time so as to be unable to see outside it. More likely, he was afforded a glimpse beyond the chronological curtain, into the ineffable, and was driven mad by what he saw. His comprehension might just have been too simple for the vision.

I should like to explain it to him, but I cannot complete a sentence in his presence.

I should like to explain to him that time is like a ball riddled through with tubes that pass through it (and through one another). The inside of each tube is made of the same stuff as the outside surface of the sphere. It is not a solid skin, though. It is a wall of threads braided around threads, each reinforcing the other, like steel bridge cables, only of finer material. Most go about their day-to-day lives incognizant of the structure, as unaware of time's velocity as they are of the motion of the air, until the vortex of caducity sweeps them along to their doom.

I am afraid that my brother has already been carried away by that cyclone. He is unable to still his tumbling thoughts long enough to focus on the structure. To exit time, one must, paradoxically, use time in an effort to learn to control it.

I have begun my exercises thusly:

To slow time down, I bore myself with meditative regimens. Ennui is dolorific to one's sense of time and, I believe, to time itself. It has a preservative effect on the constitution, slowing the heart and mind, keeping decay at bay.

I have also, at my peril, experimented with differing methods of speeding time up, hurtling myself toward my nemesis in order to see, more acutely, the tendrils that hold me captive, in an effort to find chinks in the eternal armor. The problem here is, the more I look in this way, the finer and finer resolution I see. The cable-like structure is repeated ad infinitum, and the more time I spend (the monetary metaphor is not lost on me) trying to unravel the wall towards which I speed, headlong, the less time I have to solve the puzzle. It's like trying to capture the Cheshire Cat in a room whose walls are covered in smiling wallpaper. Time laughs at me as I try to solve its riddles. I am mocked for my desperation. I don't smile much anymore.

IV. Contrariwise

"What do you have?" Tweedledee asked glumly. "Halve the answer," Tweedledum replied. The mixture of cheerfulness with a tone of command in his voice sickened his twin.

"Half the answer? The closer I get to the answer, the quicker it recedes."

"Re-seed the question." Again, that condescending tone.

"You are maniacal."

"You are the one in manacles," Dum danced in circles around his brother.

Dee fumed, then his temper burst.

"Stop this prattle!"

"RATTLE?!" Dum suddenly grew enraged. "What have you done with my nice, new rattle?"

"Not again!" Dee put his face in his hands, nearly sobbing with frustration.

"Of course," Dum said, in a calm voice that evoked unpleasant memories in Dee, "we must have a battle."

"Of course," agreed Dee, accepting this burden with a heavy heart. "But you will need to get yourself dressed."

"I am fine in trousers, thank you. Only The Queen wears dresses around here," he pointed to his hips with both hands, circling them around as a ballerina might or might not.

"Then we will forego armor," Dee declared.

"It is a foregone conclusion," Dum stated.

They each retrieved sabers—The Queen had had them each turn in their umbrellas, etc, when she bestowed knighthood on them for their careful attention to points of honor (though their bravery, or lack thereof, was never mentioned in the ceremony), and had replaced them with Polish sabers, though Dum would mumble to himself, as he fetched his weapon, that there was little pole-ish about the swords. In fact, they were rather saber-ish sabers, but he dare not utter the word "saber-ish," lest he invent a new word and thwart himself in his effort to destroy The Word. If he created more words, he would never be able to pry open the necessary chinks in the armor of time.

Arm more, neither had. Dum's and Dee's biceps and triceps both flexed and sagged in the same big-boned, age-worn way. They approached each other from foot and head of hill, Dee galumphing down, Dum shambling up (though it was no sham. Rather, it was the best charge he could muster at his age and weight). Rage filled their eyes, their mouths were twisted in the midst of their war cries, their nostrils were large and pulsating for lack of air, their organs began to fail, and Dee thought he might piss himself, less from fear than from incontinence.

"Huraaargh!" Dee screamed.

"Rarhuuurgh!" Dum yelled.

The clash of steel against steel served as counterpoint to their strained grunting in a symphony (more a duet, actually) of sweat and sparks. Blades twirled and bodies spun as each sought the soft flesh of the other, like the Walrus and the Carpenter contending with oyster knives. But neither of these opponents were so naïve as those salty little morsels. No, Dum and Dee had learned well the art of the killing stroke, both offensively and defensively, so it seemed impossible for one to gain the advantage of the other. Besides, both were old and tired, which precipitated this whole situation in the first place.

This possibility, the single most undesirable occurrence in an infinity of possible futures, had dawned on Dee in his many ponderings and contemplations, as if he had been given a prophetic glimpse through the time that he had so powerfully desired to escape. The present impasse, however, was hardly premeditated. But this would not stop Dum from realizing, if he could read Dee's thoughts, that it was meditated upon previously. But what Dum could not know was the one trick that his brother had concocted for just such an occasion, this exact occasion, in fact. It was an obvious trick, but effective.

It consisted of two words:

"THE CROW!"

As Dum craned his neck to see The Crow, Dee's saber zwisched through neck, tendon and bone, sending the beanie, sans occupant, rolling past the DUM-inscribed collar, to the ground.

"I've been Dee-capitated!"

Dee swore he heard the words from Dum's mouth as the head fell. Guilt exploded inside him. He dropped the saber and ran to look into his brother's fast-fading eyes.

"Dum! Come unto me!" Dee cradled his brother's cranium.

"I am going un-to you. In fact, I am going very far away, indeed . . . " The voice trailed away into the distance, like the sound of wind blowing away into a wooded valley.

V. Nohow

Queen Alice was much more merciful than the old queen. She had, of course, seen to it that Dee was locked away so as not to be a danger to the rest of society. But she let him keep his head attached to his body in a rather comfortable cell, and there is something to be said for that. He was even allowed whatever books he wished and all the writing materials he needed to keep himself busy. The Cheshire Cat came to visit him from time-to-time, but not out of friendship and not for any particular reason whatsoever. Dee did not appreciate the Cheshire Cat's visits, anyway, as these sudden appearances out of nowhere, for no particular reason whatsoever, tended to interrupt his reading and writing.

These are Dee's final words, as discovered by the warden:

"It is coming. The luxury of time afforded me, interrupted only by the unannounced visits of the pesky Cheshire Cat, is becoming compressed. My discomfiture grows at an ever-increasing rate. I am caught in a chronological Zeno's Paradox, coming ever-closer, but unable to catch the answer that will deliver me from the chase.

"It is coming, and I wonder if Dum, those many years ago, was able to escape its grasp at my hands or through his own mechanism in the split second before steel bit flesh, my brother slipping between the skeins to the outside. Perhaps that is how I heard his voice—the last echoes down the walls of time as his soul abandon his body and traveled outside of both ever and never.

"Tonight, I cross the asymptote. Perhaps I have given in to despair, but 'suicide' is far too crude a term for the ritual entrance into the mysteries of timelessness that I am about to undertake. Zeno be damned. He never existed on this side of the glass anyway, I've only read about him in fairy tales written by under-sexed men who prey on little girls' fancies. My greatest fear is that he, Zeno, dictates the laws of that place outside ever and never. Soon, I shall know for myself. Forever or never at all."

each thing I show you is a piece of my death

Gemma Files and Stephen J. Barringer

"There is nothing either good or bad, but thinking makes it so."
— *The Tragedy of Hamlet, Prince of Denmark*,
William Shakespeare.

From a journal found in a New Jersey storage unit, entry date unknown:

Somewhere, out beyond the too-often-unmapped intersection of known and forgotten, there's a hole through which the dead crawl back up to this world: A crack, a crevasse, a deep, dark cave. It splits the earth's crust like a canker, sore lips thrust wide to divulge some even sorer mouth beneath—tongueless, toothless, depthless.

The hole gapes, always open. It has no proper sense of proportion. It is rude and rough, rank and raw. When it breathes out it exhales nothing but poison, pure decay, so awful that people can smell it for miles around, even in their dreams.

Especially there.

Through this hole, the dead come out face-first and down, crawling like worms. They grind their mouths into cold dirt, forcing a lifetime's unsaid words back inside again. As though the one thing their long, arduous journey home has taught them is that they have nothing left worth saying, after all.

Because the dead come up naked, they are always cold. Because they come up empty, they are always hungry. Because they come up lost, they are always angry. Because they come up blind, eyes shut tight against the light that hurts them so, they are difficult to see, unless sought by those who—for one reason, or another—already have a fairly good idea where to start looking.

To do so is a mistake, though, always—no matter how "good" our reasons, or intentions. It never leads to anything worth having. The dead are not meant to be seen or found, spoken with, or for. The dead are meant to be buried and forgotten, and everybody knows it—or should, if they think about it for more than a minute. If they're not some sort of Holy Fool marked from birth for sacrifice for the greater good of all around them, fore-doomed to grease entropy's wheels with their happy, clueless hearts' blood.

Everybody should, so everybody does, though nobody ever talks about it. Nobody. Everybody. Everybody . . .

. . . but them.

(The dead)

July 26/2009
FEATURE ARTICLE:
COMING SOON TO A DVD NEAR YOU?
"BACKGROUND MAN" JUMPS FROM 'NET
TO . . . EVERYWHERE
By Guillaume Lescroat, strangerthings.net/media

Moviegoers worldwide are still in an uproar over *Mother of Serpents*, Angelina Jolie's latest blockbuster, being pulled from theatres after only four days in wide release due to "unspecified technical problems." According to confidential studio sources, however, the real problem isn't "unspecified" at all—this megabudget Hollywood flick has apparently become the Internet-spawned "Background Man" hoax's latest victim.

For over a year now, urban legend has claimed that, with the aid of careful frame-by-frame searches, an unclothed Caucasian male (often said to be wearing a red necklace) can be spotted in the background of crowd scenes in various obscure films, usually partially concealed by distance, picture blur or the body-parts of other extras. Despite a proliferation of websites dedicated to tracking Background Man (over thirty at last count), most serious film buffs dismissed the legend as a snipe-hunt joke for newbies, or a challenge for bored and talented Photoshoppers.

But all that changed when the Living Rejects video "Plastic Heart" hit MTV in September last year, only to be yanked from the airwaves in a storm of FCC charges after thousands of viewers confirmed a "full-frontally naked" man "wearing a red necklace" was clearly visible in the concert audience . . . a man that everybody, from the band members to the director, would later testify under oath *hadn't been there* when the video was shot.

"You know the worst thing about looking for Background Man? While you're waiting for him you gotta sit through the crappiest movies on the planet! C'mon, guy, pick an Oscar contender for once, wouldja?!"
— Conan O'Brien, *Late Night with Conan O'Brien,*
    November 18, 2008

Background Man has since appeared in supporting web material for several TV shows (*House*, *Friday Night Lights* and *The Bill Engvall Show* have all been victims) and has been found in a number of direct-to-DVD releases as well, prompting even Conan O'Brien to work him into a monologue (see above). *Mother of Serpents* may not be the first major theatrical release to be affected, either; at least three other films this summer have pushed back their release dates already, though their studios remain cagey about the reasons. The current consensus is that Background Man is a prank by a gifted, highly-placed team of post-production professionals.

This theory, however, has problems, as producer Kevin Weir attests. "Anybody involved who got caught, their career,

their entire life would be wrecked," says Weir. "Besides the
fines and the criminal charges, it's just totally f---ing
unprofessional—nobody I know who *could* do this *would* do it;
it's like pissing all over your colleagues." Film editor Samantha
Perry agrees, and notes another problem: "I've reviewed at
least three different appearances, and I couldn't figure out how
any of them were done, short of taking apart the raw footage.
These guys have got tricks or machines I've never heard of."

Hoax or hysteria, the Background Man shows no signs
of disappearing. However, our own investigation may have
yielded some insights into the mysterious figure's origin–an
origin intimately connected with the collapse last year of the
Toronto-based "Wall of Love" film collective's Kerato-
Oblation/Cadavre Exquis project, brainchild of experimental
filmmakers Soraya Mousch and Max Holborn . . .

From: Soraya Mousch sor16muse@walloflove.ca
Date: Friday, June 20, 2008, 7:08 PM
To: Max Holborn mhb@ca.inter.net
Subject: FUNDRAISING PITCH DOC: "KERATO-OBLATION"
(DRAFT 1)

To Whom it May Concern —
     My name is Soraya Mousch, and I am an experimental
filmmaker. Since 1999, when Max Holborn and I founded
Toronto's Wall of Love Experimental Film Collective, it has been
my very great pleasure both to collaborate on and present a
series of not-for-profit projects specifically designed to push —
or even, potentially, demolish — the accepted boundaries of
visual storytelling as art.
     Unfortunately, given that film remains the single most
expensive artistic medium, this sort of thing continues to cost
money . . . indeed, with each year we practice it, it seems to
cost more and more. Thus the necessity, once government
grants and personal finances run out, of fundraising.
- - - - - - -

(mhb): <yeah, say it exactly like that, that'll get us some money
[/sarc]>
- - - - - - -

To this end, Mr Holborn and I have registered an internet domain and website (kerato-oblation.org), through which we intend to compile, edit and host our next collaborative project, with the help of filmmakers from every country which currently has ISP access (ie, all of them). The structure of this project will be an <u>exquisite corpse</u> game applied to the web-based cultural scene as a whole, one that anybody can play (and every participant will "win").

WHY KERATO-OBLATION?
Kerato-oblation: Physical reshaping of the cornea via scraping or cutting. With our own version — the aforementioned domain — how we plan to "reshape" our audience's perspectives would be by applying the exquisite corpse game to an experimental feature film assembled from entries filed over the Internet, with absolutely no boundaries set as to content or intent.

WHAT IS AN EXQUISITE CORPSE?
An "exquisite corpse" (*cadavre exquis*, in French) is a method by which a collection of words or images are assembled by many different people working at once alone, and in tandem. Each collaborator adds to a composition in sequence, either by following a rule (e.g. "The *adjective noun adverb verb* the *adjective noun*") or by being allowed to see, and either elaborate on or depart from, the end of what the previous person contributed. The technique was invented by <u>Surrealists</u> in <u>1925</u>; the name is derived from a phrase that resulted when the game was first played ("Le cadavre exquis boira le vin nouveau."/"The exquisite corpse will drink the new wine."). It is similar to an old parlour game called <u>Consequences</u> in which players write in turn on a sheet of paper, fold it to conceal part of the writing, then pass it to the next player for a further contribution.

Later, the game was adapted to <u>drawing</u> and <u>collage</u>, producing a result similar to classic "mix-and-match" children's books whose pages are cut into thirds, allowing children to assemble new chimeras from a selection of tripartite animals. It has also been played by mailing a drawing or collage — in progressive stages of completion — from one player to the next; this variation is known as "<u>mail art.</u>" Other applications of the game have since included computer graphics, theatrical performance, musical composition, object assembly, even architectural design.

- - - - - - -

(mhb): <don't know if we need all this history, or the whole exquisite corpse thing -- just call it "spontaneous collaboration" or something? keep it short>

- - - - - - -

Earlier experiments in applying the exquisite corpse to film include *Mysterious Object at Noon*, an experimental 2000 Thai feature directed by Apichatpong Weerasethakul which was shot on 16 mm over three years in various locations, and Cadavre Exquis, Première Edition, done for the 2006 Montreal World Film Festival, in which a group of ten film directors, scriptwriters and professional musicians fused filmmaking and songwriting to produce a musical based loosely on the legend of Faust.

- - - - - - -

(mhb): <the montreal things good, people might actually have seen that one -- one more example?>

- - - - - - -

For your convenience, we've attached a PDF form outlining several support options, with recommended donation levels included. Standard non-profit release waivers ensure that all contributors consent to submit their material for credit only, not financial recompense. By funnelling profits in excess of industry-standard salaries for ourselves back into the festival, we qualify for various tax deductions under current Canadian law and can provide charitable receipts for any and all financial donations made. Copies of the relevant paperwork are also attached, as a separate PDF.

  For more information, or to discuss other ways of getting involved, either reply to this e-mail or contact us directly at (416)-[REDACTED]. We look forward to discussing mutual opportunities.

With best regards,
Soraya Mousch and Maxim Holborn
The Wall of Love Toronto Film Collective

- - - - - - -

(mhb): <for crissakes soraya DON'T SIGN ME AS MAXIM -- if I have to be there at all its just max, k?>

8/23/08 1847HRS
TRANSCRIPT SUSPECT INTERVIEW 51 DIVISION
CASEFILE #332
PRESIDING OFFICERS D. SUSAN CORREA 156232,
        D. ERIC VALENS 324820
SUBJECT MAXIM HOLBORN

D.VALENS: All right. So you had this footage for what, better than six weeks—footage apparently showing somebody committing suicide—and you didn't ever think that maybe you should let the police know?
HOLBORN: People send us stuff like this all the time, man! The collective's been going since '98. Most of it's fake, half of it has a fake ID and half of the rest doesn't have any ID at all.
D.VALENS: Yeah, that's awful lucky for you, isn't it?
D.CORREA: Eric, any chance you could get us some coffee?
HOLBORN: I don't want coffee.
(D.VALENS LEFT INTERROGATION ROOM AT 1852 HRS)
D.CORREA: Max, I'm only telling you this because I really do think you don't know shit about this, but you need to do one of two things right now. You need to get yourself a lawyer, or you need to talk to us.
HOLBORN: What the fuck am I going to tell a lawyer that I didn't already tell you guys? What else do you want me to say?
D.CORREA: Max, you're our only connection to a dead body. This is not a good place to be. And your lawyer's going to tell you the same thing: the more you work with us, the better this is going to turn out for everyone.
HOLBORN: Yeah. Because that's an option.

From: 11235813@gmail.com
Date: Wednesday, June 25, 2008, 3:13 AM
To: submissions@kerato-oblation.org
Subject: Re: KERATO-OBLATION FILM PROJECT

To Whom It May Concern --
    Please accept my apologies for not fully completing your submission form. I think the attached file is suitable enough for your purposes that you will find the missing information unnecessary, and feel comfortable including it in your exhibition nevertheless. I realize this will render it ineligible for

competition, but I hope you can show it as part of your line-up all the same.
    Thank you.

VIRTUAL CELLULOID (vcelluloid.blogspot.com)
Alec Christian: Pushing Indie Film Forward Since 2004

<- <u>Rue Morgue Party</u> | <u>Main</u> | <u>Rumblings on the Turnpike</u> ->

July 23, 2008
"Wall of Love" Big Ten Launch Party

Got to hang out with two of my favourite people from the Scene last night at the Bovine Sex Club: Soraya Mousch and Max Holborn, the head honchos behind the Wall of Love collective. The dedication these guys've put into keeping their festivals going is nothing short of awesome, and last night's launch party for the next one was actually their *tenth anniversary*. Most marriages I know don't last that long these days. (Doubly weird, given Max and Soraya are that rarest of things, totally platonic best opposite-sex straight friends.)
    For those who've been under a rock re the local artsy-fart scene over each and every one of those ten years, meanwhile, here's a thumbnail sketch of the Odd Couple. First off, Soraya. Armenian, born in Beirut, World Vision supermodel-type glamorous. Does music videos to pay the bills, but her heart belongs to experimentalism. Thing to remember about Soraya is, she's not real big on rules: When a York film professor told her she'd have to shift mediums for her final assignment, she ended up shooting it all on her favorite anyways (8mm), then gluing it to 16mm stock for the screening. This is about as crazy as Stan Brakhage gluing actual dead-ass *moths* to the emulsion of his film *Mothlight* . . . and if you don't know what *that* is either, man, just go screw. I despair of ya.
    Then there's Max: White as a sack of sheets, Canadian as a beaver made out of maple sugar. Meticulous and meta, uber-interpretive. Assembles narratives from found footage,

laying in voiceovers to make it all make (a sort of) sense. Also a little OCD in the hands-on department, this dude tie-dyes his own films by swishing them around in food-color while they're still developing, then "bakes" them by running them through a low-heat dryer cycle, letting the emulsion blister and fragment. The result: Some pretty trippy shit, even if you're not watching it stoned.

Anyways. With fest season coming up fast, M. and S. are in the middle of assembling this huge film collage made from snippets people posted chain-letter-style. You might think this sounds like kind of a dog's breakfast, and any other self-proclaimed indie genius you'd be right. But S. took me in the back and showed me some of the files they hadn't got to yet, and man, there's some damn raw footage in there, if ya know what I mean; even freaked *her* out. So if you're looking for something a little less *Saw* and a little more *Chien Andalou*, check it out: October 10, the Speed of Pain . . .

From: Soraya Mousch sor16muse@walloflove.ca
Date: Wednesday, June 25, 3:22 PM
To: Max Holborn mhb@ca.inter.net
Subject: Check this file out!

Max --
        Sorry about the size of this file, I'd normally send it to your edit suite but it's got some kind of weird formatting -- missing some of the normal protocols -- I don't have time to dick around with your firewalls. Anyway, YOU NEED TO SEE THIS. Get back in touch with me once you have!

From: Soraya Mousch sor16muse@walloflove.ca
Date: Wednesday, June 25, 3:24 PM
To: Max Holborn mhb@ca.inter.net
Subject: Apology followup

Max: Realized I might've come off a little bitchy in that last message, wanted to apologize. I know you've got a lot of shit on your plate with Liat (how'd the CAT-scan go, BTW?); last thing I want to do is make your life harder. You know how it goes when the deadline's coming down.

      Seriously, though, the sooner we can turn this one around, like ASAP, the better -- I think this one could really break us wide open. If you could get back to me by five with something, anything, I'd be really grateful. Thanks in advance.

      See you Sunday, either way,

      Soraya.

From: Max Holborn mhb@ca.inter.net
Date: Wednesday, June 25, 4:10 PM
To: Soraya Mousch sor16muse@walloflove.ca
Subject: Re: Apology followup

s.--

      cat-scan wasn't so great, tell you bout it later. got your file, i'm about to review. i'll im you when it's done.

      m.

TRANSCRIPT CHAT LOG
06/25/08 1626-1633

<max_hdb>: soraya? u there?
<sor16muse>: so whatd you think?
<max_hdb>: jesus soraya, w?t?f? who sent THIS in? even legal to show?
<max_hdb>: I didnt get into this to go to jail
<sor16muse>: message came in from a numbered gmail account, no sig – check out the file specs?
<sor16muse>: relax max – we didnt make it, no way anybody cn prove we did, got to be digital dupe of a tape loop
<max_hdb>: yeah, I lkd at specs – these guys know tricks I don't. u can mask creation datestamp in properties to make it LOOK blank, bt not supposed to be any way to actually wipe that data out without disabling file
<sor16muse>: my guess is the originals at least 50 yrs old
<sor16muse>: max, we cant NOT show this
<max_hdb>: gotta gt somebody to lk/@ it first – im not hanging my ass out in th/wind
<sor16muse>: why don't we meet @ laszlos? he can run it through his shit, see what pops

<max_hdb>: don't like him. his house smells like toilet mold,
	hes a freak
<sor16muse>: whatever, hes got the best film-to-flash
	download system in the city doesnt cost $500 daily
	rental, so just grow a fucking pair
<max_hdb>: you know he tapes every conversation goes on in
	there, right? wtf w/that?
<sor16muse>: (User sor16muse has disconnected)
<max_hdb>: and btw, next time you wanna show me shit like
	that try thinking about liat first
<max_hdb>: (User max_hdb has disconnected)

July 26/2009
"BACKGROUND MAN", Lescroat,
strangerthings.net/media
(cont'd)

"That original clip? Hands down, some of the scariest amateur shit I've ever seen in my life," says local indie critic/ promoter Alec Christian, self-proclaimed popularizer of the "Toronto Weird" low-budget horror culture movement. "A little bit of *Blair Witch* to it, obviously, but a lot more of early Nine Inch Nails videos, Jorg Buttgereit and Elias Merhige. That moment when you realize the guy's body is rotting in front of you? Pure *Der Todesking* reference, and you don't get those a lot, 'cause most of the people doing real-time horror are total self-taught illiterates about their own history."

Asked if there's any way the clip might be genuine, rather than staged, Christian laughs almost wistfully. "Some people still think *Blair Witch* was real; doesn't make it so," he points out. "Anyway, think about how hard it would be to shoot this using World War One technology and logistics, at the latest, which is what we'd be looking at if it was real—and if it was filmed later but aged to look older, then everything else could have been engineered as well. Sometimes you just have to go with common sense."

TRANSCRIPT EVIDENCE EXHIBIT #3 51 DIVISION
CASEFILE #332
RECOVERY LOCATION 42 TRINITY STREET BSMT
DATE 8/20/2008

Item: 89.2 MB .MPG file retrieved from hard drive of laptop SONY
VAIO X372 s/n 10352835A, prop. M. Holborn, duration 15m07s.

0:00 – (All images recorded in black-and-white monochrome.)
Caucasian male subject (Subject A), 40s, est. 6'1", 165 lbs, dark hair,
wearing black or brown suit appearing to be 1920s cut, shown sitting
in upright wooden chair looking directly at camera. Room is a single
chamber, est. 8' x 10', hardwood floor, one window behind subject,
one door in right-hand wall at rear. No painting or other decoration
visible on walls. Angle of light from window suggests filming began
early morning; light traverses screen in right-to-left direction,
suggesting southward facing of window and room. Unknown subject
has no discernible expression.
0:01-4:55 – Subject A rises and removes clothes, beginning with
detachable celluloid collar. Each garment removed separately, folded
and placed on floor. Care and placing of garment removal suggests
ritual purpose. Subject is shown to be uncircumcised. Subject
continues no discernible facial expression.
4:55-5:19 – Subject A resumes seat and looks straight into camera
without movement or speech. Enhanced magnification and review of
subject's right hand reveals indeterminate object, most likely taken
from clothing during removal.
5:20-5:23 – Subject A opens object in hand, demonstrating it to be a
straight razor. Subject cuts own throat in two angular incisions,
transverse to one another. Strength and immediacy of blood flow
indicates both carotid and jugular cut. Evenness and control of
movement suggests anesthesia or psychosis. Review by F/X
technicians confirms cuts too deep to have been staged without use of
puppets or animatronics. Subject maintains lack of facial expression.
5:23-6:08 – Subject A's self-exsanguination continues until
consciousness appears lost. Subject collapses in chair, head draped
over back.
6:09 – Estimated time of death for Subject A.
6:11 – Razor released from subject's fingers, drops to floor.
6:12 – 13:34 – Clip switches from real-time pacing to timelapse
speed, shown by rapidity of daylight movement and day-night

transitions. Reconstruction analysis specifies 87 24-hour periods elapse during this segment. Subject's body shown decomposing at accelerated pace.

7:22 – Primary liquefaction complete; dessication begins. Clothes left on floor have developed mold.

10:41 – Dessication largely complete. Rust visible on blade of razor. Fungal infestation on clothes has spread to floorboards.

13:10 – Subject's cranium detaches and falls to floor.

13:17 – Subject's right hand detaches and falls to floor.

13:25 – Subject's left arm detaches and falls to floor. Imbalance in weight causes remains of subject's body to fall off chair.

13:34 – Decomposition process complete. Footage resumes normal real-time pacing.

14:41 – Subject B walks into frame from behind camera P.O.V. Subject B's appearance 100% consistent in identity with initial Subject A, including lack of circumcision and identifiable body marks. Remains of Subject A still visible behind Subject B.

15:01 – Subject B bends down in front of camera and looks into it. Subject B shows no discernible facial expression.

15:06 – Subject B reaches above and behind camera viewpoint.

15:07 – CLIP ENDS

TRANSCRIPT EVIDENCE EXHIBIT #2 51 DIVISION
CASEFILE #332
RECOVERY LOCATION 532 OSSINGTON AVENUE BSMT
RESIDENCE LASZLO P HURT DATE 8/19/2008
AUDIOTAPE PROPERTY OF LASZLO P HURT

(IDENTIFICATION RETROACTIVELY ASSIGNED TO VOICES FOLLOWING CONFIRMATION FROM M HOLBORN AND S MOUSCH OF CONTENT)

V1 (MOUSCH): (LOUD) . . . see, here it is. Never see it if you weren't looking for it.

V2 (HOLBORN): (LOUD) Shit. He really does have his own place bugged. What's this for? Legal protection?

V1 (MOUSCH): (VOL. DECREASING) Maybe, but I think it's really just because he wants to. Like his whole life is a big cumulative performance art piece. Sort of like in that Robin Williams movie, where people have cameras in their heads, and

Robin has to cut a little film together when they die to sum up fifty years of experience?

V2 (HOLBORN): Yeah. That really sucked.

V1 (MOUSCH): I know. Just . . . keep it in mind, that's all I'm saying.

(BG NOISE: TOILET FLUSH)

V3 (HURT): Sorry about that. I haven't got new filters put in on the tapwater yet.

V2 (HOLBORN): That's . . . okay, Laszlo.

V3 (HURT): Yeah, you want some helpful input? Try not patronizing me.

V1 (MOUSCH): Laz, come on.

V3 (HURT): Yeah, okay, okay. So I reviewed your file.

V2 (HOLBORN): And?

V3 (HURT): First thing comes to mind is a story I heard through the post grapevine, one of those boojum-type obscurities the really crazy collectors go nuts trying to find. Though this can't be that, obviously, the clip would be way older, not digitized—

V1 (MOUSCH): People digitize old stuff all the time!

V3 (HURT): Really? Yeah, Soraya, I get that, actually; do it for a living, right? Look, the upshot is that you do have some deliberate image degradation going on here, so—

V2 (HOLBORN): I knew it, I knew it was a fake. Thank Christ.

V3 (HURT): I'm not finished. There is image degradation, but it wasn't done through any of the major editing programs; I've run your file through all of them and tested for the relevant coding, and this thing's about as raw as digicam gets. I'm betting whoever sent this to you digitized it the old brute-force way, like a movie pirate: Physically projected the thing, recorded it with a digital camera, saved it as your .mpeg, and sent it to you as is. Whatever the distortions are, they're either from that projection, or they were in the source clip all along.

V1 (MOUSCH): So . . . this could be a direct copy of that original clip you were talking about. The urban legend boojum.

V3 (HURT): Yeah, if you wanna buy into that shit.

V2 (HOLBORN): And when Laszlo Hurt tells you something's too weird to believe . . .

V1 (MOUSCH): Max, don't be a dick; Laz's doing us a favour. Right?

V2 (HOLBORN): Yeah, okay. Sorry.

V3 (HURT): (PAUSE) Way I heard, it goes back to this turn-of-the-century murderess called Tess Jacopo . . .

8/23/08 1902HRS
TRANSCRIPT SUSPECT INTERVIEW 51 DIVISION
CASEFILE #332
PRESIDING OFFICERS D. SUSAN CORREA 156232,
          D. ERIC VALENS 324820
SUBJECT MAXIM HOLBORN

D.VALENS: Jacopo. That was in Boston, in the 1900s—she was a Belle Gunness-type den mother killer, right? The female H.H. Holmes.
HOLBORN: Why am I not surprised you know this?
D.CORREA: Mr Holborn, please. Go on.
HOLBORN: The story isn't really about Jacopo herself. What happened was, this guy who'd been corresponding with Jacopo in prison, her stalker I guess he was, he managed to bribe a journalist who was on-site at her execution into stealing a copy of the official death-photo and selling it to him. Guess he wanted something to whack off with after she was gone. Anyway, a couple weeks later this guy's found in his flat, dead and swollen up, the Jacopo photo on his chest.
D.CORREA: How did he die?
HOLBORN: I don't think it matters. The point is, somebody there took a photo of the photo, and that became one of the biggest murder memorabilia items of the 20th century. You know these guys, right— kinda weirdos who buy John Wayne Gacy's clown pictures, shell out thousands to get Black Dahlia screen-test footage, 'cause they think they'll unearth some lost snuff movie they can show all their friends . . .
D.VALENS: I'm not seeing what this has to do with your film clip, Mr. Holborn.
HOLBORN: Okay. This is where the urban legend kicks in. See, Jacopo's mask slipped a bit during the hanging, so you can just barely see a sliver of her eyeball, and the story says if you blow up and enhance the photo like a hundred times original size, you're supposed to be able to see in the eyeball the reflection of what she was looking at when she died. Like an asphyx.
D.VALENS: Ass-what?
HOLBORN: It's the word the Greeks used for the last image that gets burned on a murdered person's retina, like a last little fragment of their soul or life-force getting trapped there.
D.CORREA: And under sufficient magnification, you're supposed to be able to see this?
HOLBORN: "Supposed to," yeah. Thing is, everyone who ever tried this, who actually tried blowing up their copy of the Jacopo photo?

Went nuts or died. Unless they burned their photo before things got too bad. That's supposed to be why it's impossible to find any copies.
D.CORREA: Why? What did they see?
HOLBORN: How the fuck should I know? It's a spook story. Maybe they saw themselves looking back at themselves, whatever. The point is . . . it's not about what those people saw, or didn't. It's about the kind of voyeuristic obsession you need to go that deep into this shit. And Laszlo said that was what the clip reminded him of. Somebody trying to make some kind of, of—"mind-bomb," was the term. An image that'd scar you so badly, the mere act of passing it on would be enough to always keep its power alive.
D.CORREA: Uh . . . why?
HOLBORN: Excellent question. Isn't it?

From: Liat Holborn <liath@ca.inter.net>
Date: Thursday, July 3, 10:25 AM
To: Soraya Mousch <sor16muse@walloflove.ca>
Subject: Max and me

Dear Soraya,
        I was talking to Max last night about how we're going to try to handle the next few months, and it came out that for whatever reason, Max still hadn't filled you in completely on our situation. I think he finds it pretty tough to talk about, even to you. Upshot is, the last CAT-scan showed I have an advanced cranial tumour, and Dr. Lalwani thinks there's a very good chance it could be gliomal, which (skipping all the medico-babble) is about the least good news we could get. Apparently, it's too deep for surgery, so the only option we have is for me to go into a majorly heavy chemo program ASAP. So I'm going to be spending a lot of time in St. Michael's, starting real soon now.
        My folks've volunteered to foot a lot of the bill, which is great, but poor Max is feeling kind of humiliated at needing the help – and of course he totally can't complain about it, which just makes it gall him even more. The reason I'm telling you all this is because (a) I want the pressure of keeping this a secret to be off Max, and (b) I know how much you depend on Max this time of year, and I don't want you to think he's bailing on you if he has to take time out for me, or that he's finally gotten fed up with you, the Wall of Love, or your work.

(Actually, I'm pretty sure the festival's the only thing that's kept him stable this past little while. I hope you know how much I appreciate the support you give him.)

Could you show this e-mail to Max when you get a chance, and apologize to him for me when he blows his top at my big mouth? :) He doesn't feel he can shout at me any more about anything, obviously. But I really think things'll be easier once all the cards are on the table.

Thanks so much for your help, Soraya. Come by and see me soon – I want you to get some photos of me before I have to ditch the hair.

Much love and God bless,
Liat

P.S.: BTW, I'm also totally fine with accidentally seeing that thing you sent Max, that file or whatever, so tell him that, okay? *Impress it* on him. He seems to think it "injured" me somehow – on top of everything else. Which is just ridiculous.

I have more than enough real things to worry about right now, you know?
– L.

8/23/08 1928HRS
TRANSCRIPT SUSPECT INTERVIEW 51 DIVISION
CASEFILE #332
PRESIDING OFFICERS D. SUSAN CORREA 156232,
        D. ERIC VALENS 324820
SUBJECT MAXIM HOLBORN

HOLBORN: We were on about the third or fourth draft of the final mix when we started splicing in the clip—
D.VALENS: Splicing? I thought you said this was purely electronic.
HOLBORN: It is, it's just the standard term for—look, do you want me to explain or not?
D.CORREA: We do. Please. Go on.
HOLBORN: We broke the clip up into segments and spliced it in among the rest of the film in chunks; we were even going to try showing some shots on just the edge of subliminal, like three or four frames out of twenty-four. This was a few weeks ago, beginning of August. And then it started happening.

D.CORREA: What started, Max?

HOLBORN: The guy. From the clip. He started . . . appearing . . . in other parts of the film.

D.VALENS: Somebody spliced in more footage? Repeats?

HOLBORN: No, goddammit, he started popping up in pieces of footage that were already in the film! Stuff we'd gotten like weeks before, from people who never even saw the clip or knew about it. Like that performance art piece in Hyde Park? Guy walks by in the background a minute into the clip. Or the subway zombie ride, you look right at the far end of the car, there he is sitting down, and you know it's him 'cause he's the only one not wearing any clothes. This was stuff nobody ever shot, man! Changing in front of our fucking eyes! Christ, I saw him show up in one segment—I ran it to make sure it was clear, ran it again right away and he was just fucking there, like he'd always been in the frame. The extras were fucking walking around him . . .

(FIVE SECOND PAUSE)

D.CORREA: Could it have been some kind of computer virus? Something that came in with your original video file and reprogrammed the files it was spliced into?

HOLBORN: Are you shitting me?!

D.VALENS: Dial it back, Holborn. Right—now.

HOLBORN: Okay, sorry, but—no. CGI like that takes hours to render on a system ten times the size of mine, and that's for every single appearance. A virus carrying that kinda programming would be fifty times bigger than the file it rode in on and wouldn't run on my system anyway.

Besides, it kept getting worse. He didn't just show up in new segments, he'd take more and more prominent places in segments he'd already, corrupted, I guess? Goes from five seconds in the background to two minutes in the medium frame. I'd get people to resend me their submissions, I'd splice 'em in to replace the old ones and inside of a minute he's back in the action. It was like the faster we tried to cut him out the harder he worked at—I don't know—entrenching himself.

ERROR MESSAGE
404 Not Found

The webpage you were trying to access ("http://www.kerato-oblation.org/cadavrexquis") is no longer available. It may have been removed by the user or suspended by administrators for terms-of-use violation. Contact your ISP for more information.

TRANSCRIPT CHAT LOG
08/07/08 0344-0346

<sor16muse>: max, wtf
<sor16muse>: the sites gone. like GONE
<sor16muse>: did u do that? ur only other one w/password
<sor16muse>: wtf max, were supposed 2 b live tomorrow
                    WHY
<sor16muse>: u there?
<sor16muse>: max, u there? need 2 talk.
<sor16muse>: laz sez he maybe has an idea who sent the file,
                    and why. need 2
<max_hdb>: im not going 2 b here, back
<max_hdb>: don't know when.
<max_hdb>: liat had episode. bad. in hosp. st mikes.
<max_hdb>: u ever want 2 talk in person, that's where ill b.
<max_hdb>: (User max_hdb has disconnected)
<sor16muse>: (User sor16muse has disconnected)

8/23/08 1937HRS
TRANSCRIPT SUSPECT INTERVIEW 51 DIVISION
CASEFILE #332
PRESIDING OFFICERS D. SUSAN CORREA 156232,
          D. ERIC VALENS 324820
SUBJECT MAXIM HOLBORN

D.VALENS: So who was that guy? In the film?
HOLBORN: No idea. It's not like he—
D.CORREA: And what's it got to do with Tess Jacopo?
HOLBORN: Nothing, directly. But it's like Internet memes, man; Laszlo understood that. Stuff gets around. Maybe this guy heard about

the thing with the photo, and thought: Oh hey, wonder how that'd work with a moving picture. Maybe he just stumbled across the concept all on his lonesome, or by accident: I don't know. But . . . he did it.

D.VALENS: Did what, Holborn?

HOLBORN: He put himself in there. Made himself an asphyx.

D.CORREA: So he could live forever.

HOLBORN: Yeah. Maybe. Or maybe just . . . so he could . . . not die. Maybe—

(TEN SECOND PAUSE)

HOLBORN: Maybe he was sick. Like, really sick. Or sick in the head. Or both. Maybe it just seemed like a good idea, given the alternative. At the time.

D.CORREA: So what did happen to the Wall of Love mainframe, Max?

HOLBORN: I crashed it. (BEAT) I mean—I told people there was a big Avid crash and the whole server got wiped . . . actually, I used a magnet. Like Dean Winchester in that "Ghostfacers!" 'Supernatural' episode.

D.VALENS: What?

HOLBORN: Doesn't matter. Ask me why.

D.CORREA: . . . why?

HOLBORN: Because I thought maybe I could trap him there, like he must have trapped himself inside that loop. Because he probably didn't think about that, right? When he was doing it. How it wasn't likely anybody was really going to watch that sort of shit, once they figured out what it was, let alone show it in public. How probably it would just end up left in the can, passed from collector to collector, never really watched at all, except by one person at a time. One . . . very disturbed . . . other person.

I thought I could stop him from going any further, so I crashed my own mainframe, without telling Soraya. But . . .

D.VALENS: . . . it didn't work.

HOLBORN: Well. Would I even be here, if it did?

CYBER-CRIME OFFICE,
TORONTO POLICE SERVICE 51 DIVISION
EXCERPTED REPORT
DETECTIVE LEWIS McMASTER (CYBERCRIME) SUPERVISING
DETECTIVES ERIC VALENS, SUSAN CORREA (HOMICIDE)
CONTRIBUTING
Casefile #332: Notes

INITIAL CONTACT:
Aug 14 2008 – CyberCrime received anonymous email sent from
Hotmail account created that morning, with copy of "suicide guy"
.mpg attached. Flagged as "harmful matter". Email noted .mpg was
sent to kerato-oblation.org as experimental film clip submission;
identified source of original message, webmail address
11235813@gmail.com.
[Hotmail account eventually traced through Internet café to Laszlo
Hurt, known member of local Toronto "collector" circuit; Hurt now
missing, presumed deceased based on evidence found in subject's
apartment. —EV, SC]

INVESTIGATION:
August 15 – Flagged file screened and sent for forensic analysis, results
inconclusive. Source of original submission email traced to Google-
owned server in Newark, New Jersey, United States of America.
August 16 – Established contact with Detective Herschel Gohan of
Newark CyberCrime Unit, who persuaded server admins to cooperate
with investigation; message back-tracked and triangulated to establish
physical location and address of originator machine. Address is
confirmed as unit #B325 of E-Z-SHELF storage locker facility, 1400
South Woodward Lane, Newark. Facility manager, Mr. Silvio Galbi,
provides name of renter ("John Smith"), confirms unit prepaid for six
months with cash. Mr. Galbi refuses to cooperate with search request
without a warrant.
August 18 – Warrant issued for search and seizure operation at 1400
South Woodward, Unit #B325, by Judge Harriet Lindstrom. Operation
executed under supervision of Detective Gohan. Contents of unit as
follows:

    1. Unclothed body of unidentified male, Caucasian, est.
    premortem age mid-20s, seated on floor in pool of waste.
    2. One (1) empty film canister.
    3. One (1) 35mm film projector, set up to project upon unit
    interior wall.
    4. One (1) 35mm film reel mounted in projector, est. 15
    minutes in length, confirmed on-site to be original of
    transmitted .mpg file.
    5. One (1) white cotton sheet at base of same interior wall;
    tape on corners indicates sheet was hung on wall.
    6. One (1) SONY video camera, with tripod, set up focused on
    same interior wall.

7. One (1) TV monitor, with built-in VCR and DVD player.
8. One (1) DELL laptop computer, with built-in wi-fi modem.
9. One (1) Coleman oil lantern, fuel supply depleted.
10. Pile of empty water bottles.
11. One (1) Black & Decker emergency brand power generator.
12. Fifty (50) gallon gasoline containers, empty.
13. Two (2) six-socket power bar outlets.
14. One (1) tube-gun of industrial caulking sealant.
15. One (1) journal with handwritten notes.

Galbi confirms he accepted illegal payment to lock unit on "Smith's" written instructions without confirming contents, in violation of state safety and insurance regulations. Galbi arrested and cited.

FORENSICS:
Examination of laptop hard drive reveals series of webcam captures which suggest basic chronology of events as follows:

1. Unidentified male (UM) arrives in unit roughly two weeks before email sent to kerato-oblation.org.
2. UM uses video camera to record digital copy of original film reel from wall projection (distortion visible in .mpg file caused by loose fabric in sheet).
3. UM uses laptop to program recorded file into continuous video loop on DVD.
4. UM arranges laptop and webcam to face DVD monitor, setting DVD on continuous play and webcam on indefinite record.
5. UM remains seated in front of monitor for majority of remaining time, urinating and defecating in place. Time-signatures confirm he created .mpg file, wrote submission email, then waited until death was imminent to send it, on date above.
6. Final action of UM on morning of death was to use sealant gun to caulk up door, rendering unit virtually airtight. This prevented odors from escaping unit, and retarded decomposition by hindering evaporation of fluids from the body.

AUTOPSY:
Body shows no sign of struggle or restraint. Autopsy reveals primary cause of death as oxygen deprivation, aggravated by starvation and dehydration. Probable date of death on or around June 25 2008 (date

on which .mpg file was sent to kerato-oblation.org). Corneas of victim preserved by airtight environment, and found to be deformed on both exterior and interior surfaces, damage suggesting both physical and heat trauma to tissue. Computer reconstruction of deformation suggests artificial origin, as pattern appears to portray a fixed image: the face of suicide victim in original film, in close-up still frame. Pathologists unable to establish cause or method of corneal deformation.

RECOMMENDATIONS:
Unidentified male's selection of Holborn/Mousch as recipients suggests foreknowledge, possible contact. Recommend either Holborn or Mousch be brought in for further questioning.

From: Det. Herschel Gohan <hgohan@newarkpolice.gov>
Date: Thursday, August 21, 7:20 AM
To: Det. Lewis McMaster <lewis.mcmaster@torpolservices.net>
Subject: Notification: Evidence compromise

Lewis —
     Bad news. We had a fire in our station evidence locker last night; looks like some meth really past its sell-by date may have spontaneously cooked off. Nobody hurt, but we lost some critical evidence on a number of cases, including, sorry to say, your film-nut-in-the-storage-unit material. The film reel's melted, the laptop motherboard is gone, and most of the other equipment's unusable now. I've attached .jpgs to document the losses; I'm hoping this'll be enough for your dept. to maintain provenance on your own stuff.
     Sorry again; call me if you need to know anything not covered by the pictures.
     — Herschel

8/23/08 1928HRS
TRANSCRIPT SUSPECT INTERVIEW 51 DIVISION
CASEFILE #332
PRESIDING OFFICERS D. SUSAN CORREA 156232,
        D. ERIC VALENS 324820
SUBJECT MAXIM HOLBORN

HOLBORN: So I went home after crashing the mainframe, and I didn't go upstairs, because I thought my wife was asleep. And I wanted to let her sleep, because . . . she'd been in pretty bad shape, you know? She'd only just finished her chemo, she hadn't gotten a lot of . . . sleep . . .

But then I turned on TCM, to relax, and they were playing Richard Burton's adaptation of 'Dr. Faustus,' which was made the year before I was born, and—in the scene in the Vatican? Where Faustus is throwing pies at the Pope? I saw him. That guy.

Stuck around, kept watching; the next film was from 1944, and he was in it too. In the background, until—it was like—he notices me watching him. Turns and smiles at me, raises his eyebrow, starts —coming closer.

I swear to God, I jumped back. If Cagney hadn't been in the way—

And then it was Silent Sunday, some all-night Chaplin retrospective, and . . . yeah. There, too.

Everywhere.

So . . .

D.VALENS: Obviously not.

HOLBORN: Obviously.

[TEN SECOND PAUSE]

HOLBORN: My wife wasn't asleep, either, by the way. Just in case you were wondering.

D.VALENS: Aw, what the fuck—

D.CORREA: Shut up, Eric. [To HOLBORN] Look, you can't be serious, that's all. Are we supposed to believe—

HOLBORN: I don't give a fuck what you believe. Seriously.

D.CORREA: Okay. So what about the disappearance of Laszlo Hurt?

[FIFTEEN SECOND PAUSE]

HOLBORN: I don't know anything about that.

D.VALENS: And again: We should believe you on this . . . why?

[FIFTEEN SECOND PAUSE]

D.CORREA: Mister Holborn?

HOLBORN: . . . you know, I don't know if you guys know this or not, but . . . my wife? Just died. So, in the immortal words of every 'Law And Order' episode ever filmed—charge me with something, or let me go. Or fuck the fuck off.

From: gmail@ca.geocities.mail.com
Date: Saturday, August 16, 9:45 PM
To: Soraya Mousch <sor16muse@walloflove.ca>
Subject: RE: LASZLO ANSWER ME

Hi. This is the administrator at gmail@geocities.com (00:15:32:A3)
Delivery of your message to {lazhurt@geocities.com} failed
after <15> attempts. Address not recognized by system.
      This is a permanent error; I've given up.

>Laszlo, it's Soraya, would you CALL ME PLEASE? I've left
>about twenty messages on your voicemail, Max and I have a big
>problem and we need your HELP! Where the fuck are you?
>Call me!
>S.

From: <help@geocities.com>
Date: Monday, August 18, 8:55 AM
To: Soraya Mousch <sor16muse@walloflove.ca>
Subject: RE: Account Tracking Request

Dear Ms. Mousch,
      Sorry it took us so long to get back to you; we get a lot
of backlog on weekends. I'm afraid I have to admit we're
stumped on this one. I personally went through our server
records day by day over the registration period you specified,
and as far as I can tell, we have no record whatsoever of a
"Laszlo Hurt" on our roster. I've checked under the "lazhurt",
"laszloslabyrinth", and "hurtmedia" addresses and their variants,
as well as with our billing department, and there's just no
indication that this Mr. Hurt was ever a Geocities user.
      I realize this may be an unwelcome explanation, but it
sounds to me like you may have been a victim of an attempted
phishing scam using dummy-mask addresses. I'd get your
computer checked for viruses and malware right away.
      Again, I'm sorry we couldn't be more help.
      Best regards,
      Jamil Chandrasekhar
      Geocities.com Tech Support

From: Soraya Mousch <sor16muse@walloflove.ca>
Date: Saturday, August 23, 11:01 PM
To: Max Holborn <mhb@ca.inter.net>
Subject: Blank

Max, I'm just so sorry.
      – S.

YOUR COMFORT SOUGHT
IN THIS TIME OF GRIEF

With sorrow we announce the passing of Liat Allyson
Meester-Holborn on August 23, 2008, beloved daughter of
Aaron and Rachel Meester and wife of Maxim Holborn.

Funeral service to be held at
St. Mary's Star of the Sea Catholic Church,
8 Elizabeth Avenue, Port Credit, Mississauga
Tuesday August 26, 11:00 A.M.

Commemorative reception
to be held at the Meester residence,
1132 Walden Road #744, 3:00 P.M.
Confirmations only

From: Max Holborn <mhb@ca.inter.net>
Date: Tuesday, September 2, 2:31 AM
To: Soraya Mousch <sor16muse@walloflove.ca>
Subject: look closer

s.–
        hospital released the file on liat to me today. was going
over it. couldn't sleep. found something.
        the attached .jpg's a scan of the last x-ray they took, just
before she crashed out. look at the upper right quarter, just up and
right of where ribs meet breastbone. then do a b-w negative
reverse on the image in your photoshop, and look again.

it's not a glitch. it's not me fucking with you. look at it. call me.

– m.

SURVEILLANCE TRANSCRIPT 14952, CASEFILE #332
9/19/08 2259H-2302H 416-[REDACTED] TO 416-[REDACTED]
WARRANT AUTHORIZED HON. R. BORCHERT 9/9/08

(CONNECTION INITIATED)
MOUSCH: Hello?
HOLBORN: You never answered my e-mail.
MOUSCH: What did you want me to say? I read it, I looked at the scans you sent. That . . . could be anything, Max. A glitch in the machine, some lab tech sticking his hand on the negative—
HOLBORN: Soraya—
MOUSCH: —and even if it's not, what's it matter? What difference can it make? (PAUSE) I'm sorry, Max. I didn't—I'm sorry.
HOLBORN: Uh huh.
(PAUSE)
HOLBORN: So . . . I hear you put your stuff up on eBay. Going Luddite?
MOUSCH: Well, uh . . . no, I'm just switching disciplines. Going non-visual. Film's . . . all played out, y'know? I mean, you've noticed that.
HOLBORN: Yup. Good luck, I guess. (BEAT) Everything just back to normal, huh?
MOUSCH: . . . hardly . . .
HOLBORN: You really think any of this is gonna help? Dropping anything with a lens like it's hot, cocooning?
MOUSCH: I don't . . .
HOLBORN: You remember what I told you, at the hospital?
(FIVE SECOND PAUSE)
MOUSCH: . . . I remember.
HOLBORN: That guy killed my wife, Soraya. Just because she saw him—over my shoulder, right? When she didn't even know what she was looking at. She's fucking dead.
MOUSCH: Liat's dead because she had a tumor, Max. Nothing we did made Liat die.
HOLBORN: What do you think he's going to end up doing to us, Soraya? After he's fucking well done with everybody else?
MOUSCH: Look . . . Look, Max, Christ. Liat, Laszlo, even that crazy fucking moron dude who made the clip in the first place, let alone sent it

to us . . . (BEAT) And why would he even do that, anyway? To, what . . . ?
HOLBORN: I don't know. Spread the disease, maybe. Like he got
tired of watching it himself, thought everybody else should have a
crack at it, too . . .
(FIVE SECOND PAUSE)
MOUSCH: I mean . . . it's not our fault, right? Any of it. We didn't
ask for—
HOLBORN: —uh, no, Soraya. We did. Literally. We asked, threw it
out into the ether: Send us your shit. Show us something. We asked
. . . and he answered.
MOUSCH: Who, "he"? Clip-making dude?
HOLBORN: You know that's not who I'm talking about.
(TEN SECOND PAUSE)
HOLBORN: So, anyhow, 'bye. You're going dark, and I'm dropping
off the map. I'd say "see you," but—
MOUSCH: Oh, Max, Goddamn . . .
HOLBORN: —I'm really hoping . . . not.
(CONNECTION TERMINATED)

OFFICE OF FORENSICS
TORONTO POLICE SERVICE 51 DIVISION
EXCERPTED REPORT
Casefile #332

Final analysis of X-ray images taken of Liat Holborn (dcsd) shows no
known cause of observed photographic anomaly. Hand-digit
comparison was conducted on all possible candidates, including
Maxim Holborn, attending physician Dr. Raj Lalwani, attending nurse
Yvonne Delacoeur, and X-ray technician John Li Cheng: no match
found. Dr. Lalwani maintains statement that cause of death for Liat
Holborn was gliomal tumour. Conclusion: Photographic anomaly is
spontaneous malfunction, resemblance to intact human hand
coincidental.

Following lack of forensic connection between Maxim
Holborn and Site of Death 1, and failure to establish viable suspect,
this office recommends suspension of Case #332 from active
investigation at this time, pending further evidence.

July 26/2009
"BACKGROUND MAN", Lescroat,
strangerthings.net/media
(cont'd)

One year later, the crash which brought kerato-oblation.org/
cadavrexquis down—melting the server and destroying a
seventy-four minute installation cobbled together from random
.mpg snippets e-mailed in from contributors all over the world
—has yet to be fully explained, by either Wall of Love founder.
While Mousch cited simple overcrowding and editing program
fatigue for the project's collapse, Holborn—already under
stress when Kerato-Oblation got underway, due to his wife's
battle with brain cancer—has been quoted on Alec Christian's
blog as blaming a slightly more supernatural issue: a
mysterious figure who appeared first in an anonymously-
submitted pieces of digital footage, then eventually began
popping up in the backgrounds of other . . . completely
unrelated . . . sections. Background Man? Impossible to confirm
or deny, without Holborn's help.

Still, sightings of a naked man wearing "red" around
his neck wandering through the fore-, back- and midground of
perfectly mainstream movies, TV shows and musics videos
continue to abound. Recent internet surveys chart at least
five major recent blockbusters (besides *Mother of Serpents*)
and three primetime television series rumored to have
inadvertently showcased the figure.

At the moment, the (highly unlikely) possibility of pan-
studio collaboration on a vast alternate-reality game remains
unresolved, while at least three genuine missing persons
reports are rumored to be connected with a purported
Background Man personal encounter IRL. The meme, if meme
it is, continues to spread.

Neither Mousch nor Holborn could be reached for
comment on this article.

————————————————————

. . . and up they come—
(the dead)
Crawling through the hole with their pale hands
bloody from digging, their blind eyes tight-shut and their
wide-open mouths full of mud: Nameless, faceless, groping
for anything that happens across their path. With no easy end
to their numbers . . .
(For once such a door is opened, who will shut it
again? Who is there—
—alive—
—that can?)
No end to their numbers, or their need: The dead, who
are never satisfied. The dead, who cannot be assuaged.
The dead, who only want but no longer know what, or
from who, or why. Or just how much, over just how long—
here in their hole which goes on and down forever, where time
itself slows so much it no longer has any real value—
—can ever be enough.

OPEN THE DOOR AND THE LIGHT POURS THROUGH

Kelly Barnhill

WHAT HE WROTE:
My dearest Angela,

I have spent weeks dreading what we must do today, and even as I write this, I am not entirely convinced that it is right. We are, and have been, and will be for the foreseeable future, overrun with soldiers, which is to say, *our dear American guests*. (Which is worse, love, their public drunkenness, or their incessant leering?) Far better, my darling, that you should be far away from this nursery of convalescing men, and far from the multitudes of explosives that spin like vultures in the sky. London will be flattened before the year is up, if the rumors are true. How could we not be next?

My family members, yes, are tiresome. The house, yes, is drafty and unpleasant. But the grounds are lovely. And if you cannot paint the sea, perhaps you could paint the wood. Or paint the sea from memory. Or paint me from memory. Or

paint a memory of me. Dear god, my girl, but I shall miss you.
Ever yours,
John

WHAT HE DID NOT:
W   John watched the train wait at the platform with Angela's pale, lovely, and utterly petulant face framed by the greasy window. She would forgive him in time, of course. She always did. And for the things that she did not know, she had no need to forgive.

The train shuddered, then rumbled, then slid out of sight. John stood still, watching the empty space where Angela's face once was, as though a shadow of his wife was still hung in the air, like a ghost. Unaccountably, he shuddered and his skin was damp and icy cold. He breathed in, deeply, through his nose, luxuriating in the smell of oil and smoke, and faintly, he was certain, the smell of lavender and lilac that was ever his wife.

He missed her.

And yet, he did not.

Shivering again, he rubbed his arms briskly with his long, narrow hands. Hands that were meant to entertain; fingers that could coax music from reluctant instruments and a sigh from hesitant lovers. Hands that now produced documents, perfectly accurate and deadly quick, for his superiors in the RAF. His instruments lay untouched and abandoned in the music room. His lovers—well, that was a different story.

He turned and headed out of the station.

The day was fine again, the fifth in a string of fine days, with a warm sun set in a cool blue sky with a bracing wind coming up over the water. The Promenade was beset, as usual, with soldiers—big, strong jawed Americans with their strange shimmer and stink, their arms weighted by simpering girls. There were English soldiers too, but by comparison they were pale, worn, their edges fraying to dust and light. And they were without women.

He cut through the gardens into a street of row houses followed by innumerable streets with innumerable row houses. A man stood framed between a doorway and a shuttered window, leaning against the house. The door was red, the shutters, green. The man was trim and pale and *clean.* He shimmered. He did not smell like lilacs or lavender. And yet. John approached the man and leaned where he leaned. The bricks were warm and solid. They smelled of sun and oil and smoke. Without a word, they both slipped inside the red door and disappeared.

In the weeks that followed, John tried to piece together the events following the departure of his wife, though for the life of him, he could not. He did not know how long he leaned. Similarly, he did not know how long he had been inside. A gentleman does not, after all, keep time in such circumstances. Nevertheless, over the course of the late morning and early afternoon, the wind increased, and began to rattle at the windows, at the plaster, at the door. Later, John heard the sound of moaning. And whether the moaning was the wind or the lover or something else entirely, John could never be sure.

Until he was. And by then, it was too late to do anything about it.

W*HAT SHE WROTE:*
Dear John,

It was a disaster, my love, and it was all your fault. When one travels, one should be rested and fresh, and am neither (and I believe you know why, you naughty man). As you suggested, I had my sketchbook on my lap, and prepared myself to draw my last images of the sea before I was delivered to that den of stuffy rooms and tiresome conversation that is the place of your birth, but instead of a picture, all I have are the first intimations of wind before my hand drifted to the side of the page and I drifted to sleep. So the sketch is ruined, the painting is ruined, and you, dear husband, are dreadful.

To make it worse, I missed my stop at Westhoughton, as I was fast asleep, dreaming of you (my love, you wretch). The train stopped with a terrific jolt just outside of Bolton, in view of the station, though not pulled in. Whether it was a faulty engine, or that we simply ran out of fuel, I do not know. No one could say. In fact, no one spoke to me at all. The other passengers milled about outside of the train for some time, muttering, the lot of them, like idiots. I marched myself to the desk and attempted to ring the bell, which did not ring, and I immediately began to hate the war. Now in addition to sugar and jam and beef, we must also, apparently, give up bells. And I, the sea; and you, your wife.

What will be next?

The man did not turn away from his telephone as I tried to talk to him, and instead just jabbered endlessly about the train. What was there to say about the train? It didn't work, clearly, and it had, evidently, devoured my trunk.

A kindly man with a truck agreed to give me a lift, though he did not speak either, deaf and dumb, poor man. But I listened as the station guard gave him directions to Westhoughton, and then repeated the directions, not once but three times, the poor, dear simpleton, and then wrote them all out. So I sat next to him on the cart as we drove. He never once glanced upon me—I daresay he is little used to female companions, so I drew his portrait for him and left it on the seat with a note. I assume he liked it, because as I walked down the track to your infernal mother's house, I could hear him weeping. Weeping like a child.

As I wept. *Then.* When we were children. How strange that I should think of that now!

Forever yours,

Angela

W*HAT SHE DID NOT:*
      She should have been thinking of greetings and directions. But as she walked down the well-trod track that led to the dark hulk of her mother-in-law's family home, she barely noticed where her feet touched the earth. For all she knew, they might not have touched the earth at all. What she did notice was memory. A memory so sharp it pricked her tongue. After a while, she tasted blood—a cool, sharp and sour taste in her mouth, like light and shadow blurring into one.

      When Angela was a child, John spent the summers at her family's home, as their parents were all musicians and spent the summers playing endlessly in the garden. John, being four years her senior, had little time for Angela the child, and spent most waking hours in the company of her elder brother, James, who, some years later died of pneumonia while a student at Oxford.

      One summer, however, when the boys were thirteen and Angela was nearly nine, James had taken ill with a fever and could not be seen for two weeks. Angela found John in the library, pouring over a stack of books. Angela the child sat next to John and patted him on the thigh. John rolled his eyes and made a pretense of pouring more heavily into his book.

      "What are you doing?" she asked.

      "Watching," he said, not looking up from the page.

      "Watching what?" she asked.

      "Ghosts," he said, turning the page. In later years, Angela would come to know John's expression of aggressive not-looking as one of his signature methods of avoiding unpleasant conversations. But she was young and bored and had not learned to hate anything. Not yet.

      "What ghosts?" she asked.

      John sighed deeply and rolled his eyes again. He shut the book with an impatient snap and looked at the little girl, a malicious glint in his thirteen-year-old eyes. "Well, it's an old house, isn't it? The older the house the more spirits haunting it. Thought everybody knew that."

"I don't believe you," she said. Her voice wobbled. She swallowed and bravely set her chin as she met his eye.

"Well, it's a true as I'm sitting here. Look around you. You can see 'em trapped in every window."

Angela looked up. She saw them. *Saw them.* In each window stood a face—pale, dark eyed and livid. Each with a pink slash for a mouth. Each with seaweed hair and seafoam skin. Each moving softly, as though underwater. Angela screamed and covered her face with her hands. She wept for each face, each pink mouth. She wept for things lost and forgotten and for something else that she could not name. John laughed loudly, with gusto, and slapped Angela hard on the back as though they were both men.

"Poor little idiot," John said both kindly and unkindly. He glanced up at the windows. He saw nothing, expected nothing, and assumed, condescendingly, that an overactive imagination was the source of the tears. "Poor little thing." He kissed the top of her head, turned and left the room, still laughing. The door shut with a hollow click.

The ghosts remained in the windows for the rest of the day. Only Angela saw. She shut her eyes when she could and stared at the floor when she could not. Her parents thought she was ill and sent her to bed.

The next day, Angela started to paint. She painted faithfully every day thereafter, often for hours at a time. That same day, upon seeing Angela smeared with graphite and paint and dust, concentrating mightily on the page, John decided that she would one day be his wife.

She was, he said, the only girl for him.

It was mostly true.

W*HAT he wrote:*
My darling,

I set out today, prepared to be cross. Deeply cross, if you must know. When the post arrived, I tore through the stack of envelopes looking for the clean, sure stroke of your most beloved hand and found it was nowhere to be seen. Is this, I asked, what a devoted husband should expect from his wayward wife?

In the meantime, Mrs. Wooten at the teashop, scolded me this morning for not sending my beautiful wife away from this unholy den of lusty soldiers.

—They pant after her like dogs, the poor little lamb, she said, smacking her wooden spoon upon the counter with a deafening crack.

—My dear lady, said I, I sent her to my mother's house not three days ago.

She did not believe me, of course, and insisted on calling me everything from a horse's ass to a fiend-of-a-man, unworthy of the angel who is my Angela. She insisted that she had seen you just that morning, sitting in your chair by the sea, painting a landscape of wind. She said that your hair was undone and you had a carpetbag at your feet.

And just as I was about to speak ill of you my dear, I placed my hand in my pocket and withdrew your letter. How it came to be there, I'm sure I don't know, but I assume I must have slipped it in without even thinking. Oh, to see your lettering, my love! Oh to hold the paper once held by your dear fingers. Perhaps this is what happens when we force the artist into the office instead of the studio—a weakened mind, my dear. I do hope you'll forgive me for it.

Mrs. Wooten, I'm glad to say, was pacified, my darling. And so am I.

Ever yours,
John.

WHAT HE DID NOT:
Although he had offers for company the previous night, he opted to sleep alone. The wind continued to hiss at the windowpane and insinuate itself between the cracks. The

brass bed beneath him creaked and whined each time he shivered. Eight times he attempted to sleep. Eight times he slept, though briefly and not well. Eight times he woke to a dream of Angela. Angela, seated by the sea, her hair undone and sailing like tremulous notes in an insistent breeze. Angela, whose long fingers were brought to her mouth as she puzzled over her paints. Angela, whose head was cocked curiously to the side, listening to a far away sound of twisting metal and dying engines—the percussive slap of compressed explosives hurtling themselves into the sky. She listened as though hearing music. A smile played upon her pale pink lips. John woke in tears. He did not know why.

*W*HAT SHE WROTE:
Dearest John,

It is official. Your mother is not speaking to me. I do not know what I have done to offend her, but whatever it is, will you please inform her that it is your fault, and I, as usual, am blameless. I arrived last night in the dark and though I knocked endlessly, the house was silent. So, like a thief, I entered your mother's home by stealth and settled into your old room. The next morning, at breakfast, I greeted your mother and sat down across from her. She ate her egg and sipped her tea—she *hoards* it you know—and said nothing. I was dying for tea. *Dying* for it, darling. Yet no place was set, no breakfast called for. I was glad to see that dear old Charles was still in her employ, though he did not speak to me either —doubtless, on his mistress's orders. Once, I tilted my head in an utterly charming way and fluttered my fingers towards him. He looked at me then, managed to raise his eyebrows in hello before turning quite white and staring at the ground.

—Everything all right, Charles? Your mother said with toast in her mouth.

—Fine, madam, Charles whispered. I wondered if he was trying not to laugh.

And your mother said—Would you be so kind as to ring my son, I'd like to speak to him.

—Speak to him, *indeed*, I shouted (yes, dear, I *shouted*. But honestly what would you have done?) but your mother ignored me.

—It is not possible, madam, Charles said. There was some amount of trouble last night and the lines are down. Your mother asked what sort of trouble, and of course, Charles did not know. No one knows anything anymore; we just soldier on like good little Britons. *You* might know, of course.

Do you?

Ever Yours,

Angela

*W*HAT SHE DID NOT:

The only room with proper light was the music room, so she carried her sketchbook and carpetbag to the third floor, stopping at the dumb waiter and placing a note which read, "Tea and sustenance to the music room at ten o'clock, if you please," and sending it on its way.

Each morning, a large rectangle of sunlight brightened half the room and fell, like silk, to the ground. When Angela visited as a child, she would position her body just so within the rectangle, and listen to their parents play while enjoying the sensation of the sun on her skin—the press and weight of light. She sometimes wondered if the light could somehow penetrate her small body, or perhaps radiate through it, if the outline of her hands and torso and spindly legs would somehow dissolve, leaving only heat and faded color behind.

The music room was quiet and dusty. It was clear that the room had not been used since the death of her father in law six year earlier, which meant that it would likely never be used again. The light slanted cleanly through the dusty space of the room, defining angle upon angle, shadow and pale illumination. She could sketch the room, of course. Perhaps she would. She stood upon the lit rectangle and tilted her face towards the window. The sun beyond was a bright crack on a brittle blue sky. Normally, she would squint, but now she found that she had no need. She stared open eyed at the sun, drinking it in. She looked at her hands. The were faded, translucent, lovely. This did not strike her as odd. She was, of course an artist. She lived on light. She sat and sketched a woman fading into the sun. Then, she slept. She did not know for how long.

Later, Charles came in with tea. No one was there. He saw a sketch on the table.

Go away, he whispered.

He didn't mention it to anyone else. He didn't touch the sketchpad.

W*HAT he wrote:*
My darling,

I regret to tell you that I have, apparently, been sacked. Or not *sacked* per se, but temporarily relieved of my duties. Fortunately for the two of us, I will remain on the rolls, which is good because I don't know how I would eat otherwise. I might have considered joining you in West-houghton, but the rails are closed for the time being. Only military business now, and rarely at that. It is oddly quiet without the regular churn of the engines, and I never thought I would miss it, but I do.

I do not know what I have done to deserve the ire of my commander, and though he said they were overstaffed, I know for a fact that it is a lie. Every man in the room cowered under the stacks waiting on their desks. He was not, however, unkind. He told me to divert myself, that I would be back on my feet in no time, and to have a stiff upper lip and so forth, which was nonsense because I shall still be paid and will apparently return after a suitable time. Suitable for what, they would not say.

But fortunately, after an unpleasant day, I came home and discovered that your letter was not in the post basket with everything else, but was resting prettily on the mantel, which means that our dear Andrew must have seen it and brought it in as a surprise. Don't worry about my mother. I'll write to her. Everything will be beautiful.

     Yours,

     John

W*HAT HE DID NOT*:
He celebrated his newfound free time by enjoying a lovely afternoon with his shining American, accompanied by three liters of a lovely Cotes du Rhone from his jealously guarded cache of wine, drunk directly from the bottles. The American spoke little, drank much, and was exquisitely, brutally, beautiful. The walls shook. The bed moaned. The American left at sunset, pausing, once, at the door, and slipping away without a word. There was more wine left. While drinking, John read and reread Angela's letter so many times, he began to recite it.

When he woke, he squinted at the slant of light penetrating his room. He rubbed his eyebrows and between his eyebrows and blinked. Then, he blinked again. A girl stood in the slant of light. A pretty girl staring first at the sun, then at her hands. John cleared his throat. The girl turned to him, smiled and vanished. John fell heavily back onto the pillows. The girl, of course, looked like Angela, and was Angela. But it could not have been, so it must not have been. He sat back up and the room was empty, as it should be.

He yawned and noticed the letter from Angela was now on her pillow. He had, apparently, resealed it, de-creased it, and placed it where her head should go. He laughed at himself, at what drink can do to a man. He wrapped himself in a robe and padded into the kitchen. The letter was there, too, sealed and unopened. He opened it. It was the same letter.

Three letters leaned against one another in the fireplace, their edges now seared with the remains of yesterday's coal. Two floated in the W.C. Six had been slipped between the door and the jamb and stuck out like nails waiting to be hammered in. And somewhere quite close, a girl was singing.

John gathered the letters in his hands and stood by the window. Bringing the paper to his nose, he closed his eyes and breathed them in. Lilac. And lavender. He let them fall; they spun like dry leaves, and scattered on the floor. He sat down and wrote to his mother.

W*HAT she wrote:*
Dearest John,

Today I sang in your honor, and I found that I could not stop. All day I have been here, drawing portraits of light. Singing odes to light. I open my mouth and light hangs upon my lips, drips from my tongue, spills down my front, and pools at my feet. Charles came in with tea (Did I want tea? Do I even drink tea? It's strange, but I have only a vague notion of the *substance* of tea. I believe it is not unlike the consumption of light.) He is so pale, poor man. I took his hand. His skin was papery and cool. My hand slipped over it like graphite along the clean space of an empty sheet. He shivered. I could not feel him shiver—not with my hands, anyway. But I *felt* it all the same. *Within,* if you understand. *Do* you understand? You always did understand. Or at least the thing that I believe to be you always did understand.

There was a day when I learned to see. And the learning to see and the making of art and the loving of you were bound inextricably together. There is much now, my dear, that is unbound, but those three remain. Should I think this odd, my love?

Once, there were people in the window. Do you remember, John? Their mouths were pink and open, and their hair floated like seaweed. It floats still. Charles told me to go away, but you would never tell me so.

Not you, John.

Never, ever you.

Ever yours,

Angela

W*HAT she did not:*
She knew to avoid the windowpanes. The people inside were clearer to her now, clearer than they had ever been. She had always seen them, ever since that day when she was a child. But never directly. They hovered vaguely at the corners of her eyes, the glass clearing itself every time she stared straight on.

But now they sharpened; they defined themselves. They pressed their long fingers on the glass and called her name. They were desperate, trapped. Their cold, pink mouths were open, toothless, hungry—an uneven gash in a cold white space. She knew without being told how they tried to move through light, how they were caught, trapped in glass, how they couldn't get out. Their eyes were blank, black—hollow pits where once there was a soul or a self or at least *something*, but now was not.

It was not a fate she would choose. She kept to the center of the room, moving only through open interior doors. She waited for someone to open a window or a door to the light. She waited a long time.

Her drawings littered the floor. Her letters too. How they reached their destination was a mystery, though she knew they did. She made something. She *was*. She would, she decided, remain so. Charles did not pick up the papers she scattered on the floor. He avoided the music room altogether. He averted his gaze when she wandered into his quarters at night. He shut his eyes at the seaweed wanderings of her waterlogged hair. Charles clapped his hands over his ears when she opened her pink slash mouth.

Open the door when the light pours through, she sang. *openthedoorwhenthelightpoursthrougopenthedoorwhenthelig htpoursthroughopenthedoorwhenthelightpoursthroughopenth edooropenthedooropenthedooropenthedooropenthedoor,* she sang, and sang, and sang. After two days of her ceaseless song, he opened the door. She poured herself into the light, and she *was* light, and line, and space, and negative space, and thought, and the lack of thought, and being, and nonbeing. She *was*. She knew it.

W*HAT HE WROTE:*
    My darling,
        Have you noticed any strange doors that you find yourself wanting to go through? On the edges of your vision, have you noticed, well, a sort of *veil* or some similar shimmering substance? A light, as it were. Have you found yourself wanting to know the location of, say, a long dark tunnel—one that, perhaps, has an attractive endpoint? I do not say this to cause you to feel alarm or to rush you into anything for which you may or may not be prepared. I only write this (my dear, my precious, my heart's sweet angel) on the off chance that you may be—er—putting anything *off*, as it were. You know, for my sake.
        What I mean to say, my love, is that if you should happen to, as it were, *run into* (assuming, of course, that one does run in this, er, *condition*) anyone that has been, well, *gone* for some time, and you feel yourself wanting to, I mean to say, *go*—you know—*along* with them, please my darling, do not tarry on my account. I will be fine, my love.
        Your most Affectionate Husband,
        John

W*HAT HE DID NOT:*
    He wondered if it would be James—beautiful, sickly James. James of the downy hair. James of the willowy limbs.

James of the seafoam skin. James who loved him, but not *like that*. James of the irritable lungs. James of the bloody cough. James, red lipped, pale to the point of tranluscency and dead in his arms. John knew that if James came for *him*, there would be no question of crossing over.

Angela, darling, lovely, lucky, and, yes, quite dead. And *not*. Not, as well. And that was the trouble, wasn't it?

Though he had guessed it well enough on his own, someone at the office had thought to slip a copied report— classified, of course, and probably treasonous for its mere exit from the fortified walls of the RAF offices—detailing the known facts of the train crash. The number of souls aboard. Lost, all of them. All, all lost. And Angela—angel, angel Angela—who wasn't supposed to be there, but *was,* and now she *wasn't*.

And yet.

The letters massed in the corners. They smothered the fire in the grate and mounded over the sink. They poured across the floor, particularly near the windows. They seemed to prefer light. Before he had sat down to breakfast, John swept the letters into great piles at odd intervals throughout the house. And yet they multiplied. At ten a.m. the American opened the front door. He did not knock.

"What's with the letters?" he said.

"It's complicated," John replied. He tugged at the folds of his dressing gown. It was dingier than it should have been. Angela always saw to such things. On another day he might have been embarrassed, but his mind was cluttered, dusty, over-exposed. His American, on the other hand, was pressed, shaved and clean. He shone brightly in the doorway. John squinted and gasped.

"Of course," the American said, keeping his eyes slanted to the floor. "I'm leaving."

"When," John asked. He also did not look up. Light poured in from all directions. It swirled across the floorboards. It stirred the letters in their piles.

"Tomorrow," he said, and before John could speak, he added, "and don't ask me where. I can't say."

"Of course." The light intensified. John shaded his eyes. He sweated and squinted.

"Are you—" the American cleared his throat. "I mean, have they found out—told you for sure. About your wife." He said the word "wife" as though pronouncing a word in a foreign tongue. "Is she—"

"Yes," John said while clearing his throat. "Which is to say. We assume. In all likelihood."

"Terrible thing," the American said, unstraightening, then straightening, his tie.

"Yes."

"If I don't—you know. If I don't see you again. I—"

"Of course, of course," John said, running his fingers through his hair, watching with growing panic how the letters spread like mold across the surface of the ottoman, stacked themselves higher and higher on the desk, spilled down the edge of the table. The American didn't seem to notice. John wondered briefly if they should embrace, declare their love, plot an escape. He wondered if they should begin making plans to settle in the Lake District, raise lambs, live on milk and bread and young meat, live on wine and sex and song.

"Well then," the American said, and opened the door. The light poured in. John fell to his knees, raised his hands to the light, "Oh! God!" he said, but the American turned and left without a word. He left the door open.

W*HAT SHE WROTE:*
Dearest,

Once there was a boy who loved a boy who did not love him back. Once there was a girl who loved a boy who loved a boy. Once there was a girl who loved a boy who loved her back, *mostly.*

If love is light and food is light and life is light, are we always in day? Are we doomed to never sleep?

Ever Yours,

Angela

Dear John,

I dream of your hands. I dream of fingers as they played along, across, and in. I dream how a moan becomes song and song becomes art and art becomes light. Your light enters me and I shine forever.

Ever Yours,

Angela

Dear John,

adooropensawomanlovesalifeblendsintolightandlightandlight

ever yours

ever

ever

WHAT SHE DID NOT:
There are three things that seem important to her now: Firstly, that light is useful. Particularly when one has no form, but still has substance. Light is a vehicle, though unreliable, particularly given the climate. Secondly, though the body dissolves she still feels the opening of the mouth, the electric nerves of the fingertips, the hungry scoop between what once were her thighs. Thirdly are doors. There are doors that remain impenetrable, doors that yield to the gentle insistence of her will, doors that lead her from place to place. There is a door that she needs to find. But what or where it is, and of what use, this is a mystery.

She slides through space—time too, from what she can tell. The moments of her life unfurl before her, an elegant geometry, all angles and arcs and perfect reasoning. She sees a boy who showed her to see ghosts—which is to say *death*—

which is to say *art*—which is to say infinity. She sees another boy with pale skin and a red mouth, coughing blood into a napkin. She sees the red mouthed boy floating away on harmonics and dissonance and brutal love. She sees another— her *Other*—dissembling, dissolving, despairing daily.

She is light. She is song. She is the art behind art— which is to say, *infinite*. As a formless substance, she sees her Other kneeling in the doorway. As light she pours through the door. As art she lands upon his open mouth. As song she slides what used to be her fingertips into the secret grooves of his throat. She plucks out melody and harmony—line, phrase, space, negative space. She draws dissonance and counterpoint. She lays her mouth upon his mouth. He tastes lilac and lavender and oil and smoke. He sings of bent metal and burning wood and beautiful soldiers and poisoned waters and multitudes of airships hurling themselves against the geodesic sky. He sings of a war that will never end. He sings of lost love, lost art, lost music, lost nations, lost women and lost men. He sings her name. He never, ever, stops.

ROSEMARY, THAT'S FOR REMEMBRANCE

Barbara Krasnoff

I remember.

When I was a girl, I loved going to the beauty shop. It had light blue walls, I think, and a radio. I sat under the dryer wearing a pink smock, reading the latest issue of Vogue, and listening to . . . what was her name? . . . to one of my friends talking about her latest boyfriend. It was nice.

Kay's is nice, too. The woman in charge comes to greet us; she has bright yellow hair and thick glasses and she says hello to me, not just to that woman who is standing next to me (should I know her?) the way a lot of people do. And she wears a name tag on her pink smock so that I always know her name; it says "KAY" with tiny purple flowers entwined around it.

Even though I've only lived in this neighborhood for . . . well, for a few years (I remember that I grew up in Williamsburg and brought up my children in Canarsie; I remember those years very well), Kay's looks like all the beauty shops I ever knew. Once, I remember, I went to a new one, and it had deafening music and strange machines and tall boys talking loud and winking at the others when they thought I didn't see. (I know I'm old. I can't help it. They'll be old one day too, and why don't they understand that?)

Kay smiles at me, takes my coat and my pocketbook, and helps me sit down in one of the chairs while the woman who's always next to me goes and sits in front of the salon and takes out a little, um, thing and talks into it.

"And how are you today?" Kay says while she puts a towel around my neck and then covers me with a flowery cape to protect my clothes. I'm fine, I say, although we both know I'm not fine at all. I'm disappearing. Bit by bit.

I don't know why and neither do they. The doctors, I mean. Tests are inconclusive. (You see? I can understand these things; I've got a Masters in History, after all.) They say it past me, to the woman who says she's my daughter (although my daughter is bright and small and energetic, not tired and sad like she is), but I listen. And sometimes I remember.

Kay chats to me while she dampens my hair and takes out her scissors. I had beautiful hair (I have photos), thick and brown. Jack used to run his hands through it and beg me not to cut it, although long hair wasn't really the fashion and I really looked better with short. Now, I look in the mirror and it's all dull gray and I can see parts of my scalp showing through; it makes me want to cry, more than the wrinkles and the pieces of my life that have disappeared.

I start to get up, to get away from the mirror, but the moment I start to move Kay swings the chair around so I'm looking instead at the TV set that's been set up high on the back wall. "There," she says. "You don't mind facing the wall, do you? It's so much easier for me." She chatters on, about her friend's daughter who is pregnant and miserable; about how the weather has been unseasonably icy and why do they call it global warming when things are getting colder?

Beneath the TV set, a young Asian girl with a sour expression carefully works on the nails of an old woman with bright orange hair (am I that old? Surely I'm not that old) and nods, and says we've ruined the world and that one day we'll wake up and all the oxygen will have disappeared from the earth. She says it with satisfaction.

On the TV, a man walks around the streets of a foreign country (because nobody else is speaking English), and stops in a marketplace and talks to a man who is frying foods in a little booth, and tries some of the foods, although it looks extremely unappetizing. (Let them eat what they want, I told my sister when she tried to make her kids eat their vegetables, and what was her name again?)

"There you are!" says Pat (no, not Pat, that was the woman who cut my hair when I was a girl, this is Kay, it says so on her name tag). "Ready for the dryer?"

Kay puts a pillow on the chair so I can sit comfortably and settles me in. She puts a magazine on my lap and brings over a small can of ginger ale, placing it carefully on a table next to the chair. "There," she says. "We like to make our ladies comfortable. Ready?"

I nod, and look up at her. She takes her glasses off and smiles, and wait, something is wrong—her eyes are striped, completely striped through the pupils and the iris and the whites, all green and silver. I want to call out, to warn somebody, but I don't know who here will help me and then she pulls the dryer down over my head like a giant upside-down cup and turns it on.

Something hums and grabs my head and my brain and where am

I smell morning and hear eggs frying and there is sunlight coming through the gauze kitchen curtains Catherine! it's a school day young lady do you know what time time time is on our side and her eyes are getting cold it's cold outside please stop blowing bubbles in your milk round like a hairdryer yes honey your tie is on the hanger does he still love love me do don't tease the bye baby bunting have a good day at the office, dear, and don't forget and there he goes and she goes and they go and it's quiet and oh the baby's crying but what is that sound and where did everyone go and what was I going it's all going it's all

"There now," a voice says. "That didn't hurt a bit, did it?"

There's a woman standing over me wearing a smock with flowers and a tag. I suppose it's a name tag, but I can't read it, it's just squiggles. I'm in a . . . a . . . someplace with a lot of women and it looks nice, but something is missing.

The woman smiles at me and bends down. "It's all right," she whispers, and her eyes are pretty stripes and somewhere under her voice is something, a hissing or a crackle. I can't tell what it is or what she is. "I can't," I tell her. If I could only. But. "I just can't. They're missing."

"Don't worry," she says. "We've got them. We've collected them from you and many like you, and we'll keep them safe long after you and yours are gone." She puts on a pair of glasses and raises her voice. "Now, let's go back to the chair and I'll comb you out."

She helps me up and takes me to a chair. I sit, and look at the old woman in the mirror, and wonder who she is.

WHEN WE MOVED ON

Steve Rasnic Tem

We tried to prepare the kids a year or so ahead. They might be adults to the rest of the world, but to us they were still a blur of squeals that smelled like candy.

"What do you mean *move?* You've lived here *forever!*" Our oldest daughter's face mapped her dismay. Elaine was now older than we had been when we found our place off the beaten path of the world, but if she had started to cry I'm sure I would have caved. I hoped she had forgotten that when she was a little girl I'd told her we'd stay in this house until the end.

"Forever ends, child," her mother said. "It's one of the last things we learn. These walls are quickly growing thin—it's time to go."

"What do you *mean?* I don't see anything wrong—"

I reached over, patted her knee and pointed. "That's because the house is so full there's little wall to be seen. But look there, between that sparkling tapestry of spider eggs and my hat collection. That's about a square foot of unadorned wall. Look *there*."

She did, and as I had so many times before, I joined
her in the looking. I was pleased, at least, that this semi-
transparent spot worn into our membrane of home provided
clear evidence: through layers of wall board like greenish
glass, through diaphanous plaster and thinnest lathe, we
could see several local children walking to school, and one
Billie Perkins honored us with a full-faced grin and a finger
mining his nose for hidden treasure.

"Is that Cheryl Perkins' boy?" she asked. "I haven't seen
her in years." She sounded wistful. It always bruised me a bit
to hear her sounding wistful. I've always been a sloppy mess
where my children are concerned.

"You should call her, honey," her mother said, on her
way into the kitchen for our bowls of soup. My wife never tells
you what's in the soups she serves—she doesn't want to spoil
the surprise. Some days it's like dipping into a liquid
Crackerjack box.

Elaine had gone to the thin patch and was now poking
it with her finger. "Can they see us from out there?" Her
finger went in part way and stuck. She made a small
embarrassed cry and pulled it out. A sigh of shimmering
green light puffed out in front of her, then fell like rain on
the floor.

I handed her a cloth napkin and she busily wiped at the
slowly spreading stain. "They just see a slight variation in
color," I replied. "It's more obvious at night, when a haze of
light from the house leaks through."

She smiled. "I've noticed that on visits. I just thought
it was the house sparkling. It's always been." She stopped.

"A jewel?"

"Yes. That's not silly of me? I always thought of it as
the 'jewel on the hill,' so when it seemed to sparkle lately, to
look even more beautiful than ever, I thought nothing of it."

Of course she has been using this phrase since she was
a little girl, but I said "What an interesting comparison! I'd

never thought of it that way before. But I like that, 'The Jewel on the Hill.' We could paint a sign, put it up on the wall."

"Oh, Daddy! Where would you find the room?"

This was, of course, the point of the conversation, the fulcrum about which our future lives were to turn. A painting can become too crowded in its composition, a brain too full of trivia, and a house can certainly accumulate too many plans, follies, acquisitions, vocations, avocations, heart-felt avowals, and memories so fervently gripped they lose their binding thread.

All about us floated a constellation of materials dreamed and lived, attached to walls and door and window frames, layered onto shelves and flooding glass-fronted cabinets, suspended from or glued to the ceilings, protruding here and there into the room as if eager for a snag. There were my collections, of course: the hats, the ties, the jars of curiosities, monstrosities, and mere unreliabilities, the magazines barely read then saved for later, and later, all the volumes of fact and fiction, and the photographs of fictive relatives gathered from stores thrift and antique or as part of the purchase of a brand new frame, bells and belts and pistols and thimbles, children's drawings and drawings of children drawing the drawings, colored candles and colored bottles and colors inexplicably attached to nothing at all, my wife's favorite recipes pasted on the walls at levels relative to their deliciousness (the best ones so high up she couldn't read them clearly enough to make those wonderful dishes anymore), and everywhere, and I mean everywhere, the notes of a lifetime reminding our children to eat that lunchtime sandwich as well as the cookie, don't forget piano practice, remember we love you, and please take out the trash. Our notes to each other were simpler and less directive: thinking of you, thinking of you, have a great day.

In one corner of the living room you could see where I had sat reading a year of my sister's unmailed letters found in a shoebox after her death, each one spiked to the wall after reading, feeling like nails tearing through my own flesh. And near the windows kites and paper birds poised for escape through sashes left carelessly ajar. An historical collection of our children's toys lay piled against the baseboards, ready for the sorting and elimination we'd never quite managed, and floating above, tied to strings were particularly prized bits of homework, particularly cherished letters from camp, gliding and tangling with the varied progress of the day. And the authors of those works, our precious children, preserved in photos at nearly every age, arranged around the ceiling light fixtures like jittering moths, filling with their own illumination as the ceilings thinned to allow the daylight in. Gathered together I thought each child's history in photos could have been portraits of a single family whose resemblances were uncanny and disturbing.

There were trophies mounted or settled onto shelves for bowling, swimming, and spelling, most candy bars sold and fewest absent days. And the countless numbers of awards for participation, for happy or complaining our children always did participate.

Some of the collections, such as the spider eggs or selected, desiccated moth wings I couldn't remember for sure if their preservation had been intentional. Others, like the gatherings of cracks in corners or those scattered arrays of torn fabrics were no doubt accidental, but possessed of beauty in any case and so needed to stay.

These were the moments of a lifetime, the celebrations and the missteps, and I wondered now if our children ever had any idea what they both stepped in and out of on their average day in our home.

"What's going to become of it all?" our daughter exclaimed. She moved through the downstairs rooms unconsciously pirouetting, glancing around. She'd seen it all before, lived with all but the most recent of it, but blindness comes easy. I could see her eyes trying to remember. "You can't just throw it away!" she cried, when a rain of doll's heads from a decayed net overhead set off her squeals and giggles.

"You kids can have whatever you like," my wife replied from the passage to the kitchen. "But thrown out, left behind, or simply forgotten, things do have a way of becoming *gone*. Which is what is about to happen to your lunches, if the two of you don't come with me right now!"

Within the sea of salt and pepper shakers (armies of cartoon characters and national caricatures with holes in their heads) that covered our kitchen table my wife had created tiny islands for our soup bowls and milk glasses. I had the urge to sweep that collection of shakers off onto the floor, just to show how done with this never ending tide of *things* I'd become, but I knew that wasn't what Elaine needed to see at that moment. She stared at the red surface of her soup as if waiting for some mystery to emerge.

"Sweetheart, we just don't need all this anymore."

"You seemed to need it before," she said to all the staring shaker heads.

"It's hard to explain such a change," I said, "but you collect and you collect and then one day you say to yourself 'this is all too much.' You can't let anything else in, so you don't have much choice but to try to clear the decks."

"I just don't want things to change," she said softly.

"Oh, yes, you do," her mother said, patting her hand. "You most certainly do. Everything has an expiration date. It just isn't always a precise date, or printed on the package. And you would hate the alternative."

I'd been distracted by all the calendars on the kitchen walls, each displaying a different month and year, and for just that moment not sure which one was the current one, the one with the little box reserved for *right now*.

Elaine looked at her mother with an expression that wasn't exactly anger, but something very close. "Then why bother, Mom? When it all just has to be gotten rid of, in the end?"

"Who can know?" My wife smiled, dipping into her soup, then frowned suddenly as if she'd discovered something unfortunate. "To fill the time, I suppose. To exercise—" She turned suddenly to me. "Or is it 'exorcise'?" Without waiting for an answer she turned again to her soup, lifted the bowl, and sipped. Done, she smiled shyly at our daughter with a pink moustache and continued, "our creativity. To fill the space, to put our mark down, and then to erase it. That's what we human beings do. That's all we know how to do."

"Human beings?" Elaine laughed. "You know, I always thought you two were wizards, superheroes, magical beings, something like that. Not like anybody else's parents. Not like anybody else at all. All of us kids did."

My wife closed her eyes and sighed. "I think we did, too."

Over the next few weeks we had the rest of our children over to reveal something of our intentions, although I'm quite sure a number of unintentions were exposed as well. They brought along numerous grandchildren, some who had so transformed since their last visits it was as if a brand-new person had entered the room, fresh creatures whose habits and behaviors we had yet to learn about. The older children stood around awkwardly, as if they were reluctant guests at some high school dance, snickering at the old folks' sense of décor, and sense of what was important, but every now and then you would see them touch something on the wall and gasp, or read a letter pasted there and stand transfixed.

The younger grandchildren were content to straddle our laps, constructing tiny bird's nests in my wife's gray hair, warrens for invisible rabbits in the multidimensional tangles of my beard. They seemed completely oblivious to their parents' discomfort with the conversation.

"So where will you go?" asked oldest son Jack, whom we'd named after the fairytale, although we'd never told him so.

"We're still looking at places," his mother said. "Our needs will be pretty simple. As simple as you could imagine, really."

I looked out at the crowd of them. Did we really have all these children? When had it happened?

I suspected a few strangers had sneaked in.

"Won't you need some help with the moving, and afterwards?" Wilhelmina asked.

"Help should always be appreciated, remember that children," I said. A few of them laughed, which was the response I had wanted. But then very few of our children have understood my sense of humor.

"What your father meant to say was that moving help won't be necessary," my wife said, interrupting. "As we said, we're taking very little with us, so please grab anything you'd care to have. As for us, we think a simple life will be a nice change."

Annie, always our politest child, raised her hand.

"Annie, honey, you're thirty years old. You don't need to raise your hand anymore," I told her.

"So what are you really telling us? Are we going to see you again?"

"Well, of course you are," I said. "Maybe not as often, or precisely when you want to, but you *will* see us. We'll still be around, and just as before, just as now, you'll *always* be our children."

We didn't set a day, because rarely do you know when the right day will come along. We'd been looking for little signs for years, it seemed, but you never really know what little signs to look for.

Then one day I was awakened early, sat up straight with eyes wide open, which I almost never do, looking around, listening intently for whatever might have awakened me.

The first thing I noticed was the oddness of the light in the room. It had a vaguely autumnal feel even though it was the end of winter, which wasn't as surprising as it might normally have been, what with the unusually warm temperatures we'd been having for this time of year.

The second thing was the smell: orange-ish or lemon-ish, but gone a little too far, like when the rot begins to set in.

The third thing was the absence of my wife from our bed. Even though she always woke up before me, she always stayed in bed in order to ease my own transition from my always complicated dreams to standing up, attempting to move around.

I dressed quickly and found her downstairs in the dining room. "Look," she said. And I did.

Every bit of our lives along the walls, hanging from the ceiling, spilt out onto the floors, had turned the exact same golden sepia shade, as if it had all been sprayed with some kind of preservative. "Look," she repeated. "You can see it all beginning to wrinkle."

I'd actually thought that effect to be some distortion in my vision, for I had noticed it, too.

"You know what you want to take?" she asked.

"It's all been ready for months," I said. "I'll be at the door in less than a minute."

I ran up the stairs, hearing the rapidly drying wooden steps crack and pop beneath my shoes. When I jerked open the closet door it seemed as if I was opening the door to the outside, on a crisp Fall day, Mr. Hopkins down the street is burning his leaves, and you can smell apples cooking from some anonymous kitchen. I brushed the fallen leaves from the small canvas bag I had filled with a notebook, a pencil, some crackers (which are the best food for any occasion), and extra socks. I looked up at the clothes rod, the rusted metal, and nothing left hanging there but a tangle of brittle vines and the old baseball jacket I wore in high school. It hardly fit, but I pulled it on anyway, picked up the bag, and ran.

She stood by the front door smiling, wrapped in an old knit sweater-coat with multi-colored squares on a chocolate-colored background. "My mother knitted it for me in high school. It was all I could find intact, but I've always wanted to wear it again."

"Something to drink?" I asked.

"Two bottles of water. Did you get what you needed?"

"*Everything* I need," I replied. And we left that house where we'd lived almost forty years, raised children and more or less kept our peace, for the final time. Out on the street we felt the wind coming up, and turned back around.

What began as a few scattered bits leaving the roof, caught by the wind and drifting over the neighbor's trees, gathered into a tide that reduced the roof to nothing, leaving the chimney exposed, until the chimney fell into itself, leaving a chimney-shaped hole in the sky. We held onto each other, then, as the walls appeared to detach themselves at the corners, flap like birds in pain, then twist and flutter, shaking, as the dry house chaff scattered, making a cloud so thick we couldn't really see what was going on inside it, including what was happening to all our possessions, and then the cloud thinned, and the tiny bits drifted down, disappearing into the shrubbery which once hugged the sides of our home, and now hugged nothing.

We held hands for miles and for some parts of days thereafter, until our arthritic hands cramped, and we couldn't hold on any more no matter how hard we tried. We drank the water and ate the crackers and I wrote nothing down, and after weeks of writing nothing I simply tore the sheets out of the notebook one by one and started pressing them against ground, and stone, the rough bark on trees, the back of a dog's head, the unanchored sky one rainy afternoon. Some of that caused a mark to be made, much did not, but to me that was a satisfactory record of where we had been, and who we had been.

Eventually, our fingers no longer touched, and we lost the eyes we'd used to gaze at one another, and the tongues for telling each other, and the lips for tasting each other.

But we are not nothing. She is that faint smell in the air, that nonsensical whisper. I am the dust that settles into your clothes, that keeps your footprints as you wander across the world.

PINIONS

The Authors

Claude Lalumière (lostpages.net) is a Montreal writer and editor. His first collection, *Objects of Worship*, is a 2009 release from ChiZine Publications. Claude has edited eight anthologies, including *Island Dreams: Montreal Writers of the Fantastic*, *Open Space: New Canadian Fantastic Fiction*, and *Tesseracts Twelve: New Novellas of Canadian Fantastic Fiction*. His fiction has been featured in the "year's best" series *Year's Best Fantasy*, *Year's Best SF*, and *The Mammoth Book of Best New Erotica*.

About "Three Friends," Claude writes: "Being an editor as well as a writer (and, as many writers will tell you, a nitpicky editor who often makes his writers work through multiple drafts), I'm always a bit wary when a story of mine is accepted but then simply published as is, with no editing. Surely, my stories can't be as perfect as I think they are. It's the editor's job to correct me of that self-satisfied assumption and highlight all those blemishes that I was too close to see. Any good editor should do at least that. Sometimes, it's only a question of careful copyediting. But sometimes . . .

"For me, it's always a thrill when I find an editor who truly gets, at a gut level, what I'm trying to do. Such an editor is not merely a glorified copyeditor but, rather, a collaborator. Such an editor will lead me to push my stories as far as they really need to go, will spot when I—despite my best efforts—took a shortcut but shouldn't have, will not let me get away with anything, will show me where I faltered and did not do my story justice, will say exactly the right thing to make me understand my own work better.

"I was fortunate enough that 'Three Friends'—a story I'd been struggling with for many years—found such an editor in the talented and keenly insightful Mike Allen, whose perspicacious comments and steadfast enthusiasm allowed me to finally mold my long-suffering 'Three Friends' into a satisfying shape."

To which the editor shuffles his feet, grins and says: "Aw, shucks."

Leah Bobet lives and works in a little apartment in Toronto built on consecrated ground. Her fiction has appeared in *Interzone, The Mammoth Book of Extreme Fantasy*, and *Realms of Fantasy*, and her poetry has been nominated for the Rhysling and Pushcart Prizes. Other information, miscellany, and trivia can be found at http://www.leahbobet.com.

Talking about "Six," Leah says the story "was started mostly to play with one of my favourite apocalypse plans: how, after the fall of civilization, I might turn my apartment building into a vertical farm. The idea of sixes—drawn from a themed writing challenge run with friends every spring—brought in what life would be like for the sixth child of a seventh son and, with it, what life might be for children in the usually adult fantasy-of-competence genre of apocalyptic fiction."

Marie Brennan is the author of four novels, including the *Onyx Court* series of historical faerie fantasies. The most recent book, *In Ashes Lie*, came out from Orbit in June, and features the destruction of most of seventeenth-century London. She has also published nearly two dozen short stories, in magazines such as *Talebones*, *On Spec*, and *Beneath Ceaseless Skies*. More information can be found on her website, www.swantower.com.

Here's how she describes the origins of "Once a Goddess":

"I've said before that I pillage my academic fields (anthropology and folklore) for material; this is a more direct example than most. In the summer of 2001, while cataloguing articles for the index Anthropological Literature, I came across a piece by an Indian scholar, regarding the living goddess Kumari. There are a number of Kumaris in Nepal, of which the Kathmandu one is the most prominent, but I can't tell you a lot about them; what stuck with me was not the specifics of that religious situation, but the problem of what happens to those girls after they cease to be Kumari. You grow up as the living avatar of a goddess, and then one day, you're a normal person again—with no idea how to live as one. That loss, and the question of what one does afterward, lodged powerfully in my brain. I had the title almost immediately, but it took me seven years (and five aborted drafts) to get from that to a working story."

Ian McHugh lives in Canberra, Australia, but would rather be closer to the beach. He is a 2006 graduate of the Clarion West writers' workshop and the 2008 grand prize winner in the Writers of the Future contest. A list of his fiction publications is available at ianmchugh.wordpress.com, including links to stories available free online. His big writing projects for 2009 are a graphic novel of his Writers of the Future story with Bob Hall (hallhammer.deviantart.com), who illustrated it in the *Writers of the Future 24* anthology, and a novel set in the same fantastical alternate Australia.

Of "Angel Dust" he says: "The story is set in a fantasy universe I've been kicking around for a while. Early iterations of it can be found in *Andromeda Spaceways Inflight Magazine* and the All Star Stories anthology *Twenty Epics*. 'Angel Dust' had its genesis after a friend told me that Korean fairy tales sometimes begin with the line 'Back in the days when tigers smoked cigarettes,' and trying to think of my own version of 'Once upon a time.' The line I came up with didn't survive redrafting, but maybe I'll find a story for it one day."

Ann Leckie is a graduate of Clarion West. Her fiction has appeared in *Subterranean Magazine*, *Strange Horizons*, and *Andromeda Spaceways Inflight Magazine*. She has worked as a waitress, a receptionist, a rodman on a land-surveying crew, and a recording engineer. She lives in St. Louis, Missouri.

Asked for a note on "The Endangered Camp," she replied: "Back in 2004, I read an interview with John Joseph Adams, the notorious Slush God of *Fantasy & Science Fiction*. The interviewer asked him what kinds of stories did he wish he saw more of in the slushpile, and he said he wished he saw more dinosaur fic, more stories about Mars exploration, and more post-apocalyptic stories. I said, entirely in jest, 'Who'll be the first to send in a post-apocalyptic dinosaurs on Mars story?'

"About a week later it dawned on me—dinosaurs had an apocalypse! All I had to do was get them to Mars! It took me a while to figure that bit out, and by the time I wrote the first draft, during Week 4 of Clarion West, I read another interview with Mr. Adams in which he added skyhooks to the list. It was too late to add a skyhook to the story, but if I'd known I'd have tried to cram one in there. I think, ultimately, it's better without the skyhook."

Mary Robinette Kowal is the 2008 recipient of the Campbell Award for Best New Writer. Her short fiction has appeared in *Strange Horizons*, *Cosmos* and *Asimov's*. Mary, a professional puppeteer and voice actor, lives in NYC with her husband Rob and nine manual typewriters. Her first novel, *Shades of Milk and Honey*, will be published by Tor in 2010.

Here's how she says "At the Edge of Dying" came about: "While I was living in Iceland, I was talking with a friend of mine who told a story about her upstairs neighbor. The woman apparently claimed to be a psychic but was always on the verge of death. We speculated that the reason she was a psychic was because she was so close to the other side. Bing! The idea of magic that was tied to how close you were to dying popped into my head.

"The setting is very loosely based on Hawaii, where my husband grew up. He often talks about how the more obviously volcanic parts of Iceland remind him of the Big Island and it seemed natural to translate the story there."

Saladin Ahmed was born in Detroit. His fiction has appeared in *Orson Scott Card's Intergalactic Medicine Show* and *Beneath Ceaseless Skies*. His poems have appeared in journals including *The Brooklyn Review* and in anthologies such as *Abandon Automobile: Detroit City Poetry*, and *Inclined To Speak: An Anthology of Contemporary Arab American Poetry*. He lives in Brooklyn with his wife, the songwriter Hayley Thompson.

Saladin says that "Hooves and the Hovel of Abdel Jameela" is "actually a prosification of a very short poem I'd written years before. The poem consisted entirely of a single image—an old man somewhere in the medieval Islamic world defying the narrow-minded by declaring his love for a hooved woman. Translating this image into a story, of course, introduced deeper demands in terms of plot and character. These demands eventually led to the story that appears here. The characters' names, by the way, are vaguely allegorical— 'Abdel Jameela,' for instance, might be roughly translated as 'servant (or slave) of beauty.'"

Tanith Lee was born in North London (UK) in 1947. She didn't learn to read—she is also dyslectic—until almost age 8, and by 9 she was writing. After grammar school, Lee went on to work in a library. This was followed by various other jobs. In 1974, DAW Books of America, under the leadership of Donald A. Wollheim, bought and published Lee's *The Birthgrave*, and thereafter 26 of her novels and collections.

Since then Lee has written around 90 books, and approaching 300 short stories. Four of her radio plays have been broadcast by the BBC; she also wrote two episodes for the TV series *Blake's 7*.

Lee writes across many genres, including Horror, SF and Fantasy, Historical, Detective, Contemporary-Psychological, Children and Young Adult. Her preoccupation, though, is always people.

In 1992 she married the writer-artist-photographer John Kaiine, her companion since 1987. They live near the sea, in a house full of books and plants, ruled over by two Tuxedo cats.

Here's what caused her to write "The Pain of Glass," a new tale set in her famous Flat Earth milieu: "A conversation between my husband, myself and a friend of ours which involved a broken window, brought forth the phrase 'a pane of glass.' Given my sort of mind I instantly visualized the pain of the pane—and then the flat earth drifted through the back of my thoughts, a beckoning mirage . . . the rest is the story."

Joanna Galbraith grew up in Brisbane, Australia, but now spends her time writing and teaching English in Basel, Switzerland. Her stories have appeared in a number of print and electronic journals including the first *Clockwork Phoenix* anthology. Her first novel *The Uncanny Abilities of Philomena Philpott* is scheduled for release in 2010.

Joanna says "The Fish of Al-Kawthar's Fountain" came to her while sitting beside the courtyard fountain of the

Al-Haramein hotel, Damascus, Syria. Mesmerised by the water and the fish reeling round in it, she distinctly remembers thinking she saw a couple of fish exchange pleasantries or at the very least a few bars of an old madrigal in perfect harmony. Of course, in hindsight, she realises it was probably just the intense heat and overwhelming fragrance of apple nargileh but she still relishes that idea that fish can hold a tune.

She wrote this story for the *Majnun* who took her camel riding at three o'clock in the morning. For more information on Joanna's writing go to www.joannagalbraith.com.

Born in the Pacific Northwest in 1979, **Catherynne M. Valente** is the author of *Palimpsest* and the *Orphan's Tales* series, as well as *The Labyrinth*, *Yume no Hon: The Book of Dreams*, *The Grass-Cutting Sword*, and five books of poetry. She is the winner of the Tiptree Award, the Mythopoeic Award, the Rhysling Award, and the Million Writers Award and has been nominated for the Pushcart Prize, shortlisted for the Spectrum Award and was a World Fantasy Award finalist in 2007. She currently lives on an island off the coast of Maine with her partner and two dogs.

Here's what Cat says about the origins of "The Secret History of Mirrors": "I had the idea for this title three years ago, springing from a conversation with Sonya Taaffe, and have been struggling to write a story to go with it ever since. Ultimately, it was learning a little about how to make mirrors that triggered the right tale. I wanted to talk about fairy tales and how their mirrors are so terribly similar, but also about what a mirror is, both physically and spiritually, what it can be, and how learning one thing can change your understanding of everything else. One of the best things fiction does is allow us to see plain objects differently, to see their resonance, to see them as a connection from the real world to the world of magic. I wanted to do that for the mirror in my hall.

"Also: lesbian nuns. Go with what you know, right?"

Forrest Aguirre's fiction has recently appeared in such venues as *Asimov's*, *Farrago's Wainscot*, *Hatter Bones*, and *Avant-Garde for the New Millenium*. He has received a World Fantasy Award for his editorial work, and has most recently edited *Polyphony 7* with Deborah Layne. He is currently completing work on his second novel, *Archangel Morpheus*, and is working through his third novel, *Panoptica*.

He writes that "Never nor Ever" was "a reaction to the realization that I am, now, genuinely middle-aged. In this tale, I harked back to two characters from my childhood, filtering my view of their growing older and facing death through the lens of Derrida's deconstruction and the fractal analysis of chaotic systems. I also recently began fencing again (in order to find my youth again, no doubt), and have done some in-depth study of dueling. Honestly, I just plain wanted to finish the sibling challenge that was begun, but never concluded, so long ago, in Wonderland."

Gemma Files won the 1999 International Horror Guild award for Best Short Fiction with her short story "The Emperor's Old Bones." Since then, five of her stories were adapted into episodes of Showtime's *The Hunger* TV series, she spent ten years teaching people how to write screenplays, published two collections of fiction (*Kissing Carrion* and *The Worm in Every Heart*, both Prime Books) and two collections of poetry (*Bent Under Night*, from Sinnersphere Productions, and *Dust Radio*, from Kelp Queen Press). Her novella *Words Written Backwards* is available from Burning Effigy Press, and her short story "Marya Nox" will appear later this year as part of *Lovecraft Unbound*, a Lovecraft-themed anthology edited by Ellen Datlow.

        Stephen J. Barringer's first publication was the SF short story "Restoration," in *On Spec*; he has since won first and second prizes in the short story competition for the long-running Toronto Trek/Polaris media convention, and has written several gaming products for various RPG systems, as well as a radio play adaptation of E.F. Benson's "The Room In The Tower" that's supposed to be seeing production Real Soon Now. He also does a lot of business proposals and copywriting, but that isn't nearly as much fun.

(In case you're wondering, Barringer and Files are married, with one son.)

When they were interrogated about "each thing i show you is a piece of my death," the following transcript was the result:

STEVE: The secret to a successful collaboration, especially for two writers who each have their own voice, is either (A) to create a third voice that's a seamless fusion of both separate voices, or (B) take advantage of the differences by juxtaposing them. "each thing," as an essentially epistolary story, was a perfect candidate for approach B, with each of us trading off different viewpoints and sections as inspiration and familiarity suggested. We're both huge fans of the read-between-the-lines, corner-of-your-eye school of dread seen in films like SESSION 9, or the stories of Ramsey Campbell, and of finding the creeps in a story's implications rather than its depictions, so the actual process of writing was remarkably straightforward: each of us could stand at a different angle and take various shots at an agreed-upon target, then fit them all together afterwards for optimum effect.

GEMMA: Coming from a film criticism/film history background, I've always wanted to tell a story revolving around that Holy Grail of cinematic urban legends, a haunted film. I'd also covered a lot of Toronto's experimental scene over the years, and wanted to work that stuff in as well, to give it added cultural oomph—thus the idea of the Internet-driven exquisite cadaver project. Add characters, and things fell together fairly quickly.

STEVE: I came in about halfway through the process to help organize the background and fill out the technical side of things. One aspect I really glommed on to was the chance to prove wrong the old canard that clinical, expository writing can't be scary. My own background is straight out of the old school of world-building, rules-logical SF&F, with a large side-order of professional business writing; I've always loved the craft required for good exposition, and the idea of describing something utterly horrible in as detached and clinical a way as possible was a terrific challenge.

GEMMA: Oddly, the oldest part of the story itself is probably the wrap-around, which sprang fully-formed into my head a good three years before I ever figured out what it should end up being attached to. But here's facts: Without Steve, the rest of this story probably wouldn't've come to fruition at all—not as quickly, at any rate, or by the specified deadline, either. Like Background Man and his image-drunk initial enabler, I couldn't've done it without him.

Kelly Barnhill's work has appeared in journals such as *Postscripts*, *Weird Tales*, *Underground Voices*, *Space and Time*, and *The Sun*. Her first novel was recently purchased by Little, Brown and is due to be released in the spring of 2010. She has received grants and awards from Intermedia Arts, The Loft, and the Jerome Foundation. She also writes funny nonfiction books for children—a job that allows her to be nosy and curious, to think like a fourth grade boy, and to assemble amalgamations of weird, creepy and disgusting facts for a living. It is, she feels, the Greatest Job in America. She lives in Minneapolis with her three evil-genius children, her astonishingly handsome husband and her emotionally unstable dog.

And on the writing of "Open the Door and the Light Pours Through," she says: "This story grew in fits and starts, arising from free-written sketches in different notebooks, for different purposes. I didn't even realize that I was writing about linked characters until I had nearly enough material to weave into a semi-coherent story. This actually happens quite a bit with me. Stories, I've found, have their own intelligence and sense of purpose. They are wily and full of tricks, and my own plans, alas, end up being rather meaningless.

"I can, however, tell you what I was thinking about at the time: My husband's grandmother was a war bride, originally from Southport. She met an American on leave, and they married soon after. And then he left on some of the most dangerous missions in the war. During that time, she wrote to him every day, knowing full well that it was unlikely that he'd see any of them. Knowing as well, that it was more than likely that she'd never see him again. When I wrote this story, I was thinking about their early courtship, and how a letter can be to someone and no one at the same time, as well as her American husband (my husband's grandfather) at the end of his life, in the grips of severe dementia and confusion, the elements of himself slowly unraveling. That kind of dissolution of the Self is something that fascinates and haunts me—and then works its way into fiction, in this case, with letter-writing ghosts. Because really, what else is a ghost going to do with her time?"

Barbara Krasnoff's short fiction has appeared (or will soon appear) in a variety of magazines, including *Space and Time*, *Electric Velocipede*, *Doorways*, *Sybil's Garage*, *Behind the Wainscot*, *Escape Velocity*, *Weird Tales*, *Descant*, *Lady Churchill's Rosebud Wristlet*, and *Amazing Stories*. Her work can also be found in the anthologies *Things Aren't What They Seem*, *Such A Pretty Face: Tales of Power & Abundance*, and *Memories and Visions: Women's Fantasy & Science Fiction*.

Barbara is also the author of a non-fiction book for young adults, *Robots: Reel to Real*, and is currently Features & Reviews Editor for *Computerworld*. She lives in Brooklyn, NY with her partner Jim Freund and lots of toy penguins. Her Web site can be found at brooklynwriter.com.

She confides when explaining "Rosemary, That's For Remembrance" that "Kay's is real. It is an old neighborhood hair salon where local women, most of them elderly, come to have their hair cut, colored and permed by middle-aged beauticians who chat with them about their husbands, their grown children, their health, and their problems with the world. Some of these women are still strong, sharp, and feisty, but others have become slow, bewildered, and ill, depending on walkers and the kindness of strangers. You can't help but wonder what happened to the people they once were."

Steve Rasnic Tem has new and forthcoming short stories in *Black Static*, *Asimov's*, *Interzone*, and in the anthologies *Phantom* and *Polyphony*. *Invisible*, an audio collection of some of his newer stories, is scheduled for release by Speaking Volumes. In November Centipede Press will be publishing *In Concert*, a collection of all his short story collaborations with wife Melanie Tem. In 2008 Wizards Discoveries published *The Man on the Ceiling*, a reimagining and expansion of their award-winning novella.

Asked for notes on "When We Moved On," he explains: "My favorite stories both to read and to write these days tend to be the ones that explore the magic of the everyday. They often have this deceptively simple, inevitable quality about them, and I find that when I myself am writing one, when they're ready to write, they come about as if I were recounting a story told to me a long time ago. It's that 'when they're ready to write' that's the difficult part. You can't schedule them—at least I can't. They usually come out of ideas I've been meditating on for a very long time. Oftentimes these stories take years to arrive.

"Some seemingly ordinary events in the life of a family have almost mythic significance for those who have gone through them. They shake us to our foundation. They make us children again. Events such as a road trip, a birth, a death, a move."

Mike Allen prefers to have fun writing confusing and bizarre introductions and bury the vague *raisons d'etre* for the *Clockwork Phoenix* series in the back where only the most dedicated bookworms will find them. He has said when asked that "the idea's to find stories that combine compelling, offbeat tales with beautiful and unusual storytelling, stories that both experiment and entertain. For certain, some stories are more unusual than beautiful and vise versa" (*Enter the Octopus*, 9/29/08). He's also said, "I've begun to find the traditional competently-plotted-story-competently-told to be a bit of a drag. I want stories to take more chances in how they tell the stories they tell. On the flip side, much as I enjoy the games played in more experimental works, I often find that they end feeling incomplete and unsatisfying, that they end up forgettable because they lack emotional punch. They leave no mark. In putting *Clockwork Phoenix* together I searched for stories, that for me, occupied the happy middle between the two, that were adventures both in how they read and what they said." (*SF Scope*, 8/19/08). That's his story and he's sticking to it.

Drawing on an example in Steve and Gemma's novelette, he unwisely feels the need to add that the significance of the title *Clockwork Phoenix* is similar to the phrase "exquisite corpse," an interesting juxtaposition of words that in and of itself means nothing. Although Catherine Asaro recently suggested to him that he should instead be claiming it stands for an obscure principle of theoretical physics.

Aside from the two *Clockwork Phoenix* volumes, Mike edited two volumes of the *MYTHIC* anthology series and has for ages been editor (and sometimes publisher) of the poetry journal *Mythic Delirium* (www.mythicdelirium.com), which published a new poem by Neil Gaiman in its 10th anniversary issue earlier this year. His writing achievements have been as esoteric as his tastes in fiction: though he is still trudging through a first novel draft at this writing, he has three times won the Rhysling Award for best speculative poem and seen his work reprinted in the *Nebula Awards Showcase* series. He's the author of two hefty book length collections of poetry: *Strange Wisdoms of the Dead* (a *Philadephia Inquirer* "Editor's Choice" selection) and *The Journey to Kailash*. One of the original poems from the latter collection will be reprinted in Ellen Datlow's *Best Horror of the Year Vol. 1*.

A former president of the Science Fiction Poetry Association, he gave a presentation on "The Poetry of Science Fiction" at the Library of Congress in December '08. He also gave several presentations that year extolling the literary work of his late friend, the legendary pulp fiction writer Nelson Bond.

His own fiction has appeared most recently in *Weird Tales* and *Tales of the Talisman*, with more forthcoming in *Cabinet des Fées* and the Norilana Books anthology *Sky Whales and Other Wonders*. His creepy second-person present-tense interior monologue horror story "The Button Bin" was a finalist for this year's Nebula Award. His website is www.descentintolight.com and his blog on LiveJournal is http://time-shark.livejournal.com.

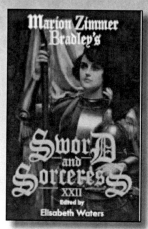

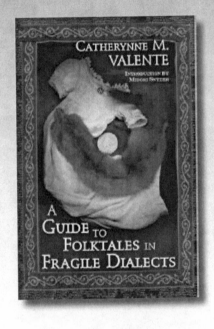

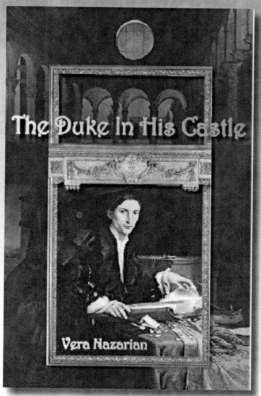

Printed in the United States
149427LV00002B/142/P

9 781607 620273